BEWITCHED WITH A KISS

"You need only ask, Ransom." Aurora's hand lightly rode the sculpted curve of his muscled arm to his broad shoulder, her finger circling the gold ear loop he always wore. "I willna lie to you. Ever." Her fingers sank into his long bronze hair.

"Aurora," he groaned, tilting his head into her soothing touch.

"You've been by me side, havena you?" Blue eyes held haunting amber.

"Aye," he managed, his body tensing, his fierce desire simmering to a boil.

Aurora's eyes sparkled with teasing. "And this concern pressed you to strip me naked and lay me in your bed."

"Shokai saw to the former, I the latter," he confessed, his gaze dropping briefly to her bare shoulders, the swell of her bosom barely hidden by the quilt.

"I swore I wouldna lie upon your sheets alone, Ransom."

"You didn't choose to be here."

"Remember that, m'lord." Her hand curved his neck, flattening to spread across his leather-covered chest.

"Why do you do this, Aurora?"

"Pleasure," she whispered, pressing her lips to the bare skin exposed atween his vest. He groaned, low and rumbling, but couldn't draw back as her mouth seared up his throat to his jaw. "Give to me, Ransom," she murmured against the curve of his mouth, husky words tempting him to the absolute edge of his will. "For I crave the taste of you . . ."

TODAY'S HOTTEST READS
ARE TOMORROW'S SUPERSTARS

VICTORY'S WOMAN   (4484, $4.50)
by Gretchen Genet
Andrew—the carefree soldier who sought glory on the battlefield,
and returned a shattered man . . . Niall—the legandary frontiers-
man and a former Shawnee captive, tormented by his past . . .
Roger—the troubled youth, who would rise up to claim a shock-
ing legacy . . . and Clarice—the passionate beauty bound by one
man, and hopelessly in love with another. Set against the back-
drop of the American revolution, three men fight for their
heritage—and one woman is destined to change all their lives forever!

FORBIDDEN   (4488, $4.99)
by Jo Beverley
While fleeing from her brothers, who are attempting to sell her
into a loveless marriage, Serena Riverton accepts a carriage ride
from a stranger—who is the handsomest man she has ever seen.
Lord Middlethorpe, himself, is actually contemplating marriage
to a dull daughter of the aristocracy, when he encounters the
breathtaking Serena. She arouses him as no woman ever has. And
after a night of thrilling intimacy—a forbidden liaison—Serena
must choose between a lady's place and a woman's passion!

WINDS OF DESTINY   (4489, $4.99)
by Victoria Thompson
Becky Tate is a half-breed outcast—branded by her Comanche
heritage. Then she meets a rugged stranger who awakens her
heart to the magic and mystery of passion. Hiding a desperate
past, Texas Ranger Clint Masterson has ridden into cattle country
to bring peace to a divided land. But a greater battle rages inside
him when he dares to desire the beautiful Becky!

WILDEST HEART   (4456, $4.99)
by Virginia Brown
Maggie Malone had come to cattle country to forge her future as
a healer. Now she was faced by Devon Conrad, an outlaw
wounded body and soul by his shadowy past . . . whose eyes
blazed with fury even as his burning caress sent her spiraling with
desire. They came together in a Texas town about to explode in sin
and scandal. Danger was their destiny—and there was nothing
they wouldn't dare for love!

Available wherever paperbacks are sold, or order direct from the
Publisher. Send cover price plus 50¢ per copy for mailing and
handling to Penguin USA, P.O. Box 999, c/o Dept. 17109,
Bergenfield, NJ 07621. Residents of New York and Tennessee
must include sales tax. DO NOT SEND CASH.

LION HEART

AMY J. FETZER

ZEBRA BOOKS
KENSINGTON PUBLISHING CORP.

ZEBRA BOOKS are published by

Kensington Publishing Corp.
850 Third Avenue
New York, NY 10022

Copyright © 1995 by Amy J. Fetzer

Zebra and the Z logo Reg. U.S. Pat. & TM Off. The Love-gram logo is a trademark of Kensington Publishing Corp.

First Printing: March, 1995

Printed in the United States of America

*This novel is dedicated to
the* real *Aurora,
Aurora Vasquez Laster,
Staff Sergeant, USMC.*

*You're the epitome of a true heroine; feminine grace and
dignity, strength, and a gentle heart unmatched.
Thanks for listening to every joy and woe and tiny story
idea that plowed through my brain, and mostly,* mi amiga,
for backing up my job with you-know-who.

A *very* special thanks
to
Jodi Greenfelder

The phone ringing and a stressed voice saying, "Tell me if this sounds right?" will follow you into the next life. I could never have finished this one without you, pal.

Chapter One

The Ottoman Empire
1756

Sword and man were one.

Toledo steel and experience wielded over flesh and bone and muscle like an impatient surgeon.

No parry was wasted.

No thrust overjudged.

Execution and completion within the realm of silence.

The tempered edge of his cutlass met the yielding flesh of his attacker's chest, carving a deep slice from shoulder to rib cage, exposing bone and a beating heart. Blood curtained, instantly drenching the man's billowy garments, his agonized howl muffled beneath Ransom's quick hand. Ran took mercy and hastened his death. The palace guard collapsed to the floor as Ran pressed on, dispatching the last sentry with a soundless cut to the throat.

The alarm rose, sudden, deafening, like a Newgate herald.

Damn and blast.

He'd hoped to do this quietly.

The advantage was lost.

The stone corridor, wet with seepage, echoed as he shouted, "Domingo! Get your friggin' Spanish carcass down here and help me!" Boot heels thumped on uneven stone, his predatory gaze darting into each shadowed cell for his captured crewmen. "Watkins! Ducks! Dahrein!"

"Here, Capt'n." Thrice came the reply from various points as distant footsteps bespoke the rapid approach of more guards.

Bloody hell.

Behind him Domingo Avilar, followed by three crewmen, met the bottom of the curved staircase, yet naught was left to do but pick their way over the bloody debris as their captain lent his shoulder to the wood door, slamming and slamming until the ancient hinge gave. With the hilt of his grandfather's sword, he impatiently broke another lock. Men stumbled into the dank hall, shielding their eyes from the flickering torch light. The strong aided the weak, Ransom noting each cut and bruise and vowing retribution.

"Step lively, lads. We have company," Ran ordered briskly, tossing his crew a dead man's dagger just as a fresh pack of guards rounded the corner from another maze of tunnels.

For an instant the turbanned men froze before the dark, blood-splattered specter standing amidst the carnage.

And in that sliver of a silence, Ran heard a voice.

Feminine.

Lonely.

His ears pricked to the hollow sound, and his gaze sharpened on the wood door at the end of the corridor. The only one with edges completely sealed in masonry. A tomb.

Grievin' mothers.

Ran's eyes snapped to the guards before him, then to the door, and his crew recognized the determination written in the dangerous look. Ransom's long legs took him rapidly toward the crypt, his bloody sword momentarily discouraging intervention as his crew gave close cover to his right. The guards protested. Two fled, some discarding their weapons and putting up shielding hands; others brandished a wicked assortment of blades, each daring Ransom to try the door. The instant his hand touched the lock, the guards attacked, the scuffling men jolting his body against the door. Ransom cursed, sheathed his blade, and wasted the last of his powder and shot to obliterate the chains and lock, then yanked the links from the guide.

White smoke, shouts, and the ring of metal and death punctured the heavy air as he bent, sliding one broad hand into the oblong slot at the door's base and gripping the wood; the other clamped onto the broken lock. Muscle flexed and bunched as he pulled. A fine white powder sanded his dark hair. Turkish protests grew louder.

"Dahrein!" Ran grunted, freeing wood and stone. "What say they, boy?"

"They talk no sense, sahib," the Indian said, a dagger in one hand and a curved scimitar in the other, threatening the guards as he covered his captain's back.

Ran quickly wedged around the door. "Enlighten me, Dahrein. Now!" The screams didn't need translation as soldiers lunged, trying to wall Ran inside with whoever lay beyond. His men retaliated and once inside Ran growled, "Sweet Christ!"

Another door stood before him, thick wood freshly sealed in drying mortar.

By all that is holy, 'twas never any intention of letting her out. With no way to offer food or water, Ran knew this woman was sentenced to a slow death. Why in God's name would the Sultan do this to one of a gender he considered naught more than vessels to serve man?

"They say an evil infidel lies beyond. Most powerful, sahib," Dahrein said in a rush as he darted forward to lop off the tip of a Turkish nose. "They insist, most heatedly, sahib," the youth called over his shoulder, "that you do not release it."

"Bloody rubbish," Ran scoffed, grabbing a lit torch and igniting the next.

Domingo advanced, his rapier slicing a path to Dahrein, and with the freed crewmen, they wedged themselves between the entrance and their captain, battling the assortment of pirates and castle guards while Ransom pried loose the decaying portal. Foul curses rang through the dungeon as he encountered yet a third wood and stone shield.

He was about to say to hell with the whole rotten mess, that he hadn't the patience nor the men to waste, when the voice beckoned him again.

" 'Tis only one more, sir."

Something inside Ran's chest shifted, jabbing him. She's but a woman, he thought, searching through the small barred window of the cell. 'Twas black as oily pitch, the torch several feet behind him obscuring a decent look, but the sound of chains rattling made his rage burn dark. His booted foot suddenly connected with the rusted chains and locks, once, twice; then he smashed the remains with his sword hilt, a ruby falling to the muddy stone as he shouldered open the crypt and stepped inside.

"Great Neptune's balls!" he hissed, sliding on smooth wet rock.

"Och. 'Tis a poor greeting, thinks I." Dry, melodic, and very Scottish.

He blinked, forcing his eyes to adjust and sift shadow from the startling vision afore him.

She was crucified to the wall, with chains shackled to her wrists and feet and spread too wide for any balance. She appeared to hover in the air, yet he knew her back had to be flat against the stone, and Ran, a man who adored the pleasures of women and especially their softer parts, realized that beneath her stained and tattered shroud lay bare skin. What crime did this speck of a female commit to warrant such an unholy barricade? Was she in league with the Black Spy?

"Have we the time for introductions, sir?"

The casual comment snapped him from gawking further, and he glanced around for a shackle key.

" 'Tis none. My freedom was never in question," she said, not the least bit dispirited.

An uneasy sensation rippled over his spine as he strode to her, examining the simple joining pins of her bonds. Sweet Mary, could the wench read his thoughts? His gaze on her delicate wrist, he heard the *plink* of metal. Her hand was suddenly free, touching his shoulder, and he flinched, cursing his childish reaction and glaring at her.

" 'Twould appear you need naught of my assistance." Within the flickering shadows he saw her lips curve, phantom slight and knowing. "Why did you not escape on your own?"

China blue eyes studied him like a cool breeze to his skin as he rescued her wrist. "I am aware of my strengths, sir, and my every weakness." Her husky voice caressed his senses. "I couldna be movin' that door, could I now?" She shrugged one bare shoulder, sending the sheer garment lower and exposing the deep valley between her breasts. " 'Twas simple enough to have patience til you came to me."

Til you came to me. He stilled, scowling. She spoke as if she'd been expecting him, yet he knew no one was aware of his plans. Dismissing the notion, he knelt and quickly pried open the shackle at her foot. "You are so certain 'twould be aid arriving and nay the executioner?"

"Oh, aye," she said, and he wondered if he imagined the laughter in her voice.

A dozen questions filled his brain with no time to demand answers, and Ran called himself a fool for coming near the lass. That she didn't cower or even express relief was a point he didn't easily dismiss.

She stepped on his bent thigh, small toes gripping, and instinctively Ran caught her waist as he released the other ankle. His fingers flexed, shaping the woman's skin. Firm and yielding. His blood rushed. Why did she not reek of the stench of her prison? She had to have been here for at least four days, he thought, estimating the dryness of the mortar. He straightened, lowering her to the floor. Her legs buckled and she fell against him, warm supple hills melting against his body as she grasped his arms for support.

He wished he could see her face.

The clatter of swords and the explosion of gunfire forestalled a proper look as he immediately tossed her over his shoulder, knocking the air from her lungs.

"Ahhh, beggin' your pardon, sir, 'tis a most undignified position of rescue."

"I could show you several others, lass, that offer a great deal more pleasure." His broad hand clamped on the back of her thigh, adjusting her to his comfort. "I guarantee."

A heartbeat of silence, then she said, "Taking to boastin', are you now?"

Ran chuckled lowly, liking the way her voice rose defiantly at the end of a sentence, and could almost feel her smile against his back.

"Careful with that tongue, lass." His fingertips brushed higher, teasing the sensitive curve of her buttocks as he headed for the door. "I could still leave you behind."

"Och, after breakin' all those doors?" she said, gripping his wide leather belt for balance. " 'Twould be such a waste, thinks I." She gave the leather a sharp tug. "Stop." He did. "I canna leave me sack!"

A hand appeared beside his face, finger pointing and Ran cursed women and their possessiveness to frippery as he bent so she could scoop up the leather satchel from where she indicated.

"My thanks. 'Tis fortunate, thinks I, that they wanted naught of me and mine." Her tiny laugh spoke of secret satisfaction as he carried her from the prison. "Wait!"

"Hush, woman, a moment's delay will find us a guest of this place." That his men were forced to use their guns meant decreasing odds against escape.

"But you've lost a stone." He halted, frowning at the plump backside tucked close to his face. "From your sword hilt, a red stone. 'Tis by your left foot, near the toe." In the waning torchlight Ran squatted, feeling the ground and feeling like an idiot for believing her; until his fingers touched the polished gem. His brows rose, and he dropped the gem in his pocket, continuing on his quest without offering thanks.

"You must save Shokai."

"And who might that be?"

"My guardian protector, of course."

"Of course," Ran mocked, his gaze on the fray beyond the broken doors. "Be certain to pay him well for his services, lass. 'Tis such a fine job he's done you."

"Oh, do not let your eyes make you a fool, sir," she said with a hint of mystery. Something tangled atween his calves, and her cry of pain matched his graceless stumble. "But you might try openin' them a wee bit wider! Leave off me hair!"

Saucy wench, he thought as she tossed the silken rope up over his shoulder, smacking him in the ear. "Cease your yapping or I'll cut this mess." He removed the heavy braid from his view and pressed on.

"Nay, you willna." Her certainty annoyed him. "Now get Shokai," she commanded in a regal voice. He ignored her, overtaking the next passage, his hard steps punching her breath as she squirmed violently. "Help him!"

He gave her rounded buttocks a stinging slap, effectively stifling her rebellion. "You're not in a position to be giving orders, lass." He unsheathed his cutlass before he met the corridor filled with men and mameluke swords, and was grateful his crew had managed to at least retake the ground beyond the woman's cell.

"You're refusing me?" she squeaked, twisting around to look at him and banging her head on the wall. "Och, you are, are'na you?" Ran didn't respond. " 'Tis nay good, this." She rubbed her bruised skull. "You're a ruthless mon, aye. And I dinna see this. 'Tis me own fault," she prattled on, though no one was listening. The moment he stepped around the stone portal the battle grew wild, and he knew they'd kill the lass.

"Baynes! Watkins! Left flank. Dahrein, the right!" His hard gaze met Domingo's near the end of the hall and his first mate nodded. The way was clear. If only he could get to it.

"Aye, Watkins, you do that, laddie, and Dahrein, to that tunnel. There!" She pointed in front of Ran's face, blocking his view. He groaned and batted her arm back, his sword tip hitting the ceiling so abruptly it rained sparks and he nearly lost his grip. The woman belonged in a booby hatch, he decided, turning the blade downward and using the curved hilt to protect his hand as his square fist dropped the palace guards Domingo had thoughtfully left standing. As if Ran needed the exercise. All for a female daft enough to get herself imprisoned in the belly of the sultan's palace. Trouble, mischief, she was already, and Ran knew if he didn't discard the shapely baggage, his life would be naught but muck. She kicked and squirmed, calling out for her protector and insisting he go back for him. Not bloody likely. By now the entire fortress was alerted, and the web of tunnels offered the dangerous vulnerability of assault. Too many lives were wasted this night. And his own would not be among them. Ran hastened his pace, flipping the sword into fighting position to separate a guard's ear from his head as he considered what distorted bit of chivalry possessed him to aid the wiggling woman.

"Cease or you will kill us all!" He tightened his grip on her thigh.

Surrounded by his men, he met the steps of the curved staircase, but her insistent squirming unbalanced him. Abruptly he set her to her feet, prepared to exhaust his anger on the perfect target as she stumbled back, flipped her braid over her shoulder and glared up at him.

It was his first clear look at the lass and Ransom Montegomery had never witnessed such fiery beauty afore this night. Coal black hair laced with thin veins of blood red was woven into a braid, caught high and loose at her crown. Her sculptured face was still vivid from being carried upside down, yet blue eyes, bright with anger and disappointment, widened and narrowed on various points of his body until they came to rest on his face. Ran felt like a pig on the auction block. She snubbed him as if he'd come up lacking, then slung the satchel strap over her shoulder and spun about, retracing the path to the cells.

The braid swished, grazing the floor, her shapely bottom swaying beneath the thin shroud. A luscious piece, he thought, absorbing the sight and forgetting the danger her stroll would cost them. Ran took a step, sword drawn.

Suddenly wounded Barbary pirates and palace guards scrambled aside, cowering on their knees and shielding their faces as she walked sedately in their midst.

"Will you look at that, sir?" a crewman said. "They're bleedin' terrified of her!"

"Oh, Rom!" Dahrein croaked from behind his captain.

"What say you of this, Ran?" Avilar asked calmly.

"I do not ponder overmuch on the doings of females."

Yet, men trained to give their lives for their master trembled like frightened children, rocking and praying.

Ran's conscience bade him quickly follow, though not a soul moved as the lass slipped just inside a darkened tunnel. Directly behind her, Ran stood rooted to the floor, his slashing sable brows drawn tight as he glanced warily around. The poised stillness intensified. He heard naught but labored breathing and moans of pain and unquestionable fear. Then she tipped her head back, her lashes sealing away blue crystal light as her face went serene and flawlessly still. Like a statue, she was; even her breathing seemed to cease. He held his own, not knowing what to expect, if anything a'tall. Slowly her arm rose, chest high, her palm out as if she expected something to be dropped in it. Ran heard the *chink* of fallen metal, the scrap of wood to stone and his scowl deepened, his gaze darting to her, to the blackness of the tunnel, then scanning the niddering Turks shrinking on the ground, afore coming back to the murky tunnel.

Soundlessly, a short, thin, gray-haired man appeared from the shadows. Ran lurched, sword poised.

Her hand floated in the air just above the blade point. "Do not hurt him," she whispered, her husky voice steaming over his body, then a bit louder, "He has come, Shokai."

Slanted almond-shaped eyes darted to Ran, assessing and judging in one glance. *"Hai,* Empress. This I see."

"Empress?"

" 'Tis naught but a pet name," she whispered again and Ran felt that heady sensation, as if her voice had the power of touch. " 'Twould be best, thinks I, if you followed this time, Shokai. Neh?"

"Hai." He bowed low, and the three-pronged comb securing his topknot glittered in the torchlight.

Ran rolled his eyes heavenward. Great Neptune! This was her protector! This wrinkled apricot of a man! He spun about, expecting to fight his way free of the corridor again, yet the guards made no move to attack, pressing themselves closer to the damp stone walls, heedless of their wounds as she swept past him. Her pace was leisurely, snapping the remnants of his tolerance. What woman was she to walk among armed pirates without a care?

"Who the friggin' hell are you?" he demanded, temper igniting.

As if she had the hourglass of the universe at her fingertips, she paused, turning slightly. The delicate motion wrapped the overly long transparent gauze tightly to her body, revealing every lush hill and valley, the darkened tips of her high plump breasts, the voluptuous swell of her hips. Her black braid marked the curve of her spine as she tilted her head, her mouth pulling into a beguilingly feminine smile. The air staggered in his chest. There was something incredibly secretive and powerful in this lovely creature.

"I am named Aurora Lassiter, m'lord rescuer." Her lashes swept down, briefly, a black stroke against pale white. Then she met his gaze. "And they fear," she waved a sculptured hand to the cowering guards, "only what they can not understand."

A half-dozen strides brought him before her and she looked up, unaffected by his suppressed rage.

"And what, little pest, is that?"

The old man moved silently behind them.

She shrugged. "That I knew you would not allow me to perish in here."

Ran grunted in disbelief. "Apparently not a very successful prediction, lass, for we aren't free yet," he said, wrapping an arm around her waist, then slinging her, bottom up, on his hip. "And if you keep interrupting my gallant attempts at rescue," he warned, his stride quick and merciless, "I shall make a gift of you to Ali Pasha."

Clutching her braid and her precious sack off the ground, she muttered at his dirty boots, "Och. Your mother dinna beat you enough as a lad, thinks I."

Chapter Two

Aurora Lassiter was a mystery that Ransom Montegomery had no desire to investigate. She'd already cost him valuable time to find the remainder of his crew. Captured during a skirmish with Salé pirates and taken as slaves, they were scattered over the Ottoman Empire like rice in the sea. 'Twould take weeks, mayhaps months to find them all. And now they no longer had surprise to their credit. Ran's enemies would be prepared. And when the Sultan discovered he'd freed his prisoner, the wily bastard would demand her return.

Or Ransom's head.

Damn and blast, he should have kept to his own this night!

Her bag slapped against the back of his calves in time with his footsteps, and Ran knew she was in pain, hanging upside down like she was.

"You think I canna travel on me own power?" she said in a gasping voice.

Ran noticed her accent got heavier when she was miffed.

"You weigh naught and your frailty will slow us down," he answered, callously transferring her to his shoulder like a sack of grain. He heard her sharp loss of breath as her soft belly impacted with muscle and bone, and she clutched his shirt, muttering something about his lack of sympathy for those a "wee bit" smaller than he. In defiance to her immodest position, her hands climbed up his back, pushing herself up right.

"Och, 'tis dangerous to be so far from the ground, thinks I," she said, awed.

Ran glanced up and a reluctant smile spread across his face. Shielding her eyes as if the torchlight were too bright, she scanned her backwards surroundings like the crow from his perch atop the mizzen mast. A booby hatch, he thought, the only proper home for this lass.

She looked down at him and the impact of her energetic smile made Ran slow his steps. His gaze darted to the plump breasts jiggling in front of his face, and he suddenly itched to shape their magnificence beneath his palms. Loosening his grasp so she slipped low enough to look him in the eye, the delectable push of her body gave Ran a splendid inventory of her lush figure. Shaped like a ship's watch glass, she was luxuriously ripe and full where most women of her small size were naught but bones. And she wasn't wearing a stitch beneath the shroud.

"You've outdistanced your men, sir," she said, wrapping her arms around his neck as if they were anything but strangers. His gaze dropped briefly to the charm hanging from a cord about her neck.

" 'Tis a frequent occurrence." He paused to scoop up her legs, holding her high against his chest. Supple flesh yielded to the hardness of his own, the scent of warm spice and crushed mint on damp skin enveloping him, creating intoxicating images he'd no time to consider. Blast. 'Tis best to ignore her, he decided and concentrated on his footsteps, darting from shadow to arched alcove, then up a steep curve of narrow stairs. But as if to mock his decision, he felt her stare and spared her a cool glance. She smiled. Aye, pitch the lass first chance of freedom and get on with business, he thought and immediately turned his face from her intense blue eyes.

Aurora welcomed the feel of her rescuer's strong arms surrounding her like a new cloak, yet she sensed he was determined to dismiss her. 'Twould do nay good, she thought as he ascended the stairs two at a time. 'Twas just so.

For in her dreams afore the summer solstice Aurora had

seen him. Well, mostly his eyes really. Dark and bronze as
the rest of him. Och, but the man was certainly pleasant to
look upon. Long-limbed and thickly muscled, his counte-
nance was brooding, his tanned face carved sharp with concentration and framed in waves of long hair the rich shade
of freshly turned earth. A quick stirring heated her body,
dampening the woman-spot atween her thighs. 'Twas the
same as when she envisioned those eyes afore, yet stronger
now, though 'twas the first occasion she'd seen him in the
flesh. Och, and what *fine* flesh it was, she thought, her gaze
dropping to the golden marble of his skin exposed between
the lacings of his black shirt. The ache grew, spread, and she
yielded to it, toying with the small gold loop piercing his
lobe. Dark eyes glared at her, and she returned it with a
sweet smile.

He frowned.

She confused the poor man. But then, she confused most
everyone. And on occasion, she thought ruefully, even her
beloved Shokai. 'Twas not something she bothered fixing.
'Twas just so.

That her vision had materialized into a living human
being was a wee shock to her, for in the past she'd never
been very accurate, or she'd be closer to finding her father
by now. Yet the fierce predatory eyes haunting her visions
most definitely belonged to this man. But what of the pranc-
ing lion with the coat of deep red? She hadn't discerned the
significance behind the beast of her dreams, only that the
soul possessing those golden eyes would help her. 'Course,
she'd no notion of the trouble she'd find herself in—this
time, and although his refusal to help Shokai was an unexpected disappointment, he *had* come for her.

Whether she'd see him again after this night or nay, she
couldn't say. Nor did she care. Pleasures were few to her,
and whether 'twere of the heart, the mind, and now, och, of
the flesh, she savored each as the precious gifts they were.

"You canna defend yourself, carrying me like this," she
whispered suddenly.

He arched a brow, then glanced behind himself. "Would

you rather be across my shoulder?" Ran challenged, sensing his thoughts open to the lass and not liking the invasion.

"I'd rather be free of this wretched place."

Darting a swift look at his unwanted companion, he briefly considered adding to the Sultan's private stock, then with a smirk, decided 'twas unfair for even His Royal Debauchness to be sacked with such a peculiar female. Besides, he reasoned, ducking into the alcove afore a sculptured door, the man intended for her to die.

That thought sent a twist of outrage spinning through Ransom, and he immediately crushed it. He needed naught to interfere with his life now, especially an addle-pated female with breasts beautiful enough to mount on his wall. But questions kept ricocheting through his brain. Why sentence her to slowly waste in loneliness and starvation? Why not execution, if her crime was so dastardly? And what offense could one so small and weak have committed? Nay, 'twould be of no consequence, he reconsidered. Even the most educated in the Ottoman customs could insult the sultan unintentionally. And pay with an arm, an eye, or a life.

Releasing her legs, he tucked her close to his side, flattened himself against the cool stone, then peered ahead. The palace teemed with shouts and the slap of footsteps, and Ran looked to where they'd come to be certain his men followed. Those helping the weak were slow and cautious. Her old man was a stooped phantom amongst them.

"God of thunder, but yer a braw lad," she murmured, and he glanced down at the woman called Aurora. She stared up at him with beautifully wide eyes, the top of her head scarcely reaching his shoulder.

"So says the one who *dinna* beat me enough." He went back to watching the progress of his men.

"Did she give you a name?"

"Aye."

When he didn't answer, she elbowed him in the side.

He scowled at her, the day's growth of beard and shaggy hair darkening his features.

"A prissy one, is it now?" One slashing black brow lifted. "Or 'tis a secret mayhaps?" she said in a stage whisper.

His lips quirked with a saboteur's smile. "Ransom."

Her assessing blue eyes prowled boldly over his body from head to foot and back, and Ran felt the uneasy combination of heat and a winter's kiss.

"Och, such a mighty name," she said in a husky tone that robbed him of all thought, save one. His blood rushed. His sex thickened. She stripped him bare in that one glance. His gaze drifted over her face, to the smudge of dirt on her cheek, the half-inch scar at her left temple, and the satiny sheen of her pale skin, afore it lowered to the scarcely covered breasts cushioning his side. Her chest rose and fell, the dusky crests shielded in thin gauze plumped and molded to the fabric. The lush sight beckoned a man's touch, and his eyes moved indolently over her shrouded form to the darkness he could see at the join of her thighs. His breath quickened as he slowly brought his gaze back to meet those gloriously blue eyes. Her gaze never wavered. The air filling the inches atween them grew heady and tart like red wine. Sensuality clung to her like perfume, fragrant and veiled, and for a instant Ran imagined she took on the look of a cat. He watched, captivated as her tongue slicked across the creamy fullness of her lower lip. By God, if ever a maid needed ravishing—ah, damn and blast!

That she could unravel his tightly clenched control with naught but a glance infuriated him. "For what crime did the Sultan imprison you?" he demanded suddenly, softly, breaking the spell atween them.

Such a closed man this, Aurora thought, assigning his behavior to that masculine need to dominate bloody near everything. "He dinna." She wiggled close, bracing her head in the crook of his shoulder. "The Sultana did."

The move was far too comfortable and enticing for Ran's liking, and he pushed her back apace. "Explain this."

"You willna 'tempt revenge?"

He sighed, irritated. For revenge she had to, at first, mean something to him. "Nay."

"She poisoned her sister's infant son. The terrified mother

risked her life and sought me out. I was able to give the child back his life."

Ran's features sharpened, his sable brows drawing tight. The bitter rivalry atween the Sultan's women was common knowledge, each fighting to maintain his devotion; yet above all else the prince prized boy children, his heirs. But if this lass had saved the child's life, 'twas an act which did not requite imprisonment. Forthwith, Ran found it difficult to believe much of what she said and glanced into the stair-well, judging his men were waiting for a certain calm afore preceding.

"And how did you perform this . . . feat?"

The words unsaid did not go unnoticed by Aurora.

" 'Twas merely a purgative necessary to rid the babe of the poison. The Sultan's first *kadine* dinna believe I possessed the knowledge, infidel that I am." She smirked. "The birth of her sister's babe meant a wait in line for the throne, for the life she carries now." Aurora briefly closed her eyes, horrified over what she'd witnessed. "The Sultan's rage was a sight to behold when he confronted us, and the *kadine* knew she would lose her life and insisted she'd nay have done such a murderous thing 'twere for *my* presence in her prince's kingdom." She tilted her head back, sarcasm dripping with each word. "I twisted her mind, you ken? Made her pour that foul concoction down the babe's throat til the pitiful thing vomited his blood and bowels." She let her breath out, sinking into the masculine strength surrounding her. "Naught I could say mattered, for the Sultan believed if I, a mere woman, could give and take life without benefit of a weapon, then I most certainly must be evil beyond even Mohammed's dreams."

Ran heard the pain in her words and recognized that it went deeper than this tale. She lifted her gaze, and he saw the gloss of unshed tears that refused to fall.

"I'd never take a life, Ransom." Her voice was a broken whisper. "Would rather die meself." She swallowed. "You ken?"

His name on her lips, the lilt of her burr sapped him of his well-harnessed restraint.

"I ken, lass," he said, giving her a squeeze and not knowing why he believed. She relaxed against him in a subtle
wave. Her hand came up to rest lightly on the center of his
chest, and the touch scorched the somber cloth to his skin.
The tender gesture was as seductive as a slow wet kiss, luring
him, and his mouth suddenly throbbed to feel hers beneath,
the smoothness, the flavor. His groin tightened painfully,
straining his breeches, and he ducked his head closer. She
met his gaze; his toured her face, her body, then returned to
that incredibly lush mouth.

Ran toyed briefly with rational thought. But excitement,
lust, and the mist of danger hovered round them, tempting
him to take what those feline eyes promised. His mouth
touched hers, a taste, nothing more, afore he was roughly
jolted, nearly crushing her against the wall. Swift rage sent
him whirling about, dagger poised as the alcove filled with
familiar faces. Sweet saints, he might have been murdered
whilst trying to climb atween her thighs!

He glared accusingly at Aurora, but she didn't look up.
She didn't have to, for his censure held the sting of a slap.
You are lying to yourself, Ransom, she thought. The influ-
ence, 'tis yours as well. Aurora had had no notion 'twould
be like this when they met, only that they *would* meet. But
this obstinate giant, she'd already discovered, was not much
on understanding that the mind was rarely in match with
the heart.

" 'Tis yonder," Ran gestured with his chin, his deep whisper loud in the hollow corridor. He was glad 'twas dark
enough that the others couldn't see the telltale bulge in his
breeches. Sweet saints, the woman could tempt a bleedin'
priest!

His men stared at her, quite thoroughly, and she knew
'twas for the garment scarcely covering her body. Lusty
beasts, she thought, and inched a wee bit behind her rescuer
as she met Shokai's gaze. The old man's thin eyes glanced
at Ransom, then Aurora, afore he shook his head as if the
pair's doings were as transparent as her clothes.

Ran and Aurora taking the lead, the group picked their
way to the next alcove, the sound of Turkish commands

growing louder. 'Twas level with the courtyard, Ran knew, and in the inky darkness he brushed his palm insistently back and forth over the sculpted wall.

"Bloody hell!" he hissed, finding naught. "I know 'twas here afore!"

Like the flow of a breeze, Aurora ducked beneath his outstretched arm, grasped his hand and placed it over the carved head of a stone bird. In the dark he sent her a thin glare and pressed. The wall receded. Motioning to his men to follow, he captured her wrist and stepped inside.

The passage wasn't wide enough for her to walk beside him, yet Ran didn't release her hand. It dwarfed in his palm, slim and delicate yet with the strength and callouses of hardship. It made him wonder how a beautiful, slightly daft Scotswoman managed to find her way onto Turkish lands.

In scarcely a whisper he warned her not to speak and she obeyed as his footsteps became measured and soundless in the tunnel. Having discovered the secret cavern quite by accident, Ran moved slowly on unfamiliar ground. He'd no idea if hc was leading his men into a fathomless pit or to freedom. He slowed his pace when he heard muffled voices, feminine giggles, and the laughter of children. His brows rose.

"The Sultan's path to his women," he murmured caustically.

"Nay, 'tis the promenade of those who fall from his favor," she whispered.

To their death, he thought, sensing the end of the tunnel and bending deeply to accommodate the shrinking ceiling.

"Damn, it leads nowhere!"

"Ochaii, but you give up too easily, Ransom," Aurora chastised, wedging herself around his broad body to stand afore him. In the dark she pressed her fingertips to his lips when he made to speak. "Listen. Do you not hear it?"

He held his breath. A whisper of wind, a thin howl, and it beckoned his hand to skim the wall. The breeze cooled his palm and his knuckles hit protruding stone. He shaped a lever and pulled, praying the floor didn't vanish beneath his feet and cringing as the stone scraped stone. Moonlight showered him, lighting the ground below. Ran leapt into the silver darkness, his feet hitting packed sand. Turning to aid the lass, he found her already at his side. He grabbed her hand.

The clatter of hooves on stone cracked the air like shattering glass and Ransom took off like a pistol shot, long powerful legs propelling him into the narrow maze of the city just as armed soldiers atop the swiftest of stallions burst from the palace gates. Shokai and the eight crewmen scattered as the guards divided and gave chase. Gunfire fractured the night. Ran scooped Aurora up in his arms and darted around a peddler's empty cart, nearly toppling it and giving away his location. The crew would head to the sea, to his ship.

Snatching a *tcharchaf* from a drying line as he passed, Ran swept the fabric over Aurora, its murky shade meshing them together with the night as he pulled her to the ground and rolled under the cart.

"Fionn's fairies, you're crushing me!"

He shifted, clamping a hand over her mouth.

Dust and pebbles kicked up as hooves thundered past their hiding place, yet Ran made no move to flee. He had no ammunition for his pistol; defense from this position was suicidal. She mumbled beneath his palm, and he pressed harder as foot soldiers demanded they show themselves, the clank and crush of their mamelukes hacking through baskets and shattering pottery.

Footsteps receded, but still he waited, wishing she'd cease her squirming. Cautiously removing his hand from her mouth, Ram's glare warned her not to talk afore they slipped from beneath the cart.

He had to get to his ship afore the Sultan burned it.

"Someone comes," she whispered, suddenly yanking him into the shadows and throwing the *tcharchaf* over them both.

The soulful bray of a camel painted the new silence.

Somewhere, a baby cried.

" 'Tis no one," he snarled softly, annoyed over the waste of precious time.

"Wait," she insisted, pulling him back, her body fitting fully against his. Ran's arms surrounded her and for a instant he forgot, forgot the castle guards, the danger, the penalty he'd suffer if caught. He could think of no more than Aurora, the taste he'd but sampled, the push and give of her voluptuous body. He swept her up against him and pressed her back to the wall. His mouth found hers within the dark cocoon of fabric. Heat and mint and spice exploded through his senses. And her jolt of surprise was lost in the frantic pulse of desire.

The thunk of spurred boots chimed past their hiding place as he filled his palms with the curves of her buttocks coaxing her legs around him and wedging himself atween the nest of her thighs. He thickened and warmed and rocked, and like the opulent swell of warm honey, Aurora ripened against him, answered, and drew his strength. She moaned and plunged her fingers into his hair, capturing him closer, taking him into her mouth, clinging and stealing his breath.

She flourished. His blood roared and his hands scooped beneath her garments and did what he'd been aching to do touch supple feminine flesh, naked and sizzling; upending his world.

She strained against him, begging for more.

His head reeled; his pulse throbbed, and she tasted like ginger. His mouth opened wide on hers and Aurora accepted the hot thrust of his tongue, sucked and battled; and Ransom thought he'd rip apart with his need to have her

Here.

Now.

Quick and hot and unforgiving.

Her hands scrubbed his shoulders, his chest, the flatness of his stomach, and a wild shudder passed through him, inside him, around him, and the demand to release himself and push into her body nearly drove sanity from his brain. The stinging heat of passion rode him with the primitive gait of stallion. Pushing. Pushing. He would come—here. God almighty, without even the wet glove of her womanhood grasping his erection, he would come!

He jerked back, the burn of his climax receding afore it unmanned him like a schoolboy. His chest heaved to drag dry desert air into his lungs. Her leg slid down his like the wrap of a snake around his calf afore her feet touched ground.

"Great Neptune," he rasped against her mouth, then abruptly put space and discipline atween them. He felt chilled and empty and, damn her, weak. The *tcharchaf* slid from his shoulders as she wrapped it around herself, hiding the contrast of her pale garments and her aroused body from his sight. She said naught, but touched her fingertips to her swollen lips.

Ran turned away from the carnal temptation, grinding his teeth and gathering command of his body as he peered around the wall to search the pitchy night for their pursuers.

Freedom was attainable.

When he turned back, Aurora Lassiter was gone.

Aurora.

A thick salacious rush of excitement poured over his body as her image focused in his mind's eye, and he drew up his knee to ease the heaviness in his groin. He smelled the tartness of apples and tried to siphon dream from reality. But then she called to him, and he turned his head to see her, poised on the edge of his sleep, his bed, her arms outstretched like wisps of pale smoke, inviting him to embrace her. He blinked, certain 'twas not as he saw. Her black hair was unbound, caught in a breeze that didn't exist. Her breasts, voluptuously full and round with desire, beckoned his touch, his mouth, and he reached for her. The mist churned and her shrouded figure receded into the dark, leaving him empty, drenching in his need for her.

His breathing swift and his brain confused, Ran leaned up on his elbow and scanned the darkened cabin. The sweet scent of apples permeated the warm air, yet the familiar creak of ropes and rigging, the waves battering the sleek hull, told him 'twas but another dream.

Bloody damn.

He flopped on his back, shielding his eyes with his arm and banishing all thoughts of the wench. 'Twas useless to try, he warned himself, his body still pulsing. Since their first meeting three weeks ago her likeness rode the waves of his memory; slashing brows like an upward stroke of black on pale skin; her smile—feline subtle, yet hinting of innocence behind the ripeness of her full lips, her luxurious kiss. And her hair—God, how he wanted to feel the silken madness draped across his chest, sifting through his fingers, rivers of velvet black spread in an erotic veil over her shoulders, revealing but a hint of her lush womanly mounds.

His body flickered with desire and he groaned. He was torturing himself, thinking along this path. But her every nuance and gesture lay imprinted beneath his skin, teasing his days and taunting him when he was alone and greedy for the feel of a woman beneath him. By God, but that lass was fashioned to be loved—nay, worshipped—by a man!

And in the recesses of his mind he marveled how swift his passions overtook his control; how he shifted from being annoyed with her, her chatter, to wanting her so fiercely he thought he'd explode. And she gave him what he craved, again and again. So untamed. And be it running for her life or pressed atween the wall and his body, he sensed a wonder for adventure in her, a will to enjoy whatever trouble she encountered as much as her sudden freedom.

He rolled onto his stomach, but the masculine ache sent him on his back again. Damn and blast, he thought, smashing his fist into the bedding. That she could demolish his composure even in the privacy of his sleep rankled him, and with a disgusted sigh, he sat up, reaching for his breeches. He shoved his feet into the pant legs and stood, straining the fabric to manage the last buttons.

Ran cursed his lust. 'Twas all it was. And he recognized that he would never see the lass again and dismissed her from his thoughts. Regardless, locating his crew and departing from this barren land was his only priority, for more than his identity was at risk.

The ship lurched as sails cracked, filling with wind and pulling the forty-gun flagship deeper into the gulf.

A scratching rattled the door, and Ran lit the grease lamp aside his bed afore he bade the crewman enter.

Dahrein slipped around the wood portal, in one hand a tin pierced lantern, the other bearing a small tray, the aroma of Arabic coffee steaming from the delicate china cup.

"A most pleasant sleep, sahib?"

"Nay, 'twas not," Ran muttered more to himself, shoving his hair back off his forehead, though it did no good, the dark maple-hued waves falling in his face once more as he shrugged into his shirt. Tucking it into his breeches, he cursed the blue-eyed woman to perdition.

"So sorry, sahib," the youth consoled, shuffling across the great cabin to set the tray on Ran's desk. "Perhaps it is too much of this?" He proffered the fragile cup in outstretched hands, turban head bowed atween.

Ran's gaze scanned the youth, the lad's thinness showing through the yards of fabric swaddled about his body. After two years aboard his ship the boy had gained little muscle.

" 'Tis doubtful, Dahrein," he said, taking the cup. The scent of cardamom-laced coffee filled his senses and he inhaled deeply, banishing memory and lust to where it belonged; controlled and suppressed.

As Ran settled his hip against the desk, sipping the hot brew and studying the maps scattered across the surface, Dahrein darted around the cabin, searching about the commode, under the desk, at the bench afore the aft windows until his puttering tried Ran's patience.

"What in the devil are you looking for, boy?"

The Indian straightened, his face flushing. "Why, the apple peelings, sir."

Ran tensed, his gaze sharpening on the boy as he set the cup down with a snap.

"They will bring the rats."

The boy looked expectantly at Ran, but he could offer no explanation. 'Twas naught but a friggin' dream! Ran grabbed his spyglass, heading to the hatch.

"Sahib?"

"There were no . . . apples!" he growled, flinging open the door and stepping over the threshold.

"If you insist," Dahrein said as Ran slammed the wood

shut. Dahrein glanced around, then lifted a map and peeked beneath. He sniffed. "I do not kill rats, sahib."

Domingo Avilar smiled lazily as his captain climbed the ladder onto the quarter deck, motioning for the cockswain to give over the helm and banishing all from the privileged area. *A foul mood again, it seems.*

"Could you not rest, *Capitán?*" he asked lightly, popping an olive into his mouth.

Ran offered no more than a grunt, glanced at the stars, then returned his gaze to the horizon and the glow of the city beyond.

Studying his superior, Domingo rolled the olive in his mouth, then turned his head to spit the pit over the rail afore he spoke. "She has paid a visit upon your dreams once again, *sí?*"

"You press the line, puppy," Ran warned without sparing a glance.

Domingo smiled, selected a mango from the wooden bowl at his side and, with a thin blade, pared a slice. "There are things even a man such as you cannot hide." Bringing the flat of the knife to his mouth, he slid the juicy sliver atween his lips.

Ran shot him a side-glance, and the first mate's gaze dropped meaningfully to the bulge in Ran's breeches.

"So. 'Tis an offer you're making, Mister Avilar?" Ran said, smoothly arching a brow. "I never thought you to be a backgammon player."

Domingo choked on the mango, the color draining from his face at the vile implication. "Nay!" he insisted, spitting the food aside. "Mother of God, do not even suggest such a thing!" He pushed a jeweled hand into his wavy black hair and glanced at the captain. Ransom's shoulders shook suspiciously as he continued to stare at the horizon and Domingo relaxed back into his perch by the rail. Sodomites didn't exist on the *Red Lion* and Ran's hand-picked crew assured it.

"You need a woman, Ran."

"Do I, Mister Avilar?"

"Sí. Sí," Domingo began, quite willing to advise. " 'Tis what?" He waved another pared slice. "The fourth night you've woken for your watch in such a, shall we say, frustrating state of readiness?" He popped the sweet mango into his mouth.

"Your constant interest is a comfort, Domingo," Ran mocked dryly.

"Shall I find you a woman, my friend?" he slurped around the fruit. "I know many."

"I need not your aid, beard splitter." The Spaniard's persistence on this subject annoyed him.

Domingo tried to look affronted at yet another insult and failed. Shrugging, he said, "I merely enjoy the company of the fairer sex, that is all."

Ran scoffed, his gaze measuring the Latin. "You enjoy naught but to roger any female willing to spread her thighs for you, Dom. I don't doubt you sire a by-blow every time we weigh anchor." His clipped tone cut with the edge of bitterness. " 'Tis a sightable difference in enjoying the gentle company of a woman *without* pushing her on her back and riding her like the seas."

Domingo Avilar knew when to retreat from a tender subject. He picked up the bowl and stabbed his blade into a papaya as he skirted the captain. He almost expected to be cuffed for his impertinence. "And what of this raven-haired nymph with the power to bring men to their knees? Eh, *Capitán?"* He balanced his favorite flat-bottomed bowl on his head as he climbed down the ladder. "Would you not like to *enjoy time* with her?"

A nymph, a spirit. Apt name, Ran thought, especially after tonight.

"I would," Dom pestered cheekily, and Ran nailed him with a glare meant to maul the flesh from his bones as the first mate disappeared from his sight. Domingo grinned. Even if Ran would rather die than admit such a weakness, the Englishman possessed feelings for the little *señorita.* Domingo decided this pleased him. *Sí,* it pleased him very

much to watch the inflexible man fall vulnerable for the first
time since his exile.

The Maghreb
Port of Tripoli

"*Sib nee finah lee!*" Aurora squirmed in Achmed's grasp.
"You will unhand me or face embarrassment, thinks I."

"Hold your tongue afore I cut it from your throat,
woman," the merchant snarled as he dragged her toward his
caravan. She strained against him, wishing she could make
him a eunuch, and he pinned her with a thin glare and
warned, "My master will be most displeased if you do not
cooperate."

Through her sheer veil Aurora's gaze darted to the
women already in the small cart; huddled, shrouded in fabric and guarded by huge men with wickedly curved swords.
Not again, she agonized, realizing the youth she'd paid to
take her to the ship had betrayed her to this sweaty merchant. Kelpie's mischief, she'd only wanted to buy passage
from this brittle land!

"Populatin' the country with more fools is a crime, thinks
I," she muttered, struggling to peel his thick fingers from her
wrist.

He heard and twisted her arm behind her back. Pain shot
up to her shoulder as his beefy arms mashed her against the
fleshy wall of his chest. He smelled of dates and rotting
teeth, and her empty stomach revolted.

"It is not necessary for you to speak—ever," he stressed
with a low chuckle. "Be sweet and soft and *silent* as a
woman should. Spread your legs and warm his divans," he
said darkly, her fingers turning purple beneath his grip,
"and perhaps my sire will make you his most beloved."

Clutching her leather sack, Aurora trembled with outrage, tired of being treated as an object for barter, trade, or
sale. If she and Shokai hadn't been separated in the crush of
the *souk,* this foul pig of a man would never have spoken to
her thusly. He'd assumed she was a harlot, since he'd found
her alone and without any male kin to defend her. Other-

wise, her family would be obligated to kill her for such a loss
of *ird,* of honor.

Theirs not hers, she thought, as her knee shot up into his
groin. Her lack of height and the heavy layers of the *abayeh*
kept her movements slow and weighted, and he did naught
but grunt. An instant later his curses littered the air as he
backhanded her across the face, the veil doing naught to
cushion the blow. His pleased smile was lost in the folds of
flesh and beard as she stumbled, her legs nearly folding
beneath her.

She went still, so still Achmed scowled, his bushy brows
drawing down into one. He studied her, trying to see her
face beyond the thin mesh *burqu'* and wondering if he'd hit
her too hard and damaged his merchandise. He'd kill her if
she forced him to lose even one dinar that her sale would
add to his purse. Foreign women were a scarce and costly
commodity, one his master insisted share his bed. And this
one was a virgin.

He could smell it.

Ignoring the pain burning through her jaw, Aurora
closed her eyes and narrowed her thoughts. Achmed The
Fat, as she'd dubbed him, needed a decent bath and a lesson
in underestimating a Scot.

Achmed's black eyes widened as the fastenings of his
cloak suddenly popped free. Stunned horror masked his
craggy features when the garment slid slowly from his
shoulders, pulled by an invisible hand. His hold on her
tightened to bruising panic. His neatly wrapped turban
sagged to one side, and his gaze swept up in confusion,
attempting to see yet without success as the decorative cord
dropped to the ground, the bright fabric unwinding in the
brisk hot wind.

Releasing her sharply, he grabbed at once for his turban
and the ornate belt slipping down over his hips, and Aurora
snatched opportunity, running into the crowded *souk.*
Achmed clutched frantically at his drooping pantaloons,
shouting commands for his men to recapture his merchandise or lose their fingers.

Aurora ran, children and chickens scattering from her

path. Her legs tired quickly, her breathing difficult through the *burqu'*. Encased from head to feet in white fabric, she was not garbed for swift movement, and the colors of the Sultan's house threaded in the trimming, further hindered her escape. But she knew naught of such things. Shokai had *found* the garment, and now she'd destroyed his plans and, great Stones of Stennis, lost his precious coin again!

As Aurora darted around people and peddlers, the recognizable colors and her hasty steps made men grab for her. Women were naught but property, and a handsome reward could be garnered for returning her to her master. Her master! Och, and there were those who said *her* people were barbaric! She respected the Islamic beliefs, obeyed the customs as best she could manage, yet wished they'd cease attempting to make her the emir's newest mattress!

Something or someone caught her disguise, the renting of fabric loud, exposing her face. People looked away in fear of the Sultan's retribution, and Aurora immediately drew the torn veil across her face, covering all but her eyes and commanding her legs to move faster. Glancing behind to gauge the pace of her pursuers, her body hit solid matter.

Her breath left her, and she and the pedestrian went down hard in the center of the open street, his body scarcely softening the impact. Sprawled across the poor man like a discarded rag, Aurora lifted her head, blew a wisp of hair from her mouth and stared into achingly familiar amber eyes.

"You!" he hissed, gripping her shoulders, his gaze sharpening on her red, swollen jaw. "Great Neptune, what do you here, woman, dressed like . . . that?"

"Causin' a stir, thinks I." She glanced briefly over her shoulder to see Achmed The Fat and his piglets advancing. "Och, yer lookin' fine, Ransom." Her fingers brushed adoringly over his lips, as if reliving the taste of his smoldering kiss. "But, alas," she shrugged, "I canna linger to chat." The last words came out in a rush as she scrambled off, banging him in the head with *the sack* in the process afore she ran into the crowd.

Ran leapt to his feet as a half-dozen *burnous*-clad men

plunged into the marketplace, heading in her direction. At the commotion Domingo looked up from sampling a leg of roasted mutton and glanced atween his captain and the fleeing figure. Ran dressed the first brigand's hide with a punch to the jaw that lifted the Arab off his feet and into a vender's cart. Dry wood cracked and splintered as the Spaniard immediately jumped in to defend his captain's back, sword and pistol banished on a hearty challenge, a chunk of meat atween his teeth.

"Take no lives this day, Dom," Ran warned, plowing his square fist into a soft stomach.

"I shall do my utmost, *Capitán,*" he assured around the food and to prove it he shoved the pistol into his belt, using only his sword to keep the Arabs from passing. He swallowed. " 'Twas she, was it not?" Domingo inclined his head behind him as the pair back-stepped.

The innocent remark touched off a dark frustration seething in Ransom, the weeks of her image destroying his sleep, the memory of her mouth moving lushly beneath his, hungry and wild, answering his primal urges in the pitch black corner of his lust, and like a taunted serpent his body uncoiled, feet and fists striking with stinging precision to bone and flesh, toppling her pursuers like water jars from a ledge. Breathing heavily, he swiped the back of his hand across his mouth, then looked to where she'd fled.

"Go, *Capitán.*" Domingo grinned, motioning Ran to follow the conscience smeared across his tanned features. "I shall deal with these peasant dogs," he said, poking one of the fallen men with the point of his sword. Ran hesitated, his gaze level with warning, and Domingo threw up his hands, Toledo steel winking in the hot sun. "No killing! I swear on my sainted mother's grave!"

"You're mother isn't dead, Avilar," Ran retorted, then headed deeper into the city, his eyes trained on the glaring white of her robes.

Aurora. Even her name evoked images of mystery and seduction.

Like an ivory phantom, she swiftly negotiated the narrow sun-baked avenue, the cream-hued walls of a building briefly masking her movements. By God, how had the lass managed passage here and so quickly, he wondered, shifting agilely around peddlers, piles of crockery, then ducking beneath hanging sheets of striped fabric.

Bursting into the cramped street, Ran shouldered people, crates, and horses aside and atween the congestion, he caught a glimpse of her protector, Shokai, standing upright as a youth and wielding a staff, clipping attackers behind the knees, then driving the blunt end into another's ribs as anyone able tried to capture the Sultan's lost prize. Stacks of merchandise toppled and crashed, animals scattered, doves took flight, and hawkers shouted as Aurora skirted carts and awning-shaded tables, Shokai defending and moving with her.

Ran called her name. Her gaze searched the crowd, then collided abruptly with his. From the distance, he could see naught but her smiling blue eyes, yet felt her presence as if she'd reached across the separating yards and touched him.

Hastening around the tables, jumping over fallen goods, he shoved an irate vender from his path and advanced as she and her protector back-stepped from the fratch that had turned into a free-booting street brawl. A stray camel obstructed her from his view and impatiently, he shouldered the beast aside.

Aurora took a step, absorbing his masculine power like rain to this parched land.

"Aiee! Only a stubborn fool would walk back under the whip!" Shokai said, recognizing the reason for her delay and smoothly barricading her path. "Flee, Empress," he commanded.

"But—"

Shokai deflected another attack, his voice patient, but winded. "A single post cannot hold up a sagging house, child."

With a longing glance at the bronze Englishman, Aurora fled.

Shokai knocked another assailant off his feet, and for an instant the way was clear. Ran advanced. Shokai pointed the staff at Ran.

"Better to cover the fish than chase the cat," he said, then bowed shortly, swiping a melon and dried fish from a cart and stashing it beneath his ragged clothes afore he turned away, his ancient form swallowed by the shadows.

Ran didn't give chase. 'Twas obvious she neither needed nor wanted his help—this time—and he was considering the old man's cryptic remark when the merchant and his lackeys spirited past like a pack of rabid dogs sniffing her trail.

Ran stuck out his leg, tripping the one man he recognized. Achmed hit the packed earth like a slab of raw meat.

"I see a lengthy stroll in the desert has done naught to curb your foul habits," Ran said archly, his booted foot nudging the Arab onto his back.

The first mate skidded to a halt. "You insisted I not kill a single one," Domingo said in explanation as he immediately took up post aside Ran. *"Capitán?"* Avilar did not like the look on his captain's face. It reeked of vengeance.

Suddenly Ransom grabbed a fistful of garments and dragged Achmed to his feet.

"He beat her." Savage anger manifested in his tone.

And Achmed unsheathed his dagger from within his vest, but lost the opportunity to strike as an English fist slammed down on his wrist. The dagger dropped to the ground, pain thrumming up his arm as a blade point tucked neatly under his bearded chin. He swallowed cautiously, staring into dark gold eyes blazing with promised retribution, then darted a look for his men. The Spaniard's pistol held them at bay. Around them the market resumed as if naught had transpired.

"Why do you hunt that woman?" When Achmed hesitated, Ransom pressed the dagger, pricking his skin.

Achmed winced, suddenly fearing she belonged to the English pasha and gambled on a lie, to play the peasant and beg his way out of this.

"You have interest in her? Achmed will find her for you. Ahh, I shall lay her at your feet, sire, wrapped in silks like the *kadine* of your English sultan."

"My patience grows thin, slaver," Ran gritted in a deadly

voice as he drew the blade across folds of flesh. Blood colored the man's burnous.

"Sheik Rahman ibn il Abduli seeks her!" the trader said in a foul rush of fetid breath. Ran's eyes flared, then narrowed, hot and predatory. "Of this I swear!" Achmed insisted. "He but heard her speak and swore to have her."

Ran stared for a moment, then flicked his blade across Achmed's jaw. Blood bloomed. "That is for striking her," he said, then thrust the slaver aside. Achmed stumbled and fell on his rump, holding his cheek and glaring at the Englishman. Ran gestured for Domingo to join him as he sheathed his blade at his waist and turned back the way he'd come.

"You do not go after her?"

Ran's shoulders rose and fell in a gesture of indifference. "She chose to flee." Again, he thought.

"I saw the old man force her to run, from more than your presence. And this Bedouin prince, Abduli, he is dangerous, *si?*" The man's reputation for stealing foreign women was legendary, as was sending them back to their families; irrevocably shamed but reputedly well loved. "Surely you cannot blame her and allow her to travel without protection."

"She has a guard."

Avilar scoffed. "And where did you find this woman, Ran?" There was a hard silence and then, "Did you offer your protection?" Both knew the answer. "Ahh, then she continues to fend for herself, for she has no reason to trust you with the life everyone seems to covet." Avilar snatched a pear from a cart and tossed a coin at the vender. "And such a pretty life."

"Basta ya¡" Ran slashed a hand through the air for silence as four more of his crew fell in step at his heels. "We have far too much to accomplish, Mister Avilar, to be mucking after a troublesome wench."

"Aye, 'tis bad luck, that one," Baynes said from behind, and Ran stopped and turned, waiting for an explanation.

"Ahh . . ." The crewman glanced briefly at his boots, then met Ran's piercing gaze. "No one'll talk, capt'n. Not even fer a fistful of gold." Baynes shrugged his thin shoulders. "We'll not find a flapping jib in this city. I'm thinking they believe yer in the sack with the Sultan and," his tone accused, "his woman."

Ran stared beyond them, at nothing and at everything. Bloody damn! he thought. It had taken weeks and several pieces of gold to get this close to finding his missing crewmen and now, because of a few moments with Aurora, he was blackened. "Think of those men, Avilar, lost to us now, suffering torture and living in God knows what filth, then wonder why I want naught to do with," his voice grew to a roar, *"that woman!"*

Domingo smiled in the face of Ransom's rage. "You are rid of her, as you've wished. So, why then, my friend," he shrugged, his palms out, "are you staring so intensely at the spot where she vanished?"

Chapter Four

El Djezair
Algiers
Pirate Stronghold

The door swung wide on limp leather hinges, banging against dingy cracked walls and drawing the attention of the occupants within the crumbling inn. Twilight's glow vanished, blotted out by the bulk of a man so tall and broad shouldered he was forced to duck and shift sideways to enter.

The breeze, dry and hot, stirred sand and dust around his booted feet.

All sound ceased.

Eyes locked on the beast with deep red hair and scraggly beard, traveling from the rakish tilt of his cavalier's hat to the wicked jumble of jeweled knives and paired pistols thrust in a wide waistband of leather. His hooded eyes scanned each corner and crevice of the room, pausing once, twice, then returning to the occupants, his gold chains and blades winking in the dull light as he gestured with the flick of a gauntleted hand. Behind him, five heavily armed men filtered inside, their presence a clear threat to anyone who'd dare cross their path.

Slave traders, hinted on the air and curious faces turned away, the dregs of society praying none would recall their existence.

A slim brown-skinned man in a soiled *throbe* hovered at

the leader's side, dipping and half-postulating like a skittish
mouse seeking a morsel of cheese. The leader shoved him
away and chose a place at a low table, dropping his bulk
into a desert-parched chair that threatened to splinter under
his weight. Immediately the innkeeper brought a tray bearing six small steaming cups of coffee, setting it on the table's
center. His back to the wall, the red-haired pirate looked at
it with obvious disgust, yet knew no spirits could be found
in the lands of the Prophet. His compatriots took up a
serving, then stationed themselves at the windows and exits.

Speculative murmurs hummed discreetly, like the flutter
of a sparrow's wing, yet not a soul put voice to thought as
the pirate cupped the porcelain and drained the cardamom-
laced coffee. No one moved or spoke, the tension hunching
shoulders and sending hands to weapons as the innkeeper
laid a platter of sugared dates, nut meats, and figs before the
red-headed man. He relaxed comfortably in the chair, drawing a thin-bladed knife and stabbing a fig. Only then did the
patrons dismiss the intruder, returning their attention to
food and drink.

A turbanned man appeared afore the table, and as if not
noticing his presence, the pirate sampled hungrily from the
platter, then gestured with the blade for the visitor to sit. He
did, and two more pirate-guards flanked the newcomer. The
pirate waved them off.

"What is your pleasure this time, my pasha?"

The pirate swiped his mouth with his sleeve. "Spices. All
that is to be had," he answered in Arabic, popping a syrupy
date into his mouth as he flung a coin in the other's direction.

The Arab caught it, testing his teeth on the circle of gold
before secreting it away beneath the folds of his dark tattered cloak.

"When and where, Foti?" the pirate demanded, his gravelly voice carrying through the noisy room.

Foti glanced around suspiciously, then relaxed back into
the chair, his cool dark eyes unmasking his greed.

"I find the goods you seek will cost you more."

The pirate's gauntleted fist shot out, grasping the folds of the *throbe* and drawing the merchant across the rickety table.

"Spill the words afore I pare you open and decorate this hovel with your entrails."

Nose to nose, Foti stared into the amber eyes of a beast on the prowl for fresh meat. "Careful of your hide, my pasha." His brave smile revealed blackened teeth as his gaze flickered to the robed men shadowing his commrades, curved swords directed at their tender gullets.

"You think to rob me this night, peasant?" The pirate twisted his fist, tightening the garments around the merchant's neck enough to assure Foti he'd allow his crewmen to do battle for the precious cargo's location.

Foti opened his mouth to protest, but the pirate interrupted with "Me thinks the heat has made you mad," as Foti felt a sharp sting in his testicles. He didn't bother to look, knowing the pirate was dangerously close to piercing one just as he had the fig.

"Would my pasha be interested in a livelier cargo?" With the knife still poised on Foti's future, the pirate's eyes narrowed dangerously, and the merchant, hoping it was interest he saw and not anger, rushed to say, "A vessel, in six days' time, docks in Tangiers before setting her sails for the Colonies."

"I deal in spices, not pounds of human flesh." There was a soft gasp from somewhere to his left, and the pirate glanced to the side, studying the room's occupants; a hooded man scooped food from a bowl with two fingers, shoving it in his mouth as insects crawled over his table; the innkeeper cuffed a boy who swiped too slowly at the dirt; a rat skittered across the floor unnoticed.

"If the infidels are careless enough to be taken captive," the pirate brought his gaze back to the merchant as he shrugged, "then it is *kismit,* my pasha. The fools are worth ten times the value of a few herbs."

The pirate's smile was brittle and calculating, his eyes never breaking contact as he released the merchant, then gestured to one of his men to join him. The merchant hovered over the cups of coffee. As the sun set, a deal was struck and broken, then struck again.

Lamps were lit, the muddy darkness glowing gold.

And the boy shifted closer, his rag skimming the tables as the haggling intensified; the pirate demanding a manifest, Foti refusing. The innkeeper emerged from a curtained-off room, scowling at the youth as he marched over and grabbed his arm, tugging impatiently. But the youth was far too interested in the deal than keeping his job and yanked back just as the pirate leaned forward to offer his bond.

"Oh, nay! Do not!"

Ransom's head jerked up, his gaze searching out the intrusion as his hand slid immediately to his knives.

"Relax, sit; is nothing," Foti coaxed his infamous guest, trying to bring the bargain to a close and coin into his pocket. He put himself between the pirate and the interruption. "The boy is impudent as the young will be," he soothed further, and cast a meaningful glare at the innkeeper.

"How can you be party to this?"

Again the voice, Arabic, yet unmistakably familiar. And Ransom shot to his feet, the chair toppling backwards to the dirt floor as he stared into the crystal blue eyes that had tormented his dreams for the past weeks. Sweet saints, he thought, grinding his teeth nearly to powder. What was *she* doing *here?*

Foti was slower to rise, his eyes shifting suspiciously between the red-haired pirate and the boy. "What is this? You seek to drive up the price with games, *ahmar* pasha?"

The lad broke the innkeeper's hold, rushing forward, and Foti's eyes rounded as the ripe shape of feminine hips and thighs molded to the robes.

"A woman!" Foti glared at Ran, unsheathing a curved knife. "You deceive me with a *woman!*" he bellowed as if the last word wasn't fit to remain on his tongue.

The room erupted in instant chaos, men grappling to see the unveiled female for themselves as Ran reached, pulling her over furniture and tucking her protectively to his side.

Her sloppily wrapped turban sagged and the thick black braid secreted inside the cloth fell.

Men scrambled wildly, mad for a piece of her.

"Grievin' mothers, pest, but you've made a muck of things—*again,*" Ran stressed as he carved, pierced, and sliced in defense.

"Dinna shelve the blame with me!"

"By God, 'tis where it lies!" With his meticulous plans destroyed, Ransom was uncertain whether Foti suspected his true motives, yet fleeing the country in all haste was his only choice; leaving his captured men behind, the consequence.

Three Algerines charged at the couple and Ran bellowed, "Domingo, take her!" and shoved her toward his first mate as fist met flesh.

Domingo grabbed, pushed her behind him, then, eager for a fight himself, sent her toward another crewman. "Quincy, take this," he shouted, joining the fray to cover his captain's back.

Quincy flashed a grin at Aurora, then propelled her into the arms of his comrade, both men deciding they were all better off if the interfering woman were left to the fates.

Aurora felt like a pendulum, bouncing from man to man, until a crewman was struck with a blade and she found herself alone in the middle of the frackus. A man grabbed her from behind, dirty hands mauling her, his body banging rhythmically against her buttocks as he tried to lift her robes. Ran retrieved his knife from an Algerine's thigh and spun about to catch the sight an instant afore her head snapped back into the Arab's face. Blood spurt from his hawk nose as she shifted, ramming her elbow into his gullet. The Arab folded and she brought her clasped fists down against the back of his neck, sending him to the dirt floor.

Ran was momentarily stunned at both her swift, clipped motions and the remorse on her face as another robed man threw himself in her direction. Ransom lunged, deflected the attack, clamped an arm about her waist, and backed toward the door; and amongst the slamming fists and flashing knives, the hooded man set aside his empty rice bowl and

stood, sliding a wood staff from beneath his beggar's cloak.
The beggar swung, expertly clearing a path to the exit, and
as Ran's crewmen closed ranks, allowing escape, he recognized her ancient protector.

"Domingo! Castille! Forge ahead and make way our freedom," Ran commanded once beyond the door, his burden
like a slippery fish in his grasp. He tightened his hold til she
gasped for air, then, certain she'd cease fighting him long
enough to listen, he hissed in her ear, "By all that is holy, if
you knew 'twas me, why did you not keep silent?"

"Och, and 'twas not a shock to see you primped and
painted like a Spanish peacock!" she returned in heated
whispers, and Ran set her to her feet with more force than
necessary, propelling her down the street, Lougière, Quincy,
and a wounded Baynes a few feet behind.

"What have you to do with that man, Ransom? Are you
in truth a slaver?"

Slaver. The word sounded like a curse from her lovely lips
and he looked down at her soot-darkened face, her blue eyes
glittering with revulsion as she wiggled beneath the *throbe,*
freeing *the sack* from beneath and jamming her hand inside.

"Foti Kafar is . . . is . . ." she foraged deeper into the bag.

"Pig fodder?" Ran supplied, urging her along and glancing back; Shokai was naught but a shadow moving up
behind.

"Aye, aye. The man possesses no soul, only those of the
innocent!" She halted, and one by one slapped the contents
of her bag in his hand, forcing Ransom to stop in the center
of the street, cup his palms, and juggle a jumble of pouches,
bottles, pebbles, and candles. "He thinks naught of tearin'
fathers and mothers and children—oh, Ransom, *the children*—from their homes and families!" She paused and met
his gaze with honest question in her own. "Have you naught
but stones in your heart, m'lord?"

"Sweet saints," he growled to the heavens. "I should have
let them have you!" The woman's thoughts shifted faster
than the winds. A silver dagger and a small latched box
topped the unbalanced stack and he blasted her with,
"What do you woman? We must make haste!"

"A wee moment, Ransom. Have patience," she scolded as if they weren't about to be set upon by the foulest creatures of this land.

Footsteps approached, warnings sounded.

"Baynes!" Ran demanded, catching a loose candle stub and feeling foolish and very husbandly.

"They near, sir," the young man reported, holding his arm.

She slipped a tiny pouch inside Baynes's shirt front, giving it a pat. "Wet it to a paste, lad, smear on the *cleaned* wound," she said, holding open the sack, and Ransom knew he looked ridiculously grateful as he dumped the pile inside. "Twice afore each sunrise."

Baynes stared from her to the suspicious lump in his shirt as Shokai appeared, parting the group with his staff and taking his place at Aurora's side.

Her gaze flew to Ransom's, her words ringing with a finality that soured his gut.

"Farewell, m'lord rescuer." She turned away, the odd pair slipping into an alley, figures quickly fading into the dark.

Though he could not reveal himself, a tiny spot inside Ransom begged not to let her leave holding such horrid images of him.

In three strides he was upon her, lightly catching her arm. She turned, her expression so blandly unaffected he imagined she'd already put thoughts of him aside. He called himself vain for feeling stung, yet the prick to his pride made his voice harsh.

"Will you sentence without trial?"

"I heard you speak the words." The disappointment in her voice struck him like a blow.

He pulled her closer, staring deep into her eyes. "Look at me, pest, and tell me you believe in truth I'd sell a life for a fistful of gold."

Aurora's gaze swept his features, probing beneath dirt and henna-dyed hair, unkempt beard and clothing bespeaking his trade—to the man, to the spark of need disguised in his amber eyes, hiding the true strength of his heart. A clear pool of water flashed in her mind, and her misconceptions melted like warmed honey as she reached out, her fingertips grazing his jaw, sliding softly over his lips.

"I've judged and done so poorly. Will you be forgivin' me, Ransom?"

For a splintered moment he came unhinged, his muscles slackening, loose and floating toward her, and he had the strange sensation of falling. He leaned closer; her mouth lay a whisper beneath his, tempting, her lush curves swathed in boys clothes beckoning he take her with him, now, afore she vanished, and he ached, God, how he ached to taste the almond flavor hovering on her lips.

"Captain! A handful comes, at five knots!" Lougière called urgently and Ran twisted a look at his gray-haired quartermaster, armed and prepared to defend his back.

Unsheathing his cutlass, Ran's gaze snapped to Aurora, but Shokai was pulling her into the dark.

Ran took a step toward her.

"Gone, all me mates gone 'cause of that fool woman!" Baynes cursed, sword in hand as he threw the pouch where she'd disappeared.

Ran's features darkened, sudden and sharp, and he turned his back on her, striding past his men and taking the lead. Damn and blast! If not for her, 'twould never be a fight yet to finish, nor missing crewmen to pay the debts of his weakness.

Ran was vulnerable, dangerously so, and more determined to dismiss his unwanted feelings for the Scots lass. Yet even as he led his crew to safety, the haunting fragrance of ginger lingered where she'd touched, reminding him how glorious a temptation she was.

Above them yellow light shone from an open window of the inn, a solitary figure watching, listening; then slowly, shrouded hands grasped the latch and sealed away the night.

Chapter Five

"Prepare to cast off!" Ransom roared, doffing his gloves as he strode up the gangplank. Crewmen scrambled and made ready to sail, securing yard and boom and standing clear of the captain's temper, for their leader rarely raised his voice and his terse commands boded ill.

Dahrein met Ran at the rail.

"Sahib?" The boy darted around him, nervous and eager to speak, but Ran didn't notice.

"Not now, Dahrein." Damn interfering female, Ran thought, slapping gloves against his thigh as he strode toward the passageway.

"But I must warn—"

"Be gone, boy!"

Dahrein stopped and the abruptness of it made Ran halt. He tore the feathered hat from his head, blowing out a breath afore he gestured for the boy to join him. Ran opened the hatch and stepped over the raised rim, waiting for Dahrein to do the same, then moved down the companionway to the great cabin. Ran paused at the door, turning to the boy. Dahrein bore that same look, expectant, prepared to give his life for his benefactor, and Ransom wished the lad would think more of himself than of his captain; Dahrein's harsh childhood and gentle heart made him deserving of so much more.

Ran dropped a hand to Dahrein's thin bare shoulder with a gentle weight. "I beg your forgiveness, lad."

Dahrein's odd pale eyes widened. Sahib had never spoken to him in this manner, giving him concern over the cause.

"What is it that you wish to warn me about?"

"A woman." He poked the air toward the cabin door. "In there, sahib."

Ran's lips thinned, his features darkening. Domingo, up to his waistcoat in woman, thought it amusing to present his captain with a luscious tempting female now and then. And Avilar was the one man who knew why Ran always sent them packing, disappointed but with a purse filled with coin.

"Tell Mister Avilar to report in two minutes. By the Gods, I'll cut off his toes for this!"

"No, sahib!" Then more calmly, "No, I do not think this one is a gift from the Spaniard."

The boy's frown, adult and deep with speculation, sent Ransom's thoughts colliding. He stared at the door. Aurora? Nay, she could not have beaten him to the ship, even if she knew its location. But then . . . Ran shoved open the door and froze on the threshold. Her back was to him, a dark shawl wrapped about her shoulders and head. His heart pounded as she rose stiffly from the chair afore his desk and turned, and Ran hoped his mouth was shut for in truth he was stunned and, secretly, a little disappointed. But the woman was lovely, pale, delicate, her narrow shoulders encased in somber black, the thinness of her body accented by the unappointed gown, yet there was a sereneness about her, almost ethereal.

Nay, she was definitely not one of Domingo's women.

"State your purpose, mistress, I am a busy man."

She flinched at his first words and Ran found himself annoyed with a weakness he never witnessed in Aurora.

"You—you are Ransom Montegomery?"

Ran measured the dark-haired woman against his crew's safety, then nodded tersely.

"Then I am your sister."

Ran snickered meanly. "I am a bastard, woman, and have no sisters." He strode across the massive cabin.

"A half sister," she corrected, blushing at his rudeness. "We possess the same father."

Ran's stride faltered as he tossed the last of his disguise on the worn brocade chair adjacent the porthole.

"You have proof of this, of course," he said from behind his desk, removing his weapons and laying them neatly aside.

"Yes, ah, certainly."

When no evidence was forthcoming he glanced up to see her attention locked on his blood-covered knives. Her gaze flew to Ransom and she swallowed visibly, taking a step back.

"The proof, mistress." Grievin' mothers, she looked prepared to swoon!

The woman shook herself, her hand trembling as she opened her reticule and dipped into the sack. "I am Rachel Ortiz," she said as she offered a gold ring. Ran eyed first the piece and then her afore accepting it. "My mother is—was—a courtesan." Ran looked up, stared briefly, then returned his study to the ring. "Granville Montegomery spent time with my mother in Madrid. I am the product of their brief affair." She offered no shame in the confession, and Ran admired her for the small dignity. "I was sent away as a babe to a convent and have only recently learned of my mother's death. She left me no legacy, Señor Montegomery, nothing but a letter explaining my parentage and that ring as proof. Your—our—father gifted it to her."

"A ring means naught." He set it on the edge of the desk in front of her, yet she made no effort to reclaim it.

"Mayhaps these will be the confirmation you desire?" She lifted a parcel from the floor beside the chair, placing it carefully, almost reverently, on the desk and sliding it across to him. With amazing speed Ran sliced the securing string and unwrapped a small stack of letters. His father's handwriting glared at him from the pile and he grasped one, peeling it open. They were love letters, disgustingly passionate, speaking of loneliness and need for the woman he called Rosa and the child she would give him.

Rage, warranted and yet controllable, churned inside

him, and he forced his gaze away from Rachel. Ransom wanted to smash something, wanted to have the pleasure of tossing this bit of fluff off his ship and bidding her a fruitful life far from his sight. But he could not. He'd been raised with a chivalrous code; Rachel Ortiz was his sister, though of that Ran could be no more certain than to hear it from his father's own lips. He would do as expected of a Montegomery. 'Twas the final stone to the heap already piled high with troubles.

"What do you want of me, sister?"

Rachel's shoulders relaxed and she sank dramatically into the chair. Ran looked to the heavens, shook his head, then offered her a glass of water. She sipped, and he settled his rear against the edge of his desk, muscular arms folded over his chest.

"I am alone," she began in a tiny voice, staring at the glass clutched tightly in her hand. "I've nowhere to live, no prospects of marriage—"

"Are you a virgin?" he interrupted, and her head jerked up, her white skin blooming red. Ran wasn't affected by her unschooled reaction. "If I'm to provide . . ." He paused. " 'Tis what you ask of me, is it not?"

She nodded, her eyes round as saucers.

"Then I must be aware of your attributes as well as your lack," he said, coming around the side of the desk and dropping lazily into a chair, "if I'm to see you properly wed and bedded."

Her red cheeks seemed to flash with embarrassment, and her eyes took on a sharpness he hadn't expected.

"You are a cold man, Ransom Montegomery. And incredibly heartless."

"I do not deny who or what I am, mistress." He shrugged indifferently. "And 'twould benefit you to never forget 'tis so, for 'tis I who is sacked with finding a match for a dowerless bastard sister."

She could not hold his gaze and dropped her own to her lap. A flicker of sympathy flamed inside him, and he cursed his callous manners, but skittish weak females were utterly useless in this part of the world, and he imagined Rachel

would fit nicely into proper English society. That she was
raised in a convent, pure as Irish linen, would provide her
with an enticing lure for a young conquesting buck and
mayhap her questionable background would be over-
looked. She was, after all, a Montegomery. Ran nearly
laughed at the absurdity of that, yet kept his face impassive.
His lineage blackened him like a bleedin' plague, and afore
him sat another sin of his father's debauched life.

She winced as he sat upright and struck flint to a blood
red candle, then grasped a quill lying across an ornately
carved silver writing box, dipping it into the well. He slid a
scrap of paper from a stack and scribbled quickly.

"Make ready yourself in three hours," he said and when
protested he cut her off with, "We sail with the morning's
tide in four. I will send my man as escort that you may
retrieve your baggage. Be forewarned, this ship meets with
another in ten hours and you *will* be on it."

"Am I to know to where you are packing me off?" she
said with a spark of defiance. He looked up, sprinkling sand
on the missive, shaking and folding it, then tipping the
candle and affecting his seal without taking his eyes from
her.

"To my home, Rachel. You will be well tended in a
manner befitting my sibling." There was no gentleness in his
tone, only the ring of a man used to giving orders and
expecting them to be implemented. He stood and strode to
the door, calling for Dahrein. The boy appeared, head
bowed. "Dahrein. This is Mistress Ortiz, my . . . half sister."
Ran introduced her briskly, ignoring the lad's shocked look
as Rachel rose and joined them. "Bid you see her properly
settled in a vacant cabin and post Mister Castille at her
door." Ran looked at Rachel, his eyes unyielding. "You will
not show yourself on deck, and you will obey my directives.
Is that understood?" He refused to explain that a woman in
this country, let alone aboard his ship, was reason enough
for mutiny, and he hadn't the time nor the desire to beat his
crew into submission over so frail a female. One look from
the one-eyed Castille and she'd banish herself to the cabin
regardless, he thought with a crooked smile. "This will as-

sure your *homecoming,"* the word stuck in his throat as he handed her the sealed letter, "upon your arrival."

Dahrein stared intensely at the woman for an improperly long moment, then, with a bland expression, waited for her to follow.

Rachel paused afore the raised-rim threshold, her hand resting lightly on Ran's forearm, her glossy black eyes lifted to meet his.

"Thank you, brother. I would ask for the ring and letters when you have satisfied your misgivings."

With that, she lifted her skirts and padded after Dahrein.

Ran shut the door with a snap, spun on his heels, and stormed across the great-cabin, halting behind his carved desk.

He yanked open the right drawer and withdrew a latched box, dropping it onto the cluttered surface. He stared at it for an instant, then flipped the catch, the lid, and plucked a ring from the velvet. Snatching up the one Rachel had left, he compared the two.

"Blast you, Father!"

Screaming at him in confirmation was the spread eagle of the House of Montegomery.

"Is this the legacy you leave me? And how many of your bastards will seek me out for a piece of your name!"

A gloved hand tipped, spilling coins into a robed man's palm. The recipient plucked one from the pile, biting it afore secreting the remainder in his purse.

"Where and when?"

Again the cloaked figure thrust out a hand, slapping a scrap of paper in the other's fist.

The robed man read the missive. "I risk much for this." He jingled the purse.

A pistol appeared, the long barrel pointed at his gullet. The robed man grunted and turned away.

* * *

It was a hovel.

But to the woman lying on the dirty cushions 'twas a palace. Though she'd sprinkled pennyroyal on the cushion to disguise the odor of the last soul who'd slept there, 'twas far better to have softness beneath her skin than the unyielding skin of mother earth. Snuggling beneath the threadbare carpet she used as a blanket, Aurora toyed with her amulet and gazed at the stars, clear and bright through the hole in the wall cut to resemble a window. She wondered if Ransom was searching the heavens this night, using the pinpoints of light to guide his ship to his next adventure.

She sighed, rolled over onto her back and blew out a breath.

He was gone, of that she was certain. Just as she'd felt his presence, the heat of his gaze, the width of his powerful shoulders, the weight of his boots as if they pressed down on her heart the moment he'd stepped into the inn, the emptiness tearing at her now bespoke his absence. Though she'd experienced little of him, she missed that sensation of warmth and safety.

Aurora knew he blamed her for "mucking up" his plans, whatever they were, yet 'twas the scraps of information she'd gathered which brought her to that crumbling pesthole and, dangerously into his path. She hoped the young lad Baynes had used the powders on his wounds; her toadstone ring had heated to nearly burn her finger, warning her of the taint of poison in the open wound.

"Shokai?"

"*Hai*," came from the lump stretched afore the door, protecting her with his life.

"Why do you think he was dealing with Foti?"

"A leader owns many faces, child."

"I suppose." Her sigh blended to a light laugh. "Great stones, but did you see those hideous boot he wore? To beyond his knees with gold tassels. And that red hair. Och, 'twas a sight."

Shokai offered no more than a grunt, but he'd always been a man of few words.

"Has it occurred that our information on me father has

brought us into the path of the Englishman thrice in three fortnights?

Shokai shifted to his back, old bones cracking in the dry silence. "When two paths are struck, who is to say they will not cross?"

"You think he knows something?"

"Ee-ayy!" Almond-shaped eyes flashed at her, and Aurora recognized the command to think things through afore taking a wild guess.

"Nay, he couldna," she said, satisfied the three seconds of contemplation were enough to know. Shokai groaned, muttered to himself in his native tongue and rolled over, dismissing her.

"Ransom does not care for me, thinks I."

She thought Shokai laughed, but couldn't be certain.

"Och, he has a fierce lustin' fer me, aye, but enjoyin' our meetings, nay." She sighed loudly, her thoughts clouded with images; the luxury of his kiss, feeling the exquisite heat of his big hands on her body, and discovering if he was that exquisite warm bronze color all over. Aye, 'tis likin' that I am, she thought, then gasped, images gone dark and her head suddenly pounding.

She sat up sharply.

"Shokai!" she screamed afore the door shattered.

Chapter Six

Ran lurched out of the chair and moved to the port window, bracing the flat of his palm against the frame. The ship rocked, knocking the pier, and though his gaze remained fixed on the lantern-lit vessels in the harbor, his mind was on the crewmen he'd lost.

"So, Foti was incorrect," he said unnecessarily.

"Not quite," Domingo put in. "The ship will be in Tangier, unfortunately not for another fortnight, mayhaps even two."

Ransom muttered a curse and turned back to the long polished table lined with his officers. Two chairs were empty, a reminder of the price paid.

"What we do now, Capt'n?" a sailor asked from the far end, nervous over his new position.

"Pray, Willy, 'cause if that wench 'adn't given up the captain—"

Domingo sent Baynes a quelling glare. "We can hardly fault the lady."

"Why the bloody hell not? If she ain't ruinin' any lead we got, we're draggin' her out of a bleedin' frackus every time we see the wench."

"I believe 'twas our captain who did the dragging." Domingo met Ran's gaze, smiling in spite of the unimpeachable glare he received.

"An' what's a female doing in a men's place dressed like a lad?"

They looked to Ran, but he refused to speculate. He'd

done the like constantly since they'd parted in the street
two days ago, though forming an objective opinion wa
impossible, for he knew naught of the woman's past. Ye
'twas the markings he'd glimpsed on her silver dagger tha
bothered him still. 'Twere familiar. Nay, not so much tha
he could recall them as a whole but only in part. Was it th
never-ending knot that captured his attention in that fleet
ing moment or merely the swirled silver hilt, smooth from
frequent handling? And grievin' mothers, why did she no
use the weapon in her defense, for 'twas obvious he
strength was outmatched regardless of her ability to dres
down the Arab. And why was she there, in that shop, at tha
moment? How long had she been waiting? Disguised her
self, why then did the fool woman give them both up to th
pit brimming with thieves and marauders? She had to hav
known the dangers!

God's blood, he couldn't think of her without the anger
wouldn't allow himself the privilege; his control would fa
ter, weak to her beauty and energetic charm and the explo
sive desire he felt whenever he looked into her clear blu
eyes.

"Think she's followin' us?" the coxswain put to his com
rades.

"If she is, that means we've a spy aboard the *Lion?*"

There was a strike of silence then, "Scuttlebutt like that
earn you a blade in yer back, Mister Baynes," came from
the usually mute bosun, Connor Lockewood.

Leelan Baynes glanced down at his dinner plate, the
grabbed his copper mug and drained his ration of preciou
rum, realizing the rashness of his comment and the rumor
such speculation could cause. He rubbed his wounded arm
and the ship's surgeon bid him let him attend it again
Baynes nodded, yet kept his face impassive, regretting th
loss of the medicine the woman had given him, for augh
must be less painful than being lanced and drained.

" 'Tis well the lass is gone, then," Lougière said, swipin
his lips with a napkin, then tossing it across his plate as h
came to his feet. "I've the first watch," the quartermaste

eminded his captain, then sauntered from the cabin,
Lockewood following.

Ran dropped into his chair, toying with a fork and listen-
ng to the discussion, mostly concerning Aurora and her
strange little guard, with half an ear, for nothing could be
accomplished until the slave ship, *Black Star,* made her
rendezvous in Tangier. That they could be sailing into a trap
hadn't been far from his thoughts, and as he considered and
discarded possible weaknesses in his plans, he filled the
cracks with precautions to be implemented. He trusted his
men, and though earned at heavy cost, Ransom knew from
experience that if a man wore a mask long enough, he would
not recognize the uncovered face in the mirror.

"You may take your leave of me," he said without moving his gaze from the fork, and when men hastily departed,
he added, "But not of this ship."

Disappointed groans accompanied an "Aye, aye, Capitán," from the Spaniard as he snatched a half-loaf of bread
from the table, tearing off a chunk as he left.

Dahrein entered, moving on shoeless feet to pile a tray
with soiled plates and flatware. Impeding the lad's duties
Ran went to his desk, sinking into the Moroccan leather
chair and propping his feet onto the polished surface.

Taking up a whetstone he put a fine edge to his favorite
blade.

"Capitán?" Domingo called from the threshold, and only
Ran's gaze shifted as he worked blade to stone in smooth
practiced strokes.

"Mister Avilar," Ran muttered dryly, then noticed the
worry creasing the Spaniard's usually smiling face. He slid
his booted feet to the floor, brows drawn tight as Domingo
stepped back to allow someone passage.

A hooded figure appeared and Ransom immediately recognized the hunched shape.

Aurora's guard.

For the love of Neptune, how had he managed passage
here, within hours of the *Lion*'s docking? And to find the
ship in such a congested port?

Without waiting for permission, the old man shuffled slowly into the cabin, his wood staff ticking off each step.

Ran's heart tumbled strangely in his chest, for one fact stood out.

Shokai was alone.

Head bowed, the man stood motionless as Ran gestured for Domingo to step inside. Closing the door behind him, Domingo took his place to the far left of his captain, bracing his elbow on the high back of a chair, his shoulders pressed to the cabin wall.

"You could be aboard for only one issue, old man. What mishap befell your 'empress' this time?"

"A beautiful woman comes to learn much grief, my lord."

"I do not believe for a moment that woman's troubles lie within the contours of her face."

"But when even the finest perfume is gone, the scent will surely fade."

"Well, you have your wish, Ran."

Ran slanted a chilling look at Domingo.

"You wanted her gone, now it appears the lady has been abducted. Am I correct?" the Spaniard asked Shokai, and the Japanese guardian nodded. "Now, *Capitán*," Domingo said with relish. "Whose desire for the woman is grand enou—"

"Abduli," Ran rasped caustically, his fingers flexing on the knife hilt, his grip fading his knuckles white.

"Hai," Shokai clipped, his bow faltering.

"And you've come to bid *me* fetch *your* charge?" Ran's muscles clenched.

"Hai."

"Never," Ran snarled and threw the knife. It thunked into a block of wood fastened to the beam, the gouged center marking hours of practice. By God, Shokai knew not what he was asking!

"My lord—"

"Nay!" Ran stormed across the room, yanking the dagger from the block. "Find another champion, old man. I've lost the appetite for rescue."

"But a spirit cannot be free inside the gilded cage."

Ran dropped his head back onto his shoulders and blew out a breath, Shokai's words striking a penetrating blow. The gilded cage. The *hareem*. The thought of Aurora spending even one moment veiled and hidden as no more than the sexual plaything for the Bedouin soured in his mouth. Great Neptune, he would tear the city apart searching for her if her captor were anyone else, but to bargain with the Bedouin . . .

"Nay. I cannot." Rending open the wounds of his past for a woman he hardly knew was unthinkable.

"Then you willingly allow the desert prince such a bright star?" Domingo asked, but his captain remained silent. "*Madre de dios,* you know the ways of the Qur'an! He will claim her and she will be lost behind *his* walls." Ran's face darkened with molten rage, and Domingo pressed his suit. "Ah well, mayhaps she will be happy to be *rogered* by the famed prince, for 'tis reputed no woman can resist his—"

"Enough! I do not give a fig to rumors. And you, Mister Avilar," Ran jabbed the blade in the Spaniard's direction, "have crossed the line!"

Domingo's face remained impassive, but inside he marveled at the explosive vent of emotion. Ransom Montegomry was usually subdued, controlled, and dangerously ruthless.

"Maidens and fish do not keep," Shokai added fuel to Ran's indecision, and though Ran doubted Aurora was an innocent, the image of Rahman plying his mastery to her flesh spirited unbanked rage through his gut.

Shokai swayed, then abruptly crumbled to the floor. Ran went to his side, gently turning him over, and with the blade cut open his cloak to the cool air. It was then he saw the lash marks on the old man's thin chest. Spitting a curse, he bellowed for his surgeon.

"Ransom." Domingo nudged, and when Ran followed the Spaniard's gaze, he saw the bloody footprints marking the floor and carpet. His attention flew to Shokai's bare feet. The soles were ground raw. "He must have walked the entire distance," Domingo whispered, awed.

"A fool's wisdom comes when he is hurt." Shokai's voice

was weak and gravelly as he laid his wrinkled hand on Ran'
arm. "Condemn the crime, not always the criminal."

"Are you saying Abduli is not responsible for this?"

"Great villainy is often called loyalty, my lord." Ra
wasn't certain the old man's comment absolved himself o
Abduli's men. The surgeon arrived and Ran gave orders t
tend the old man. As Shokai was carefully carted from th
cabin, Ransom stood near the aft window, feet braced wid
apart, his gaze clinging to the full moon and seeing th
woman he'd challenge more than the desert to set free.

*I have weakened to you again, little pest. And I care naugh
for it.*

"We are vulnerable in this port, Domingo. Take the *Lio*
to waters beyond Tangier and remain anchored for no les
than five nights, then make port two miles west. We wi
wait there."

Domingo hid his satisfied grin, knowing his captain wa
in no mood, but could not resist a final pinch. "Tell me
Ran, what was it that changed your mind? What the pluck
little dove would do to you if her protector died, or imagin
ing her writhing beneath Abduli with more than her arm
locked around him?"

Ran's head barely shifted for a look at his first office
half his face covered with a waterfall of maple brown hai
A brow arched, eyes sharp and menacing with controlle
fury.

"Forget that I asked," Domingo said and quickly quit th
cabin.

As the door slammed shut, Ran raked his fingers throug
his hair. A second later the jeweled dagger whispere
through the air, sinking into the wall nearly to the hilt.

Chapter Seven

Dry desert wind whipped and swirled, snapping fabric walls. Sand hissed angrily at the delicate barriers, white granules seeping through the well-seamed skin. In a large open area of the steepled tent, surrounded by small curtained rooms, *throbe*-clad men talked softly, eating, drinking. Women, shrouded in black from head to foot, shuffled behind them, serving, taking away soiled dishes, silent, unobtrusive, unseen.

Beyond the tent walls someone plied talent to a flute.

A dark-skinned man, regal in his bearing, reclined on a dais in the curve of the tent wall. An intricately patterned wool carpet covered the ground before him, upon it platters of dates, pomegranates, peeled figs, and dried Turkish apricots. He sampled none of it, offered no comment to the conversation, yet Aurora felt the sheik's gaze on her as he brought the hookah to his lips, drawing in the sweet-smelling smoke. She kept her head bowed, refusing the man the satisfaction of eye contact, not caring a wee bit for the smugness lurking in those pebble-black depths.

From the moment his men unrolled her threadbare carpet to deposit her at his feet like the spoils of war, she'd refused to speak, aware her accent and the unusual pitch of her voice had enticed him to abduct her. And he'd made no effort to disguise his plans for her. Sequestered for two days

in the women's quarters, bathed and plucked of body hair,
oiled and massaged, Aurora felt like a well-seasoned leg of
mutton prepared for a feast. 'Tis the sheik who'll be doin'
the feastin', she thought realistically. And doin' it on me.

'Tis a slave I've become.

Cailleach, Mother of All . . . Aurora prayed; how long
could her protective spell keep the raven-haired Bedouin
from bedding her? And with no notion of where they'd
taken her, Aurora doubted a single member of this encamp-
ment would defy their handsome leader to lend her aid for
an escape. If only she'd sensed the intruders sooner, mayhaps their flight would have succeeded, but to lose her freedom at the cost of Shokai's well-being was an aspect of this
adventure she couldn't accept. Oh, Shokai, her heart cried.
How did he fare? He'd done his best, she knew, but youth
and numbers pitted against one man were foul odds to
vanquish. And for that reason, Aurora abhorred the man
nested within the mound of elegant pillows, his leg bent and
elbow propped there.

'Twas anger she felt and helplessness, and she was familiar with neither emotion. Aye, her temper was a fierce and
ugly thing she controlled, for it enhanced naught in her life,
but Aurora believed 'twas a flaw the Goddess bestowed to
enrich her, make her stronger. The sheik and his arrogant
actions thus far were not to be held accountable. 'Twere
naught but catalysts, for 'twas the way of this country. Her
own people were notorious for kidnapping and ransoming
heirs of a clan, the snatching ofttimes leading to war, but
Aurora held no hope of such romantic nonsense. She had
no clansmen to champion her.

*Och, 'tis a foin crock of it you've landed in this time, Aurora
me lass, an' wi' nary a way oot.*

Again she felt the sheik's gaze upon her, prying beneath
the layers of fabric and veils, and she suspected his
thoughts.

He had to have this woman. Beneath him, above him, to
fill her sweet flesh and ride her like the Sahara winds til the
fierce ache he carried was satisfied. Yet even now Rahman
could not understand what kept him from the delightful

ask. By right she was his, yet the one innocent brush to her
hand felt as if he'd committed some heinous crime against
Allah.

And Shiek Rahman ibn il Abduli refused to force any
woman.

Yet the sandalwood fragrance of freshly washed skin and
hair and the gauzy veils hiding her curves were driving him
to distraction. He had not lived so long in the west to have
forgotten the seductive pleasure of removing each layer to
uncover the lush treasures beneath.

And it was time to sample her.

He reached.

Muffled hoofbeats blistered through his lust, shouts of
warning renting the air.

The woman's gaze flashed up, eyes as blue as the dawn
sky meeting his, then shifting to the tent flaps. Rahman
clapped and women scattered, men taking up arms. His
captive rose to join the other women, but a slash of his hand
kept her from fleeing. She immediately bowed her head,
trying to cover her hands, and Rahman suddenly thought
the submissive position incredibly uncharacteristic of a
woman he did not know.

The commotion intensified and Rahman's hand shifted to
the hilt of his sword, yet his pose remained relaxed as his
man entered, whispering in his ear.

A towering hooded figure burst through the tent entrance.

Two guards halted him, their swords crossing his chest.

"Is this how you treat a guest, Abduli?" Wind whipped at
his cape, an inky swirl of black around his booted calves.

"When the guest is you."

The woman tensed, her head slowly tipping back, and
Rahman watched her sky-dawn eyes grow round as coins.
Just as quickly, she bowed her head. Abduli frowned at her,
then returned his gaze to the intruder.

"I've no taste for killing this night, Bedouin. Beg off."
The guard's confident snicker was instantly cut short, and
Rahman's gaze dropped to the blades poised atween their
legs. His features darkened with annoyance and with a flick

of his wrist, his liege men cleared a path, allowing passage
The man advanced, yanking on a rope looping his wrist
then impatiently dragging Achmed forward by the ear.

"You send this dog to do your bidding?" came in Arabic
as the visitor released the merchant at Rahman's feet.

The visitor ignored the guards flanking him again, their
swords poised to disembowel at the slightest command.

"I care not how he does his job, *Ahmar Asad*. Only that
he does."

"Apparently not. Then you condone deliberately dishon-
oring her?" He pointed to Aurora.

Rahman shot to his feet. "What lies you speak!"

"She was not alone when Achmed stole her. Her family
was with her."

Rahman bellowed in outrage, his black eyes hard as
stone, and Achmed immediately prostrated himself before
his master, salaaming and begging forgiveness. Rahman
barked a few words in Arabic and his personal guards came
forward, jerking Achmed off the floor.

"Cut off his hand that he may never know the touch of a
chaste woman." Aurora gasped, glaring at Rahman, and he
felt the cut of her gaze.

"You would prefer his head?"

Vehemently, she refused the offer.

"Then his hand it will be."

The guards dragged Achmed away and Aurora looked to
both men in the hopes of ceasing this madness.

Pushing his hood back, Ransom ignored her, refusing to
spare her a glance, for if he but gazed into those lovely blue
eyes he would not accomplish all that was necessary to free
her. The balance was incredibly delicate, the customs with
a life of their own. Ransom's only hope was to bargain,
shame, or reason her freedom into his hands.

He would not leave without her.

Alone but for Aurora, the two men stared, nose to nose,
silent and challenging.

Ransom's gaze flickered insolently down the sheik's lean
form clothed in a billowy white shirt, white breeches, and
dark knee boots.

"You look more the English pasha than the Bedouin prince," Ransom said, the *kaffiyeh* covering Abduli's head and secured with a thick cord the only significance of his race.

Rahman mimicked the glance. "And you dress well as the desert baron, Montegomery," he retorted just as arrogantly.

Aurora groaned at the fashionable discussion occurring when her freedom was at stake. Both men looked at her, but she kept her head bowed.

"What ails you, Abduli, that you cannot find satisfaction in so many woman and must take captives," Ransom paused, "to get what your body needs."

Rahman laughed, sluffing off the insult to his manhood. "I satisfy them all and need more, Englishman." Abduli turned away and dropped to the cushions, leaning close to Aurora and toying with the folds of her robes.

Ran clenched his fists at the open display. Had Abduli taken her to his bed already? Had he tried the luscious body, found it to be pleasurable, and now refused to bargain for her? It drove Ran mad to think on it.

"She is not of your people, Bedouin, and is not obligated to your customs."

"Ahh, but she is mine by right. And," Abduli shrugged, "the merchant has paid the price for his stupidity."

"Does the loss of his hand undo the dishonor to your name?"

Rahman's shoulders tensed, his glare hot, brown fingers pulling the sword a few inches from its sheath in open threat. "Do not question *my* name, English!"

Aurora inhaled sharply and the sheik's gaze snapped to her, sketching her bowed head, the flow of her garments, then with a gentle push beneath her chin, Abduli tipped her head back. Again the sensation that he should not have touched her thus swept over him and he frowned, leaning back a fraction; yet could not take his eyes from her.

Forgetting the Englishman's taunt, he whispered something and dark lashes swept up.

Aurora stared into his raven black eyes, not knowing

what he was about. Silently she thanked the Goddess for sending Ransom, yet she also recognized the powerful desire Rahman displayed only for her. He would fight, mayhaps kill, to maintain his possession. Och, 'twas an honor many women would covet, for his striking good looks and lean muscular form could entice any female into his bed. Except her.

"I want to make love to you," he whispered in Arabic.

Well, Aurora thought, arching a brow. He was certainly going to try.

"I promise nights of scented pleasure and to want for nothing in my house." His finger slid across her veiled lips and he groaned, the touch sweeping him with an odd mixture of denial and desire. "To feel these upon my body, mine upon yours, little blue eyes, is but the beginning." He leaned closer, ignoring the forbidding sensation, and lowered his voice. "I want to put my fingers inside you, feel you grow wet for me, so I may give you the pleasures you were made for."

Och, another takin' to boastin', she thought, yet remained impassive, his lusty talk stirring naught within her even as he whispered close to her ear, "Imagine me inside you, little one, sliding smooth and warm within your—"

"You cannot keep her," Ransom bit out, unable to submit to another moment.

Abduli's gaze sharpened on him. "You dare dictate what I can possess, English?"

The challenge was clear, but Ransom was aware of nothing but Aurora, and the portrait of her naked and straining for Abduli's possession devouring his soul.

"She is mine, Bedouin."

Abduli stiffened and Aurora flashed a look at Ransom, utterly stunned at the daring claim. Sheik Abduli glanced between the Englishman and his captive, instantly recognizing the fire she denied him, was bestowed on the pirate. Fury surged in him, the foul taste of impending defeat souring his ardor. "Have you entered my camp to claim my slave for yourself?" Abduli stood, facing his adversary.

Ran tore his gaze from Aurora. " 'Tis your dishonor, Abduli. She is a protected woman."

Abduli waved him off. "Many of my women have families, English, and few will see them again, but here," he gestured to the empty tent, "she is *my* slave."

My slave. Naught but the possession of her body, Ran thought, and his next words came unbidden. "Then sell her to me."

Abduli's brows rose sharply. He never expected such an offer from this man. Yet when he glanced down at the woman and her eyes remained fixed on the pirate, he realized the undeniable emotions they exchanged were the will of Allah.

But that didn't mean he had to like it.

Pulling Aurora to her feet, he drew her between himself and the Englishman, then folded his arms across his chest. "Can you pay the price, pirate?"

Ran shrugged, black cloth shifting on powerful shoulders. "You have yet to put a name to it." Though he could feel her bright blue eyes on him, he kept his gaze on the Bedouin.

"Long rifles."

It didn't surprise Ransom that Abduli knew he'd brought the long rifles, and 'twas only as a courtesy the weapons weren't being used on him now. But they were a last resort.

Ran shook his head. "Too much for one insignificant woman." Purchasing Aurora like a bolt of cloth ground on his last nerve and he could feel her fuming beneath the veils as the sheik settled his hands on her shoulders with a possessive weight.

"Rifles, molds, and powder." He needed them, desperately, and Montegomery knew it. Yet if the Englishman were here merely as her protector, then Rahman would see the man pay the consequence for his arrogant demands.

Aurora suddenly found herself swept up into Abduli's arms. Ransom took a threatening step, his heart hammering in his chest. Would he keep her and the rifles?

"The weapons for a night's desire, *Ahmar Asad?*"

Her panicked gaze shot between the two men an instant

before the sheik thrust her into Ransom's arms like unwanted baggage. Ran could do naught but accept the shapely bundle, and as he hefted her snugly in his arms, both men knew 'twas as solid as his word of bond.

"Claim her as a man claims his bride." Rahman's lips curved in a cynical smile. "And remember I have ears, Ransom Montegomery." He gestured with an elegant wave to the far left of the tent. "I will know."

Ran had no choice and wordlessly shouldered his way beyond the sheets of silk, striding to the center of the curtained room and unceremoniously dumping Aurora on a mound of pillows. Before he could turn completely away she raised her leg and kicked the back of his knee. Ran went down with a jolt beside her. He stared at her, shock painted across his usually stoic face as she peeled away the veils and scarves.

She propped her head in her palm. "Dinna be treating me like that again, Ransom Montegomery." She wagged a finger beneath his nose.

Ran's lips twitched. He admired her tenacity and courage.

" 'Twas well you held your tongue out there, woman, for I saw my plan dying at your feet."

She sat up sharply. "You brought weapons strictly to purchase me?"

Ran twisted away. Purchase. A soul for a cache of rifles. "Do you question the means to your freedom," he glanced back over his shoulder, "or the act itself?"

"But guns, Ransom, are for naught but to take life. Innocent life."

He turned toward her, propped on his side, forcing his gaze from straying to the loosened robes and the plush figure hinted beneath. "In the desert, little pest, 'tis either defend or die. Abduli needs new weapons and with them, mayhaps he will find his time more occupied and," he eyed her pointedly, "lessen the chance that he will steal defenseless women for sport."

"I was nay defenseless," she huffed.

"But you are here." He waved to the lavishly appointed tent.

"Aye, and so are you." She poked his mighty chest. "And dinna be excusin' the rifles so cleanly."

Ran was in no mood to argue, for 'twas a month's manifest he'd relinquished for her, but it was apparent she wasn't going to let the subject die. "Abduli's people need protection, lass, at least for the children—from warring tribes."

She stared at him, crystal blue eyes unblinking for what felt like an eternity. "You always find me tender spot, don' you now, Ransom?"

Ran groaned at the image her words produced, for 'twas not the softness of her heart his mind dwelled upon. Needing to occupy his hands before they found their way beneath her robes, he yanked at the ties securing his cloak, pulling it from his shoulders and flinging it aside. His gaze touched on the small brazier warming the room and a kettle, then the platter brimming with sweet gooey delicacies; and for an instant the vision of her pushing a sugary date into her mouth, then offering him the chore of licking the heavy syrup from her fingers and lips flashed in his mind. He swallowed tightly, then shoved the platter aside. God's blood, to spend a night with the lass will be merciless torture!

"Why have you done this, Ransom?" came softly on the desert air. He didn't look up. " 'Twas a far journey and surely at great cost to your ships and men."

"Aye." He flicked the gold fringe of a pillow.

"Well?" she pestered, kicking off her slippers.

Ran lifted his gaze and recognized the honest concern for his welfare. It endeared her to him, gave him a fierce need to wrap her in the cloak of his protection and smother her with kisses 'till she'd naught to think on but pleasure. But as she shifted to draw her tiny bejeweled feet beneath her robes, the pampered evidence of her captor's intentions slapped him in the face.

She was prepared for Abduli's bed. Would she have submitted freely or fought the Bedouin?

"Such a fate is deserving of no man or woman." He rolled

over and came to his feet. What other words could he speak? 'Twas truth no human deserved to be sold or traded like a pound of meat, and without doubt 'twas the only solution to free her into his care; but to tell the lass the image Domingo seeded in his mind burned like salt in an open wound, pushing him to travel across the desert for two days without stopping? *Never.* Though 'twas a relief to find her unharmed, to speak the words was to relinquish a weapon he could not afford to give. Especially to this woman. For reasons he cared not name, the lass herself was force enough to make him face the Bedouin.

Damn and blast!

Ran paced.

Aurora watched, pulling on the rope of hair stuffed down the back of her *abayeh* and unwinding the braid. His booted feet wore a crevice in the carpet-covered sand, tension building with his every step. Patiently, she waited for the explosion.

'Twas not long.

"Rahman wanted you."

So, that was it. She rubbed her scalp, loosening the braid. "Aye, 'twas made quite plain."

"So fiercely he will not allow us to leave until he is certain I have," he stalled and she lifted her gaze, "possessed you."

"Och," she waved negatively. "He is simply angered that *he* couldna."

"Nay, his purpose now is to insure the bargain *sealed,*" the word clawed in his throat, "so that I cannot take back the rifles."

"I see." She nodded gravely, disgusted with the handsome sheik. Her virtue was naught but loose coin to Rahman.

" 'Tis a surprise you have not been ravished." Question lingered in his voice. She didn't notice.

"Had you not arrived," she shrugged, "then mayhaps 'twould be so, m'lord, yet at least for a time, the sheik couldna breach me protecting spell."

He stopped, his expression brimming with sarcastic

doubt. "A spell. Of course," he said flatly. Good God, the lass actually fancied herself a sorceress!

She sighed, lying back and stuffing pillows beneath her head. "You've a narrow mind and a chillin' heart, Ransom."

"This you have mentioned afore," he muttered dryly, his gaze darting to the shifting curtain, his body gone still. "And so, the walls *do* have ears."

Aurora leaned upon her elbows and patted the space beside her. "Well, then we canna deprive them," she whispered. "Can we now?"

Chapter Eight

"What?" he practically shouted, then lowered his voice, stretching toward her. "Surely you jest, woman."

Aurora hid her smile.

Och, puir mon. Those eyes couldn't get any farther out of their sockets, she thought, marveling to find him at a loss. Then it was gone, suppressed, controlled. Again, patting the pillow, she watched with pure feminine pleasure as he strode slowly toward her. The *Lord* and *Lady* were generous to this man, she thought as her gaze traveled from his dusty booted feet up thickly corded thighs and beyond, to the lean hips cradling his masculine power and the chest loosely swathed in black, so wide her arms scarcely fit around. A longing she felt for no other climbed through her body, her desire to feel that strength beneath her palms splashing her with quick heat. She accepted it for the sweet pleasure it was and pressed her gaze upward to his face. No measure of emotion shaped his features, yet his eyes held the faint flickering of confusion as he settled to the silken bedding, the nut brown mane of hair briefly shielding his chiseled face. With a toss of his head, he flicked it out of view and met her gaze. Amber eyes smoldered with suspicion.

He was a fine man, the past hour proving much, and she would like nothing more than to succumb to her desire for such a powerful lord. Aye, 'twould only make her stronger to be linked with the Englishman, but for him, 'twould be an act of physical gratification. Nothing more. And Aurora knew he would never allow it to be otherwise.

"What are you about, lass?" he asked cautiously, his gaze traveling down her lush body in a gentle caress.

Aurora flopped back on the pillows, panting. "Oh, Ransom," she cried softly, then purred, a deep throaty growl that robbed him of strength. "Aye, 'tis a way you've about you." She rolled to her side, grinning devilishly in the face of his deepening scowl. "Ochaii! What a braw lad you are. Mmmmmm," she hummed, closing her eyes and lightly shaking her head.

Ran's smile was reluctant and, if anything, skeptical over the success of her antics for the ears beyond the curtain, but sweet heavens, he thought, sinking onto his elbow, the lass was a constant unexpected delight.

She nudged him. "Come on," she whispered. "If we've a performance to give, then 'tis best it be that of two."

Was she mad? He couldn't. 'Twas impossible to not feel the fool and give the makings of pleasure without the pleasure itself. He swore it. But when her writhing grew more animated, her hands smoothing down over her breasts, her belly, Ran could do naught but watch the sensual glide, his loins heating, his heart accelerating. She was tutored. She must be. For no other female could drive his lust to such heights without ever touching him! Then she did, her fingers curling into his shirt and pulling him close.

"Join me or the prince will believe I canna please you." Her tongue passed over her lush lips, and she panted a touch louder.

He couldn't take it. "By God, woman," he growled, pressing her back to the cushions, "I shall give you something to moan about in truth!" His mouth captured hers like a clap of thunder. He molded, plundered, his fingers gripping her jaw as his tongue pushed deeply inside.

'Twas a mistake.

For she answered with the gale of a storm, clawing at his shoulders, stroking his wide chest, the thickness of his arms. She wanted this, ached for his kiss, and until this moment didn't know how much. She savored him, the weight of his chest to her breasts, the twist of his fingers in her hair and the erotic power he yielded with naught but his mouth.

Tongues thrust, waging a fiery duel, and Ran shuddered, his body rock hard and throbbing to be sliding into her silken depths. And when she drew back he knew, 'twas not enough.

"Think the ears are satisfied?" she asked, breathless, smoothing her hand down the flatness of his stomach.

"Nay," he murmured against her lips, taking them again and again, shaping, licking, and nipping. Then his hands came into play, sliding down her shoulders, over her breasts, and she arched into the heavy pressure. He rubbed gently as if scared to touch, then glided lower over her shrouded flesh, seeking the hem.

And she let him, wanted him, embracing the pleasure he gave, his name whispering on her lips as he ground a hot path down her throat. He tugged fabric and the garment slid from her shoulder. Ran eagerly sought her mouth again, but hesitated when his gaze caught on the richly embroidered vest beneath her clothes. It was like cold water to his passion, and he sat back abruptly.

Her chest rising with each needed breath, Aurora leaned on one elbow, frowning. What made him cease, she agonized, breathless, yet said naught. His caustic gaze raked her body. Embarrassed and not knowing why, she covered herself. His eyes flew to hers, and the rage glittering in the golden depths startled her.

"Ransom?" She reached.

He flinched. He hated it, the clothes, the fact that she wore them, and the significance in his life the scandalous attire represented. The *hareem.* Slave to passion. Slave to the laws of *one* man. Misery and death to any who disobey.

He rolled away and quit the room, halting just beyond the curtain when he recalled 'twould not be safe for her to be left alone.

Damn and blast. Ransom thought he was resigned to the culture he detested. Nay, twas the unfaithfulness of the hareem he despised. The unfaithfulness of man to the laws of life. But Aurora was no part of his silent war. By God, what must she think of him? To take her to passions' door, then slam it in her face! Everything surrounding him in this camp made him angry, burrowing thorns into his pride, and 'twas unfair to subject the lass to his own hatreds and doubts. How was he to explain his behavior?

Beyond the curtain tucked in the far corner of the tent, Sheik Rahman ibn il Abduli watched the Englishman. The songs of passion had filtered to him as he smoked, and he was about to allow them complete privacy when Montegomery appeared. He stood still now, head bowed, a dark specter silhouetted against the pale glow from beyond. He was aroused, painfully so, Rahman thought with sympathy. And since he was resigned to never possessing the woman's attentions, Rahman was no more than curious as to what had cut the lovers' play from its path.

Then she appeared, a few steps behind Montegomery. The breath clung in his throat and Rahman thought Allah had come to take him away, for her sensuality was beyond a man's dreams. Her hair was unbound, grazing the floor around her feet, and the light from within their chamber cast a hazy outline of her body against the single layer of cloth. She was naked beneath, her breasts plump and high, the darker centers taut with desire, her waist shaping inward like a fluted glass afore gently swelling into ripe rounded hips.

Allah, you are cruel to deny me this exquisite creature.

She took a hesitant step, whispering Ransom's name, and the Englishman jerked a look at her so possessive, Rahman felt the unaccustomed sting of jealousy.

Ran gazed into her bright eyes, her discomfort and concern ripping a hole in his anger. Without will, his eyes lowered to the robes. Gone was the costume, the jewels from her ankles and wrists, and briefly he glanced into the tent, but could find none of it. How had she known 'twas the garments that bothered him so? Could she truly read his thoughts and know that to see her, a woman so full of energy and life clad thusly, was further bane to his anger?

"Come inside, m'lord," she coaxed in a husky whisper, grasping his fingers. "This pain you hide," his gaze sharpened defensively, "will not find ease this night."

" 'Tis another of your predictions?" Though his expression was harsh, his voice was gentle. "When will I find it?"

She took a step away. " 'Twill come to you, thinks I," she glanced back to add, "when you are ready."

Then 'twill never come, he thought, her fingers feeling incredibly fragile in his grip as he allowed her to lead him back inside, toward the divan. And Ran discarded his bitterness, focusing on her; the shift of her figure beneath the cloth, the sweep of her hair as she settled to the bedding. She lifted her face, her eyes a calm sea blue as she tugged. Ran sank to the softness beside her.

She smiled, slight and knowing as when he first looked upon her, and questions he'd held at bay flooded to his lips.

"What brings a Scotswoman to this parched land?"

Aurora slid gracefully to her knees at the foot of the divan, her hesitation to answer clear as she hovered over the brazier, flipping back the lid of the small kettle to check inside. "I've a quest to fulfill," she finally said, then glanced up, easily reading his doubt. "You dinna believe women can have such a need? You've a—"

"Narrow mind," he finished. "Aye, thin as a string by your estimation. Attempt to stretch it, pest, and tell me what holds enough worth to take you so far from your home."

She snapped the lid shut. "I have no home, Ransom." Pain hinted in her words. "Though when I left Scotland I'd no notion the journey would bring me so far."

"The reason?"

Her gaze faltered, for to reveal such would bring him into her problems and he'd done enough on her behalf. " 'Tis private, this quest." Her expression beseeched him to understand. "You're not offended?"

"Nay, lass, we all have secrets." She looked relieved and he told himself he cared not, for he was eager to be apart from such an intuitive woman; but that she never asked for his help, or invited him into her secrets, left him feeling a touch bereft. She already knew much of him and he naught of her, he realized, following her moves as she prepared coffee, telling himself there was naught else to look upon.

"Why does Rahman call you *Ahmar Asad?*"

Ran offered no comment and suddenly her clear blue eyes

held him prisoner as if she'd a grip on his throat. He could tell she was searching her mind for the translation. She found it, her eyes widening.

"The Red Lion? The pirate?" came in a whispered squeak, half in question, half in shock.

Still he said naught, his features impassive, and he commended his restraint when her gaze slithered suggestively over his body, ending at his face.

She smiled, feminine pleased, and something inside him shifted loose. "Och, notorious company I'm keepin', neh?" she murmured, then wisely changed the subject. "How is Mister Baynes' wound?" She measured and stirred, her breasts swaying gently beneath the voluminous fabric, cloth brushing her nipples. Good God! Did she not know the erotic picture she presented?

"Bloody awful," he bit out harshly, and she looked up, frowning. "He did not use your *potion.*"

Stirring the coals, she shook her head, disheartened as she set the pot to boil. " 'Twill be a high price for such a prejudice, thinks I." She wasn't going to waste time trying to convince the unschooled on the value of nature's cures. 'Twas just so.

"By the by, where is that sack of trinkets?"

Her lips twisted sourly over his choice of words. "When Achmed took me he left it behind." She positioned herself at his feet. "Mayhaps, Shokai has it."

Ran recalled he did. "You do not ask after the old man?"

"He came to you, Ransom, therefore I know he is well tended."

Grievin' mothers, she was trusting. And he refrained from telling her about the man's wounds, for the *Lion*'s physician was seeing to his care and while they were reluctant prisoners, naught else could be done.

Hesitantly she grasped his boot, tugging, and Ran helped her ease off one, then the other. "Why do you this, woman? I need no such pampering."

Neatly she placed them aside. "You've traveled far for me, Ransom, and I can see this place displeases you more than it does me." She shifted enough to pour coffee into a tiny cup. " 'Tis but a wee bit of comfort I offer." She held it out to him. "Naught else."

Her arm outstretched, Ran looked from the cup to her, then leaned forward to accept it, his eyes skimming over her in one sweep as he reclined back onto the cushions. The amulet rested atween her breasts, teasing his gaze. He sipped, watching her intently as she folded the layers of the *abayeh,* veils and head scarves. She rose, placing them on a chest set off to the side, and Ran stifled a groan; for the dim light offered him a luscious sample of her ripe womanly fullness, her plush belly and thighs and the dark treasure atween. He considered throwing a coverlet over her and ending his personal torture. But his imagination refused to play the gentleman and be deterred when she scooped up the platter and set it within his reach. She popped a date into her mouth as she climbed on her knees onto the divan, and the image he'd created earlier took on life as she licked the syrup from her fingertips, unaware of his thoughts.

Thank God, he decided, for he swore on occasion she could read them.

Attempting to discard the pattern of his imagination, he set the empty cup aside and focused on his appetite. She sat slightly above him on the mound of pillows, and as he gathered a handful of nuts and then relaxed, he found her close to his back. He flinched, nearly choking as her hands rested on his shoulders, but she didn't seem to notice and dug her fingers into his muscles.

"Och, Ransom, you've rocks 'neath your skin."

And in me breeches, he thought. He tried to ignore her, even pull away, but she continued the skilled grind and push on his shoulders and neck and he groaned, long and rumbling. It felt bloody good, and as she kneaded the muscle and sinew, tension slowly fled. Ran had never been treated thusly and though it smacked of the subservience of the *hareem,* he knew there was not a submissive bone in this woman's lush body unless she deemed 'twas so. A smile curved his lips as he rolled his head back on his shoulders and she scooted further up on the cushions, her fingers plowing softly into his hair and easing his head onto her soft lap.

"Close your eyes," she whispered into his comfort and he did, nimble fingers moving in small circles over his scalp, smoothing the lines of his face. 'Twas rhythmic, soothing, and Ran felt on the verge of dreams.

She was seducing him into her care.

And he feared . . . into her heart.

Chapter Nine

'Twas dangerous. This vulnerability.

For he ached to touch her, *really* touch her. Yet he was
careful not to, for he recognized the explosiveness when he
did. But sweet mother, he was burning to turn into her arms
and feel the plushness of her body against his own. And let
her, for this moment, soften him.

His life was harsh, possessing none of the gentleness he
experienced at her hand. Not even in his youth. His past and
the shame were constant companions, his bastardy a taint
he chose to openly wear. He needed it that way and took
little pleasure for himself, for to indulge would lead down
the path he'd no intention of traveling, repeating his father's
sins against the innocent.

'Twas why he'd been celibate for the past ten years.

Populating foreign ports with illegitimate heirs was not
the mark Ransom wanted to leave on the world. To see the
slave trade squelched into the sea was. His sex would not
rule him. 'Twas *his* choice, personal and private. Though
the lack of release of his baser need left him a touch frustrated in the beginning, he'd adjusted easily to the absence.
No longer did he miss coupling for the sake of a few moments of primal gratification. And with months at sea, long
physically draining hours of work, the absence of women on
his ships and in the Moslem-ruled ports, 'twas an easy
enough vow to maintain.

Until Aurora.

No other tempted him like this trouble-seeking Scot.

No other person, man or woman, could sense his thoughts and emotions without speaking, like her. She unnerved him and intrigued him, and even with his eyes closed he could see her vibrant beauty, feel the earthy sensuality she wore as if layered over her fragrant skin, unaware of the power she wielded.

His blood rushed. His manhood flexed with thickening need.

Ahh, God, help me, he thought, wanting to lose himself to the desire she created. But he couldn't. Not now, not with her, for the consequence was too high for his conscience to bear. Avilar would be laughing if he saw him now, testing fate with his head pillowed on soft, scented thighs, her fingers sifting gently through his hair, her humming tugging on the strings binding him to his vow.

Temptation riding him, Ran thought it best to direct his lusty thoughts elsewhere.

"How old are you, lass?" Harmless subject, he thought, though his voice sounded strained to his own ears.

"Five and twenty," she answered easily.

He opened his eyes and twisted to look at her. She smiled, her strokes never ceasing.

"I thought you much younger." He imagined her but seven and ten. 'Twas comfort to know he hadn't had these lecherous thoughts for a girl.

"And you, m'lord, are three and thirty, aye?"

His features pulled taut. "Aye," he muttered, stunned by her accuracy, then settled to her lap again. "How long have you known the old man?"

"He is called Shokai." A tightness pricked her tone. "We met nine years ago. He saved my life."

" 'Tis a frequent occurrence for most men you encounter?"

"None but two." She bent and planted a sweet kiss to his forehead, whispering, "And I thank you, m'lord rescuer," afore drawing back. "Shokai is from Nippon . . . the Japans, neh?"

He flashed her a knowing glance, aware of that fact. "His loyalty to you is unmatched."

"Aye." She shifted, curling her body around his shoulders, then propping her chin in her palm and looking quite studious. "Like a father, he is, but oftimes more *sempai* than friend," she sighed, "though he doesna say very much."

"Sempai?" His eyes sketched her features, from the long lashes framing bright blue eyes to the midnight black hair draping over her shoulder to pool on the cushions like a river of shimmering velvet.

"Old one, more learned," she explained. "We are but students to their wisdom and experience. Shokai-san is very inciteful."

She loves him, Ran thought, unreasonably jealous of the ancient man, and without caution he reached out, capturing a gleaming lock and sanding it atween his fingers. Wrapping it around his fist, he brought it to his nose, inhaling deeply.

"God's blood, but you always smell so inviting."

"Would you care to be so near if I dinna?"

He chuckled, snuggling against her belly and breasts like a child, then realized what he was about and jerked back, embarrassed.

"Nay, lay sweetly, Ransom," she coaxed. "If 'tis where you find a wee comfort, I'll not begrudge you your pillow."

He hesitated, a grim battle plain in his amber eyes, the muscles of his body firming with resistance, and Aurora sought only to ease his turmoil, no more, and reached out to brush the unfettered strands from his face. He tensed further, his hooded eyes suspicious. The aura of the predator clung to him, the hunt inbred as if 'twere another of his senses, calculating, efficient. She didn't have to ask to know he'd had little love and gentle caring in his world; his edges were dangerously sharp, jagged. And yet 'twas this unyielding strength that drew her, the dark suppressed power. Like the hot coals hidden beneath white ash, 'twas there, deceptively perilous to touch, a warning of heat, yet she didn't fear the burn. She longed for it.

Her fingers whispered over his jaw, sinking into the hair at his nape and still he resisted, fighting not to close his eyes and succumb to his own need. He was near, propped on his side as she was, yet his long body lay in the opposite direction. His hands were still, marking a line atween them.

"Do you fear me, Ransom?" she challenged softly, drawing her hand back.

He did, for she was like a shifting wedge, forcing it's way beneath his well-tooled armor. "You are a most unusual woman."

She arched a brow. "You seek what is not there. I am no different than any other of my gender, except that I care naught to hide behind the wall of society and the will of a man." She paused, staring deep into his eyes. "For I have known neither."

An outcast, he thought, the loneliness in her confession touching a barren spot in his heart, filling it swiftly. 'Twas a common thread they shared.

"Yet you come to a land where women are treated as less than sheep?"

"The ways of Islam are not mine, Ransom. But for a time I can adjust enough to survive." Her gaze dropped to the pillow, a finger tracing the pattern. " 'Tis simply the path my journey has taken."

"Aye, constantly into mine."

She looked up, grinning mischievously. " 'Tis *kismet,* you think?"

"Nay, I do not." He scowled. " 'Tis but a woman who cannot keep herself out of men's affairs."

Aurora laughed, a warm throaty purr that stole beneath Ran's skin. "You would find your life much simpler, pirate lord, if you realized men do not rule the universe."

"In this land they do."

His disgust apparent, Aurora frowned. "But you are so familiar with the ways of Islam, I had thought surely you were—" He stiffened, the sudden motion like a shot of pain jolting through his long body and into hers.

"Nay!" Abruptly he rolled away to the edge of the divan, his elbows propped on his knees, his gaze on his clasped hands. "Nay," he repeated harshly. "I am *not* a Moslem."

"And yet you were so readily accepted into this camp?"

He turned his head to look at her. So much resentment and fury in those eyes, she thought, wanting to comfort him.

"My presence has been accepted, though on exceedingly thin terms." His glare sharpened, his next words a furious snarl. "Because Rahman ibn il Abduli is my half brother."

"How fortunate to have a brother," she rushed to say, and an angry growl rumbled in his chest as he thrust off the cushions.

Does he despise the brother, or that they shared only one parent? Aurora couldn't understand his resentment. Abduli was his family! No matter the sheik's beliefs. Och, would that she could claim such a privilege. But Ransom wanted naught of his brother, mayhaps even hated him, and she recognized the magnitude of his sacrifice on her behalf.

She slid off the cushion, her movements instantly drawing his attention, and Ran watched as her graceful steps overtook the space separating them. She brushed rivulets of black hair back off her shoulder and the perfume of her skin rose up to greet him. She stood within inches, the heat of her shaping the plush contours of her body to his, and when she looked up at him, her gentleness and compassion spread into him like the warm fingers she plied to his muscles.

His shoulders sagged. "Aurora." Questioning and apologetic.

"Nay, dinna speak on it further." She laid her hand to his broad chest. "To dwell brings you pain, and I canna bear to lay witness." He wrapped an arm around her waist, drawing her flush to his body as calloused fingers gently pushed beneath her chin, tipping her head so that he could capture her mouth. The press of his lips was tentative, chivalrous and courtly, and Aurora gasped softly at the balmy feel of his mouth moving slowly over hers. 'Twas a tender kiss, more loving than any other they'd shared, filling an emptiness in her; yet the splendid energy their touch produced— ignited swiftly. He was suddenly possessive, hotly plying his mastery with lips and tongue, and she sank into his embrace, her hand caressing up his chest to his jaw, fingers driving into his hair.

He groaned at the luxurious feel of her touch, his arms

tightening around her, one hand seeking the curving shape of her spine, her buttocks, and pressing her to his need. She flexed against him.

The natural way she responded to his kiss, his caress, was like a dam breaking, flooding him with her desire, making it more a part of him than anything he'd ever shared with a woman. He wanted it to go on forever and yet he wanted it to die, now and quickly. For she was deadly to his way of life, the life he *must* lead, *would* lead without interference from anyone.

Suddenly he drew back, breathing heavily, his gaze on anything but her as he dropped his arms and put space atween them. "Get you to bed, woman, we leave this place at sunrise."

This time, when he turned to leave, he didn't stop.

Chapter Ten

Och, there was simply no pleasing the man, Aurora thought, scanning the tent for her slipper. Not privy to the games of the upper crust, she'd no notion of what the man was about. One moment he was kissing her with all the tenderness and passion of a man devoted, the next he was putting her aside like soiled laundry. She'd woken in the middle of the night to find him sleeping on the floor near the entrance, and the lack of warmth sent her to his side. Abruptly he'd roused and put her to bed as if she were a child. No coaxing would bring him to the divan. She'd only wanted the warmth of his great size, for the desert nights were incredibly cold, but Ransom Montegomery had refused her even that. So she'd stolen his cloak.

" 'We depart this place at sunrise.' " She mimicked his deep tone to no one. Hah! 'Twas well past, and the morning had not brought the pirate back to the tent, she mulled, her gaze darting around the pillows and furniture littering the tent, searching.

Ransom entered the confines to find Aurora on her hands and knees, her rounded bottom puncturing the air as she sent an assortment of pillows, cushions, and clothes over her shoulder in wild search for God-knew-what.

"Great Goddess, how can one beastly slipper—Ah ah! 'Twas a wee chase you've lent me," she said to the shoe, sitting down and jamming it on her foot.

Ran grinned. "Do you oftimes converse with footwear?"

She shot him a hot look. "Do you oftimes slink into a chamber unannounced?"

His smile fell. 'Twas not the compliant woman of yester-eve staring at him, but a woman bereft. Or simply a poor riser?

Ran ignored the urge to smooth her ruffled feathers and crossed the room. She was a knife to the thread of his commitments, and it was best, he'd decided this morn, that they depart and quickly.

Shaking out his cloak, he swept it over his shoulders, immediately assailed with her scent clinging to the fabric, and with that, the memory of finding her curled snugly in the cocoon of his body. He likely wouldn't have stirred from sleep had she not slept so restlessly, her hands straying beneath his shirt for warmth. Ahh, 'tis well not to dwell upon it, he thought, securing the frog at his throat.

A sudden barrage of gunfire made her jump, and he glanced up from his task. His lips twitched. The scarf on her head and a dried apricot clenched atween her teeth, she looked the frightened mouse as her rounded eyes shifted from the area beyond the walls to him.

" 'Tis a war you've started, thinks I?"

"Abduli practices with his new toys."

"You taught them how to fire the rifles?" Her tone said he'd done quite enough by using the weapons as barter.

" 'Tis how I've spent the morn." When her gaze narrowed, Ran felt compelled to add, " 'Twould be no more than handing a loaded weapon to a child, if I did not."

He waited for her concession, not knowing why he should bother. It came in a short nod afore she swept the veil across her face, shielding all but her eyes, and he wondered if she donned the little vest and silken pantaloons of the *hareem* beneath. Shoving his knives into his waistband, he scanned the floor for any forgotten possessions, his gaze halting on the costume half hidden beneath the satin cushions. His eyes flew to hers, then lowered down over her body. Sweet mothers, how was he to travel for two days across the desert with the alluring notion of her nakedness parading through his brain!

Aurora's brows furrowed as she secured the *burqu'*. For a

moment he looked as if he'd delight in tossing her on her back and ravishing her. Then it was gone, the brief impression masked beneath the dark aura that continually called to her.

She smiled beneath the gauzy shield as he flicked the cloak off his shoulders like a mantle. He did look the Bedouin now, his head wrapped in the *kaffiyeh,* the securing cords threaded with gold. Sheets of black covered his long hair, a length left to draw across the lower portion of his face when they traveled the desert. The collection of knives in his wide belt proclaimed him the warrior lord, and the weapons drew her gaze to his waist, his lean hips, and the gloriously molding fit of his dark breeches disappearing into his boots. Och, he was a bonney man, she thought, and afore her study, his masculinity thickened, defining length and shape within the shroud of fabric. Her gaze flew to his. He scowled meanly. She smiled, her eyes giving way to smugness that he was not immune to her, and she stifled a laugh when he grasped her shoulders and propelled her out of the tent.

Outside, she halted, head bowed, waiting for him to proceed.

"Show naught of that boldness again, woman," he hissed from her side.

" 'Tis you who are displaying your," she choked, *"boldness."*

He arched a brow, watching her shoulders shake. "Do naught to anger Rahman now, lass." Faint pleading coated his tone.

"Aye, m'lord," she whispered, then giggled.

Briefly Ran looked to the heavens and shook his head, praying for an attack of patience in this already tremulous morning. No amount of stern admonitions within himself had prepared him for the delectable sight of her lying across the divan this morn, still asleep. Yards of black hair tangled about her body, she looked the seductive Delilah, her robes twisted snugly, outlining womanly curves and hiked up to reveal shapely legs. He'd wanted to sink to the cushions then and wake her with generous kisses, but he could not allow himself to be beguiled again and left her alone. The tenta-

tiveness of their stay bade him to prepare a smooth path for
their departure, for this morning his half brother had made
it clear he would rather have Aurora in his bed than the
rifles in his arsenal.

Ransom made it clear he would kill to keep her.

He strode toward his horses, the coal black stallion
stomping to be off, its docile gray mate now free of the rifles
and spices. One of Rahman's followers had prepared the
packs for travel and Ran checked their security, then turned
to Aurora, lifting her onto the back of a gray mare. Expertly
she slipped her leg over the horse without revealing an inch
of skin to the gawking men, yet Ran scowled that she would
ride astride afore them.

Rahman strode across the sands, handing a rifle to one of
his men afore they departed to give their leader privacy. The
sheik glanced to his brother, then up at the woman. Her
gaze remained lowered as his traveled over her.

"You are free to remain," he said softly, keeping question
from his tone.

Ransom stepped atween Rahman and Aurora's horse.
"She is mine, Rahman. I have claimed her. Thoroughly."

Brothers of half fought a wordless battle. "Is this true,
little blue eyes?" Abduli gritted, then looked up at Aurora.
"Does my brother claim your heart?"

For the first time since leaving the confines of the tent
Aurora looked up, yet her gaze did not touch the seeking
black eyes of the sheik, but fell on her rescuer. Ran was
staring at his half brother when he felt her possession, like
a whisper of warm fingers across his cheek; yet not even a
breeze grazed his skin. Cautiously he looked back over his
shoulder at Aurora. What trickery was this?

"Nay, m'lord."

Ran paled visibly.

"A man canna claim a heart, thinks I," she said, reining
around, "if one doesna beat in his own chest."

Abduli busted with laughter, and Ran swung up into the
saddle as she sped off across the desert. The sheik was still
chuckling as Ran gave chase, the pleased sound grating
down his spine.

He'd blister her bottom for toying with their freedom.

But Aurora was swift, though she soon recognized the heat of the desert would kill the horse and slowed. Ran crested a small hill, moving up beside her.

Hesitantly, she looked his way. "Dinna scold, Ransom, I couldna help it. Abduli wished I'd disclaim your words, yet I couldna lie."

He scoffed. "Insisting I've no heart is not a lie?"

She looked into his disgruntled face, pulling the veil from her own. "Oh, 'tis a heart in that mighty chest, Ransom Montegomery," she said sweetly. "Whether 'tis beating or nay, is the question."

"Saucy-mouthed wench," he muttered, his lips tugging in a reluctant smile.

"You look less intimidating when you smile, Ransom."

Her voice was low, intimate, and a rush of memory flooded over him: the feel of her wrapped in his arms; the excited gleam in her eyes when she discovered Rahman was his brother; the way he responded to her every nuance, and her unawareness of her allure.

And the loneliness she hid.

Aurora, he realized, was a complicated woman. And he found he wanted to know more about her, but his mission bade him leave her to her own devices and continue on alone. Yet when she was near, 'twas far too easy to discard his priorities and bend to the attraction they shared. He must maintain control, or he'd be lost for certain.

"You're doin' too much thinkin', Ransom."

Her voice broke into his thoughts and he blinked.

"I see it in your eyes. You find a little pleasure, then discover a reason not to enjoy it."

A brow arched sharply, and she thought this a cynical manifestation of his character.

"Those who depend on me number greatly, lass. I can not fail them for my own . . . dalliances."

Guilt shadowed her bright eyes. "I apologize if my circumstances have caused harm to you and your purpose."

Feeling contrite, he waved her off. " 'Tis but a delay and a few rifles."

"Yet 'twas to your brother you forfeited them."

He could tell by her tone she was curious about his relationship with Rahman, but he refused to elaborate. 'Twas naught else to say. They shared the same father. As he did with several others, he thought bitterly, recalling Rachel and that she now resided under his roof and in his care. So far Ran knew he was the eldest. Not that it mattered.

"Do you despise your brother because of the sire you share? Or is it your sire you hate for giving you a half sibling?"

Ran's gaze snapped to her, his eyes hard and probing. By God, the woman was either guessing aloud or possessed with the talents of the Black Spy. Regardless, she touched a nerve. "You pry where you are not wanted, woman," he rasped caustically. "And I warn you not to press."

She drew herself up, ripe with indignation. "Dinna dismiss me like a child, Ransom, for you know I am not."

He spared her an insolent glance. " 'Tis naught of your affair."

"Ochaii! Two brothers barter for me like bulls called to mating and you say this!"

" 'Twas a path to the end." Tension burned in his shoulders, yet his voice was calm.

"I know you might have used else but rifles to make the exchange!"

She was right, blast it. " 'Tis done, now be silent."

" 'Twill make a long trip longer if we dinna speak."

"You, madame, chatter enough for us both and say naught I care to hear."

Her expression fell. " 'Tis truth, you have no heart."

That stung. "Aye, and I do splendidly without it! And by God, without you!"

He kicked the horse to a swifter gait, and Aurora watched as he charged across the sand like a desert lord, his cloak whipping out behind him like the wings of a hawk.

Her lips curved, her heart picking up pace at the powerful sight of him; then she kneed the beast and followed.

'Twould be at least a day afore they would reach a city or

a port to meet with his ships. And that day possessed a night. Even if his heart and mind did not want her, Aurora knew his body did. And the evening promised to be very cold.

Chapter Eleven

Tangier

Icy wind bit into her robes and Aurora shivered, constantly surprised that the searing heat of the day could turn so frigid after the sun made its descent. But nothing compared to the chilling silence of her escort, or the painful clarity behind his intentions.

He wanted naught but to rid his life of her as quickly as possible. He need not have spoken the words, for the impenetrable wall he'd thrown up atween them at the beginning of their journey remained intact, and butting against it left her peevish and ill tempered.

She'd been cast out of villages, denied lodging and friendships for her unrestrained behavior and beliefs, but naught, she realized, wounded her as much as Ransom's dismissal.

And she didn't understand the why of it.

Nor could she sense aught beyond the image of darkness, flat and barren, filling her mind. 'Twas impenetrable, this mental shield. Not that she could ever actually *read* his thoughts, but on occasion, if she prepared herself to accept, she could feel his unguarded emotions; like capsules of oil caught in a pool of water, a sudden stirring separated them, and within action or conversation, 'twas simple enough to understand what brought them so close to the surface. But not now.

For not once in the previous days did he touch her or look her way. No amount of teasing or cajoling brought him back to her. And any notion she had of the cold night drawing him back to, at least, speaking with her, banished when he continued on relentlessly, traveling from dusk to the dawn, spending only short interludes during the day to sleep and rest.

Och, to be free of this horse will be pleasure enough, she thought, glad to finally see the lights of the city ahead. An unexpected lump grew in her throat, and she swallowed it down. She would be with Shokai, she reminded herself, and off in search of her father. Just the pair of them, as it had always been. Putting Ransom from her mind was her only choice. But afore it had been easier, for she'd experienced only the single earth-shifting kiss in the darkened alley and naught of the rich desire they shared, nor the part of him that felt needy for a gentle touch. She would miss him.

'Tis nay fun a'tall, this.

They rode the edges of the city toward the sea, the ocean's moisture hanging in the air, and she inhaled the dampness, parched skin absorbing greedily.

"I love the sea," she murmured into the wind and he cut her a sharp glance. She didn't return the gesture, and drew the veil across the lower portion of her face as she allowed him to take the lead, following as they skirted the heavily traveled streets toward the seclusion of a rock-faced jetty.

Aurora did not question the reason behind their clandestine approach, for caution permeated his constant surveillance of the darkness beyond. He was an outlaw of the seas and likely avoiding a less-than-pleasant reception.

The sudden crush of waves came to her and together they quickened their pace, the full moon lighting the shore and sea with a dusting of silver. Water foamed violently, spewing geysers as it hit the jetty, calmed, then roared again with unleashed power. Aurora sighed, sealed away the sight and drew on its magnificence, the crescendo beating the shore and filling her with pulses of strength. She could leave Ransom, now. If she asked the Goddess for help, she would find the source within herself to walk away as he so wished.

Her veins hummed with the rush of blood, her heartbeat slowly accelerating. 'Twas the night of the waning moon. A powerful evetide, she knew, and was wise not to waste this night. She channeled her thoughts to the beast atween her thighs. The horse picked its way behind Ransom's steed, sure-footed and dainty across the rocky shore and yet, the closer they came to water, the less she was fain to be parted from him.

A spatter of patterns and images filled her mind, the power of the night giving her the piercing awareness of her surroundings. She tried to forage through the jumble of sensations and visions and discover the clearest source. Something was wrong, but her slim grasp on the visions slipped when Ransom grabbed her reins, jerking the horse to a halt.

Her eyes flashed open, the uneasy feeling clinging to her skin.

" 'Tis bleedin' dangerous to ride like that!" His features were thrown in shadow, his amber eyes glowing with angry concern.

"I was not at risk, nor was the beast." She leaned forward and stroked the horse's gleaming neck. As if agreeing, the horse bobbed its head. "And with you runnin' me into the ground, 'tis the only source of rest I've found."

Surprised by her acid tone, he gestured toward the water. She followed the direction and saw a longboat scraping the shore, crewmen leaping out to draw it farther onto the beach. Domingo dealt commands, the exactness of them muffled by the crashing waves as Ransom dismounted, motioning for her to remain. Domingo splashed up the beach and met his captain, their heads together in heated conversation. Ran shoved his fingers into his hair, then glanced at Aurora, his handsome features offering a brief portrait of his remorse. Panic swelled in her, for it was more for another being than for her. She slid from the saddle, gathering her robes and racing to the two men.

She grabbed Ransom's arm, then Domingo's. Her breath came quick and shallow. " 'Tis Shokai!" she gasped, her hands trembling, and Ran's eyes flared. "Why did you not tell me?" she cried.

Grievin' mothers, how could she know? "I meant to warn

you, lass," Ran offered lamely, wanting to ease the stark fear in her eyes. "But saw no reason to grieve you when we could not reach him til now."

"Take me to him."

Ran looked at Domingo, then jerked his head toward the longboat. The Spaniard's quizzical gaze lingered on Aurora for a moment afore he walked away and immediately gave orders to set it afloat. And as Aurora climbed in, Ran gathered their possessions, ordered two men to remain with the horses til signaled, then tossed the bags into the skiff. Lending his shoulder to the bow, he sent the craft into the surf, then leapt inside, immediately taking up position aft and steering the craft toward the *Red Lion.*

Aurora sat in the bow, her small white hand clutching the rim, her eyes on the night-shrouded flagship a few hundred yards ahead. She looked at no one. And Ran wondered how she knew her man was dying. Aye, he thought, if the ship's surgeon was correct the old man had but hours left in this world. It would destroy her, Ran thought as the skiff bumped the *Lion*'s hull.

Ran called out to her but she was heedless, latching onto the rope ladder and hoisting herself up the side of the ship without aid. Her robes gathered in her fist, her bare legs exposed, she moved with the grace and speed of a cat, shaking off helping hands as she met the rail. Ran stepped around his crewmen and ascended, overtaking the expanse and swinging his leg over the polished railing in time to see two crewman holding her by the arms, refusing her passage. She struggled, a barrage of Gaelic blueing the air afore she kicked one man in the shin, then twisted, slammed her back to the other's gullet, clamped both hands on his wrist, and with little exertion, sent him over her shoulder onto the deck. Ran froze, glancing from the fallen man to her, then to the second still clutching his calf. Aurora ran toward the portal and crewmen followed.

"Leave off!" Ran commanded as she slipped into the passageway. He strode after her, tossing a disgusted glance at the sailor still sprawled on his back and trying to catch his breath, then followed.

A long sorrowful cry pierced the walls of the forty-gun flagship, stopping him in his tracks on the ladder. The hairs on his nape stood on end, a chill drawing up the skin on his arms, as the woeful sound spiraled down the companionway from the surgeon's quarters. Inside, the stench was unbearable, yet Aurora knelt on the floor beside the old man, tearing at the layers of her robe, using the cloth to blot seepage from his festering wounds. She plucked the hollow reed from Shokai's arms, then tore more strips, binding the surgeon's cuts.

"Aurora?"

She snapped a look over her shoulder. "Look what this butcher," she flicked a bloody hand toward the surgeon, "has done to my Shokai!" Crimson stains spattered his breeches.

Ran blinked at the spitting tigress, claws bared and prepared to slice and pare the surgeon from his skeleton.

"He is a skilled man, lass, and was offering his aid. At my orders."

"He offers naught but death!" she snapped contemptuously at the doctor, then returned her heated gaze to Ran. "What do you with me sack?"

Ran turned toward the passageway and called for Dahrein to fetch the bag, and when the boy appeared, Aurora changed, briefly, as if calmed by the youth, even offering a thankful smile as she accepted the sack. Yet when she met Ran's gaze all softness vanished. Clearly she was laying the blame for Shokai's condition at his feet.

"We must disembark this ship," she demanded in a voice unlike her own. "Now."

"Nay, Captain," the surgeon interrupted. "He is far too ill for travel."

Ran's gaze lowered to the ancient man and he tried to keep his features impassive. Shokai's chest was sunken, his rib cage protruding. The whip wounds festered, red and angry; and his raw feet showed no sign of healing. Beside his bare thin arms lay the surgeon's knives and a bowl of blood. His breathing was nearly nonexistent, and Ran knew Shokai stood on death's threshold. Aurora had to see that.

"He will not survive, lass."

She turned on him like a striking viper, stunning him with her vehemence. "He will! I will see to it!"

She was fooling herself, but Ran strove for calm, his voice even. "Then do as you will, here."

"Nay! This place is unclean." She waved at the tiny cabin. "I cannot perform my . . . work in this filth."

Ran's lips thinned. The lass dares much, he thought; yet could hardly believe the same woman who'd soothed him so gently in the Bedouin tent was now glaring holes in his skin. Her robes were tattered and covered in Shokai's blood, a streak of red melted with the damp sheen on her cheek, strands of hair clung to her skin. He ached to brush it aside, take her into his arms, and soothe the sorrow he felt like a heavy draught of rum. She stood afore him, her face upturned, her liquid eyes ripping apart his control; and he faltered, conceding her request and calling for the longboat and volunteers.

Suddenly she pressed her forehead to his chest, her shoulders drooping with relief; and Ran rested his hands there with a gentle weight, rubbing tenderly. She tilted her head back, laying her trembling palm over his heart.

"Och," she whispered. " 'Tis beatin' again, thinks I."

He offered a weak smile, knowing she was masking her own misery with the jibe.

Quietly, she turned away and knelt beside Shokai, holding his limp hand. In a tongue Ran didn't recognize, she spoke to him. The old man responded with a faint squeeze of her hand, and within minutes she had him prepared for travel. An hour passed afore they pulled onto the shore, and Aurora remained at Shokai's side, speaking softly to him as they traveled into the city. He didn't respond, and Ran felt he would never utter another word.

But Aurora did. She was full of haste and righteous demands for a room at a hostelry; then once inside the narrow rented space, she confused him by ordering several buckets of boiling water and a bath.

Alone with her and her guardian, Ran braced his shoulders against the cracked wall, studying her as she washed

and cleansed Shokai's wounds, then aught within a circle of
the pallet bed and crude wood tub. Finally satisfied the
room was sufficiently clean, she turned to the small table
beside the tub. Rummaging in *the sack,* she withdrew candles, twine, flints, small velvet sacks as well as sacks of
leather and cloth. The markings on the bags were foreign,
totally unfamiliar; and Ran strained to decipher the significance of the curls and circular lettering. His eyes widened a
fraction when she placed a dented challis on the table, and
a tiny caldron atop a small brazier. The silver dagger followed, and she laid it reverently aside.

"I bid you leave me," she said tonelessly, sprinkling a
blue powder into the water, then loosening her robes. He
sensed an odd calmness in her, tranquil yet determined. It
unnerved him.

"You will bathe? Now?" She wouldn't look at him, and
he felt her distance as if 'twere a thousand leagues. How
could she change so swiftly?

"I must."

He opened his mouth to ask why she would not tend the
old man first, but she cut him off with a gentle tone.

"Do not question me on this, for I will not reveal." Nay,
Aurora thought, he was not ready to lay witness to her
beliefs and rituals. Had not his crewman refused her help
already? "Your surgeon has . . . tried his craft, now 'tis my
chance." She glanced down at Shokai and Ran heard her
quick gasp for air. Her eyes were glossy wet, yet when she
looked back to Ran, not a single tear spilled.

"I am in need of lavender. And clothing." It was a dismissal, lacking her earlier anger.

As much as he wanted her out of his life, Ran couldn't
leave her. Not without protection. His rearing forbade it,
though he'd spent the better part of their journey back
insisting he could dismiss her to her own devices when the
time came. The time, he decided, was not at hand, and he
turned to do as she bade, gladly so, for he felt the weight of
blame, thought she never voiced thus. Ran cared naught to
understand the ways of medicine, yet for the sake of his
crew, he'd seek a manner in which to placate the surgeon.

Shokai was doomed, yet if Aurora was determined to slave over the dying, so be it.

At the door, Ran paused, his hand on the crude rope latch as he glanced back over his shoulder to see her lower the robes and step into the bath. Abruptly he looked away, his mind racing for an explanation to her actions, yet the image of her naked body burned across his brain, banishing all else. He quit the room, shutting the door.

Beyond, the gray-haired quartermaster polished the barrel of his flintlock, his shoulder braced negligently against the wall. It was odd not to see Lockewood at his side. The one-eyed Castille held the same position opposite Lougière, rolling a cheroot atween his teeth, yet at the sight of their captain both men straightened.

"Remain here. Allow no one to pass." Ran looked at each man pointedly. "No one."

The splash of water penetrated the thin walls.

Then her voice came, soft and sweetly luring.

"I am mortal, loved and cared for by the Triple Goddess and the Great God. Through the Great Mother, all things are born . . ."

Ran scowled at the sealed wood, the dark look masking his confusion. Abruptly he spun on his heels and went in search for her blasted herb.

Chapter Twelve

Ran skidded to a halt afore the shattered door, his heart jumping to his throat as his gaze snapped urgently over each splinter of wood, each torn piece of bedding. Every drop of blood.

Grievin' mothers, nay! Nay!

Stepping inside, he righted a table and, beneath it, found Lougière, the quartermaster's jaw and lips swollen, blood pulsing from the gash at his hairline and trickling from his mouth. Ran called to him, bending to gently nudge, and Lougière stirred, his lids sluggishly lifting. Recognition was slow, almost frightened, and with effort Lougière pushed up on his elbow. Ran handed him a scrap of cloth, and the man blotted his skull, then turned his head to the side to spit blood.

"Castille?"

Lougière shrugged, then winced, rubbing his ribs. "Mayhaps they took him, too." He glanced around the room. "I'm thinking they thought me dead, Capt'n."

"Who be they, man?" he demanded, searching the confines. "What sort would do this to a woman and a dying old man?"

Lougière climbed stiffly to his feet, accepting his captain's help. "They came up there." He gestured to the window, and Ran stepped over rubble. " 'Twere four, in black, their faces covered. We didn't hear a thing til she screamed for the old man," he went on to say, as Ran fingered the gouges in the wall and the wood sill.

Ran's gaze scanned the area below, and he realized the intruders didn't have far to climb with the privacy wall so close to the hostelry. He'd been careless. Angry at the distance she'd put atween them and bleedin' confused by her "preparations," he hadn't seen to her protection thoroughly. *'Tis me own fault.* Damn and blast, he thought, shoving his hair off his forehead, why were so many intent on possessing this little woman? No spectators milled, yet from the look of things, it had been a battle worth witnessing. And if all within earshot had ignored the fight, then who was he to question? 'Twas bloody difficult to believe Castille was laid down so easily; the burly one-eyed Spaniard lived for his battles. And how had Aurora fared through this . . . mess? Dear God, had she cried out for his help with no offer forthcoming? Imagining her terrified pleas twisted a knot in his stomach, and he clenched his fist. The scent of lavender stirred him and he unfurled his fingers, the forgotten herb crushed in his palm.

Aurora. To where have you vanished this time, lass?

Will you survive this kidnapping? he agonized. Will your man?

Movement drew his gaze to Lougière, who was stuffing his torn shirt into his breeches and searching the mess for his weapons. He found them, groaning disappointedly at the cracked grip of his pistol, yet jammed it in his belt nonetheless. He limped to the doorway and glanced back. Ransom bent to grip Aurora's satchel, staring at the blood on the floor.

" 'Tis mine, sir," Lougière offered and Ran threw him a devastated look, stunning the quartermaster with the worry tightly etching the clean lines of his face. His eyes were unusually turbulent, yet Lougière said naught as Ran tucked the bag beneath his arm and swiftly quit the room.

"Captain?" Lougière leaned against the frame, catching his breath and his side.

"We search, Mister Lougière," he said without looking back and taking the stairs. "We overturn every bleedin' fistful of sand in this city 'til we find her."

"And if we do not, sir?" Lougière limped after him.

Ran halted at the landing, his body tense, a muscle working violently in his jaw. Then he sighed heavily and glanced back over his shoulder. "Then we sail."

Three days later it was Domingo who convinced Ran to end the search. "She is not in the city, my friend."

"She must be!" He slammed his fist against the rail, yet continued to study the wharf, searching, always searching, and if the situation had not turned so grave Domingo would have been amused at the harsh emotion Ran had expended in the past days.

"What pace could they set with the old man?"

"Perhaps he has been left to die somewhere. 'Twould not be unrealistic."

Ran glared over his shoulder at his first officer. "Aye. Aye, aye! Damn you, aye!" With the last he shoved away from the rail, and Domingo didn't know if Ran was cursing him or Aurora. Regardless, he knew life remained a task until they either found her or proof of her death, or Ran simply accepted the matter as done. Already he'd nearly killed three Tangierians for refusing to bend to his inquisition, and now he paced the quarter deck like a caged beast, snapping orders, growling at every inefficient move a sailor made. If he wasn't behind the men, barking at them to be faster, quicker, smoother, he was climbing the mast, repairing sail, hauling line, shifting halliard and boom, straining his body and his mind til there was naught to do but sleep. Yet thrice Domingo had come upon him slouched in his chair, awake, silent, nursing a tin mug of rum, the woman's sack within reach.

"We have a rendezvous to make," Domingo reminded needlessly.

Ran ceased pacing and shot him a caustic glance. The Spaniard fingered a belaying pin lodged in the rail, responding with a patient await-your-command look. It made Ran see red, as well as the futility of his search. By God in heaven, he thought, tilting his head back and gazing briefly at the twilight sky. A dryness sanded in his throat. Where was she? Was she hurt? Or Sweet Mother of God, dead? His chest tightened, threatening his breathing. Had the Sultan stolen her back and walled her inside a private crypt? Had Rahman gone back on his word? Did Achmed seek vengeance for the loss of his hand? The unanswered questions were slowly driving him mad. And Shokai, sweet saints, as if he didn't feel horrible enough with allowing Aurora to be kidnapped, his guilt multiplied over what his lax efforts likely cost the old man.

He'd exhausted every source to find her, from street urchin to the emir. No one would speak, no one knew a bloody thing. Damn and blast! he cursed, shoving his fingers into his hair. He felt strung tight as rigging, and not even sleep gave him a reprieve. It mattered naught. The remainder of his days were destined to be haunted by her face, her unsettling anger, her pain, and more than aught, her alluring smile, the way she soothed and aroused him like no other.

God, he missed her. He ached to feel her vitality, in the heat of her mouth, her body's warmth beneath his hands, and to mark her his own.

And he swore he would if he ever saw her again. He would!

"Capitán?"

Ran flinched and realized his first officer awaited commands. "Prepare to cast off, Mister Avilar," he said in a flat tone. "Make the night's tide and alert me," Ran glanced at the sky, judging the time and wind speed it would take to best the *Black Star,* "at seven bells." Abruptly he spun on his heels and descended the quarterdeck ladder without so much as a glance in either direction.

Crewmen skittered out of his path, but he paid them no heed, striding to his cabin. He needed sleep, aye, and sharp senses this night, for 'twas his last opportunity to regain his imprisoned crew.

By God, he needed this battle.

Seventy-two miles off the West African Coast

The *Red Lion* roared to life, her gun ports spitting angry red fire and cannon shot to splinter the slaver's mizzen. It crashed to the deck, and fo'c'sle' armory repaid shot for shot. Ran gave orders not to sink the *Black Star,* nor target the hull in any way, for all aboard the *Lion* knew slaves were housed below the waterline in the belly of the vessel.

The slave ship sent double rounds across the *Lion*'s bow, taking half the bowsprit and the capstan into the sea. And two crewmen with them.

Ran gave orders to come about, and the flagship took wind and crossed in deadly position in front of the bark. But the *Lion* was swift despite her great size, and her captain coaxed miracles from wood and rope and sail, turning his ship abruptly toward the bark, clarifying his threat to ram her port side. Ran stood on the quarterdeck, his crew suddenly silent, breathless with fear and admiration as their captain vigorously spun the wheel, turning the vessel sharply away. As the flagship veered, the *Red Lion*'s finest marksmen splattered the *Star* with a hail of cannonfire lasting no more than ten seconds, and afore the echo ceased, Ran ordered sail heeled. The flagship swept alongside the *Star* amidst the panic and carnage. Random gunfire from the slaver lit the darkness.

Ran strode to the rail, bracing his foot on the polished wood. Propping his forearm across his knee, he stared for a moment, viewing his handiwork, mentally noting to reward Foti for his information.

"Strike your colors." Ran didn't shout, the closeness of the ship and the tensing silence offering no need.

They refused, the remaining Salé pirates scampering to lift sail and catch wind to escape.

Ransom flicked his hand toward the vessel and beneath his feet cannons rumbled, leveling the slaver's main mast.

"I'm a patient man, slaver," he said when the din ceased.

"Our captain's dead. I beg quarter for the living," a youthful voice shouted, obviously in pain and panic.

Ran admired the man emerging from the dense smoke,

his blood-darkened shirt hanging limply from his shoulders. He stared across the sea at his opponent, valiant and bold as if he'd the British Navy at his disposal, then wisely struck his colors. Domingo ordered planks and Ran boarded the captured vessel, leaping onto the deck in front of the man.

He could be no more than twenty, Ran thought, waving off the offer of his sword. "You wage a fine fight." The *Lion*'s crew followed, disarming and capturing all who stood.

"Finer still, if you'd done bloody fair."

Ran's amber eyes flared with suppressed fury. Insolent whelp. "There is no fairness in the selling of lives," he snarled, leaning closer, his gaze sliding contemptuously over the officer. "Or did you not think there would be a price for the peddling of flesh?"

The slaver frowned, glancing at the flagship, then its captain. "Do you not steal them for yourself?"

Ran refused comment, his expression bland. "Shackle him."

The officer's eyes rounded.

"Mayhaps a taste of prison will be deterrent enough."

Crewmen grabbed his arms and the officer shouted, "This is an outrage! What honor have you in doing this!" Iron clamped on his ankles and wrists.

Ran knew it was bad form to imprison the captain, or rather first mate, of a captured vessel, especially afore his crew, but any thought of leniency soured as his men pried open the latticed hatch and helped the freed slaves to the deck. The stench that came with them was intolerable, yet Ran kept his features clear as they shuffled about weakly, metal clinking, several bodies marked with the wounds of a whip.

"Watkins!" The flame-haired man appeared at his side. "Get those bloody things off them. Now!"

The crew knew their jobs, yet 'twas always at this time of a raid their captain grew impatient. As prisoners crawled to freedom, Watkins met his captain's gaze, then shook his head.

So far, none of Ran's lost crew were aboard.

Damn.

Impatience riding his spine, Ran strode to the hatch, climbing down the passageway in search of the captain's quarters. The odor of sex and spoiled food permeated the tiny room, and Ran was surprised he could distinguish the two. The bunk was unmade, the floor strewn with rotting fruit and clothing. A rat crawled from the beneath the stained bed sheets and over the mattress' edge, plopping to the floor. It skittered from sight as Ran moved to the desk, brushing aside overturned bottles of rum, scraps of salted meat and scorched bread as he searched for the ship's log and rudders.

'Twould do him well to discover exactly whose slaves he'd acquired and the destination intended.

"Ran!" Domingo called as he stepped over the threshold.

"The count?" Ran didn't look up from perusing the log.

"Nearly two hundred."

There was a hard pause afore Ran asked, "Mister Bona-face and the others?"

Domingo smiled. "Alive, scarcely. Already aboard the *Lion.*"

Ran briefly closed his eyes, expelling a breath. "Have the captives made their decision?"

"They take the vessel."

Only his gaze shifted, his brows knitted tight. "There are sailors aboard?"

Domingo nodded, his lips bending in a smile. "A surpris-ing number of England's finest. Slavery, it seems, has no preference. Are you prepared to inspect?"

Ran nodded, closing the log and retrieving the rudders. It would serve no purpose to free slaves and then gift them with a sinking ship, and Domingo admired his thorough-ness as they made their way topside.

Ran thrust through the narrow passageway as the cox-swain ducked beneath a tangle of rigging, calling and mo-tioning him to follow.

Ran didn't. He had yet to deal with the slaver's crew, and the longer they remained joined at the stern with this vessel, the greater the chance they'd be spotted.

"Speak of it man," he ordered impatiently.

"I'm thinkin' you should be seein' this with your own eyes, sir."

Scowling, Ran glanced first at Domingo, who'd ceased clearing debris, then to the bow. The forward hatch. Instantly Ran handed the log and rudders to the nearest man and strode across the lantern-lit deck, shoving fallen rigging and shattered wood aside, climbing over it when he couldn't til he came to the forward hatch. He bent, grasping the iron ring, and with a mighty jerk, opened the door. The odor of fish and feces curled up to him. As moonlight sprayed the darkened hull, a pale white face was visible in the blackened recesses.

His heart slammed against the wall of his ribs, then thundered wildly.

"Aurora." Breathless, joyous.

"Och, Ransom, did you happen to find me lavender?"

Chapter Thirteen

Ran grinned hugely, baring white teeth and a dimpled cheek. She sounded as if 'twere the most natural occurrence to find her in the belly of a slave ship.

"Aye, lass," he answered, maneuvering over the ledge and down into the hull. "But in my panic, I'm afraid I crushed it beyond use." He dropped to the deck and squatted to where she huddled on the wet floor. He trembled inside, never imagining he'd be this thrilled to see the troublesome woman, regardless that every inch of her was bilgewater wet and filthy.

Sweet Jesus, he wanted to kiss her daft.

"Were you truly in a panic?" Eagerly she sketched his features, her eyes skimming over his dyed hair and heavy beard; needing to read more into his smiling face, yet daring not.

"Aye." Guilt shadowed his features, and his gaze flickered. " 'Twas my fault."

Her expression fell. " 'Twas your only reason, then?" She tried to look under his bent head as he attempted to free her shackled limbs. "Clearin' the blame?"

His gaze collided with hers. Could he confess the unceasing torment he experienced whilst she was missing, and the crushing devastation when forced to finally give up his search? 'Twas new to him, this wrenching of his vitals whenever he thought of her and could not press the words past his lips.

"If you believe so, then you do not know me well."

"Och. I dinna know you a'tall," she said matter-of-factly.

But she did, and from their first shared kiss became a threat to Ran's vows and future plans; yet at the moment not a single reason could keep him from reaching out to her.

She jerked away. "Dinna touch me. I smell of the fish-monger's leavin's."

"As does this vessel," he murmured, pushing soggy hair from her face anyway. His hand lingered at her cheek.

His eyes were soft, so tender their look, Aurora's heart swelled. She wished she were clean enough for his kisses. "Then release me again, m'lord rescuer, so I might bathe and be fitting company for my champion."

He chuckled, and Aurora's eyes widened. She'd never heard him laugh like that, easy and lacking in mockery. Och, 'twas a grand sound, like the rumble of thunder.

"Twice in the Sultan's prison you proved your talent for locks," he said, running a hand down the length of rusted chain binding her to the hull. He yanked and it tore from the brace. "Why did you not free yourself as afore?"

Aurora eyed him warily. Did he think her naught but a thief? "That horrible toad of a captain paid me a visit, hourly." She shrugged, watching his long brown fingers easily break the hinge from her ankle. The power secreted behind the effortless task was a reckoning force, and Aurora wondered if anything in this world could bind or best the pirate lord. " 'Twoulda been a whipping to pay, thinks I, if I werena bound when he visited."

His gaze jerked up. "Did they hurt you?" he demanded, scanning her body, searching for marks the eye could not see.

"Strike me? Aye."

His features hardened.

"Force a husband's rights? Nay," she said, palming his shoulder and pushing herself to her feet. The effort cost her strength and she sagged against the curved hull. Still kneeling, Ran gazed up at her. The slime-covered *throbe* molded wetly to every curve, and pore of her body and it was all he could do not to run his hands from trim ankles to plump breasts to be certain she was truly alive and unharmed.

Clenching his fists to avoid doing just that, he straightened, recognizing how volatile he was.

"Is Shokai aboard?" Ran tore his gaze from the wet material clinging to her bosom, then stripped off his shirt, dropping it over her head.

"Aye." She smiled, working her arms into the billowy sleeves. Whose eye was he protecting her from, his or the men beyond? "He's held with the others." She nodded aft, then frowned up at him. "You've attacked this ship to free the slaves?"

Ran offered no admittance. "Can you climb?" He gestured to the narrow ladder.

She studied him briefly, curious as to why he wouldn't claim such a noble act, then nodded. He stepped back, allowing her to pass, yet when she moved away from the hull, her legs buckled. He caught her close, and she gripped his arms, resting her forehead against his broad chest. Her body quaked.

He bent to whisper, "When last did you eat or see the sun?"

"With you," she murmured into his salty skin. "In the desert."

He tensed. Six days! Grievin' mothers, the slavers hadn't bothered to even feed their *merchandise* enough to see them live to their destination!

Aurora felt his rage seep beneath her skin, searing her, and she rubbed his biceps, tilting her head back to look at him. Any speck of gentleness she'd witnessed was gone.

"Release it, Ransom," she whispered. " 'Tis done."

He looked down at her, his features carved with fury, the urge to turn this ship's crew into shark fodder grinding through his bones. Then she touched his jaw, fingers sliding over his cheek, brushing loose hair from his forehead; and like a glacier shifting on warm currents, he melted a little. He bent slightly, his gaze darting from her mouth to her blue eyes and back. Aurora clung, her soft liquid body shaping to fit his hard sculptured length. His lips hovered. He was aching, throbbing, nearly out of his mind to steal a draught of her passion. But he couldn't, for to succumb to the allure of Aurora was to crack the casing of his soul.

Abruptly, he put her from him.

" 'Tis bad, the smell?"

His lips curved, his lust receding a little. "Bloody awful," he admitted with feeling, when in truth he wanted to press her against the hull and push his tongue into her mouth and his body into hers. Instead he crouched, instructing her to climb onto his back. She did, wrapping her arms around his neck as he swiftly ascended the ladder. Domingo lifted her from Ran's back the instant he popped through the hatch. He'd lay witness to the conversation, the near kiss, and couldn't lose his smile. Ran was damn near drowning in the woman's presence, and Domingo wondered how long it would take for him to succumb to the fierce desire molding his features—and his breeches.

" 'Tis good to see you fit, *señorita.*"

She smiled sweetly. "My thanks to you and your courage, Mister Avilar."

Surprise that she knew his name and his native language brightened his tanned face.

"The old man?" Ran asked, and Aurora shot him a hot look.

"Shokai. Shokai Ishido," she corrected, her lips scarcely moving.

Domingo grinned, glancing between the pair. "Aboard the *Lion,* faring surprisingly well." He looked down at Aurora for explanation, but she merely shrugged, turning her attention to the deck. She sucked in a sharp breath.

One mast was completely destroyed, another cracked like a broken bird wing at the top, their torn sails hanging like discarded rags. Gray-white smoke still colored the air, lanterns swinging with the dip of the vessel, but it was the deck, littered with bodies mangled beyond recognition, that stunned her.

"You did this?"

Ran looked down at her, wary.

"Credit my gunners, lass."

"Yet on your orders," she countered sourly. "Och, Ransom, 'tis so much killing you've done."

A sable brow arched. "Would you rather I left you to the slavers?"

"Nay, nay, but 'tis surely a way to avoid this." She flicked a hand to the armless dead man a few feet away.

"Only a coward would surrender at the first volley." He didn't like his methods questioned, for over the years they'd proved efficient with the least lives lost. If 'twere not a strong cause behind this, he would not find himself pirating the seas and breeding a price on his head.

" 'Tis more valiant a quest to save, than spill, blood."

Suddenly his sharp features filled her vision. "Will you ever find fault in the path to your freedom?" He referred to the exchange of rifles at the Bedouin camp, and she knew it. "Or is it only with me and mine you seek to question, interfere," his voice rose in volume, "reshape, and condemn?"

"I havena reshaped nor interfered. This time," she admitted reluctantly.

"Ahh, but you condemn and question my every move. By God, you are an ungrateful wench!"

" 'Tis me you're upset with, pirate lord?" she asked, planting her hands on her rounded hips. "Or has letting the blood of a few blackguards put you in this snit?"

A muffled snort came from the Spaniard and Ran looked to the heavens, drawing on patience and control.

" 'Twill make you ill, Ransom, not speakin' your thoughts. 'Tis unnatural." He met her gaze, she saw naught but a shuttered stare in the golden depths.

"Do not challenge me again." Crisp and precise, daring her to gainsay him.

Abruptly he spun on his heels.

"Ochaii! I willna bow and scrape to you, pirate, nay matter how noble your quest!" she called out as Ran strode across the slick deck. Arrogant beastie. "Your captain doesna fare well on bein' questioned," she said, folding her arms, petulant. "Does he now, Mister Avilar?"

"From anyone? No. And from you, *señorita? Never.*" Domingo tipped a bow, clicking his heels, then followed his captain.

Mayhaps she was a wee bit rash, picking apart the results

of his efforts like that. Especially afore his crewmen. Another pirate would have claimed any salable goods and sunk the vessel, the lives aboard an inconvenience. Och, it didn't matter now, for 'twas obvious he thought little of her opinion anyway. 'Twas most annoying, she decided, this control he exercised over himself, suppressing every twinkle of emotion after a tiny burst, and she wondered what bred it, for she could not imagine a child birthed with such a foul disposition. Yet she *had* witnessed the brief unfettered moments, in the alleyway at Barbary, beneath the Bedouin silks, and on the shore in Tangier. And moments ago in the cargo hull. 'Twas capped and powerful, waiting to be set free, and she considered he might be frightened by the strength. Ransom? Afraid?

Hah!

Even now, he strode amongst his enemies, weaponless but for a few knives jammed in his wide leather belt, his bronze chest stripped bare and vulnerable. He lifted the dead and the debris, muscled arms flexing with the sheen of sweat as he sent both into the sea, then ordered a longboat dropped, the slavers who refused to swear allegiance to the new captain, set adrift for their crimes. His movements were efficient, calculated, unrelenting, and she saw not a flicker in the hard mask of his face, even as he wrapped a girl-child in cloth and sent her to her grave. A multitude of people shuffled across the decks, milky white English skin shining stark against the Africans, some too weak to stand or stunned by their sudden freedom. Arabs, Chinese, even those distinctly Nordic were not spared the slaver's pressman. She was pleased to see Ran offer the slave captain's sword to a tall dark-haired man with startling green eyes, relinquishing the command of the captured vessel. His captivity left him weak and his skin sallow—Aurora knew most had been prisoner much longer than she—and as she wound the length of her hair over her arm to keep from tripping anyone, he looked up.

"Mistress." He bowed, clamped hands bracing his weight on the hilt of the sword, its tip piercing the deck. "I didn't know you were aboard."

"You're a Colonist, an American," she said with fascination, moving over loosened ropes and spilled crates to stop afore the man.

"Aye, and proudly so, miss. Evan Pierce," he introduced.

"I am named Aurora, m'lord—"

"I am no one's *lord,*" he interrupted in a caustic snap.

" 'Tis so, then." She covered his hand with her own and flinched, his agony and hopelessness spreading from him to her. "It pains you?" She nodded to his wounded leg.

He didn't look down, for fear the sight of it would remind him he would lose it soon. " 'Tis tolerable."

"It will not have to come off, sir," she said, and he stiffened, green eyes narrowing.

"What say you, lass?" Evan's gaze darted briefly to the surgeon, who'd recently informed him of the opposite, then back to her. "Have you the knowledge of a healer?" He was prepared to do anything not to lose his leg.

She shrugged wet shoulders. " 'Tis a way I've got." She never questioned her sensitivity in such matters, for to peel apart the layers of such a gift would destroy it. And it did come in rather handy at times.

"She knows naught!" the surgeon spat, taking his anger out on a tightly wrapped wound. "Full of bitter concoctions, the wench is, and naught but Satan's toys!"

"Satan is your evil, not mine," Aurora harrumphed at the doctor, then looked at Evan. " 'Tis but ill kept and needs a thorough purging," she said, ignoring the surgeon's mutterings and leaning closer for a better look. "The salt has prevented the infection from spreading too far, yet . . ."

Ransom secured a rope and looked up to find Aurora conversing with Pierce, heads bowed together, the Colonist hanging on her every word. His eyes sharpened on her hand covering his, then to the smile she offered and the masculine admiration in the look Pierce swept over her body. An unfamiliar pain, ugly and harsh and filled with righteousness, burst through Ran like the strike of a cutlass to soft flesh, pain singing through his veins, making him feel like a tortured animal as he stormed across the deck, snapping terse orders to depart immediately. He grabbed her hand, pulling her toward him.

"Remember your vow to return the Africans to their coast," he warned Evan, and the man straightened, affronted.

" 'Tis a bully, you are, Ransom. And a rude one at that." Her fingers twisted for freedom in his grip. "Now Evan . . ." She looked to the Colonist. "Hot compresses and a fortnight of tinctures. King's Clover, thinks I, should ease your pain. I can prepare—"

"Nay, you can not," Ran interrupted, and she arched a tapered brow in his direction.

"You would deny him the aid I offer?" Her challenge dared him to be so cruel after saving so many lives.

"I would divide us from this ship afore we are discovered and risk a fresh pack of wolves coming to feast," he said, pulling her toward the *Lion,* and Aurora's skin suddenly prickled.

She yanked free and rubbed her arms. "And if I choose to stay aboard?" She didn't want to, really, but she couldn't fathom remaining with the barbarian pirate when her chances of finding her father lay on land and not on the sea. Regardless that Ranson and the surgeon thought her healing powers were naught but parlor tricks and smelly concoctions, 'twas her father she sought, not their approval.

"You are welcome aboard, mistress," Evan offered, and Ran's shoulders tightened at the tender smile she bestowed the Colonist afore turning her maiming gaze back to him.

"Bring Shokai back. I shall remain."

"I do not believe I gave you the choice." Grabbing her upper arm, Ran ducked and tossed her up onto his shoulder. Aurora pounded his back, squirming, but his hold on her thighs was firm as he started across the swaying planks to his ship.

"A poultice of Sain' John's Wort and yarrow. Hourly, til 'tis nay longer red," she spouted between her cupped hands to Pierce, who was grinning madly. "Keep it soft and dinna stitch the infection inside," she warned, then leveled several ine descriptions about and at Ransom. "I am not a prize of battle, pirate. Cease this nonsense!"

Ran didn't, even as she gripped the frame of the passageway and he was forced to peel her fingers free, he continued on to his cabin, setting her none too gently to her feet. He went to his desk, withdrawing paper and quill.

"The methods Mister Pierce needs to save his leg?" Cynical, bespeaking his doubt.

Aurora checked her temper, giving a list of herbs and detailing their process, satisfied that Ransom's interference would not leave the Colonist to perish. "Ransom?"

Scribbling her words, he stilled. That voice was far too sweet and coaxing after the string of Gaelic curses she'd spat moments afore, and slowly he tilted a look at her.

"Do you perchance have me—?"

"Your bleedin' bag of trinkets, aye." He flicked his hand toward the chair. Aurora raced to it, slopping a wet trail. She rummaged, coming out with her little pouches. Within moments she had proper amounts prepared to deliver.

Ran snatched them from her, stuffed her instructions inside, then turned away, heading for the door.

"Ransom!" He halted, his foot braced on the threshold as he twisted to look at her. Continuing her search was uppermost in her mind. "I dinna wish to remain here with you."

Her words stung, deeper than he imagined. "You will. For you, m'lady, have cost me more time, effort, and men—"

Her eyes rounded. " 'Twas nay my doin's!"

"And I cannot continue my mission with the threat of your unpredictable interference hanging over me head!" he finished as if she hadn't spoken.

" 'Tis easily remedied—send me back to the *Black Star.*"

He turned fully, fists clenched. "Nay!" Dear God he couldn't, not ever!

"Evan will see me ashore," she reasoned hopefully.

" 'Tis damned unsafe, woman! Defenseless! Can you not see that?" The Colonist's name, spilling so affectionately from her lovely lips, galvanized his anger. "And though saving your troublesome life thrice over ought to be a fair amount of suffering for any man," he ground out, "it seems

I do not fear God enough as He continues to force your presence on me!"

There was a brittle pause, the bite of his words sinking into their target. Hurt sprang across her upturned face.

Wood creaked. The vessel dipped, waves battering the hull. Somewhere below decks a gun port slammed shut.

"You arrogant beast," she whispered hotly. "You think I've no life of me own to lead?" She didn't give him the chance to answer, weeks of manhandling rising like sea foam as she crossed to him. "I canna be faulted for the ways of men, *powerful* men who wish me dead, *greedy* men who see only the coin to be gained in sellin' me to men like Rahman, who wants naught but to exhaust his lust, though any *willing* lass would do. An' aye, 'tis grateful I am, for savin' me *troublesome life,"* hurt and frustration simmered in blue eyes gone dark as night, holding Ran captive, "but *I* dinna *ask* for your help." She thumped his bare chest, her accent thick and rolling. "An' I dinna care to be caught atween yer mon-wars, Ransom Montegomery. An' I am bloody ill with bein' tossed 'round like a vender's apple," her voice rose, "an' treated as if I've no purpose in this life but to be a mon's chattel!"

Glass shattered, punctuating her last word. Aurora flinched. Ran blinked and together they looked at the broken pitcher, spilled water and crockery littering the commode and deck.

Immediately she looked away, reddening. Ran scowled, dismissing the mess as the ship heeled again, and returned his gaze to Aurora. She waged a damn fine argument, and he was loosing, seeing reason beneath the haze of bruised pride; yet he could not, would *not,* concede to her demands.

"I want naught but to see you safe."

"I can swim." She tilted a look up at him. "You ken me, Ransom?" 'Twas a final jab at his imprisonment.

Yet to Ran 'twas a refusal to accept his protection, and it felt like a betrayal.

"So can I," he warned, then stepped through the hatch and shut the door, the bolt sliding home fracturing a trust atween them.

Chapter Fourteen

Ran thrust away from the cabin door, his breathing quick as he slapped his palms high on the opposite wall. Wood rattled with the force. Arms braced wide, his head bowed atween, he struggled for control.

Damn and blast!

He was in a fine twist now.

What was he thinking, stealing her against her will like that? Then to lock her in! He felt like a villain of the first water. But grievin' mothers, *that woman* tempted and tested him beyond distraction, became his worst nightmare oftimes; and now he'd settled himself deep in a trap of his own making. When he'd seen her with the Colonist, touching him, so bloody intimate, Ran had comprehended nothing beyond the painful sensation ripping through his gut and that he'd *never* felt that way afore. It intensified when she'd refused to leave the slaver. He should have left her behind, been damn pleased about it, but after a week of his imagination torturing him to insanity, he'd felt betrayed. And when she'd refused his protection, she'd thrown the gauntlet in his face. Ran could not resist the challenge.

Jealousy had pushed him. God's blood, trapped by a useless emotion! And that he'd succumbed infuriated him, as much as Aurora's disregard for her personal safety simply to see the American properly tended. Tended. Bah! The bloody Colonist's interest was plastered across his face, and 'twas not her healing arts he was wanting her to reveal!

Dear God, Ran thought with a bolt of desperation. What has become of me?

Suddenly the latch rattled and he started, turning sharply as the door creaked opened. She stood beyond the raised threshold, his shirt in her hand.

"You'll be needin' this." She offered the garment. Ran's gaze darted from the bolt to her and back. He could have sworn . . . Nay, he *did* latch it! Had she jiggled the door just so, to release the bolt? Was this some thief's trick? He turned his gaze to her, but her somber expression offered no explanation and he would not look the fool by asking. The lass was, after all, a master at locks and likely proving she could not be imprisoned, he decided, reaching for the shirt. He grasped it, but Aurora refused to let go.

Eyes collided across the threshold.

"I dinna wish to have words with you, Ransom." The *Red Lion* was already free of the slaver, *Black Star,* and no amount of pleading would make him turn back, yet 'twas her own beastly temper that kept her from recognizing his fear for her survival. Though he was a wee bit highhanded about showing it, the depth of his caring touched her. "I accept your protection." The shirt slid from her fingers.

Surprise flickered in his amber eyes as he dropped the black fabric over his head. He wouldn't question her sudden turnabout. He'd enough problems riding his back. "Good," he said magnanimously, his eyes never leaving her as he pushed his arms into the billowy sleeves. "For it will do you naught to challenge me now."

Folding her arms beneath her breasts, Aurora leaned against the frame. "Och, if yer goin' to be snippy about it, I willna make your generosity so easy to swallow."

"You already have." He softened his words with a faint smile, avoiding a look at the plump bosom outlined in thin damp fabric. Would he ever see the woman properly dressed? "That's a fine temper you've got."

"Aye." She reddened, dropping her gaze, disgust tinting her voice as she said, " 'Tis a wretched flaw I must struggle with."

Ran felt a pang of guilt, for under the circumstances, the outburst was deserving. "We all have our own, lass."

She looked up, eyes suddenly bright with mischief. "Care to list yours, m'lord?" Her gaze slid luxuriously over him from head to foot and back.

"Hardly," he muttered tightly, his body quickening in response. He crushed back the urge to do something about it. His gaze lit on her tattered garments, and it prompted him to ask, "Who has cause to send you to the slaver?" Ran suspected a strong hand in her misfortune.

Aurora released a breath. "They were covered, Ransom. Mayhaps they were mistaken and meant such a fate for another?" She shrugged. "I am known to none else in this part of the world save you and a few of your crew." She hesitated, looking away. "And mayhaps me father?"

His brows rose. "Is that your quest? Do you seek your father?"

"Aye, but 'tis doubtless he would recognize me."

How long had she been searching? Was she, like Rachel, hunting a wayward sire? And for what? "And this search, how will you continue now?"

She smiled, light and mysterious. "I need not be on land to find answers."

Ran scoffed, dissatisfied with her reply, and when a crewman started down the companionway he jerked his head, a silent order to find another route.

"You will remain inside . . ." He glanced to the bolt-lock and frowned, his suspicious gaze snapping immediately back to her. Aurora answered with a benign smile. "For your presence aboard is enough to bring mutiny to my door," he went on to say, "and I'll not have my men knifing each other for a look at you."

Aurora didn't believe such muck, but realized Ransom would court the wrath of his well-disciplined crew to see her safely under his protection. It humbled her. For he'd already risked the Sultan's fury, even bent his personal values to barter with his insolent half-brother, all on her behalf.

"Aye, but I'll be wanting to see Shokai." Soft, yet edged with demand. "He needs me."

"In time. He is resting comfortably, Aurora, and," his stern glance halted her interruption, "I give you my word, the surgeon will not touch him."

Her chin lifted a fraction. "He'll decline without me help." Her brisk tone indicated that naught would dissuade her from seeing to Shokai's health. Not he nor his captainship.

Ran admired her loyalty. "And so will you, without proper food and rest."

She nodded absently, her eyes dropping to his waist as he shoved his shirt into his breeches, then making a slow climb back up to his face. His gaze was a tight prisoner to hers, his mind suddenly vacant to aught but those crystal blue eyes smoldering with unanswered desire, sparking the memory of their last kiss, in the Bedouin's tent. Eager, heady, and incredibly hot.

His control slipped a notch. He would prove himself stronger than the cravings of his body.

"Cover yourself, Aurora, and do not think to beguile me with your soft eyes and lush charms," he said crisply, fighting his body's needs and inflicting his determination on her.

Aurora blinked, then flipped soggy hair over her shoulder and matched his tone. "One simple woman is nay enough to 'beguile' the likes of you, thinks I." She grasped the latch and nearly took off his nose as she firmly shut the door in his face.

He stared at the door. Simple? Bah! The lass was a whore. The Sultan's leavings. And he would continue to think of her thus. After all, what decent woman would look at a man with such blatant hunger and not be experienced?

One who has known no rules to society, a voice reasoned. *A woman unhindered by father, brother, husband; yielding nothing for she has never been schooled to do so.*

Bloody independent wench, giving too much faith to her herbs, powders, and mysterious words. Good God, what a bucket of bilge water that, he thought, mounting the ladder leading topside. Yet as Ransom Montegomery, captain of the *Red Lion* leapt onto the deck, he knew naught of the

truth behind Aurora Lassiter. And he swore he didn't want
to find out.

Aurora discovered several appropriate names to describe
the barbaric pirate, impolite ones, but fitting just as well.
Arrogant, overbearing, demanding, cold, narrow-minded,
cold. Och, she'd said that already. Well, he was, she
thought, plopping on the tapestry-covered bench beneath
the aft windows. She fingered the exquisite weave, tracing
the pattern, the sting of his clipped barb fading easily. She
recalled her worry for him, over what he must have thought
when he found her gone from the inn. His argument was
justified and bespoke hidden feelings for her. It made her
smile. Yet his distrust of women, smothered beneath his
disciplined exterior, gave her pause. He would fight it, forever she considered, and Aurora wondered who'd hurt him
so deeply to leave such a festering wound. Did he ever enjoy
his life? Find pleasure in a simple chat or a jest, or the sheer
joy of walking in the living world? She remembered their
time in the silken tents, his resistance to even the little comforts she offered. Or was it that they came from her?
   Och, to know the man's thoughts! Could he not see that
this secreted pain did naught to enhance his life? Her lips
curved with a rueful twist. *The mon doesna give a kelpie's wit
fer yer ways, an' likely thinks yer half mad as a result.*
   She shrugged. 'Twas no matter. She had time to know the
man afore he put her ashore.
   Abruptly the door opened and a handsome young boy of
no more than two and ten delivered a simple meal for her.
He was in the Sultan's prison, she recalled, caught unawares
by his startling pale blue eyes.
   "Mem sahib," he said, bowing like a chicken pecking
grain, his gaze darting nervously from her to the door as he
set the tray on the table.
   "My thanks . . . Dahrein." She hoped she was right.
   He grinned, white teeth against tawny skin as he backed
up against the door.
   She frowned at his behavior. "I willna hurt you, laddie."

"So sorry, my lady." He fidgeted with the tin-pierced lantern. "I know this to be true, but . . . but . . ."

"Have you not been near many women?"

He gave her a starry-eyed look. "None as beautiful as my lady."

Aurora glanced down at the coverlet draping her shoulder and knew beneath was little else but dirt and the odor of salt and sea. "Are you in need of spectacles, Dahrein?"

He looked confused. "No, I see well—Oh! Oh-ho." He grinned. "You make the joke?"

Aurora laughed softly. "Aye, puir as it was."

His grin widened as he backed out of the cabin, nearly tripping over the threshold.

"Dahrein? Will you tell Shokai I am well and safe?"

Dahrein looked reluctant, weighing the consequences of her request, then suddenly smiled again, nodding and bowing. As soon as he closed the door Aurora left the bench and dropped onto a chair afore the long polished table and devoured the meal of chicken, hard crusty bread, sliced apples, and mulled wine. It was a feast, and she was silently thankful for Ransom's success as a pirate and his bountiful stores.

An hour later she recalibrated her recent sour opinion of the pirate when Dahrein returned with three bucket-toting crewmen and pressed his flattened palm on a carved panel she hadn't noticed. Wood sprang open, inside a copper tub fitted into a space too cramped to be comfortable, and as Dahrein pulled it out, the water-stained spots on the deck marked its frequent use. Ignoring the leers from the crewmen depositing steaming water into the bath, Aurora went to her sack, retrieving powders and bottles, scenting her bath water, and the two pitchersful Dahrein left behind. Alone, she tossed off the coverlet, then shimmied out of the wet *throbe,* stepping into the tub and sinking into the delicious warmth.

The ship rocked, taking wind and speed and threatening to slosh water from her bath. Masculine voices, harsh and brisk, came to her as she scrubbed away the slime of the slave ship. Her feet were sore, and her muscles reacted to the warmth of the water, loosening and making her sleepy. She washed her hair, yards of black tresses floating in the water.

'Twas always a chore, this, but she never considered cutting it for the convenience. *'Tis too lovely to ever sheer, my sweet, too unusual.* Aurora could almost feel her mother's fingers brushing at the flame red strands framing her forehead and temples. *Like the burst of dawn.* Aurora sighed, releasing her only clear childhood memory of her mother to the recesses of her mind, and stood, taking up the pitcher and gently working the lather from her hair, a foot at a time.

'Twas the sight greeting Ran as he opened the door and, startled by the vision, gawked like a pubescent schoolboy. Liquid slickened over her naked body, streamers of black hair webbing her hips and buttocks, clinging to the back of her thighs, and Ran wished she would turn toward him, yet when her movements stilled he knew she detected his presence. She made no move to cover herself nor demand he leave, and in Ran's eyes her disregard further marked her the harlot.

Grinding his teeth nearly to powder, he tossed the clothes into the room, then backed out of the cabin, closing the door. He didn't move, couldn't move, his groin so frigging hard a single step would leave him marred for life. He gripped the latch, fingers nearly bloodless, and breathed slowly, cursing his weakness and vowing to best it.

Chapter Fifteen

The *Red Lion* was well at sea, ghosting along on zephyr winds, chasing a vermillion sun, when her captain recognized the true impact of having one woman, one unusual, saucy, yet exceedingly beautiful woman aboard his two-hundred-forty-man flagship.

'Twas like a fuse to gunpowder. His crew was tense, lying in wait for the coming explosion, grumbling to themselves over every bad turn of luck and casting the blame on Aurora's unwanted presence in a man's domain. She'd been sleeping, recovering her strength, yet now the bundle of mischief was making herself known.

"Mem sahib says she wishes to see her man, Shokai," Dahrein said. "Immediately, sahib."

"Does she now?" Ran continued to gaze through the spyglass, aware that every man within earshot listened. Although Ran hadn't set eyes on her since she'd slammed the door in his face, he thought it harmless, allowing the lad to deliver meals and bath water, yet the simple concession had given her an ally.

"She says you know you cannot keep her locked up." Dahrein frowned, confusion smeared across his face. "Why would she say this, sahib? She is so little and you are so big?"

Domingo chuckled, nearly choking on the apple slice he'd popped into his mouth. Ran sent the Spaniard a silencing glance, then looked down at the youth. Dahrein blinked, waiting a response. Bloody hell.

Unwilling to reveal her talents with the locks or his suspicions, Ran fudged. "The lady's well aware that keeping her sequestered is not my true preference." Putting her tart little bottom ashore was. "Does she have any other requests?"

"She says if you do not give your permission, she will go anyway."

"Is that so?" Ran nearly bit off his tongue to maintain an even tone. How dare she challenge him!

"Yes, sahib. She was most clear on this." Dahrein's brows knitted, replaying the conversation again to be certain, then he smiled, certain he'd repeated it exactly.

Ran growled, tossing the spyglass to Domingo, forcing him to juggle apples and knife afore discarding both and catching the valuable instrument. Ran stormed to the ladder. He didn't bother using it and vaulted to the lower deck, the impact of his weight thundering through the vessel. All eyes followed his disappearance through the hatch, then speculation murmured in his absense. In moments he stood outside his cabin. He hesitated, then yanked the door open.

Damn and blast.

The room was empty.

Kneeling at Shokai's side, Aurora pummeled roots and leaves into a thick paste. " 'Tis a hatred I felt, *sempai.*" She ground the marble peg into the cup. "The moment I neared this pile of wood and rope."

"Some see what is not there and ignore what can be seen."

"Nay." She shook her head, scooping out the paste and dabbing it to the fading slashes on his chest. " 'Twas the same when we were taken to the slaver." Briefly, she met his thin gaze. "A true and righteous fury I felt."

Shokai stared, recognizing the gravity of her discomfort. "Your glass is clear?"

"I havena 'tempted it," came, almost ashamed.

"Fear can be a foolish friend."

"I ken." Mayhaps her judgment was clouded and Ransom was right. This hatred could be from his crew, collec-

tively. "Och, I canna sense Ransom as clearly as I did this."
She focused on her task. "I canna feel him a'tall."

"A pure heart can be a window into the dark, Empress."
His voice was coaxing.

"He's jaded, Shokai. Badly so." She shrugged indifferently.

"Ahh, but the pheasant could not be caught if it did not
cry out."

She looked up, catching her lower lip briefly atween her
teeth. "Nay. I'm thinkin' he believes I'm like that redheaded
lass we met in Ceylon."

Shokai's face darkened with instant fury. "A bitter man
judges the tree . . . even afore he sees the fruit!"

"There you go, gettin' yourself in a fit over naught." She
pushed him gently back to the bed when he was wont to rise.
"I dinna care, Shokai."

"Your mouth says no and your eyes say yes."

"Then me eyes are lyin'." She blinked prettily and Shokai
grumbled.

Ran pushed loitering crewmen aside, his voice like pressurized steam as he issued orders to be about their duties or
risk punishment. As the companionway emptied, he stared
into the tiny space. The surgeon was absent, but Aurora sat
on the floor aside Shokai's bunk, her white gown, the only
suitable garment he could find, a fluffy cloud about her. A
belt fashioned from thin leather strips and fine gold chains
circled her waist, slung low on her hips with a medieval
favor. Her hair shone nearly blue in the darkly lit cabin,
only the heavy red-streaked locks caught back at her temples, and braided together at her crown. Yards of velvety
black spilled down her back to the floor, briefly drawing his
attention to her shoeless feet. A peasant angel, he thought.
The pair conversed softly in a clipped tongue, and for an
instant Ran was taken back. How many languages could
the lass speak? Gaelic, Arabic, Spanish, and Hindi, if Dahrein was to be believed.

"Aurora!"

"Dinna bark at me, Ransom. You promised," she said, without taking her eyes from the application of some foul-smelling green goo to the old man's chest. Shokai muttered his opposition, wrinkling his nose. And Ran realized he was sitting upright, his chest wounds nearly healed, and his feet; dear God, 'twas but less than a fortnight since the lass had tended him, yet the pinkness of new skin gleamed as he wiggled his toes!

She stood, dropping a kiss to the top of his gray head. Shokai scoffed, pushing her away and making a show of adjusting the forked comb binding his hair in a topknot, yet Aurora merely laughed. It died when she looked at Ransom.

After catching her at her midnight bath, he'd thought it wise to avoid another mistake and had slept on deck, throwing himself into the ship's repairs, putting his crew through their paces, mapping new courses. 'Twas monotonous work, the opportunity to regain a firm hold on his purpose, his vows; but one look at her upturned face and he knew he courted trouble.

"I'll be returnin' later, Shokai," she said without taking her eyes from Ransom. The old man muttered something in his native tongue and Aurora flushed, wiping her hands on a cloth, then tossing it in a basin.

"I told you not to leave the cabin," Ran reminded her unnecessarily, his gaze dropping briefly to the amulet lying above her breasts.

Catching her skirts, she sidled past his imposing bulk and headed up the companionway. "I canna wait 'round when there's work to be done." Ran enjoyed the swish of hair and hips, then shook himself and followed. "And I'll not be treated like slave nor captive."

Gently he caught her arm and she turned. "You are neither."

A black brow swept up. "What is it to be, then?"

Lovers, he thought, then shoved the erotic notion aside, releasing her. "A reluctant guest."

"Convenient title, m'lord," she sniffed, then stepped into his cabin. "Keeping me hidden behind these doors," she flicked a hand toward the hatch as he ducked inside, "makes you no better than your brother."

An angry flush crept up from his neck, his body still with icy calm. "I am *not* Rahman."

"True, but you've banished me to wait *your* presence."

"Yet *I* do not seek to make you my whore."

Aurora flinched at his caustic tone. " 'Tis not a position I aspire to, m'lord, I assure you," she said measuredly, then turned away. "Soiled doves lay for coin. I've no need for such wealth."

Ran scoffed, watching her move about the cabin. "Then how do you fill your belly? Where do you lay your head each night?"

"I rest with the creatures of the earth, Ransom." She plucked a fat yellow apple from the bowl centering the long table and faced him. "And dine on her fruits." She tossed him the apple and he caught it, his brows knitting.

Was that why she chose to sleep on the floor? Wore no shoes? Bloody hell, the lass owned naught but her sack of trinkets! Had her life always lacked the simple comforts? It gave him pause.

"Are you not paid for your *cures?*"

"Nay!" she answered a bit too sharply. He wouldn't understand that to do so would banish her meager powers forever.

Ran scowled at her adamance. "Surely you must find the need to replenish your potions?" The last came snidely and laced with skepticism.

"Aye, and I work, Ransom, servin' in a tavern, launderin', tendin' animals, doin' a bit of scullery, if need be. But I *dinna* accept coin for me healin' talents."

His earlier notions thawed, a little, and as he sank his teeth into the crisp apple, he watched her move about his cabin, noticing the fine polish of the furniture, the glass, the scent of sandalwood awaking him as she straightened this and that. Finally she dropped to the long padded bench beneath the aft windows, drawing up her knees and wrapping her arms around them. The windows slanted out, catching the sun's reflection on the water and casting it across the ceiling. She looked incredibly forlorn draped in the blue-white flicker and flashes of the sea. And Ran realized she wasn't making such a fuss about being confined, but that she was bored and mayhaps lonely. Sweet saints, how could he have been so blind?

"Can you read?" he asked, gesturing to the locked cabinet of books aside his bed as he crossed the room. Her gaze darted to the case, a light sparking her blue eyes.

"Aye," she said almost dreamily, and he paused at the book case, withdrawing a key from inside his leather jerkin, releasing the lock, and carefully opening the doors.

He ran his finger across the spines. "Shakespeare?"

She vaulted from the bench, rounding the foot of the grand bed and bending to peer. "That one I've read, mayhap . . ." She caught her lip, meeting his gaze. "Voltaire?"

His brows shot up in surprise and he slipped the edition free, offering it to her. She held it reverently, carefully opening the leather-bound book as if peeling away fragile petals. Her eyes scanned each word and she started to sink to the floor, but Ran caught her, ushering her a few inches back to the bed. She didn't notice, her lips moving silently, and Ran sank down beside her. She turned the page cautiously, shifting a little for comfort as Ran moved to lay on his side, munching on the apple, watching, utterly captivated by her thirst.

"Och, listen to this," she said, drawing her feet onto the bed as she read a short passage. Ran didn't hear it. He was too busy watching her lovely lips shape the words. " 'Tis amazin', this mon's thoughts." She read on, absently taking the apple from his hand and biting off a chunk, chewing and talking and waving it animatedly. Ran caught her wrist, sinking his teeth into the fruit and breaking off a bite; the only way he'd get any, he decided. She asked his opinion, then he hers, and they talked, the apple passing back and forth atween them. She scoffed at his criticism of the author, and in the next breath convinced him to see another side. Ran forgot everything but the woman, the keenness of her mind, her ability to counter any point he made. And the way her eyes lit up like blue flame when she talked, the way her gown, obviously too big, kept slipping off her shoulder to reveal a smooth golden shoulder and the swells of her breasts.

Aurora opened her mouth to bite the apple, and found it naught but a core. She looked accusingly at Ransom. He chuckled lowly and her heart did a magnificient flip in her chest.

" 'Twas mine," he answered to his crime, taking the core and volleying it into a basket.

"Then I thank you for sharin', Ransom." He was close, propped on his side, his head cupped in his palm. A big lazy cat, she thought, his hair slipping over one eye. She leaned forward, brushing it back. Her amulet swung from its silken blue cord and he caught it, realizing 'twas more than one piece.

" 'Twas fashioned by my father's hand," she said softly as he examined the loose never-ending knot of silver. "A talisman." He flashed her an intense look, then returned his gaze to the charm. The knot was the same as her dagger, familiar; yet fastened in one of the loops was a smooth circle of green stone clutched in a clawlike frame of hammered silver. "And this," she flicked at the dangling hag stone, "I found on the Isle of Iona afore I was," she paused, thinking back, "five and ten."

"There is a significance behind this?" His dry tone marked him the skeptic.

She ignored it. " 'Tis for protection, Ransom, a very powerful amulet," she whispered as if revealing a great secret. She was, but Ransom would not understand, for he chose not to. 'Twas no matter, she thought, pulling it from his grasp.

Rubbish, he thought. "It seems to have failed you, for I've yet to know a woman who can find trouble quicker than you."

"But I am unharmed," she countered with a lift of her brow.

"If 'tis true, then tell me, lass, what is this?" He brushed her gown off her shoulder, pushing the fluted sleeve down to reveal the fresh bruise on her arm above her elbow. Aurora clutched the material to her breast, looking at the mark, then to him.

Her gaze faltered.

"Well?" he demanded almost angrily.

" 'Tis your mark, Ransom." His eyes flared. "When you put me to your shoulder."

Ran's gaze shifted, from her face to the fingerprints and back. "My God, I am sorry," he whispered, sitting up and bracing his elbows on his knees. He held his head in his hands, maple brown hair shielding his features. "I'm sorry."

Aurora stared, sympathy filling her. "It doesna hurt, then or now." Her palm caressed the leather drawn tight across his broad back. "You dinna intend it, Ransom. 'Tis of no consequence."

He shot off the bed. "But *I* did that." Revulsion coated his voice, and she slipped her feet over the edge of the coverlet, coming to him, frail and delicate afore his imposing height.

"You're a braw man, Ransom Montegomery, with hands like mallets," she said, taking one and unfurling his tense fingers. She traced the lines and scars and callouses with her fingertip. " 'Tis a grand power here." She smoothed her fingers over the back, then up each digit, creating a glorious tingling. Ran never imagined such an innocent touch could be so intoxicating. He wanted to see her face, her eyes; and he gave way to impulse. His hand lifted free from hers, knuckles brushing the curve of her jaw, fingertips tilting her face up.

"But now . . . see how gentle they are?" she whispered, turning her cheek into his roughened palm and closing her eyes.

Her skin was like cream silk, kissed by the sun and warm to the touch. His thumb brushed her lips, so smooth, the shade of crushed raspberries. Her lashes swept up slowly, blue eyes filled with unfathomable tenderness. He trembled down to the heels of his boots. A part of him was tight and tensed to flee, and another, deeper and stronger, wanted to clutch her close, slowly taste the flavor of her skin, her lips, spend hours and hours knowing the feel of her breasts in his hands, her thighs clutching his.

But he couldn't. She was mark of defense, a silent war with himself, for Aurora gentled him. In a time fraught with blood and death and torturous hardship, she represented life and renewal and sustenance. A dangerous hazard. There was far too much to do, too many who depended on him. If he weakened, if he allowed such selfishness, he'd perish for certain. And take his people with him.

Yet still he bent, moving ever closer, to her face, her mouth.

A taste. 'Twould be enough. He cradled her face atween his palms. With only his hands, his lips, he touched. If he took more, he would never retreat. Never. His tongue swept her plump lower lip, wetting it and she gasped, a soft flutter of air shuddering atween them. He pressed, balmy and rolling, molding her mouth with his own, stirring with the sweetly banked fire. He could feel it in her, the flame igniting, the eagerness and energy she always possessed and gave, and when her hands came up to splay his chest, he struggled for control, to keep his hands still and not hurt her, not indulge further. 'Twas hard. Bloody painful, for her fingers smoothed beneath his vest, shaping cloth-covered muscle, the coin of his nipples, the contours leading down to his stomach; and he kissed her and kissed her, mastering her mouth, loving her only there, his tongue stroking her teeth, outlining her lips, then plunging inside. A moan escaped her, heady and begging for more, and still he resisted and she grasped the width of his belt and hung on tightly. Their breathing gushed, the wind afore the storm, and she ached for the weight of his warmth to her body, the power and strength he withheld.

He trembled, with want and passion and something else she couldn't decipher.

And Aurora thought she'd turn to flames if he didn't hold her, take her against him, beneath him.

"Sahib!" The call registered in Ran's brain seconds too late. "Oh . . . oh! Saa-heeb," came in breathless awe from the doorway.

Ran jerked back, abruptly releasing her. Aurora staggered at the separation, her legs like liquid, her mouth on fire. Ran fought to draw air into his lungs, knowing if he moved, he'd snap in two. His blood hummed in his veins, charging through his groin, making it pulse with unsatisfied desire. She met his gaze and smiled softly, and his attention darted to her bruised lips. Another mark I've put on the lass, he cursed, then glanced back over his shoulder at Dahrein. The lad looked as if he'd seen a ghost, his face ashen, then reddening with embarrassment. He swallowed, his immature Adam's apple bobbing like broken glass in his throat, round blue eyes darting back and forth atween the couple, then lowering to the floor.

"I am most sorry, sahib. Forgive this wretched soul." He salaamed.

Ahhh, God, to be caught dallying by this lad. "You've good cause to come running into my cabin unannounced?" Ran snapped, hating his weakness or that any member of his crew should witness it.

"The *Phoenix* comes, starboard at two knots." Dahrein hastily backed out of the cabin as Ran crossed the room, brushing back the curtain to examine the horizon.

"Dinna be harsh with the lad, Ransom, 'Tis nay his fault."

His gaze flashed to Aurora. Her skin was flushed, her tight nipples pushing against the white fabric, her quick breaths defining the lush fullness. By God, but she was ripe for the plucking! His fists clenched, the need to take her into his arms making his features sharp. It had been years since he'd felt this way, this vulnerable to a woman; and he reminded himself that the risks of planting a bastard in her were not worth a few moments of unspeakable pleasure. Nay. Yielding was not in his future. And 'twas folly to be near the lass.

"Need I remind you, woman, that they are my crew and 'tis my ship." He slapped the curtain down and moved restlessly about the cabin.

"Och, Ransom, you canna coddle affection with one

hand," she said calmly, softly, refusing to fuel his sudden anger, "then bat it away with the other."

His lips twisted in a snarl, and he couldn't hold back the snap of anger. "You're well educated about a man's affections, eh?"

Aurora's features tightened. "I enjoyed it, your kiss. Greatly so." She folded her arms beneath her breast, bracing her shoulder against the bedpost. "And would do it again if I dinna feel the bite of your insults a moment after."

He scoffed, flipping pages of his log. "If I but pressed the advantage," he hissed caustically, "we'd be pumping on that bed like friggin' rabbits!" He slammed the log shut.

Smoothly she arched a black brow. "Boastin' again, are you now?" He chuckled, dark and confident, and her gaze followed him around the room as he flicked at this and shoved at that. "Great Thunder, look at you!" Her hand lashed the air. "You're prowlin' this cabin like a wild beastie. Your rage is palatable and the taste is a wee bit sour, thinks I." He ground the carpet beneath his boots, pacing. "I say yea or nay to aught you ask, yet you'll not find satisfaction, for me words are taunts, pirate lord. You want me to be what I am not, to justify treatin' me so poorly."

"Is that so?" he responded with a furious glare.

"Aye. There's a gentle heart in you, Ransom Montegomery, and it doesna sit well in your belly that *I* have found it."

He stilled, his eyes softening a fraction; then liquid amber chilled to impenetrable gold. "Bah!" he growled with the flick of his hand. He headed for the door.

"You'll be wantin' to postpone going up on deck."

He didn't want to stop, but did and cast her a side-glance through a curtain of sable hair, his eyes dark and glacial.

"Your boldness is showing."

He looked down, painfully aware of what he'd find; his arousal tenting the fabric of his breeches.

"Now *that,* m'lord, you can blame on me."

He quit the room and she said naught as he sealed her inside.

Chapter Sixteen

Rabbits, was it now?

Did he truly believe she'd welcome such bitterness in her bed? 'Twas a place for powerful loving, not releasing fury. And 'twas not *his* decision alone—and that was that!

Wrapping her arms around the bedpost, Aurora blew out a soothing breath as she sank slowly to the floor. She wasn't angry, not entirely, for her skin was frighteningly warm, her lips still tingling with the fresh taste of his savage kiss, and if her wildly thumping heart broke free, she swore 'twould dance 'round the room like a wee crazed brownie. Yet while she was prepared to embrace the powerful passion they shared, Ransom obviously was not.

Puir mon.

In a sorry way of it now. She pitied the sailor who crossed his path first. Ransom harnessed aught he felt, even prided himself, she thought, on his tight efficient rein; yet when his discipline slipped, overruling the fierce need he kept bottled, he didn't know how to manage the flood, except to dam it up—moored in silence and anger as in their desert crossing. And she felt his restraint, in the trembling heat of his kiss, always so greedy, laced with a dark desperation, as if in the one tender moment he'd taken too much and would be punished for the pleasure. 'Twas a wee comfort to know she affected him, but Aurora wasn't daft. He didn't want to show the weakness, to anyone, and whether or not she did aught to constantly provoke this quick masking, she recognized the war he waged. It drew her, this secret pain and she longed for the shield of indifference to crumble. He didn't.

'Twas why he avoided her. Aye, and mayhaps his imagining her a harlot and beneath such attentions, was his only defense against the feelings he had for her? She didn't doubt he had them. She'd seen it in his eyes when he'd climbed down into the slaver's hull. But 'twas so fleeting, that. And though she'd make no more effort to convince him she wasn't a whore, Aurora admitted it hurt that he would not take her word.

But then . . . he thought her ways outlandish anyway, so what consequence was it to add whoredom to the list.

Aurora moved silently on bare feet to the tiny cabin where Shokai rested. Standing outside, she watched him sleep, breathing evenly, healthily; and satisfied at his recovery, she turned back toward Ransom's cabin.

And found her path blocked.

"What a fine plump piece you be," the seaman said, his eyes drinking in her bountiful shape, his hand smoothing roughly over her shoulder.

She batted it away. "Leave off, laddie, or you'll be regretting it."

He laughed, ugly and lecherous, clamping a hand to her shoulder again, tighter, and Aurora checked her temper with a calming breath.

"Capt'n's aboard the *Phoenix,* so who'll protect yah now, doxy?" the sailor threatened, and Aurora wondered if this was the anger she felt when she first boarded. Suddenly the dark-haired sailor yanked her close, burying his face in her bosom, and Aurora immediately grasped his wrist, her thumb digging into the apex atween that and his forefinger. The sailor straightened, his eyes widening as pain shot up his arm, numbing the limb. She twisted it and he curled low in quick agony.

"Och, I dinna wish to hurt you, laddie, but must I demonstrate further?" she said in a soft whisper, not wanting to alert any more of his friends who possessed a like mind.

"Nay, ow! Nay, leggo!"

"Promise me, as a man of honor?"

"Aye, aye, aye."

Aurora released him, and he stumbled back into something sharp and cold. The sailor lurched.

Domingo Avilar stood in the companionway, his back to the wall, a slim knife poised to slice. "The captain will hear of this." With a sharp nod, the first mate stepped aside and the sailor hurriedly skimmed past.

Domingo sheathed his blade, his features creased with concern as he looked to Aurora. "Are you fit?" *Madre de Dios,* Ran was going to bludgeon him for allowing this to happen!

"Aye. My thanks," she said, smiling, her gaze moving beyond him to Shokai, his *sai* aimed at Domingo, his topknot unwinding for lack of the securing fork.

Domingo twisted, glancing atween the two.

"Get you to bed, Shokai. I am well, neh?"

The old man nodded once, stone gray hair whipping free, and with economy of movement, he twisted it back into the skull-scraping knot and shoved the *sai* into place.

Domingo didn't realize he held his breath until the old man bowed and vanished into the cabin. "He doesn't trust anyone?" Domingo looked offended.

" 'Tis a distrust I accept, Mister Avilar." She headed back up the companionway, Domingo following. "After so many years, I am alive only as a result."

"Yet you should not have ventured from the cabin."

She paused at the threshold, giving him a side-glance. "The first mate chirps like his captain," she said tartly, then stepped into the cabin.

Domingo smiled, caught off balance by her directness. "It is safe in here, my lady. No one would dare oppose Ran, but he—we—cannot be everywhere," he said, adding his loyalty. "You are a lovely temptation."

Aurora made an indelicate sound. "Ransom holds far too much faith in me face and figure." She moved to the window bench and plopped down in a huff. "And I am nay so sheltered in the ways of men."

Domingo's brows rose. And he wondered if she were

admitting to being seasoned as a courtesan as Ran suspected or well acquainted with the working of a man's mind. Which usually lay atween his thighs. Either way the lady had no idea how truly alluring she was. "I've seen great men stumble at the feet of a beautiful woman." Like Ransom at yours, he thought, bracing his shoulder against the frame, not daring to step inside.

"Were you one of those pitiful aspirants?" she asked cheekily.

"I fear for more women than I can count." His grin lacked even a smattering of self-reproach.

"But you *do* count them," she said, his wiggling brows and roguish smile making her laugh. He was a flirt, light of heart and free with his thoughts, and likely tamed the ladies with ease, for the Spaniard cut a dashing picture of sultry masculine perfection. His black hair was wild, brushing his broad shoulders, and his mustache, though thick, was neatly combed and clipped. Raven black eyes stared at her from a sun-warmed face, his features possessing the strength of his forebears and the tiny creases of frequent smiles. Though shorter than Ransom by a hand he was still of good height, lean hipped and long legged, every inch of him accented by the snug fit of his dark breeches and long embroidered waist coat. He was bare armed, and like most of the men on this ship she'd seen, cleanly muscled.

"Ran will not like you staring at me like that," he teased, flattered.

"Och, Ransom doesna find pleasure in aught I do this week."

Domingo nearly choked on that, thinking Ransom ought to be commended for his restraint. What warm-blooded man could resist such a luscious creature? Yet she was incredibly poised and serene, her inner peace like a beacon, drawing him. And every man on this ship, he thought gravely.

"Capt'n's hailin' ye, sir," the bosun's mate said, appearing suddenly at his side. "Says ta get yer Spanish carcass topside afore ye find yerself as the *Phoenix* crow."

Domingo laughed at the pleasure the lad received in

relaying the message, then bowed to Aurora. She didn't
notice. She was staring intently at the young man. Her gaze
dropped to his arm, to the wound he'd received in Barbary.
Without seeing it, she knew it had worsened, her toadstone
ring growing warmer by the moment, warning of soured
blood. 'Twas not fatal yet, but without care . . . ? She'd no
chance to ask of his symptoms, for he left hurriedly.

Domingo recognized her concern and shrugged helplessly. "He will not come to you," he said truthfully. "Their
loyalty is to the surgeon."

"Let it be known I will offer my aid, if they wish it."
Aurora couldn't force her ways on those who would not
ask. Even the night she'd found Shokai near his death, he
had to *ask* for her help.

"Ran will be aboard the *Phoenix* taking his reports well
into the night," Domingo said, hating to leave her when she
looked so forlorn, just sitting there, staring out the aft windows.

Aurora's shoulders lifted in a heavy sigh. "I ken, *Señor*
Avilar."

"Domingo," he corrected, and she glanced back over her
shoulder, her lips curved in a smile afore he shut the door.

Aurora leaned back against the wall, drawing her legs
onto the bench and sitting cross-legged. She plucked at the
folds of her only garment, wishing Ransom would have
returned to her afore boarding the sister ship. But he hadn't
bothered, sending only messages, avoiding her.

"Ah well, he canna do that for verra long," she thought
aloud. 'Twas his cabin, his bed, he'd come to miss. And then
mayhaps, miss her.

Kneeling on the bench cushion, Aurora hovered over the
keek stane, her well-trained mind coaxing the images from
past to present in the concave glass.

Moonlight splashed on the sea, reflecting to illuminate
her face and the ceiling above. The ship was quiet, gently
rocking, the waves a soft sloshing rhythm.

A sudden squeak rent the air and Aurora flinched, shutting the box.

"Hush now, you'll wake the lot of them and then where will I be," she whispered to the dolphin poking its blunt nose through the open window. She'd slid the framed glass aside to let in fresh air, for the cabin was stifling hot, and the mammal had appeared, pestering her, swishing water as he strained up on his flukes. "Hush now." The dolphin settled.

Her hands on her thighs, Aurora stared briefly out at nothing, then closed her eyes, banishing emotion and incidental debris from her mind. The image of Ransom materialized and for an instant she savored his handsome form, then pushed him out too, bringing back the opaqueness of a barren mind. Without looking, she flipped the tiny latch and lifted the lid again.

Opening her eyes she bent and stared into the glass. 'Twas a moment in coming, the interruption weakening her powers and stamina, but she'd come beyond the childhood of her life to the present. A twisting rope appeared, the swing of it grating against rock and pebbles, a red lion and a white wolf faced off for attack, each demanding possession of the rope. The wolf had come! She sighed, relieved her father was near and alive. But the red lion? 'Twas Ransom? Why would he fight with her father? Aurora studied the image, certain she had seen all there was to see, then coaxed the glass to foretell deeper. The glass muddied blue, liquid, running red, and she frowned for it lasted but an instant.

She concentrated, coaxed and chanted. An urn, small, pear-shaped and clear as crystal, sat on a table, light flickering through its emptiness. The table was polished, the style and wood of a talented craftsman, finer than aught she'd ever see or touch, and Aurora knew 'twas the surroundings that always told her more than the objects or scenes she witnessed. A movement caught her, a flicker so faint she almost missed it. Tucked in the recesses of the urn's image was a figure, shrouded in darkness but for the shape of a shoulder, an elbow, and a bit of sleeve. Aurora could not decipher whether 'twas woman or man, and strained for clarity—

"What the bloody hell are you doing?" came the whispered inquiry and Aurora flinched, then sighed, the image gone. With annoyance she closed the *keek stane* and secured the latch. Cheese and crust! He was supposed to be aboard the *Phoenix,* she thought, doing all those man things outlaws do.

Ran closed the hatch behind him.

A chirping sound snapped his attention to the windows and the dolphin nose bobbing through the opening. Ran frowned, his expression darkening to something else as she rose up, bending over the wide sill to caress the grampus' smooth wet skin.

"Go on with you now," she shooed. "I've no time to play. The pirate's back," she whispered loudly. "Give the *Phoenix* some of that seaman's luck." The gray beast rose up on his flukes, then sank away. Aurora turned to Ransom. He looked a wee bit shocked, yet she recognized the sudden smoldering in his eyes as his amber gaze drifted over her body.

For with the exception of her silver amulet, Aurora was naked.

Chapter Seventeen

The warm air surrounding him felt heavy, damp and salty, quickening with an untouchable current. Slowly, he started toward her, his steps measured as his body and vision greedily absorbed every inch of sweet pale flesh revealed in the refracting moonlight. Blood rushed in his groin, reacting with a deadly force, and a voice in him, the one which remembered clearly the price of such a temptation, screamed for him to leave. Now.

But with her so brazenly bare and free like this, he couldn't resist the pleasure of looking at her. And by God, she was exquisite, utterly unaffected by his intrusion, he thought, his gaze skimming her waist, her rounded belly to the luxurious swell of hips and supple thighs, to her buttocks resting on her calves. Yards and yards of thick curling hair spilled over her, veiling and revealing her body in erotic splashes. The sight made his knees wobble.

"What, in the name of all that is holy, are you doing . . . like that?" He sounded far too breathless for a man his age.

" 'Tis a sweat house in here, Ransom." She flipped hair off her shoulder, exposing a plush breast fully to the gray light, and Ransom thought he'd explode the seams of his breeches. "So dinna be gettin' yourself into a fit."

"I do *not* have *fits*," he ground through clenched teeth, desire running amuck with his control.

"Of course you dinna." Smug, with hidden laughter.

"Close your mouth, Ransom. 'Tis undignified." She reached for her chemise.

Dignified! "How can you speak of dignity when not wearing a stitch?" His words fractured as she lifted slender graceful arms, dropping the fabric over her head. Her breasts swayed as she settled it in a soft film over her body, yet naught, *naught* under blue skies would ever banish the image of her nakedness from his brain. *Grievin' mothers, man. Leave. Leave now!*

But he didn't, settling slowly to the bench beside her. The familiar scent of ginger wafted to him, teasing him mercilessly.

"Clothes dinna give a person dignity, m'lord, or the ragged souls of the world would have naught to sustain them."

By God the woman had a talent for making his struggles seem incredibly inconsequential. Especially when he was coming apart with the fierce hunger that rode him constantly since he'd laid eyes on her. Tearing his gaze from her lush form, Ran searched for a smattering of control when all he wanted to do was press her back to the cushion and ravish her until she cried out for him to cease. Sharply he reminded himself of the consequences, that she seemed well at ease baring her body to him, and the significance of that; and he managed to gain a firm enough rein on his raging senses before he looked back to her.

Ran swallowed a pain-thickened groan, losing his grip.

She'd made no effort to dress further and remained poised on the bench, legs tucked to the side, pulling her hair free and spilling it over her thighs to the floor. The ship rocked, waves gently battering the hull and sending a sparkling mist through the open window. She shivered deliciously. And Ransom considered a life on the stage, for his calm appearance as he relaxed on the bench was as remarkable as it was artificial.

"What is this?" He gestured to the box and hoped she didn't see his hand tremble.

She did and studied him curiously, then darted a glance atween the *keek stane* and the man afore her. 'Twas time he knew, she decided, and slid the box to the bench atween

them. He met her gaze and she nodded permission. Long
tanned fingers flipped the lid, his eyes squinting. Unable to
see the contents clearly, Ransom rose to light a lantern,
setting it into the brackets on the sill.

The golden light showered her body, seductive, enticing;
grinding away at his restraint.

" 'Tis a *keek stane.*" He scowled his ignorance, then bent
to examine the box closely. "A skrying glass."

His gaze flew to hers. "Like a crystal ball?"

"Aye, a wee bit, but . . ." She broke eye contact.

"But?"

She shrugged bare shoulders. " 'Tis for seein' things."

"Must I pry the words from you?" he challenged softly,
watching her nervously wet her lips and aching to taste
them.

Aurora sighed. Why was she hesitating? *Because he willna
believe,* a voice chanted. *He'll scoff and laugh and call you
touched and tainted, like the others did.* Nay, she thought
with a deep breath. This was Ransom. He may not believe
in her ways, but he would not laugh at her.

Aurora lifted her gaze, meeting his with unflinching calm.
" 'Tis a tool, Ransom. I've used it since I was a child,
coaxin' the images, decipherin' the glass. Most see people
and events. Common things," she specified. "Oftimes a
warning, or the like. I dinna have such fortune." She shook
her head, always confused and disappointed over this. "I see
images that represent a deeper event." At his raised brow,
she added, " 'Tis like a wrapped box . . . I ken the outside,
but must unwrap the meaning to discover the truth inside."
Naked shoulders shifted with agitation. "The *Lord* and
Lady dinna believe me too bright a lass, thinks I, for I'm
needin' a few more lessons afore I get it plain."

The lord and lady? What have they, whoever they be, to
do with this tiny container, and why did it upset her? Ran
stared at the tapestry-covered box. 'Twas naught special; a
concave clock glass resting in a bed of velvet, shaped to fit
it snugly. A rim, from the box edge to the glass lip kept it
from slipping or breakage. And as he examined it closely,
Aurora bent forward, gently brushed his hands aside; and

she was oblivious to the amber eyes skating briefly over her face and delectable shape as she slipped a tiny block of wood from one corner, then lifted the securing rim.

Ran tore his gaze from her and removed the glass, holding it to the light. Sable brows shot up. " 'Tis painted black, Aurora, you cannot see through this." Was she trying to make him look the fool? he wondered, dropping the circle back in its place.

Carefully she replaced it just so and fastened the rim, closing the box. "I see *in* it, Ransom, not through it."

"Of course."

Her eyes jerked to his, searching his bland expression for laughter, the mocking. His disbelief she could well tolerate, his ridicule she could not.

"And this skrying—you must do bare-assed?" A sudden smile softened his features.

"I was hot," she said testily, sliding the box into her sack, then stuffing it in the drawer fashioned beneath the bench.

Ran braced his weight on one locked arm, the effort putting him closer to her. "And what, little pest, did you see?"

Her gaze swept to his. "You dinna care to know, Ransom, so why bother to ask that of me?"

She may have asked if he were having porridge for breakfast, so matter of fact her tone, but 'twas her eyes that alerted him, her challenging stare making him see how much this meant to her. And he wouldn't for his life willingly hurt her. God, he'd done that enough this day. He might not agree with her ways, nor believe them, but he'd defend the woman's right to have them.

"Tell me, lass," he coaxed softly. "Did you see your father?"

"Aye." Defensive, wary.

"And where is he hiding?"

"I dinna ken. Me father appears as a white wolf," she said patiently. "Which means he is near." She refrained from adding that wolf and lion fought, knowing such a deep connection to her would not be to Ransom's liking.

" 'Twere a crystal urn and a twisting rope, too, but I dinna ken the meaning, yet."

His sudden honest interest surprised him. "Is this the first time you've seen these images?"

She blinked. Was he truly curious or was lust nudging him along? She couldn't be sure with him staring at her, all warm and simmering hot. She wished he'd kiss her and relieve the ache churning through her body.

"Nay," she finally answered, shaking her head, black tresses waterfalling like Chinese silk. Unconsciously Ran reached out and snagged a fistful, rubbing it atween his fingers. She didn't seem to notice. "But 'twas another image, very faint, of a human, though I dinna ken if 'twas man or nay." She yawned hugely, covering it too late. "Mayhaps next time."

He smiled with tender humor, tucking a lock behind her ear. "Sleepy, pest?" His fingers trailed her jaw and as she nudged the roughness of his palm with her soft cheek, mortal strength kept him from drawing her to the hunger of his mouth.

She nodded groggily, taking up the coverlet and wrapping her shoulders. " 'Tis the drawing forth with me mind, Ransom." She drooped like syrup to the floor. "I'm nearly swoonin' with fatigue, for the task."

Ran smiled as she snuggled noisily. Still seated, he bent over her. "You are welcome to my bed, lass."

Her eyes blinked open, meeting his dark amber stare. It simmered with an unsaid message, his grin utterly rakish and playful, and she almost considered relenting, for they'd parted last on unsettled terms and he rarely showed this ease with her.

"Nay." Her lids drifted closed. "I dinna care to share your bed, pirate."

Ran stiffened and supposed he was well deserving of that. "I meant alone, pest."

One eye flashed open. "If I choose to lay upon your sheets, Ransom Montegomery, 'twill not be alone."

Ran's throat tightened, his body, behaving like a man who'd been without a woman for ten years, maintained a hearty strength, crowding his breeches. "You've a tart mouth, woman," he ground out his anxiety.

"Aye, m'lord." She patted a yawn with a blanket-covered fist. " 'Tis just so."

'Tis just so. Either take me as I am or nay, he interpreted, for Aurora didn't argue her shortcomings. And she readily accepted his. He was an outlaw, yet she cared naught for that. He'd come for her in the Bedouin camp, and she'd accepted his aid without interference, trusting him. And on the slaver, she didn't care how he was there, only that he was, trusting him. And she accepted the passion they shared with equal aplomb, trusting that he would, too. He couldn't. God above, he wished he could.

Ran stretched his long body out on the bench, his groin throbbing painfully as he shifted to his side, elbow bent, palm supporting his head. She was like a kitten, curled and snug, her back seeking the solid warmth of the wood cabinetry. And Ran shut out the sweet image of her doing that to him. Sweet saints, he'd no one to blame for this torment but himself, and the kettle was his to stew in. Yet even hip-deep in logs, casks, and crates aboard the *Phoenix,* he couldn't free his mind of her, wondering if she was unharmed or hungry . . . or thinking of him.

And in the hours they'd been apart he'd realized his disposition was no better than a taunted bear's without the sight of her to enjoy. She was simply too enticing to ignore. Voluptuous and sensual. 'Twould never be said that Aurora was not every bit a woman.

And she kissed like madness.

And she was still angry with him.

I dinna care to share your bed. Her words stung, yet in the same breath Ran recognized he'd acted the conceited fool, assuming she would welcome him when *he* chose. Toplofty bastard, you are, Montegomery. Even a harlot has pride.

Careful not to disturb her, he left the bench and went to his bed, stripping quickly and climbing atween the sheets. The book he'd given her weighted his foot and he reached for it, staring at the volume and remembering the easy companionship they shared and how natural it felt. It seemed like days ago now, and as Ransom set the edition aside, he wished for more moments like that, knowing well he shouldn't be wishing a'tall. He would bring her naught but sorrow.

Ran stood midship, hands clasped at his spine, booted feet spread wide to accommodate the dip of the vessel as the *Lion* took wind. The breeze whipped hair from his face and snapped the sleeves of his shirt.

His amber gaze skipped over the deck of his ship. Men hung from ratlines in the rigging, repairing sail, adjusting halliard. Bare chested and shoeless. Others worked at their posts, mending cannon track lines, polishing wood, threading new lanyard in dead-eye blocks.

None would look him in the eye.

One of their mates had confessed his crime. That Aurora had adequately deflected the attack was of no consequence. His crew had been warned not to touch her. Ever.

Disobedience would not be tolerated.

Carefully Ran weighed crime and punishment, and considered that his mood was already foul, for he'd spent the night in a firm state of unsatisfied arousal, listening to Aurora cry out like a lost child in her sleep. A sleep that kept her still. Loss of wages and demotion of rank would not matter to these men, for they shared equally in the prize of captured ships, several duties assigned to each to maintain the massive flagship. Nay, harsher measures were the only recourse for keeping Aurora safe when he was not with her.

"Twelve lashes."

His tone bore none of the rage simmering beneath the surface, even as the sailor paled. Mates stilled at their jobs as the lash struck mercifully, swiftly, welting bare flesh. The seaman flinched, yet valiantly kept silent and the *Lion*'s master remained impassive, like a spire of carved granite. Crewmen stared bleakly from their mate to their superior as the man was led away.

The message was clear.

The lady was beyond their limits.

Ran turned away, shooting Domingo a disfiguring glare afore heading toward the hatch. Shokai stood motionless, half blocking Ran's path. Eyes met and clashed. Shokai nodded ever so slightly. Approval? Ran was not certain, yet as he strode past, the old man's words stopped him cold.

"Reveal this and the lion withers to shape a rat."

Ran was amazed he could understand the cryptic remarks. "I care not, old man. The pair of you will not be aboard long enough to make a difference."

Shokai inclined his head amidship, where the punishment was dealt, reminding Ran that at least one person had already influenced his life. It angered him to realize it and he quickly slipped into the hatch, taking the ladder rungs two at a time.

"No lord can rule without sometimes playing deaf and blind," he heard afore the ancient man disappeared from sight.

Heading to his cabin, Ran mulled the old man's remarks and the caliber of woman he protected. He would not lie to her. If she asked, he would reveal, but beyond that 'twas no longer her affair and he would not volunteer. Ran pushed open the door, expecting to find her awake, and frowned when he discovered her slumbering still, her hair rippling across his carpet like spilled ink. His body and mind reacted immediately to the sight of her, remembering every detail of the voluptuous body revealed to him the eve afore. God's blood, but she was a lovely spirited creature.

She stirred fitfully, drawing the coverlet over her shoulders, murmuring in Gaelic. What tortured her dreams to upset her thus, exhausting her enough that she'd not heard Dahrein enter to prepare his bath? Or had using her *keek stane* truly taken such a costly toll on her strength, he wondered as he unbuckled his sword and belt, laying them quietly aside. Reaching for the platter Dahrein had left, Ran watched her sleep, breaking off a crust of bread and shoving it into his mouth. He chewed, tilting his head for a better look at her, then realized he was moving closer and stopped. Twas best to avoid the lass and begone afore she woke.

Briskly he stripped and stepped into the tub, lathering his palms and scrubbing with a vengeance.

Blasted prick. Ruled him every time he was near the wench. *I dinna care to share your bed, Ransom,* vibrated in his head. Get her off the ship, he reminded, and he'd no longer have such ill-fitting breeches.

The splash of water stirred Aurora and she opened her eyes slowly, the display filling her vision robbing her breath less. She remained still, her gaze following the rub of his hands across the work-sculpted marble of his chest, then down over his flat stomach. Her body jumped to life, awake and aching for his touch. Lather foamed, making little sucking sounds as he rubbed beneath his sinewy arms, then soaped his hands again.

Och, a giant of a mon, she thought as he reached for a pitcher, tilting his head back and sluicing water over dark sudsy locks. More water splattered on the deck than in the tub, tinged with red dye. He was just too big, his knees poking well over the rim, and where she'd been able to sink completely beneath the water, he was scarcely in it. Like a child in a bucket, she thought, snuffing out a laugh. His amber gaze instantly collided with hers, his lips thinning.

Ran set the pitcher aside with more force than necessary. God's blood! he cursed, feeling incredibly vulnerable with her lying on her side, watching, him naked and marooned in the tub.

She rose slightly, propping her torso on one bent elbow. The chemise strap slipped off her shoulder. She watched him intently, glad the awful red henna was gone.

"Do you always find a man at his bath so fascinating?" he rankled from the other side of the room.

" 'Tis a first for me, m'lord." She waved. "Please continue." Her lips twitched with a smile as he slapped a hand over the wedge of soap. "Och, you wouldna have such a lack of privacy if you dinna take me aboard, so dinna be squawkin' at me."

He scrubbed, scowling, knowing 'twas truth.

"You missed a spot," she said with a grin, pointing to her elbow but nodding toward him. Ran looked and scrubbed.

And Aurora climbed to her feet, dragging the coverlet with her as she strolled about the cabin, feeling his warm gaze following her as she paused at his desk to examine the copper lion head of his buckle. Ran watched her fingertips dip into every crevice, smooth the hammered copper as if to memorize the contours, and wondered what it would be like to have her touch him that way, then shook himself, desperate to get out of the cabin. He attacked his foot.

"Who fashioned this?" she asked, her eyes on the growling lion-head clasp.

He shrugged. " 'Twas a gift of my crew." The answer indicated the whole, and her face held a frown as she resumed her promenade. She plucked a dried apricot from a tray on the long table and popped the sweet fruit into her mouth, aware Ransom watched suspiciously.

"You've soot on your back," she said, passing close to the tub and flicking water in his face.

He frowned meanly and she snatched the wet sponge from his hand and squashed it across his face. Ran sputtered soap and sponge fragments, stunned and appalled.

"Woman!" His features darkened.

" 'Twas hopin' I could wash away that scowl."

She was grinning. He wasn't, and reached for the sponge. Aurora stepped back and arched a brow, daring him to come after it. "Soap," she urged hand out, fingers wiggling.

Refusing to be baited, Ran reached for a length of cloth, toweling his hair. "I do not need aid in my bath, Aurora."

If ever words were spat, she thought. "Are you askin' me to go fishin' for it?" She nodded toward the cloudy water atween his thighs.

Grievin' mothers, Ran thought, looking to the heavens, the woman knew how to tempt.

Ran dunked his fist into the water and came back with the soft chunk. "You are determined to pester me, regardless?"

"Aye." The man simply did not know how to have fun, Aurora decided, stepping closer, unafraid of his malevolent stare. The coverlet fell to the carpet as she took the mushy cake, allowing her hand to cover his briefly afore she lathered the sponge. His gaze lowered to the thin chemise, to bare thighs and knees, then back to her face, following her suspiciously as she moved behind him. She smiled, plying the sponge to his broad back, efficiently, in smooth invigorating circles.

"God of Thunder, you're carved with scars," she said, squeezing the sponge, expelling thick foam over his massive shoulders.

Ransom bit down a groan, his manhood throbbing and stretching as it had since she'd roused from sleep, and now with her touching him so intimately, he felt his will dissolving, tension and heat rocketing in its place.

"I am sorry if they offend you," he snapped.

"But 'tis beautiful, they are." She outlined one, then another with her fingertip. " 'Tis so of a Pict prince, marks of the warrior, m'lord." He tossed her a quick disbelieving stare. "Aye, even the Gods had to fight for their place beside the Goddess."

"Beside the goddess?" came in a tight chuckle.

Aurora leaned close, her breast pressing deliciously to his back as she rubbed the sponge down his arms. " 'Tis the way of me ancient people, Ransom." Her words whispered across his wet skin and into his brain, storing it for later, for now he could think of naught but the woman and her seductive stroking. "Women have as much right and power to rule as men."

She drew the sponge back up over his shoulders, then reached past him to take the pitcher, rinsing away the soap. She smoothed his back, toyed with his hair, and he tilted his head back into her touch, then suddenly stiffened. Letting the misshapen sponge fall into the water, she walked around the tub to look him in the eye. Her lips twitched. He looked much like a child awaiting punishment.

"You best be getting out afore you shrivel like a fig."

Naught on him could shrivel with her so near, he thought with a self-depreciating smirk. "Then do me the privacy of turning your back."

"A prude, are you now, Ransom?" She folded her arms. "Or is it boys yer likin'?"

He shot her a dangerous look meant to carve the skin

from her bones and she laughed, tossing him a fresh drying cloth from the neat stack afore scooting out of his reach.

Ran stood, pleased she was busying herself away from him, and left the tub, wrapping the cloth about his hips. He didn't want her to see how her scrubbing affected him.

But Aurora stole a peek over her shoulder. 'Twas too grand a temptation. Her breath caught, a deep warmth coiling its way to her woman-spot. She swallowed a hungry moan, her hands fairly itching to touch him again, to run her fingers over every curve and slope of his muscled form, and she took feminine enjoyment out of watching muscle ripple and flex as he gathered clothing from chests and cabinet. Och, he is bronze all over, she realized, but from hip to upper thigh. And her curiosity was satisfied as to why, when he shoved his feet into short tattered breeches. They scarcely covered half his thighs! He wore naught else, and Great Thunder, it made him appear larger and more threatening than afore!

And there was something else she noticed.

He was aroused.

Fully. Ragingly.

All gloriously male.

She gasped. He looked up and she turned completely, not disguising her admiration and fascination with him. It nearly destroyed his composure.

"Are you pleased?" he snapped, embarrassed, impatient to be away from her.

She frowned. "Are you *that* afraid of the affections you have for me?"

He fastened the buttons over his arousal, ignoring the wet chemise clinging to her breasts and supple thighs and his fierce need to be atween them. "I've a pain in my breeches for you, woman, nothing more." Done, he headed for the door.

"Och, was it a pain that gave me the book and shared an apple?" she said hurriedly. "Or smiled down upon me in the slaver hull? Was it a pain in your breeches, Ransom, that made you cross the desert and barter with your half brother for my freedom?"

Ran faced the door. She faced his back.

"Was it?"

Her hand touched his damp shoulder, and he flinched, whirling about. He stared at her upturned face, saw her need for a confession he couldn't admit, and his frustration mounted. Suddenly he took her by the arms, pinning her to the wall with his body. His hands slid up her shoulders, her throat, her jaw, afore slipping free of her and bracing on the wall above, spread wide, hemming her in. She stared up at him. His fingers flexed on the wood.

Abruptly he bent, his mouth capturing hers, hot and pressing, his tongue prying her lips apart and sweeping deeply inside. And Aurora accepted, accepted the untamed urgency in him. She wanted him, longed for the weight of him, the enveloping heat of his big hands on her breasts; and anticipation spirited through her as his hands slid down the polished wall. He cupped her breasts, kneading, moaning into the heat of his kiss. He thumbed her nipples, hands charging roughly over her ribs, her waist, then around her, yanking up the chemise and cupping bare buttocks. He lifted, spreading her, tilting her tighter to his arousal, his big hands urging her legs around his hips.

His fingers found her, slick with raw desire, and he stroked and pressed and wanted more.

His kiss was savage and filled with fury at himself and her for drawing it out. For being here and his fault in it. For taunting him with what he could not take. Not and be the man he was. He pressed her harder to the wall, the soft apex of her thighs warming against his erection. It would be so easy, he thought. A flip of a button and he could plunge into her. So easy. He ground against her, the sheer force of him shoving her up the wall, and Aurora sensed the change in him. His kiss grew hungrier, bruising, forcing her head back; and when she tried to twist free he followed her mouth, taking, taking. Immediately she dug stiff fingertips into the softness beneath his arm. He jerked back and soundlessly her feet met the floor.

Breathing heavily, they stared.

There was pain there, in his eyes. He was like a raging

beast with a wounded soul, struggling to be saved, angry when he was left alone to suffer. His was a dark heart she wanted to crawl inside and live within, forcing out the pain. But *he* must approach her freely, if he wanted more than passion and wet kisses.

"Dinna come to me in anger again, Ransom. Ever. For you'll nay be welcomed twice."

Shoving at his chest, she ducked away, moving to the far side of the cabin. He slammed his fist against the wall and she flinched, but didn't turn til she heard the door close. Then she sank to the carpet, covering her face with shaking hands.

Chapter Eighteen

He was putting her ashore.

For three days he'd not come near her, and in two more the unwelcome pair would be out of his life. To Shokai it hardly mattered, for he thought the smelly barbarians rude and uncouth. Yet the old man wisely kept these thoughts to himself. His concern was for his charge and the torment he saw in her usually bright blue eyes.

"Have you discovered any recently signed crew?" she asked in a low voice, her unhappiness tearing the bindings of Shokai's soul. She was his world, the only child of his heart; and he would die to protect her from harm, but was unable to keep guard over her tender heart. One would think for all their travels she would have grown unfeeling with everything she'd seen, yet Aurora blossomed, her inner serenity, the way she approached the world and its creatures, the crux of who she was.

A Wiccan. A white witch. Following her ancestor's teachings, she cared for the well-being of the earth, yet it was Shokai who was forced to instruct her to use caution. Society did not look upon her as he did, with love, admiration and a fierce protectiveness, but with bitter scorn and fear. And though she was oblivious to the slurs most often, she could be easily stung. This was the first time since her sixteenth year she'd allowed anything to continue to make her unhappy. And she refused to discuss it with him.

"None in two summers. And loyalty is blind."

She glanced up from removing the last of his bandages.

"You were expectin' otherwise?" she said, and he didn't like the cynical lift of her brow. They were outcasts, nothing could bring the crew round to accepting her. Shokai had proven his ability to defend himself, but with the punishment the sailor suffered, 'twas Aurora who was not welcome.

A howl rumbled from the lower decks and her brows drew tight. Rising from her seat at the long table she went to the door, opening it a fraction. She'd been barred from wandering the ship, so Shokai had come to her, against Ran's permission, she didn't doubt.

"Dahrein." She caught the boy as he rushed by with a tray. She glanced benignly at the instruments arranged on the cloth. "Who cries out in such pain?"

"The bosun's mate, my lady." He pecked a bow. "The surgeon will take off his arm."

Aurora inhaled sharply. "Nay!" She shook her head. "Nay, 'twill do no good, 'tis not the arm that is wounded still, but the blood."

Dahrein's slashing black brows rose. "You know the healing ways?"

"Aye." Aurora looked at Shokai tucked protectively behind her, then to the youth. Her gaze darted up the passageway in indecision, then the howl came again, begging, pleading, and she stepped out of the cabin. "Take me to the lad, Dahrein."

Dahrein nodded, and she followed, Shokai moving soundlessly behind her.

"Baynes is most terrified, mem sahib. Perhaps if you tried your ways afore—"

"Only if they ask," she said as they strode deeper into the heart of the ship. Dahrein entered the cabin, yet Aurora remained beyond the doorway. The young man twisted in agony on a low pallet, his arm, hand, and fingers red and swollen with severe infection. Aurora's toadstone ring seared her finger. The wound was closed, looking like a seam in a well-stuffed couch. And the poison was on its way to the lad's heart.

"Get out!" The surgeon demanded. "We don't need your kind here!"

"Mayhaps he does." She nodded to the sailor. He lifted his head off the pillow, eyes glazed with panic and a pain so violent Aurora shuddered from its intensity. He would not last the night.

"His blood, 'tis poisoned." She dragged her gaze from the young man. "Why did you stitch it inside?"

The surgeon rounded on her, his hands stained with the sailor's blood, drained from the other arm. "Do not propose to tell me my profession, wench," he sneered. "Have you an academic degree. Have you been schooled at Leyden?"

"Nay," she answered with quiet dignity. "But your method isna helpin'."

"The arm must be amputated to heal him," the surgeon informed her, turning away to lay out a curved jagged-tooth saw.

"Nay! Oh, mother of God, nay! Don't be takin' me arm," Baynes cried, wide eyes pinned on the bone saw. "I'll be useless. Just kill me now. Please. Kill me!"

Aurora pushed consequences aside and rushed to the lad, kneeling close, whispering soothing words and stroking his damp brow. The surgeon turned back to find her in his territory and leaned over his patient, grabbing her arm. He never got the chance to speak. Immediately Shokai popped the side of his hand against the doctor's forearm with a paralyzing blow. The surgeon jumped back, but Shokai was not satisfied and swept his hand round the surgeon's like a whirlpool of wind, twisting the limb, catching more hand than wrist and bending it sharply down. The doctor sucked in air, numbing tendons stretched unnaturally as the old man backed him up against the wall, crooked fingers poised to strike his throat.

"Never touch," Shokai said, jerking the helpless man forward to meet his face.

The surgeon swallowed, the threat to his life mirrored in slanted black eyes.

"What the bloody hell are you doing?"

All but Shokai looked to the door, Ransom's massive size filling the narrow hatch. Dahrein shifted from foot to foot behind his captain.

"Shokai, release Mister Buckland. Now!" he commanded when Shokai remained unmoved, then turned his gaze on Aurora.

"Get back to the cabin." Brisk, offering no space for rebuttal.

"I canna leave him, Ransom. He needs help."

He remained impassive but for a distinct darkening in his eyes. "Mister Buckland is an officer of this ship, Aurora. You interfere with his authority and you answer to mine."

Unaffected by his threats, she felt the young man's forehead, then looked back to Ransom. "You canna let the lad lose his arm."

"And you cannot give the man false hope!"

She stood. "What harm is a shred, where there is naught a'tall?"

Ran ushered her out of the cabin, but she yanked free, refusing to move another a step. "He will die without surgery," Ran growled. "And I'll not have these men believing you can cure any ailment with your foul-smelling concoctions."

Her chin lifted. "I canna cure every sickness, aye, but 'tis an infection of the blood Ransom, not his wound. He was struck with a poisoned blade that night in Barbary," she rushed to say. " 'Twas why I gave him the herbs, then. I could feel the poison."

"Feel?" Ran scoffed. "Am I to allow you to undermine a learned physician simply to placate a wild assumption? Nay. Nay!" came louder when she opened her mouth. "For when you are gone, the surgeon will remain."

Aurora smothered her hurt and thought of the young man approaching his death. "Would you risk his limb for the sake of the physician's pride?"

Silence stretched.

Ran stared into hopeful blue eyes. Eyes he knew would darken with passion, eyes that never shed a tear but sought to soothe the woes of the universe. How like her to scrape away the crust of authority and lay reason bare and simple as a matter of pride. Any argument felt insignificant in the light of her reasoning.

When he didn't respond she pressed. "If Mister Baynes doesna want me help, I will leave. But ask him, Ransom. For the slim hope he clings to, ask."

Ran glanced into the room. Baynes squirmed in pain, his skin pasty gray, his lips chalky. His chest heaved for needed air, his left arm flame red and distended grotesquely.

"Capt'n," he croaked and Ran went to him, going down on one knee.

"What will it be, Mister Baynes?"

Leelan Baynes' gaze shifted nervously to the surgeon, who'd regained his dignity and arrogance as soon as the old man released him, then back to his captain. "What good is a one-armed bosun's mate, sir?" The words came stilted and breathy. "Cain't live wit'out me arm. I cain't." Leelan struggled with his pain and fear, not daring to cry in front of his captain, but he was terrified. "Look at the old man, sir." He paused to gasp for fresh air. " 'Member 'ow bad he was?" Ran's gaze swept briefly to Shokai and he conceded the point, for his recovery was nothing short of remarkable.

"This is the same woman you blamed for letting your mates suffer further in prison," Ran warned, aware of his own guilt in that. "And you ignored her help then."

"Aye." He looked past his captain to Aurora and she answered his silent call, coming to him. "Can you forgive me, ma'am?"

"Of course, Leelan," she whispered, kneeling beside the pallet.

" 'Nough to help me?" Desperately he clutched her hand, and Aurora's heart constricted. He was in agony, knew he was dying, and she admired his effort to keep tears suppressed.

"Aye." His tense body deflated. "But you mustna question me methods, neh?"

"I won't, I swear."

"Och now, dinna be makin' pacts with me yet, Mister Baynes." She smiled gently, then rose as Ran did. Across

the pallet eyes met, his amber stare bearing the hot warning
of the consequences should she fail the young man now that
she'd garnered his trust. Tension bristled, and for a moment
he looked about to throttle her soundly for making even the
smallest request. She did anyway.

" 'Tis been improperly tended for too long, and time is
not ours to waste. Have this cabin cleaned, thoroughly. And
he," she gestured to the indignant surgeon, "must not be
touchin' him again."

"This is an outrage!" the surgeon exploded. "He is my
patient!"

"Not anymore," Aurora said softly and left the cabin.

Ran gave curt orders to have the cabin stripped and
scoured, then followed her into his own quarters. She was
already setting out her possessions, instructing Dahrein that
cloth, needles, fresh linens, water, and a basin be placed in
the cleaned cabin, afore requesting a bath. Dahrein didn't
bother to seek his captain's permission and did her bidding
with a loyalty that rankled Ransom.

Haste was her partner and within moments she'd cleared
a chest and fanned a cloth over the top, methodically arranging a challis, dagger, pestle and mortar, and a tiny
kettle in the center, filling the latter with water and lighting
a stubby candle beneath it. She sanded herbs into the water,
presented several leather pouches, then laid a pale gray robe
afore the sea chest. Turning to the tub, she sprinkled dried
blossoms and herbs as Dahrein finished filling the copper
hip bath. Ran watched from his position near the door,
arms folded, shoulders braced against the bulkhead.

"My thanks, Dahrein."

He bowed, his face beaming with unabashed affection. "I
will be near if my lady wishes."

"I do, Dahrein. Let no one interrupt, and clear the path
to where Mister Baynes rests. No one must block it."

Ran shifted with agitation. Could she not request that of
him? But then, he'd made no effort this day to champion her
beliefs and likely she saw no purpose behind asking.

As Dahrein departed, sealing the door, Ran wondered if
she realized he was still in the cabin. Then she looked at him

and he felt the distance growing, as in the hostelry. 'Twas as if she were leaving him by small increments and he wanted to call out, demand she not do this, for he felt her slipping like cool sand through his fingers, unretrievable. Determination marked her brow, her eyes glistening in the darkened cabin.

And though he was but a few feet from her, 'twas as if she were a continent away.

"Do you wish privacy?" Why did he feel so insignificant?

"Aye. But 'tis your ship, Ransom, and I canna banish you from your home." Her shoulders lifted with cool indifference. "I ask that you not speak nor move, and I beg you, leave your anger with me outside."

His anger? Did she not know 'twas his own brutal assault on her he couldn't abide?

She didn't wait for his conformation but moved to the tub, removing her belt of leather and gold, then wiggling out of her gown, leaving both in a pile on the floor. Next the chemise fell away and she stood naked, her back to him as she stepped into the tub. She loosened the braid, then slowly lowered into the water. He could not hear her clearly but snatched bits and pieces as she chanted softly to herself. Then she sank completely beneath the surface and, like a siren rising from the sea, slowly rose and scrubbed her body and hair with the dampened leaves floating in the water.

Jasmine and clover scented the air.

The deck rocked gently like a mother's arms.

Her voice whispered in the confines of the cabin. "I call upon you, Great Mother, and give thanks and me blessin'. Banish impurities from this earthbound body. Give me strength and power to do as I must."

She left the tub, dried her body, and donned the mist gray robe. It clung to her figure like a shroud of smoke, and he was taken aback as she stood afore the chest and drew the hood over her head.

It obscured her features.

And in that moment, she left him. 'Twas beyond his comprehension how he could know this, for he could see her clearly, yet he felt the sudden absence of her. It set his nerves to tingling, drawing up the hair on his arms and neck. Aurora was no longer in this cabin, but in a tranquil place only she could imagine. And it scared him. The solid sense of it. What if she didn't return? Even as the thought entered his mind, he couldn't move, acutely aware he was privy to something remarkable, a ceremony she was trusting him to keep private.

Aurora lifted her arms wide, her voice a breath beyond a whisper.

"A null e. A nall e. Slainte." She lowered her arms. "My shield is strong and worthy. The Goddess' hands around me stay. Guide me, Lord and Lady. Empower me." She knelt and emptied a pouch into the mortar. "Strengthen this herb the earth has given me. I give thanks to its roots and leaves and flowers, for in them lie the powers of healin' and rebirth." With the pestle she pulverized the herbs, then set it aside. "Be generous, power of water, sustainer of life. I bow to your strength." Pinching from another pouch, she sanded a yellow powder into the challis, then tipped the kettle, spilling steaming water into the mortar and more into the dented cup. The scent of clove, camomile, and dandelion filled the cabin, sweet and soothing as she lifted the cup, holding it near her chest. "I give this infusion all my strength, offerin' me powers with the fruits of Mother Earth to ease the suffering of Leelan Baynes." She bowed her head, imagining his pain receding, the poison leaving his blood. She held the image of him using his arm without aid for a moment longer, then carefully placed the cup on the chest. She took up her dirk and Ran was entranced as she drew it across the stubby flame. "Pure silver and steel of my ancestors, harm not the man but the taint flowing in his veins, and free him from his agony." She wrapped the dirk in a cloth, then scooted back.

"Blessings to all who come to my aid. This spell is complete." Extinguishing the candle, she climbed to her feet, leaving the robe behind, and Ran decided he'd never known anyone so at ease with her nakedness. Lifting her gown from the floor, she slipped it over her head, then donned her belt. After carefully replacing her possessions in her sack, she gathered the cup, mortar, the wrapped blade, and a small pouch, then moved to the door. Her gaze never shifted, Ran noticed, as she opened the hatch and stepped out. 'Twas silent beyond the walls, and he heard Dahrein whisper to her. She didn't respond.

Ran rolled around the door frame to follow.

Aurora stepped into the tiny cabin, her gaze assessing its cleanliness. On the wall the flame from a single grease lamp whipped and sputtered. Leelan stared at her through fever-tormented eyes and she knelt beside him, placing her items on the floor, then pushing damp hair from his brow. He looked frightened and desperate.

" 'Twill be better, my friend. This I promise."

He nodded shakily and she rose, the pouch in her hand. She dipped her fingers inside, crushing green brittle leaves in the corners of the cabin, and the pleasant scent of mint perfumed the stale air. With each measure she asked for purification and healing to come into the room. She went to the side of the bed, helping him sit up enough to drink from the cup. He made a face, but softly she encouraged him to take more afore he sank heavily onto the straw pallet, his strength spent.

She held his gaze in her own, narrowing her concentration, giving him her energy; for the instant she entered the room she knew he was too weak to last the night.

"How do you feel?"

"Don't hurt as bad," he slurred, and she nodded, pleased the infusion was relieving his pain. His fever was dangerously high.

"I willna lie to you, Leelan. I must open the old wound." He nodded nearly imperceptibly, and she wasted no time, her moves smooth and efficient as she unwrapped the dirk and drew it across the angry slash. He winced slightly as blood curtained, the odor of infection distinct to her. She blotted and pressed his skin, over and over, and Ran's eyes widened as the swelling receded a fraction. With two fingers she scooped from the mortar, smearing the saturated herbs across the incision. She wrapped it loosely in a cloth, then encouraged Leelan to drink again from the challis. Within moments he sank into a deep painless sleep.

Aurora mopped his brow, his chest and throat. Constantly she touched her palm over the wound, holding it there as she whispered softly. A chant. A call for help.

With her head bowed Aurora prayed, beckoning the forces of water, wind, earth, fire, and spirit, and the *Lady* and *Lord* who ruled them.

Chapter Nineteen

Ran stood beyond the door; staring intently at her back, the bosun's mate lying lifeless as she freshened the herb poultice. Her sigh was audible as she swept the back of her hand 'cross her brow, but still she continued, relentlessly, for better than eighteen hours.

"Aurora?"

Without pause, she dipped the cloth, wrung out the water and wrapped the wound, and Ran turned away, frustrated and a touch angry. The distance he experienced afore her incantation maintained its strength, and he felt unrealistically confused. What did he know about such things? 'Twas utterly preposterous to him that a few words said over some herbs would lend miracles, but Aurora's faith in her ways was not to be questioned. 'Twas all young Leelan had left.

God help her if she failed.

For the wrath of two-hundred-forty mates would descend upon her, and Ran wasn't certain he could protect her.

Canvas sails fluttered loosely and without looking Ran ordered the maintop hoisted as he paced the quarterdeck, a stinging tension working in his shoulders. Crewmen exchanged a frown, a shrug, darting a glance at their captain afore returning attention to duty. Domingo looked up from the charts he studied, briefly watching his captain chew up the deck with thunderous steps, then sighed and shook his head. From amidship, Lougière observed the unusual behavior, then focused on his inventory. Dahrein worried his fingers, his tawny face marked with concern.

"You must do something, sahib. She will not answer, to anyone," the youth spoke softly as if raising his voice would interrupt the man's restless pacing. It did not. Nor did Ran respond. 'Twas nearly two days and Aurora continued to work diligently over the fevered Baynes, without food or water, without rest, yet each hour her movements grew more sluggish with exhaustion. Several times, he'd called to her, pleaded with her to take relief from her work, but she ignored him, as if he'd not spoken, had not existed.

And for a time he imagined she'd taken young Leelan into another world.

Bilge rot, he thought.

Her motions were rote, yet her voice, low and throaty, coaxed the young bosun to fight back. She'd warned them not to interrupt, that Baynes would become worse afore he regained his health. Mister Buckland thought otherwise and sought every instance to voice his pessimism til his ridicule of Aurora pushed Ran to the limits of his patience.

The good doctor was now confined to his cabin.

Ran mashed a hand over his face, then rubbed the back of his neck.

The *Red Lion* was a night's sail from its rendezvous with the *Morgan,* the ship Ran intended to carry Aurora to any shore she wished. 'Twas impossible to live with her aboard and not be enticed by her unrestrained behavior. 'Twas bloody unfair, this wild ride atween uncapped desire and bitter rage, and he would no longer place himself or her in that position, for he hadn't the strength to best his temptations.

No matter how sweetly she kissed. She had to leave. Aye, he didn't trust himself not to hurt her again. For the rapture of touching her was not for mortal man to resist.

He spun on his heels, then flinched to a stop, for Shokai stood afore him, bearing a tray of steaming mugs.

By God, the man had the uncanny ability to arrive and depart on the wind!

Wrapped in the layered garments and sashes of his heritage, Shokai stood motionless even with the rocking of the ship. It broke into Ran's worry.

He took a mug from the tray, meeting thin slanted eyes, black and fathomless and mayhaps challenging. Shokai had assumed the duties of the cook, their last killed during the confrontation with the *Black Star*. Shokai hadn't asked permission, but Ran never expected such a courtesy. This man, he learned, said little and did as he pleased. And it was clear he no longer trusted Ran, if he ever had.

"Are you well enough to be about?" Ran said, looking over the cup's rim.

"Even fish and guests stink after three days."

A smile tugged at Ran's lips as he sipped the coffee, noticing its smoothness. He had to admit the food tasted a sight better.

The din of the ship suddenly died and Ran's brows furrowed tightly, the cup coming slowly away from his mouth as narrowed eyes glanced the length of his ship.

"Ran?" Domingo said and when he turned the Spaniard gestured below.

Ran's features stretched taut. "Aurora," he breathed, and Domingo smiled to himself.

Aurora stepped listlessly onto the poop deck and turned, shielding her eyes and looking up toward the quarterdeck.

She opened her mouth to speak, but her words were cut short as her legs buckled and she crumbled slowly to the deck. Ran tossed the cup aside and leapt the rail, landing with a jolt beside her.

"Aurora? Aurora, lass?" He felt for her pulse, then immediately swept her into his arms, his angular face a map of panic and concern as he clutched her close, the eyes of every crewmen following his quick departure into the passageway. Shouldering the cabin door open, Ran shifted round the long table and crossed the room, laying her gently on the wide bed. She moaned, and he settled beside her, brushing loose strands from her face. He called to her, but she didn't respond. He rubbed her wrists and still nothing. He poured a cup of water and cradled her head in his broad hand, forcing her to drink. Liquid dripped from her lips and fear surged through him.

"Sahib?"

"Summon Buckland."

"Eee-ayy!"

Ran twisted a look over his shoulder. Shokai, his bare feet wide apart and hands on his sash-wrapped hips, looked threatening and formidable even for his advanced age.

"Wilted flowers need water and sun," he said. "Not to be clipped and pruned."

Shokai's lack of sympathy infuriated Ran and he leapt to his feet. "My God, man, look at her!" He lashed a hand. "She's undernourished, pale and—"

"Tired," was all Shokai said, then positioned himself near the door, silent, daring Ran to gainsay him.

Ran turned back to Aurora. Her gown was soiled and bloody, her complexion lightly sheened with perspiration. Dark smudges colored the skin beneath her eyes, her hands raw and red, the palms roughened with old callouses. After witnessing her spell he hadn't known what to expect; mayhaps for her to say a few words over Baynes or some such rot. But again she surprised him with her vigilance, yet her selflessness cost her more than he imagined. She was ghastly pale.

"What have you done now, little pest?" he whispered, fingering the coverlet and not daring to gather her in his arms as he wanted. She appeared near death, her breathing shallow, and Ran felt utterly lost. Had she somehow taken the poison into herself?

"Ran?"

He recognized Domingo's voice but didn't tear his gaze from Aurora.

"Baynes is asking for food."

Ran snapped around.

"Sí. You wouldn't believe how fit he looks."

With a gentle hand, Ran pulled the cover over her still form, the backs of his knuckles skimming her cheek and smooth lips afore he retreated a pace. He left her behind, with her odd little guardian keeping watch, and negotiated

the companionway filled with sailors. A path cleared and he
stopped at the entrance. Sable brows shot up, his shock
mirrored on like faces. Baynes sat propped against the wall,
flexing his fingers and arm for the audience. Including Buckland. Lockewood stood silently aside his young mate, and
when the patient met Ran's gaze, others followed. Doctor
Buckland stepped back, his face flushing deep red.

Ran ducked inside.

"She did it, sir," Baynes said, his voice gravelly. "She
promised and she did it." He rotated his bandaged arm in
the shoulder socket to prove it.

"The pain, 'twas bad?" God above if but one of his crew
received an inkling as to what she was about, there would
be hell to pay. He hoped Baynes was in too much pain to
remember aught she did.

Leelan shook his head. "Didn't feel a thing after I drank
'orse shit–smelling stuff." Chuckles rumbled and Ran
relaxed. "An' look." Baynes peeled back the bandage.
"Them's fine stitches," he praised. "With me own hair!"

Buckland bent to examine the sutured wound, marveling
that not a shred of inflammation remained.

"Have you aught to say, Buckland?"

The doctor straightened, his gaze jumping to the interested faces, ending on the healed young man. "I ask your
forgiveness, all of you. I was blind—" He choked, humbled.
"God have mercy on me, *arrogantly* blind to a method
unfamiliar to me."

Ran folded his arms over his chest, eyes dark and unfathomable. He would not reveal her spells and chants, uncertain if he understood the lot of it, but Aurora deserved an
apology. From the ship's surgeon and her captain.

"See that you make restitution to the lady," he said, then
nodded to the bosun's mate and quit the room.

Ran found Shokai outside the cabin, barricading his
path. The flagrant challenge set his teeth on edge. "Step
aside," he growled. "Now."

"You cannot set the hungry cat to guard the milk."

Amber eyes darkened a fraction, simmering with impatience. "Good God, man, I'm not going to ravish the woman! She has naught to fear from me."

Shokai scoffed. "A tender heart wounded ten times remains wounded forever."

Guilt prickled his spine. "I've no wish to hurt her, Shokai," Ran said, forcing a calmness into his voice when he realized Shokai knew more of his relationship with Aurora than he cared.

"Then do not try to graft costly pine into bamboo, my lord, for you can work in dirt and still lead a clean life."

"I am well aware of that."

A nearly hairless brow rose. "Now," Shokai snorted as if the knowledge came too late.

It had.

Regret poured over him. Graft pine into bamboo; a gentle woman into a whore.

Good God, his own life was not pristine, so why did he imagine hers would be? He remembered the callouses on her delicate hands, hands that had worked hard to save a life. Hands that soothed his anger and coaxed his desire. The dirt of a clean life. Her lack of inhibition he saw as wanton, their passion as a threat. *And who, besides you, has hurt her?*

Ran stared at the door, realizing he knew naught of the woman lying in his bed. And in hours she would be gone. He didn't know if he could do it.

Without being asked, Shokai moved aside, a sentinel over his "empress." His hand on the latch, Ran briefly studied the man who refused to look at him, staring ahead, arms folded over his slim chest. Shokai was a deadly adversary, Ran decided suddenly. For he loved Aurora, and within that love lay undying loyalty. He would not hesitate to kill for her, yet chose not to interfere in her choices, her life.

Ran opened the door and stepped inside, closing it softly. He leaned back against the frame, his gaze on the woman stretched out in his bed, and the rightness of her presence there made him frown. Pushing away from the wall, he started for her, then halted, his gaze jerking from the chest, devoid of her items, to her, to the dress lying across the foot of the bed, and the basin and rag discarded on the commode. Shokai. And the fact that he was familiar enough to remove her clothes and bathe her made Ran see their relationship in a different light. Had the man always tended her like a lady's maid? he wondered, knowing the pair had been together since she was but six and ten. Good God, 'twas no wonder the lass was uninhibited with naught but the riddle-speaking old man for company. Yet what did Shokai know then of rearing a budding young woman? The man was distant, hardly one to chatter for the sake of it.

The lonely hardships she must have suffered crushed down on him, destroying the idea of leaving her alone, and he positioned a chair aside the massive bed, dropping lazily onto the sculpted wood.

She looked unusually small lying in the soft center, like an angel in a fluffy cloud. He wanted to hold her, desperately, to give her something beyond the cool affections of a withered old man, but after bludgeoning her with an angry kiss and the knowledge he was sending her away, he didn't think she'd speak a civil word to him again. For free-spirited and optimistic as she was, there were restrictions on being with Aurora. And Ransom knew he couldn't meet the requirements.

He never left her side.

For hours she twisted and squirmed, faint whispers tumbling erratically from her lips, yet again 'twas Gaelic she spoke and he wished he could understand. Suddenly she threw off the covers, exposing her breasts, ribs, and a supple curving thigh; and all notions of gallantry fled as he looked his fill of her, his gaze sliding unrestrained over her body.

This was very ungentlemanly, he thought fleetingly, and knew when it came to Aurora, his finer qualities fell into rubbish. She was extravagantly shaped, no fat, no bone protruding, but plush and soft and decadently feminine. Exquisite. And his fists tightened as he submerged his baser lusts and grasped the satiny coverlet to shield her. As if sensing his presence, she turned to him, a sorrow-filled moan working in her throat, the side of her breast, soft and warm, grazing his knuckles, and in her sleep she arched to the faint contact, her rosy nipple pressing against his hand. He froze, hovering over her, fingers flexing, every cell of him begging to caress her, to shape her bosom to his palms, then draw a plump peak into his mouth and suckle, stroke with his tongue, hear her throaty voice cry out in erotic whispers of— Damn and blast!

Drawing a fortifying breath, he yanked the quilt to her chin, enveloping her like a package for delivery. She's weak with exhaustion, he reminded, yet even as she snuggled beneath the crisp sheets his imagination went mad, conjuring damp bodies and husky laughter, his manhood sliding wetly into her softness, her supple thighs gripping his hips. Oh, God above! Cease this madness, his brain demanded, and he dropped into the chair, tilting his head back and closing his eyes. He shifted uncomfortably, his breeches tight across his hips. Bloody hell, he thought, in this sorry state since the woman came aboard.

Why did Aurora stir him to mind-numbing distraction? In the past ten years, he'd been able to disregard female affections, his oaths holding far more power over him than his need to roger even the naked wenches Domingo repeatedly deposited in his cabin. Yet they were merely faces and bodies, so he found no difficulty sending them packing back to the Spaniard, but Aurora, grievin' mothers, the thought of her inviting him to her bed produced a totally different sensation.

Ran closed his eyes, struggled to lay a name to why. He always lacked control when he was with her, always, like the loose threads of sails, useless if 'twere to unravel, but still he stayed close, thirsting for her attention, for the way she made him feel, as if he were the only person in her world. He craved to hear his name rolling on her tongue, feel her fingers sifting in his hair, and be drawn into the soft lazy dream with no chance of waking, forgetting the harsh world beyond the walls and sinking into the madness of Aurora.

Sheets rustled and he opened his eyes, focusing on her. Abruptly he straightened in the chair, his heartbeat accelerating as she thrashed beneath the covers, not like afore but frantic, as if fending off attack, her breathing quick, her moans punctured with sorrow and an unmasked pain he'd never witnessed in her afore. Defenseless. Alone in her nightmare. And the sight knifed him in two. She called out for Shokai, for the protection of her Goddess.

Then she cried desperately for him.

And Ran answered, sitting on the bed beside her and gently shaking her shoulders. She pushed and clawed, her hair winding around her arms and throat, and he shook again. Suddenly her eyes flashed open and she inhaled sharply, eyes glossed with unshed tears searching his face. She struggled for air.

" 'Tis me, lass, you're safe," he whispered.

"Oh, Ransom," she gasped, clutching his thick bare arms. "Mister Castille is dead!"

Dark brows drew down, sharpening his chiseled features. "How can you know this, how?"

She shook her head. "I dinna ken, but he is! Oh, Great Mother, what have my troubles done to you and your people," she moaned, and tears threatened. " 'Tis me own fault!"

Ran's chest tightened. He'd never seen her like this and gathered her in his arms. "Nay, nay, nay," he soothed, tucking her head beneath his chin and rubbing her naked back. Tangled hair shifted beneath his hands. "Castille volunteered, as did Lougière. 'Twas their own choice to remain as guard. Not yours."

Her arms wiggled around his waist, clinging to his strength. "But he perished for his valiance."

"You cannot be certain." His voice held as much question as assurance.

Silence lengthened. Ran could almost feel her sorrow recede, yet still she remained nestled in his arms, trembling, and all he could think was he didn't want to let her go despite the danger of keeping her close.

"Castille was not with us on the slaver. So then, where is he?"

Ran tensed, grasping her shoulders and pushing her back to look at her face. "Are you certain?"

"Aye. Castille remained in the room."

His scowl darkened.

"I swear to you, I saw him laid down afore we were kidnapped."

"Mayhaps he rose to defend and was taken afterward?"

She bowed her head, fingering the worn edge of his leather vest. " 'Tis possible," she said, worrying her lower lip, but wasn't convinced, or the dream would not have ended with the bleakness of irretrievable loss, the desolation of energy snuffed prematurely. Yet her senses had misled her afore.

"I will try to discover to where he vanished," Ran assured, staring beyond her at nothing, one hand unconsciously stroking the length of her spine. "I promise." Aye, and the names of those who'd orchestrated her constant misfortune. He didn't doubt 'twas not her trusting nature or simply her vivid beauty that drew her into trouble. Someone had been alerted to her existence in that hostelry, and despised her enough to sentence her to a life locked in slavery.

When she remained quiet, Ran touched two fingers beneath her chin, tipping her head back. His gaze searched hers, probing. "What else do you not tell me, pest?"

She hesitated, preparing herself for his disbelief. "In me dream, 'twas hatred I felt, Ransom. Born in a selfish greed for a power I dinna ken." The memory of it made her shiver. "At first I thought 'twas as I sensed on this ship, your crew not liking me being aboard and such, but 'twas a fury I felt then, and distinguishable from this ugly hatred. Nay," she said as if she'd come to a decision. " 'Twas in the hostelry, this came to me."

He leaned back, dropping his hands. "What the bloody hell's the difference?"

" 'Tis easy to become angry, Ransom," she eyed him pointedly, "and much harder to hate."

Chagrin softened his harsh look, but question and skepticism lingered in his eyes.

"I canna explain it." She shrugged bare shoulders. " 'Tis just so."

He stared at her, images filtering in his mind's eye; her

acute sensitivity; finding her hovering naked over her *keek stane,* talking to the dolphin; her unfailing belief in her healing potions, her incantations; her success, the price of it. . . . And he suddenly burst with, "You're a bloody witch."

She arched a brow. "I am Wiccan, like you are Christian and Rahman is Moslem. A witch, aye, if 'tis what you choose to name it. Och, I see it in your eyes." She outlined his brow with a gentle finger. "You're wary of me now."

"Nay, but if another had informed me, I might be," he said honestly, wanting more of her touch. "For 'twas not as I'd expected." He looked away, fidgeting with a loose thread on the quilt. "Your conjuring, I mean."

"You were expectin' I'd sprout warts and a hump?" she couldn't help but tease.

His eyes flew to hers. "Of course not!"

"Or that I'd be stirrin' over a caldron, addin' newt guts and sheep eyes—"

"Aurora," he warned, and she ceased her needling, her face growing serious.

"Magick isna simply spells, talismans, and poppets, Ransom, nor somethin' I can show you like openin' a book and pointin', for it lies within all that is living. 'Tis here," she touched the bare skin over her heart, "and here," she tapped her temple, "it lives, too." A pause and then softly, "I've never hid this from you."

" 'Tis half the problem, pest, this bluntness of yours," he said, his lips curving, for she'd insisted her spell kept Rahman from taking her to his bed. He hadn't believed in her then, and though he was seeing her differently, he still didn't grasp the foundation of her beliefs.

"You need only ask, Ransom." Her hand lightly rode the sculpted curve of his muscled arm to his broad shoulder, her finger circling the gold ear loop he always wore. "I willna lie to you. Ever," she stressed, deciding he had enough to comprehend and refrained from telling him tales of fairy kings, seers, and water spirits. Her fingers sank into his long bronze hair.

"Aurora," he groaned, tilting his head into her soothing

touch. How could she even want to be near him when he was such a brute afore?

"You've been by me side, havena you?" Blue eyes held haunting amber.

"Aye," he managed, his body tensing, his fierce desire simmering to a boil. Hadn't he sworn just an hour afore not to put himself in this position again?

"Why?"

"You collapsed." He kept his hands flat on the bed, braced on either side of her hips. "I worried."

"And this concern pressed you to strip me naked and lay me in your bed." Her eyes sparkled with teasing.

"Shokai saw to the former, I the latter," he confessed, his gaze dropping briefly to her bare shoulders, the swell of her bosom barely hidden by the quilt. *Turn away, man.*

"I swore I wouldna lie upon your sheets alone, Ransom."

Her words struck him like a blow to his middle, slamming the air from his lungs. He swallowed, unable to move, his fingers flexing on the coverlet. "You didn't choose to be here."

"Remember that, m'lord." Her hand curved round his neck, the other flattening to spread across his leather-covered chest, and his breathing quickened.

"Why do you do this, Aurora?" Fabric bunched in his fists.

"Pleasure," she whispered, pressing her lips to the bare skin exposed atween his vest. He groaned, low and rumbling, but couldn't draw back as her mouth seared up his throat to his jaw. "Give to me, Ransom," she murmured against the curve of his mouth, and he trembled. "For I crave the taste of you."

"Sweet Jesus, Aurora." His groin tightened, his tingling senses shaping the plush body held a breath from his own. "Don't."

Her lips hovered over his, husky words tempting him to the absolute edge of his will.

"Come to me, pirate, for I seek to steal but a wee kiss, not your treasured lion heart."

Chapter Twenty

A kiss.

'Twas all she wanted.

And in it she would find the chance to slip beneath his armor and push away the pain that kept him from opening himself. To her. To anyone. In these moments, precious and scattered, Aurora witnessed the unguarded side of Ransom Montegomery, stripped bare of his controlled exterior.

He trembled for her.

He agonized over simply touching her.

And he battled demons, for this mighty pirate lord ached to release all that bound him behind his private shield . . . and succumb.

She could feel it. Like a dark cloak weighing his massive shoulders. The depth of his feelings terrified him.

And Aurora longed to show him it wouldn't hurt as he predicted, that if he wished, she would ask no more than a kiss. Aye, as much as she burned to lie with him, join with him, and feel his strength fill and satisfy her, she'd give him that.

Yet she was near volatile to have him close, and a little moan escaped as she struggled against the need to leap on him. Just the thought of him touching her naked skin sent her senses prickling with a heavy, glowing heat. Her breasts throbbed for his caress, atween her thighs moist and hot for his attention, and she bent her leg to ease the liquid burn. The motion enveloped him closer to her.

Come to me, Ransom.

Her breath teased his lips, her tongue snaking slowly across and Ran was powerless, for she coaxed the fire atween them, tasting his chin, the line of his jaw, teeth scraping, nipping. Torturing him. Luring him. Her ragged breath tumbled into his mouth, and he suddenly claimed it, deeply, thickly, his head rolling back and forth as he wildly took what she offered.

The ship rocked. Footsteps pounded the decks above.

The rush of urgent breaths and low moans filled the spacious cabin.

Ransom quaked. His heart thundered.

And he swore but hours afore he'd not tempt such again, for he'd hurt her last time; but she kissed like moonlight, silvery soft and dark.

And in synch his hands slid up her arms, stopping at the coverlet and brushing it down, exposing her. She gasped against his mouth as cool air hit her skin, arching, offering, the tender tips of her breasts grazing his leather jerkin.

He hesitated. And she tugged open the soft calfskin, dragging air into her lungs, yet refusing to cease the kiss. Touch me, she urged silently, aching to feel his hands on her breasts, her nipples tight with excitement, but still he refused even that. She spread the belted vest, small hands molding his hard male breasts, squeezing, and his mouth opened wide on hers, ravenously, his tongue plunging deeply. Her fingertips outlined his flat nipples, slowly, and his hands lifted, clenched, then opened, and anticipation clawed at her senses.

"Touch me, Ransom," she breathed on a moan. "Please."

He gripped her waist, then slid upward, palms filling with soft woman-flesh, and Aurora cried out in a shuddering gasp, the sound smothered beneath the liquid heat of his mouth. His tongue swept the sweet darkness hidden within, dueling feverishly with hers as he molded her plush breasts, his thumbs tenderly circling the sensitive nipples to taut rosy peaks.

Ransom thought he'd explode with the pleasure of her.

Her hands toured lower, down his chest, stroking his lean

ribs and Ran felt her shiver delicately as he massaged and
stroked, his lips nipping and pulling at hers. Her breath
rushed, and he drew back, staring into crystal blue eyes
afore lowering his gaze to the breasts enfolded in his hands
watching, feeling, knowing; and his steamy touch coiled the
tightness knotting in her belly.

Then he lowered his head.

Aurora swallowed repeatedly, licking her dry lips, watch
ing as his lips closed over her nipple, and she inhaled, arch
ing. He suckled, drawing the throbbing tip deeply into his
mouth. She drove her fingers into his long burnished locks,
holding him there, fingertips grazing the shape of his mouth
as it moistened and laved at her breast. That she would want
to feel every part of him that touched her aroused him to a
blinding madness, and his mouth seared a path to the plump
mate, lifting it for his caress.

She whispered his name, how glorious his mouth felt on
her skin, how much she adored his strong hands and their
gentle hold, and the huskily spoken words were like droplets
of oil to hot flame. His groin was hard as hull pine, her
moans and erotic praise tearing loose the mooring of his
restraint as he worshipped the succulent the fruit of her
breasts.

He wanted her. Feverishly. Recklessly. Years of condi
tioning himself to resist such temptation crumbled away
with her every motion, her every word. And he struggled
not to become violent, fought not to spread her thighs now
and slam into her as his body demanded, and shuddered
heavily, every muscle and pore springing wildly with un
chained passion. But she was touching him, his shoulders,
his arms, up and down the length of his thighs. And he
wanted more of it, of her. He leaned into her, easing her
slowly back onto the cushion of feathered down, hungrily
laving the tender underside of her breast, her extravagant
curves, the flesh of her throat as his hand wandered over her
waist, her rounded hip, afore sliding luxuriously beneath the
covers to the bare skin of her buttocks. He cupped, pressing
her upward, gently, as if he feared he'd hurt her, bruise her,
meshing her supple hips to his own as he lay half on her, his

mouth devouring hers; and Ran ached to be inside this
woman.

Then she curved her leg around his thigh and drove her
fingers beneath the band of his breeches and Ransom was
lost. A knife toppled free of his belt and fell to the deck.
Neither noticed. He rocked against her, his fingers seeking
her wet center, and she answered the rhythmic push, her
hands sweeping up his strong back to cradle his head in her
palms, afraid he'd tear away from her, afraid he'd bring his
anger to this bed. Aurora hungered for him, to know *him*,
beyond experiencing pleasures of his body and touch the
heart he shielded, would someday be hers, for he possessed
the one beating in her chest. She didn't want it back.

She wanted *his* in return.

His fingers found her, sliding deeply, and she gasped his
name, holding him. He withdrew and plunged, and she
pulsed with his rhythm, but when she tried to free him from
his breeches, he denied her. He couldn't, 'twould be selfish
and risky, but he ached to wipe the brutality of his last kiss
from her memory and see her find pleasure at his touch.

"Ransom, come into me. Please."

"Nay, let me give you pleasure, ahhh God, you smell so
good," he said into the cloud of hair. "Feel yourself take me
in," he whispered in her ear. "Let me give you this."

"Aye, aye . . . oh Ransom, dinna cease."

His fingertip circled the sharp bead of her sex, the motion
drawing her hips off the bed, and he shifted, his mouth
moving hurriedly over her breasts, her belly, the join of her
hip and thigh as he slid off the bed to his knees. He shoved
aside the coverlet, drawing her to the edge of the mattress.
She looked at him, up on her elbows, eager and panting and
damp. He spread her, holding her gaze as he licked the
inside of her thigh, the sweep of her hip, stroked over the
tender core of her; and she fell back onto the bed, boneless
with desire. He tasted her, deeply, drawing her leg over his
shoulder, and she clutched him, squirming, calling his name
and 'twas a beautiful thing to see; her body open, her own
hands stroking over her breasts, her belly, to hear her gasps
and whimpers and luxuriously long moans.

Then he felt her tremble, the sweet explosion poised, an he pushed two fingers inside her, delicate muscles graspin and drawing. And he gave and gave and her breath shud dered from parted lips as she twisted and clawed to feel hi weight upon her and Ransom crawled up onto the bec filled with an incredible satisfaction, her release wild an undoing him. His stroking gentled and she held him atwee her thighs, moving sexily to the fractional push. He drew back, but she covered his hand, kissing him.

" 'Tis nay enough," she breathed heavily into his mout her body quaking. " 'Tis you I want there." Her palr rubbed the length of his arousal, thick and warm beneat the breeches. She flipped open a button.

A sharp knock rattled the cabin door.

Aurora selfishly deepened the kiss.

The summons repeated and Ran drew back suddenl staring down at her, and Aurora met the separating spac and kissed him again, refusing to move, to let aught tak him from her yet.

"Dinna leave me, Ransom." She nuzzled his jaw, follow ing as he slowly sat up.

He groaned, holding her back. "I . . . can not." Air rushe into his lungs. "Not to you."

Her hand caressed his broad chest, her own breathin rapid. "Not to me, *with* me."

"Ah God, Aurora, do not say such things!" He thrust o the bed, giving her his back and staring at the floor.

Aurora opened her mouth to beg him back, then immedi ately snapped it shut, his quick retreat reminding her tha she'd asked for naught but a kiss and had received far more She would not press him further, for if she gaged his expres sion correctly, he was already swamped with sudden regre It hurt to witness it, that he could find discomfort in lovin her, yet she would accept no apologies from him, nor offe one in return. 'Twas just so, this gift they shared, and sh was patient enough not to throw it away.

"As you wish, m'lord."

He righted his clothing and with a sharp toss of his heac

flicked hair from his eyes to look at her. "As you wish?
You've naught else to say?"

She left the bed, dragging the sheet around her nakedness
as she stopped afore him. "Aye," she said, meeting his stare
and seaming the edge of his vest. "My thanks for givin' me
such pleasure, Ransom, and mayhaps if *I'd* but pressed the
advantage we'd be *pumping like friggin' rabbits,"* she
mocked.

Eyes wide, he sputtered, saying nothing.

"But if you satisfy the ache between yer thighs," she
flicked the worn leather, then headed to the door, "you may
find peace for the one in your heart."

"One has naught to do with the other," he lied, snatching
his dagger from the floor and positioning it in his belt. By
God, the woman was direct. "And since you've claimed
naught beats in my chest, I see no purpose in massacring
this . . . subject." His words trailed off as he realized she
would answer the caller thusly clad and in three strides, he
clipped her off. "Cease, woman, you're naked."

" 'Tis but a body, m'lord." She shrugged. "Who I am is
inside this shell." Her hand touched the latch and he
blocked her path, forcing her beyond the door.

"Sweet Christ, do you seek to cause a bleedin' riot?"

Facing him, she braced her shoulder against the wall,
patient, rosy, and incredibly composed. Damn her.

"Sahib?"

Ran opened the door, his gaze warning her not to move
into sight.

"Sahib?" Dahrein tried to peek inside. "Is my lady well?"

Ran looked down at the woman with aught but a sheet
held to her bosom and that done poorly. A mischievous
smile curved her lips, a cat licking stolen cream as she bared
a bit of hip and sensations barraged Ran; her flesh beneath
his palm, how sweetly she rode his mouth, her breathy pleas
for his loving and he gravitated toward her, then caught
himself. Damn, would he never learn?

"Sahib?" Impatience laced the boy's tone.

"Aye." Ran's eyes never left her. "She has recovered."

Her gaze dropped meaningfully to the bulge outlined by

his breeches. "But you havena," she whispered smugly, and
Ran's lips quirked.

"Saucy wench," he muttered for her ears alone, attempt
ing to sound chastising and failing.

"Her dress, sir." Dahrein shoved the garment into his
hand, frowning at the odd look on his captain's face. He'd
never seen him smile quite like that afore.

Ran's brows rose. " 'Tis dry? Already?"

"I hung it from the spinnaker line," the boy confessed
and Aurora smothered a laugh. Ran looked to the ceiling
then shook his head, bidding the boy to bring her a meal

"Ahh, sahib? The *Morgan* is in sight."

Ran's gaze instantly snapped to Aurora, and he felt as i
he'd been kicked in the teeth as the color rapidly drained
from her face. She'd forgotten, and Aurora's heart sank to
her knees, all thought of having a chance with Ransom
shattered, the finely wedged crack in his armor slamming
shut.

He was sending her away.

Any gentleness showed this man would not penetrate the
years of fortification, and she experienced the sharp sting o
loss. For as he lay in her arms, loving her body, he'd intended to put her ashore. As much as he silently cried ou
for her attention, he continued to view her as a threat to his
freedom, his cause, and his accursed command. 'Tis me own
fault, she thought, wanting him so deeply. Turning away
she crossed the room, hips swaying, hair swishing, the
draped length of sheet dragging behind her like the cloak of
a queen. She stopped afore the commode perched atween a
cabinet and bookcase, wrapping the sheet more securely
and sponging her face, throat, and arms.

Her dispirited expression left him with a dull ache in his
chest, and he came to stand behind her, their eyes meeting
in the small silver glass.

"Aurora." Regretful, but firm.

"Leave me be, pirate. Find me a place aboard the *Morgan,* for I ken well there is none on the *Lion.*"

The fracture in her voice sliced him in two. "You see wha

happens atween us." He gestured to the rumpled bed. *"This I cannot afford in my life."*

"Aye, 'tis plain to me now," she said tonelessly, dropping the sponge into the basin. " 'Tis more than a passion we share, Ransom." She faced him, holding his amber gaze. "And if you're believin' otherwise, 'tis a lie you alone must swallow." He broke his gaze briefly, then looked back at her. "What did you think would become of us when you sequestered me in your private quarters? Why did you even bring me aboard?"

She wanted a small admittance. She didn't get it.

"I wanted to protect you." Bloody weak words, Ran thought, for both knew jealousy commanded his actions then.

"How chivalrous. Yet now you pack me off with a freshly loved body."

He flinched. "I must. By God, you are a distraction of the worst kind!" Ran raked his hands through his hair, already second-guessing himself, for with Castille's strange disappearance he could be sending her back into the path of a murder. "Understand that I am obligated elsewhere and I cannot take you with. Ever." Aye, he'd already made too many promises, to others, to himself; and being with her, like this, was further bane for private defenses.

A short bitter laugh escaped her, and the odd sound made him uneasy. "Then surely you must keep the cold sea for your bed and this ship for your silent mistress, for they'll not gainsay you as I have." She shook her head sadly. " 'Tis a home of your own making, Ransom, and I dinna care to stand beyond the threshold, never to be let in." She drew herself up with a deep breath. "You forget I possessed a life afore knowing you, a father to find. And your *protection* has kept me from it long enough, thinks I." She turned back to the commode, her voice dropping to a broken whisper. "Shokai and I will be prepared in less than an hour's time."

Something deep inside Ran shattered. And he swallowed hard. He never wanted to hurt her, and to see her bubbling spirit calmed with lifelessness, tightened his chest like a vise.

Amy J. Fetzer

This would never cease. He would continue to hurt her again and again.

Are your bloody vows worth this, a voice blasted. Can you live peacefully after witnessing your handiwork, knowing you might be tossing aside the chance of a lifetime?

He'd thought the path of his life precut, well planned, unyielding . . . until this moment. God, he felt cheated.

Then he thought of his people, the souls locked in slavery, the half sister residing under his care; and afore he gathered her in his arms and apologized, Ran spun on his heels and quit the room.

Chapter Twenty-One

The wind gently caressed her face, its invisible power tearing loose the flame red strands at her temples. Aurora brushed them from her cheek as she stood on the deck of the *Red Lion,* the sun's warmth balmy to her skin. She breathed deeply of salt and tar pitch, grease and beeswax—of life—while above her, amidship sails puffed like boasting roosters, pulling the flagship along Triton's azure depths. Able seamen toiled at their duties as the *Morgan* drew closer, some staring at her in rapt awe, others with open disdain. A few crewmen milled closer than they ought; but she was careful to stand clear of the congested deck, hugging the rail.

No one spoke to her.

Shokai stood near, watching nothing and everything. Eternally suspicious. Yet Aurora no longer felt the fury she had upon first boarding and it eased the twist of regret churning in her stomach as she watched her new home for the next fortnight cut a watery path toward the flagship. The *Morgan,* a powerfully built vessel, midnight black, four masted, moved with a speed that amazed her, skillfully captained by Nickolas Ryder. Och now, what did it matter where she resided? For her time aboard the *Lion* was the longest she'd remained in one place since she was sixteen. 'Twas not the place but the people she would miss.

"Make ready the skiff."

Aurora tensed as the command came down, then released

the annoying sensation as crewmen cleared coils of rope afore the boarding break in the rail.

"Ma'am." She turned and Leelan ducked his head politely, crushing his knit cap in his fist, his arm bandaged to his wrist. "I didn't get the chance to thank you."

"You did, Leelan, by living. 'Tis thanks enough."

Leelan was humbled and suddenly leaned close, pecking her cheek with a chaste kiss. Aurora gasped, touching her face, moved by the gesture. He blushed, glanced around, then blushed some more.

And on the quarterdeck Ran stiffened at the tender sight, at once annoyed with his own reaction. One by one, men approached her, tentatively, as if fearing she'd bite. Yet she offered naught but one of her bright smiles, and Ran watched hardened soldiers of fortune be gentled by her. They, too, felt her nourishing spirit, Ran thought, as Buckland stepped forward. Aurora offered her hand, laughing lightly as he bowed over it like a knight begging favor. A moment later she and the doctor were head to head in conversation. Ran felt isolated, the segregation thickening with jealousy as Markus Lougière joined the group, leaning back against the rail beside her with that lazy negligent manner women found so captivating. By God, the man was ten years his senior!

Ran grit his teeth and called for his spyglass.

Domingo slapped it in his outstretched palm, so hard he glared at him.

"Was the only way you'd notice I put it there," he said, not the least bit apologetic, then lowered his voice. "I did not think to see the day you'd put a life in jeopardy for the sake of that damned oath," Domingo hissed, and Ran's blistering gaze pinned his first officer. *"Madre de Dios,* you take her from the Colonist, for her safety you claim, then hand her over to Ryder!"

"She is safe with Nickolas."

"He is a rakehell of the first water, and you know it!" Domingo clenched his fists, furious and frustrated. Aurora was Ran's last chance at happiness, the only person who'd broken through his cool exterior, and Domingo didn't want

Wish You Were Here?

You can be, every month, with Zebra Historical Romance Novels.

YOU'RE GOING TO LOVE GETTING

4 FREE BOOKS

These books worth almost $20, are yours without cost or obligation when you fill out and mail this certificate.
(If the certificate is missing below, write to: Zebra Home Subscription Service, Inc., 120 Brighton Road, P.O. Box 5214, Clifton, New Jersey 07015-5214

Complete and mail this card to receive 4 Free books!

Yes! Please send me 4 Zebra Historical Romances without cost or obligation. I understand that each month thereafter I will be able to preview 4 new Zebra Historical Romances FREE for 10 days. Then, if I should decide to keep them, I will pay the money-saving preferred publisher's price of just $4.00 each...a total of $16. That's almost $4 less than the publisher's price, and there is no additional charge for shipping and handling. I may return any shipment within 10 days and owe nothing, and I may cancel this subscription at any time. The 4 FREE books will be mine to keep in any case.

Name _____

Address _____ Apt. _____

City _____ State _____ Zip _____

Telephone ( ) _____

Signature _____

(If under 18, parent or guardian must sign.)

LF0395

Terms, offer and prices subject to change without notice. Subscription subject to acceptance by Zebra Books. Zebra Books reserves the right to reject any order or cancel any subscription.

A $19.96
value.
FREE!

No obligation
to buy
anything, ever.

ZEBRA HOME SUBSCRIPTION SERVICE, INC.

120 BRIGHTON ROAD

P.O. BOX 5214

CLIFTON, NEW JERSEY 07015-5214

AFFIX
STAMP
HERE

to see his friend die a lonely bitter man. "Ryder will cease at nothing to best a challenge to his bed."

Ran refused to comment, torrid images of Aurora's loving taunting him. Would she succumb to Ryder's prowess and offer the Carolinian her fiery kisses? Would he be charmed by her unvarnished ways and feel, as Ran did, without substance, without a will to resist her. Ran's features sharpened. Ryder resisted naught, the hedonistic braggart.

"Dios, you are a cold bastard," Domingo muttered when he received no response. "And even if you do not have the decency to bid the woman good-bye, I do." He left Ran's side to descend to the rail.

Ran gripped the spyglass and scanned the horizon, avoiding another look at Aurora and focusing on the *Morgan's* approach with a mix of relief and dread. He deciphered the signal flags the *Morgan* posted, an intricate series of sail hoist, spinnaker shift, and colors designed to relay messages atween vessels at great distance. Ran had developed it for the rendezvous, for the *Lion* was tactically vulnerable waiting in the Atlantic for his captains to report. Yet, mooring them collectively in a harbor was suicidal. Quietly he ordered his ship's colors hoisted; a pawing red lion silhouetted against black.

Aurora's laughter startled him, low, sultry, steaming over him like the sun's radiance, and he struggled not to look her way, not to see who'd brought the delightful sound to the surface. It made him increasingly aware 'twas not him. He hadn't seen her since leaving his cabin this morn, yet her sadness surrounded the *Red Lion,* as if her unspoken emotions had the power of touch. His men were quiet, the sea dull, the wind less than a cat's-paw of power, and Ran felt like a blackguard and half a fool, the disappointed looks Dahrein kept throwing him doing naught to lighten his foul mood.

Putting Aurora aside, he realized, was the hardest thing he'd done in years. But keeping her aboard meant a commitment, and he couldn't afford the luxury of permanence, nor be distracted by one who guided her life with potions and chants and spells. His missions, his oaths, must come first. They threaded his life deeply, and breaking them would unravel years of hard work and sacrifice. Business, aye. 'Twas his only true reward. Passion was fleeting—and replaceable, his father would say. Maintaining commitments and promises were not a Montegomery strength, yet Ransom decided ten years ago he would not follow that legacy.

Aurora deserved better than he was willing to give. And she deserved not to be hurt. Mayhaps if she were off again searching for her father, she'd find a man who'd be all that she craved.

I crave the taste of you, vibrated in his head, the aura of her sensuality filling his being with a strength that made him look at her accusingly. She appeared frail and cheerless, yet he knew beneath the white gown was a temptress, luxuriously shaped and ripe with want. She was an untamed colt in his bed, and her whispered pleas to make love to her tortured him now.

"Lower away," he growled, moments afore the *Morgan* swept cleanly alongside the *Lion*. Orders carried on the breeze, swiftly implemented while Aurora bid her callers farewell. She straightened her spine, waiting at the rail as Domingo lifted away the barricade. A rope ladder rolled down, and two sailors descended to man the small boat.

"Can you manage?"

"Aye, Domingo, my thanks," she said, offering him a gentle smile.

"It has indeed been a pleasure, *querida,*" he said taking her hand and bringing it to his lips.

"Och, Domingo," she said with a tilt of her head and affection in her voice. "Good life, my friend." She drew her hand back, turned to the rail, and froze. Regret, sharp and poignant clutched in her chest, the depth of it undeniably strong, and she gasped, whirling about, half expecting to find Ransom standing close, yet not one soul looked her way. Her gaze searched the ship, then unwillingly swept to where he stood at the helm, untouchable, commanding, a bronze king of his floating village, and her heart jumped

crazily in her chest. From the distance she could see his dark
amber eyes, eyes that had haunted her visions for weeks
afore she'd laid eyes upon him. He wouldn't look at her,
offered no bid good-bye. 'Twas his own choice to dismiss
the precious gifts they shared, and Aurora could not stay
where she was unwanted. 'Twas too humiliating to bear.

"Aurora?" Domingo's tone bespoke his concern.

She shook her head, waving him off as she lowered herself
over the side.

Shokai paused at the rail, hands on his narrow hips,
glaring down at the long drop as if the skiff should jump up
and allow him a more convenient descent; then he glanced
up to where Ransom stood with his feet spread wide apart,
clasped hands braced at the base of his spine.

Eyes locked and Shokai harrumphed at the fabled sea
captain, turned, and descended.

"A gift, Ran?" Nickolas Ryder called out pleasantly.
"How good of you to think of me."

"Bloody hell," Ran muttered and strode to the rail. "Do
naught but take her to shore, Ryder." Clear with an unspoken threat. God above, Ran thought, this was killing
him.

Nickolas braced his forearms on the polished wood, grinning down at the approaching skiff. Aurora felt his stare
and twisted to look at the dark-haired man. He flashed her
a rakish smile, then saluted, confidence splashed across his
tanned features. Aurora was not impressed. Though boyishly handsome, she'd seen his like time and again in the
past years. 'Tis a harlot in breeches, she decided, and it
infuriated her that Ransom would adjourn her to the hands
of a rogue.

Prepared to lambaste him for his disregard, she looked
toward the *Lion,* but he'd turned his back on her, at once
dismissing her from his sight and his life, and Aurora felt the
thick choke of hurt. She wished she could turn her emotions
away as easily.

Peering through his spyglass, the lens trained on the
windward side of the ship, Ran scanned in a one-hundred-

eighty-degree circumference. Abruptly he halted, lowering
the glass, then viewing again.

"Stand fast! Man your stations! Signal the *Morgan* to
retreat!" Bearing down on the *Lion* were three ships, gun
ports open for battle. She flew no colors, but Ransom could
smell British beef a half a world away.

At first warning, Domingo leapt to the capstan, searching
the horizon, then swearing viciously as crewmen scrambled
to stations. He met Ran's gaze across the crowded vessel
and together they looked toward the woman solemnly sitting in a dinghy atween the ships.

"Watkins, turn back!" Ran ordered over the din, rushing
downship. "Now!"

At the command, Aurora stood, rocking the little boat.
"Back? Nay, Ransom, nay!" By the Gods, he could not toy
with her like this! "And if you so much as dip that oar to
turn us back, laddie," she warned the seaman. "I'll swim the
distance."

"But ma'am, he's given me an order."

"Silence," she said with the slash of her hand, and the
man fell back as if struck.

Struggling to sit up, Watkins fumbled to catch the fallen
oar, looking helplessly toward his captain.

"Aurora, blast it all!" Ran said, glancing atween her and
the British warships closing fast. "Allow Watkins to bring
the skiff back!" Sweet saints, she was a perfect target!

"Mister Watkins can do as he bloody well pleases, but I'll
not step aboard your precious ship!"

"Damn you, woman!"

"Dinna be cursing me, pirate. 'Twas your decision, now
abide it!"

He couldn't, not leave her on the *Morgan,* not now. The
Lion was twice the *Morgan*'s size, heavily gunned, and at
that moment Ran didn't trust Aurora's safety to Ryder, not
in battle. The *Morgan* was fast and Nicholas' skill lay in
evading, sailing away unscathed.

"Captain Ryder seems the generous sort to take me
ashore. Are'na you, sir?"

"Oh, aye, my sweet mermaid." Ryder grinned hugely even as his crew scrambled to make sail. "Come see."

See her on her back in his damned bed most likely, Ran thought as he left the quarterdeck and made his way to the open portion of the rail.

"There now." She turned back to Ransom. "You've naught to worry over. And if Captain Ryder doesna play the gent, Shokai will cut off anything hanging loosely." Shokai, sitting like a stone Buddha, nodded once to agree and Nickolas laughed deeply. " 'Tis halfway I've gone now, so why return?" She held her breath, gazing up at her pirate lord.

"Because you are safer aboard the *Lion*."

Aboard the *Lion*. Not safe with me, safe in my arms, but simply sequestered aboard a grander ship. Cheese and crust, nay, she would not be at the mercy of his chivalrous whims!"

"You're besmirchin' Nickolas' reputation," she tisked, disappointed in his reply.

"Will you defend my honor, pretty mermaid?" Ryder asked, enjoying the sight of Ran nearly tearing his hair out with frustration.

"Och, yer saying you have one then?" she tossed with a sly look over her shoulder.

"Ah, love, that hurts." Though Nickolas' expression said otherwise. "Let me prove it to you."

"Ryder! Damn you man, you are not helping!" Blast her for choosing now to rebel! They were about to be blown to kindling!

Nick shrugged, as if there was naught he could do. "The lady doesn't want your company, Montegomery."

"By damned she will have it!" Ran shucked his belt, scattering knives to the deck afore he dove into the water, surfacing beside the skiff.

"Now why did you go and do that?" She glared militantly, hands on hips, the Trojan maid come to war with him. "You seek to steal me from another's protection again, pirate?" she snipped, then flailed wildly as he hoisted his arms over the edge, rocking the tiny boat. She dropped to the seat in an undignified plop. "You did that a'purpose thinks I."

"Correct, thinks me," came dryly as Ran smeared hai from his eyes and struggled for calm in the surging water "But in less than an hour this span of ocean will be a battle field." He hoped to get a reaction. He hoped for naught.

"Best tootle on back to your ship, then." She waved hin off, sparing a mildly curious glance at the ships. Her un flappability rankled him and he decided he didn't mean a much to her as he'd imagined, but he'd hurt her and she wasn't prepared to give him an inch of line.

"What do you want?" he growled, ignoring the oarsmer who listened intently.

She folded her arms, arching a black brow. *"Yer* the one come callin'."

"Come back with me . . . please."

Grittily forced and without conviction, she thought "Nay. I've a father to find and Nickolas can help me."

"I'll help you." If we live through this, he thought, crew men aboard both ships moving about like disturbed bees.

"Oh, Ransom," she said dejectedly, her stiff expression falling. " 'Tis willin' I am to be gone from your life." She held his gaze. "If you'll but let me go."

Confusion and turmoil brightened the blue eyes staring down at him, and Ran saw exactly how deeply he'd wounded her. He felt shiftless and unworthy, and for ar instant, he didn't care that the British rode the sea to claim a price on his head, nor of the more than three hundred pairs of eyes watching them intently; only that she knew he needed her, more than he thought possible, more than wa wise, and though he hadn't wanted to send her off—'twas his only choice, then.

"I can not," he admitted in a whisper. "God's blood Aurora!" he half cursed her unaffected look. " 'Tis harder than I imagined!"

Suddenly she leaned close. "Now that wasna so hard,' she said, brushing her fingers over his moist lips. "Was i now?"

"Aye, pest, 'twas." He kissed her fingertips, softening

ito his downfall, aware she'd risked her life to gain even
iose small words from him. "For I can not give what you
ant," he said, but he had, his tortured confession speaking
iore than he realized.

"Dinna be assumin' you ken what I need, pirate," she
iid tartly as Ran lurched into the boat, her acute satisfac-
ion making him frown.

" 'Tis a spell you've cast on me?"

"Hah! One to change an ogre into a troll?" she huffed,
ioving an oar at his chest.

Did that mean she wasn't satisfied, Ran wondered, his
ioulders flexing beneath the wet cloth as he brought the
iiff home.

"You could have taken me by force again," she said as
iey climbed the ladder, wondering why he hadn't.

"Nay, pest," he replied, helping her onto the deck amidst
ie chaos of rolling cannons and rushing sailors, he stared
eeply into her eyes. Thirty-three years did not make him a
ise man, he realized, for she'd answered to no one her
ntire life and he'd done naught but bully her. "Nay, not
iis time."

The bosuns' whistle shrieked, halliard hoisted, winch
vung, and the flagship took wind as Aurora searched his
rong features, trying to see what lay beneath his somber
are, but Domingo called to him. Pressing a chaste kiss to
er forehead, he turned away, his long strides over-taking
ie engorged deck, his commanding voice carrying orders
nd instilling confidence. Crewmen ran up track lines as
asily as climbing a hill, ropes uncoiling near Aurora's feet
ke swirling snakes, and she pressed herself against the rail,
ut of harm's way as Shokai vanished into the melee.

"Aurora!" Ransom gestured for her to come to the quar-
erdeck and she obeyed, weaving her way from midship to
oop deck to quarterdeck ladder. She grasped the rail, skirts
i one hand and he reached down, pulling her onto the deck
eside him. "You are safer up here, for now," he said.

Her gaze lit on the three ships bearing down on them as
e steered her further aft. "Och, Ransom, they're huge!" she
iid awed, then suddenly frowned. "But the *Lion* isna near

any markers, miles from shore, so how could they have—?

His cold stare stopped her. "We've been betrayed."

"Great Goddess!"

"Aye, lass, pray to her, for we're outgunned, outmanned and with nary a wind at our backs."

Doomed, he was saying. Aurora refused to believe it. But then he withdrew a blade from the collection at his waist and pressed it into her hand.

"If we are boarded, pest. Do not let the bastards have you. Promise me."

She stared down at the slim jeweled blade and swallowed. She could not take her life, no matter what, he had to know that. His gaze said he did, but she tucked the thin dagger in her leather belt regardless.

"When the bombardment starts, head to my cabin and stay put." His tone begged her not to fight him on this, and his wide shoulders drooped with relief when she nodded. Immediately he left her and she was filled with a sudden uncertainty, a haste to touch him one last time.

"Ransom!" She reached out as he lowered himself over the quarterdeck ladder, and he stilled, catching her hand, squeezing, aching to hold her, kiss her, ease the honest fear he saw hidden in her blue stare. But he couldn't. She should be afraid. Damned if he wasn't.

"If you've a spell to conjure the wind," he teased for her ears alone. "Now is the time, lass." He clutched her hand tightly, then released her, disappearing down to the lower deck. Aurora backed out of the way as the attacking ship rapidly covered water. Lives would be destroyed. Futures crushed. Shokai appeared at her side, and she grasped his hand.

"It is simpler to die, my empress, than to live."

She looked at him, his words sinking deeply. Ransom would defeat them. He had to. She had not lived a lonely, barren life to find him, then lose him to a bleedin' British attack in the name of some fat king.

Aurora prayed, urging the forces of wind and water to roar for her *Red Lion*.

* * *

The *Morgan* did not retreat, and Ran cursed Nickolas
Ryder as he shouted orders, and the thick-armed coxswain
spun the wheel, rudders tugging through icy water. Sail
dropped, spinnaker and yard shifted, and the flagship *Red
Lion* came about like a heaving storm to face the British
vessels, while the *Morgan* went full sail, elegant and sleek as
a delicate lady, sweeping leeward, listing dangerously and
coming to the defense of her master.

And above Triton's kingdom a line was drawn.

Ran looked back at Aurora. Wind whipped at her white
gown, her braided hair flapping like a loose rope, the sun's
gleam a blade of white ricocheting off her silver amulet, her
features cast with determination and brave defiance.

Her gaze never left him.

And he was filled with a sense of raw power, that inside
her were the secrets men sought for centuries. Peace, the
treasures of a rich life. And in that moment Ransom knew
any emotion he kept hidden lay open on his face. She
smiled, so like her, so optimistic, brimming with encouragement. And he knew he would take these bastards to Davey
Jones for this tiny woman's life.

The first volley whizzed across the *Lion*'s repaired bowsprit, plunking into the sea and sending tons of water hail-
ing across the deck. Not a man to sit still and be taken,
Ransom allowed the British warships to gain striking distance. The instant Aurora was below deck the *Lion* gunners
opened fire, emptying their cannons on the two warships
drawing unwisely close. Four volleys struck home, ripping
open the fore hull, spilling ballast and men into the sea.
Better than six balls leveled a Brit's fore and mizzen, but the
warship was not to be outdone.

She readied to fire, but the *Morgan,* lighter and swifter,
and without stores to hinder her, shifted round to sail into
the fray, atween the disabled and sinking warship, and the
two primed and ready. She didn't position to fire but hacked

off grapeshot and langrage as she moved into the wolf's den like a spitting dragon, white smoke and red fire covering her presence.

British tactics were known to a third of the *Morgan* and *Lion* crew. They were as predictable at sea as they were on land. A line and charge, no evasiveness, and Ransom's expertise was tested to the limits. For 'twas one hundred twenty cannons to his collective sixty-four.

Hot smoke and the odor of burning flesh filled the air. For hours the battle waged.

Below in the captain's quarters, Aurora observed the fight through the portside windows, captivated, glancing away only briefly as unbolted items rolled across the desk. The British ship was massive, longer from bow to stern, and through the smoke she could see the wigged captain, unmoving, allowing his crew to do battle and die while he stayed on the quarter-deck unharmed, pristine in his uniform.

A volley struck above, followed by the shatter of wood, the cry of pain as the *Lion* rocked with the force. Aurora gripped a wall hook for stability as lanterns rattled, books shifted in cabinets. 'Twas the quarterdeck, she panicked, near desperate to go help, yet knew she would only distract the crew.

But 'twas a war unfairly matched, she decided, and suddenly closed her eyes, narrowing her thoughts, then narrowing them even deeper, painting the rig lines of the warship in her mind.

"A null e. A nall e, Slainte," she chanted, drawing strength from the ancient words. Her brows drew down as she concentrated, pinpointing a tender spot, imagining the rig line snapping, the sudden slack releasing belaying pins and fluttering sail to the deck. A cheer sounded and her eyes flashed open to find the British ship draped in white tattered sail.

She smiled, pleased. She'd never tempted aught so daring afore.

The *Lion* quickly caught wind. And she watched the British warship, ringed in smoke and ablaze, grow smaller and smaller.

"Unwise women are a man's trial."

She didn't have to turn to know Shokai stood near.

"Dinna scold me, *sempai,* 'twas nay a risk, harm to none." She let out a small laugh. " 'Twas well, for me gift's never been that accurate afore."

She turned, inhaling sharply, for Ransom stood in the doorway, his hair wind-wild, his face sooty, his clothing rent and blood splattered, but his expression one of disbelief and bewilderment. She dismissed all but the bloodstains and flew to him, checking each spot. He remained motionless for her exam, his gaze moving suspiciously from her to the departing Shokai and back. Suddenly he wrapped his arm about her waist, stilling her as he brought her tightly against his body. She lifted her gaze and found him searching her face with an intensity that knocked the breath from her lungs. Then he crushed her mouth beneath his, his lips drinking in her vitality, her wild energy. And she gave it. His tongue outlined her lips, then speared atween as his hand found the curve of hip and buttocks. She clung, her body shaping to fit his.

"Ahh, pest," he breathed against her lips. "What am I to do with you now?"

Suddenly she pushed away from him. "Ochaii! Some things are laid at one's feet even the sighted folk cannot see!" She dealt him a disappointed stare. "I am not a body you *do with,* pirate. Or has war addled yer brain?" Sarcasm dripped but hurt spoke, running too deeply to have him touch her, kiss her, and not have his love. She would rather live without him a'tall. Simply said and hardly done, she thought, dropping her gaze as she said, "Call the *Morgan* to heel, Ransom. I will board her and begone."

"Aurora?"

She looked at him.

"The *Morgan* was sunk."

Chapter Twenty-Two

Sunk.

"And me down with it," Aurora muttered, dropping numbly into a chair. Her choice to return to the *Lion* spared her life, and Ran's expression clarified his hand in it, the arrogant sot. "Captain Ryder?"

"Taken prisoner." He laid spent flint lock pistols on the table.

Her gaze flew to his. "Oh, Ransom!"

"Do not fret. He will not be one for long." A boarding cutlass joined the pile.

"You sound so certain."

Only his eyes shifted. "I take care of my own, lass." The Montegomery name still held some power in the proper circles, and Ran would use it. His father owed him this.

Aurora stood abruptly, panicked. "Dahrein?"

"A few scratches. And afore you riddle me with questions, get your bag and come see for yourself."

She blinked, stunned that he'd allow her above decks *and* to tend the wounded. Instantly she glanced around the cabin for her sack, knowing Shokai would have seen to it.

"I caution you, woman," he said, gesturing to the lump lying by the door, "do not recite a single chant, spell, or whatever the bloody hell you do on my decks." She swept past him, picking up her bag. "My men are suspicious of you as it is."

She stilled from inventorying her herbs. "They think I betrayed them?" Shaking her head, she waved off her worry.

" 'Tis impossible." And Ran would defend her if need be, she was sure of it.

"Aye, but Castille is missing because of your presence. And their loyalty lies with him."

And the blame with her, an accessible target. " 'Tis wiser, then, to put me ashore?"

"Out of the question." The thought of her gone from his sight harshened his tone.

"Not even at Rabat? 'Twas where my last bit of information led."

Ran stored that for later. "Those ships *came from* Rabat, and if this vessel is so much as glimpsed, it will be blown from the water. Nay." He shook his head, his mind made up long afore. "We are in danger, for rigging can be repaired," he reminded with a pointed look, still not certain if she had a hand in that a'tall. "And I cannot favor your preferences over the lives of my crew."

Her shoulders lifted and fell in a sign of resignation, for she could not argue his point. Cheese and crust! Marooned, again. "How will you evade them?" She flicked a hand toward the aft windows and the smoking ships dormant in the water.

He shrugged. "Disappear, for a time."

"How long, Ransom?" came cautiously.

He braced himself afore he said, "Mayhaps a fortnight or two."

Her eyes widened, and when she opened her mouth to protest he kissed her, quickly, deeply, a thick swirl of erotic possession; then drew back just as suddenly, his lips quirking over her dazed expression. He crushed the urge to see if he could make her knees wobble and grabbed her shoulders, directing her out the cabin door.

Aurora shot him an annoyed look over her shoulder, nearly tripping on the threshold. "Gloating beast," she muttered, and he smiled. "Dinna be grinning all toothy at me, Ransom Montegomery. For I dinna like this a wee bit!"

"What *dinna* you like, lass?" he said close to her ear as she paused at the ladder.

Her hand on the rail, she twisted to look at him. His

teasing smile instantly vanished, for she appeared on the verge of tears.

"I canna forget you loved my body well only this morn, yet were willing to discard me. For the sake of your 'obligations.' " His features tightened with guilt. "If I'd made it to the *Morgan,* we'd not be having this chat." The crack in her voice was like a pistol ball to his chest, tearing through him with searing heat, intensifying with the knowledge that his damned pride, his indecision, could have killed her. Domingo was right. He'd nearly sacrificed her life for the sake of his oath.

"Aurora?" came soft and coaxing. "Ah, look at me, lass."

She did, and he was unhinged by the disappointment in her eyes.

" 'Tis done. You are here and alive because of it."

"But naught has changed, Ransom. I see it in your eyes, feel it in your kiss, your touch. And I fear," she swallowed, "I've been wrong about you."

"How can you speak so?" He turned her to face him fully, his hands imprisoning her arms.

" 'Tis a coldness in you I canna reach. Part of you you willna release for anyone. I thought I could enjoy the brief moments, truly I did, imaginin' I could be satisfied with only bits of your passion in the hopes of more, but even that you willna give without repercussions."

"Pest," he groaned, leaning closer.

"Nay, dinna kiss me," she said, turning her face away. "For 'tis not enough." She met his gaze, marshaling her will power. She could not live like this for a fortnight, not and want to be closer to him. "I am no longer satisfied with crumbs, Ransom. Nay. I've lived me life on them, and even if I dinna find me father, I'll take naught less than . . . your heart."

"I cannot give you that." Quick, without regret, stabbing through her like a hot dagger.

"Then I beg of you, let me be," she pleaded. "For 'tis humiliating to crave your nearness and ken yours is naught but an empty caress."

"Empty!" he hissed, slipping his hands to the guide rails

and hemming her in. "I do not have to *touch* you to feel your presence, Aurora. By God, do you know what you do to me with naught but a simple look, a innocent touch?"

"Anger you, Ransom," she said without missing a beat. "For it always ends with bitter words."

"Aye, aye! For you make me weak, Aurora Lassiter, and I do *not* like the feeling. With your thirst for life, your tender trust and gentle caring, you alone have rent apart *ten years* of my life, for you are not a woman a man can love in his bed and look blandly upon in the morn." Her brows rose at that. "Aye, I am not so blind that I cannot see beyond the supple curves and soft voice." Eyes of bronze fire slid hotly over her once afore returning to her face. "You are not a wench of slight brains and unlearned ways, and *I* crave all that you offer but I cannot have; for if I succumb I will lose more than a moment or two or a pain in my heart, I will lose my very soul."

Aurora saw the darkness of his heart, the howling beast suffering beneath the weight of some divided loyalty to his past, to whoever or whatever had turned him away from feeling anything but hurt in the guise of love. Loving was so foreign to him he could not recognize it beyond that to love, made him vulnerable.

"Och, Ransom, I dinna seek to make you weak, but stronger. For I will be, too."

His disbelief mixed with disdain.

"God of Thunder, who has filled your mind and heart with so much rubbish?"

"A string of bastard siblings warns me of loving carelessly," he bit caustically. "An unfaithful father and spineless mother prove I cannot trust even a smattering of devotion." He'd never be like his father. Never. Allowing children to live lies, pushing them on people who thought them beneath maggots eating at spoiled meat and treated them as such. Like Lady Anna Montegomery. The woman he called mother for twenty-three years.

"Nay," she whispered, eyes searching his face in new wonder. " 'Tis not the losing of love, but the gaining that frightens you. Aye, dinna deny it. You feel if you weaken to your needs, then you will be no better than your rogue father." She reached out to him, slowly brushing a lock from his forehead. "Och, Ransom, you are not that man. A babe can be prevented, this I swear," she added when his gaze narrowed. "And loving is not *only* of the flesh."

"Cease, Aurora, say nay more." Low and agonized, a portion of his soul withering each time she countered his words.

She drew back. "But surely the times you and I—"

"God above, do you not think this tears me apart?" He shook the guide rails, once, hard. "For you, above all else, are undeserving of my trials." His arms braced on the rail beside her, he studied the deck.

Her heart wrenched for him, and her hand lifted, hovering over his wind-tossed hair, then drawing back.

"But you havena told me why, Ransom? What gives you this strength of conviction?"

He lifted his head, amber eyes filled with despair and remorse.

"Murder."

Her eyes rounded.

"Aye. I killed a man in the name of my father's unfaithfulness, for a weakness of the flesh that *I* refused to see."

He thrust away, ignoring her pleas as he turned into his cabin and shut the door. Inside he leaned against the sealed wood and closed his eyes. God almighty, he had not spoken of it for years, yet the memories were painfully fresh. The accusation; that Ran, too, was one of Granville's bastards. The duel; the life Ran ended was no more than that of a pup spouting at Whitehalls. And then Anna.

She'd never shown him any tenderness in his entire life. Still he had hoped.

"You utter fool!" she'd shrieked in the opulent halls of Montegomery House. "Do you think it untrue!" A heartless cackle. An angry toss of her head. "Look in the mirror. Do you see even a hint of my blood? My God, you *reek* of her! Those slashing brows and that horrible golden skin! Your mother was naught but a whore!" Anna took delight in telling him. "Spreading her thighs for her owner, her mas-

ter! And when he was tired of her, she was given away like
a prize or a trinket. To Granville. So you see?" She stared
down her thin nose at him. "You, Lord Montegomery, were
born in a *hareem!*"

It destroyed the cultured young lord, for beyond his own
torment, an innocent man had died for a lie.

By daybreak the wounded were tended and the *Lion* was
no longer struggling to make distance, yet Ran refused to
slacken, maintaining the swiftest speed the massive ship
could attain. He was exhausted, on edge, going without
sleep, for even though Aurora had accepted Domingo's
offer of his cabin, her scent permeated Ran's quarters and
he lay awake aching for her comfort and denying his need
for it. He would never find peace, he thought as he manned
the helm, gazing at the sun's push over the horizon.

What she was thinking after last night? Did she fear him?
Was she repulsed?

"Shokai," Ran bade softly, and as the old man moved
silently to his side, Ran realized he was no longer Aurora's
shadow. Did he trust him now? Or his crew?

"My lord." Shokai bowed.

"In the hostelry, did you perchance see the attackers?"

Shokai frowned up at him. "No one ever stumbled lying
snug in a bed."

"Cease the riddles, old man. I believe someone had a
hand in your mistress' fate."

Shokai's gaze shot to where she sat on a crate, playing
cards with Dahrein, a small audience of crewmen watching
intently.

"I saw no evil. For I was blinded in pain." He turned his
attention back to the captain. "She knows none but this
ship, my lord."

Ran didn't believe for a moment one of his crew was
involved, yet considered that someone had betrayed their
position to the English authorities and her last information
on her father had come from Rabat.

"Has she crossed anyone?"

Shokai eyed him pointedly.

"I mean someone who would harm her."

Shokai folded his arms over his thin chest, his stare unwavering.

"Physically," Ran ground through clenched teeth.

"Foiled sultans, fat merchants, and desert lords."

"Those I *am* aware of," Ran said, losing patience. The Sultan was notorious for exacting punishment for even the minutest slight; Achmed wasn't stupid enough to risk losing another hand, but that alone would send any man to seek retribution; and Rahman had no motive, nor would the Bedouin go back on his word. Foti. Mayhaps Foti thought Ran would betray his deeds and sought to gain British favor by giving his location. But that still didn't explain who put Aurora on the *Black Star*.

"Revenge and envy often take the same form, m'lord," Shokai cautioned. "And a pretty woman and a bag of coins take much watching."

Beyond them Lougière limped across the deck, staring so intently at Aurora that the quartermaster didn't notice a coil of rope and stumbled inelegantly. Aurora laughed behind a fan of cards, her gaze sweeping up to the quarterdeck and colliding with Ran's. The devilish glitter in her eyes softened, pulling at his black mood, showering him with warm blue light. She flipped a card down, not breaking eye contact, and Ran sank deeper into her gaze. Had she forgiven him for risking her life? Sweet saints, he thought, he didn't deserve it.

Shokai glanced atween the two, then muttered disgustedly, "Ah, two wet birds under one umbrella" as he shuffled off, and Ran realized he was grinning foolishly and looked away, gripping the wheel spokes.

Nearly two dozen seamen witnessed the exchange and smiled.

The piercing mournful sound of bagpipes weighted the air, seeping into the cracked and splintered wood of the *Red Lion*. Above decks the ship was quiet, men caught in their own thoughts as the piper played for the downed ship and the coming of midnight. Staggering with exhaustion, Ran headed for his cabin, knowing it would be empty and disliking it well. A faint muffled noise caught his attention, and he backtracked down the companionway, listening at Domingo's door. The sound came again, smothered, and he pulled open the hatch. Huddled in the darkened corner of the narrow bunk, Aurora sobbed hopelessly into a pillow.

His knees went soft. The shock, the sound of her cries cinched his breathing. She'd never once shed a tear. Not even when Shokai was dying! God above, had he caused this upset?

"Aurora?"

She pressed closer to the wall, turning her face away.

"Begone pirate, I dinna want you here."

He couldn't leave her like this. And he entered the cabin, moving cautiously, as if approaching a frightened, wounded animal.

"Leave, I say!" she hissed.

He sat on the bunk, slowly. "Tell me what grieves you, lass."

"Your stubbornness!"

His lips curved at that. "Aurora?" The tinny music heightened, and she seemed to shrink into the wall with every note.

"Oh, make them cease, Ransom," she pleaded pitifully. "Make them cease!"

His brow tightened. "The pipes?"

"Aye, aye, aye!" She covered her ears, and her torment sank like tiny arrows into his heart.

"Ah, lass, 'tis only a salute to a downed ship."

" 'Tis a song of home. I canna bear it!"

Immediately Ran went to the door and bade a wandering crewman to see to her wishes. When he turned back she was on her knees, rocking, her arms clutching her middle. She looked in physical pain and he rushed to her, but she shied away from him, hiding behind a curtain of black hair. It clawed at his heart to see her like this, for she'd shown naught but strength and determination thus far.

" 'Tis not all you weep for. Tell me, pest," he coaxed softly, easing down beside her.

"Me mother." Almost a childish whimper.

"And where is she?"

"Dead, Ransom. Murdered." She shuddered raggedly. "I can still see her face. Och, I shouldna, after all these years, but I do."

"Is it her you dream of?"

"Aye, oh aye," she sobbed, rocking, her despair wrenching him in half. "She knew they'd come, Ransom, for she hid me in the hollow of a tree just afore. I heard her argue, then scream, over and over, for me father."

"And where was he?"

"Huntin', thinks I." She shivered violently. "Och, 'twas nay a simple death. This beast cut her, Ransom." She lifted her teary gaze to him. Tortured, bleak. "Cut me mother's beautiful face, taking her finger and an ear. Ohhh!" Her lips quivered and she looked as if she'd be sick and Ran reached for a basin. She waved him off, glancing briefly away. "She dinna find peace even then, for she moaned for me to stay hidden, not to come out. Another man came then, and," she gasped back fresh tears, "Mama spoke her last words to him."

"Your father?"

"Nay. But Papa returned, and . . . and . . . he went mad, Ransom, howling like a beast of the undead, tearin' at his hair, clawin' his face. I was terrified, for 'twas not me father but a wild creature. I'd never seen him so . . . twisted."

"Did he not look for you?"

"I couldna form the words to call out to him," she said as if it were her fault. "He vanished into the forest." She dropped her gaze to her knees and whispered, " 'Twas the last I saw of him."

To be abandoned like that, when she needed most. "How old were you then?"

"Three or four." She sniffled and shrugged as if it made no difference. "Gran found me, thinks I. I lived wit' her til she died." Her voice choked. "I left then, to find me father. I met Shokai when I was set upon by . . . thieves."

"What was he doing in Scotland?"

She looked at him. " 'Twas England," she said with a hint of petulance, "and if he wanted me to know his past, then he would have told me."

"Why do you seek a father who abandoned you?"

"He dinna abandon me!" she defended hotly. "He dinna ken I was in the tree, alive, and likely he thought I was stolen away."

"The killer argued with your mother?" She nodded, looking at him strangely. "Mayhaps she knew him or her?"

Her brow furrowed and she looked him over. "What are you sayin'?"

He'd rather cut off his thumb than to suggest, "Perhaps your father—"

"Nay, nay!" She leapt on him, covering his mouth with her hand. "Nay, dinna speak it, nay, Ransom! They loved, they loved! So deeply she gave up her family for him!"

Ran's arms wound around her as he stared into red-rimmed eyes. Her lip trembled. Slowly she released her hold over his mouth and he gathered her closer.

"Nay, nay," she moaned, slipping her arms around his neck, gripping tightly, sobbing into his shirt front. "He loved her." Her shoulders jerked wretchedly. "He did," she said through wet tears, and Ran didn't gainsay her.

He held her, his hands stroking the curve of her spine. "I believe you, lass." She squeezed tighter. "But why do you search after all these years?"

" 'Tis not *after,* Ransom. Been lookin' I have, since I was six and ten."

Nine years echoed through his brain, and he pushed her back enough to see her face.

"Dear God, Aurora, why?"

"Do you not ken he is all I have left in this world. And mayhaps he is lonely and needs me."

Needs me. Did she never think of herself?

A flood of tenderness swamped him. For he saw the motherless babe, hidden as her parent was butchered, saw the gangly young girl with no one to make her frilly dresses, weave flower garlands for her hair, or read fairy tales at her

bedside. He saw the fatherless child with none to defend her
from bullies, to warn her of the harshness of the world, to
make her toys, or hold her gently when she was frightened
by midnight goblins. He envisioned the wild lass raised in
the Highlands, collecting herbs and flowers, believing in her
spells and potions and her *Goddess.* He saw the woman-
child bravely leaving her home in search of a father who'd
selfishly surrendered to his grief and neglected his only
child.

And then he saw the woman chained to the wall of the
Sultan's prison, calmly waiting for him, and the inside of his
chest seem to expand, a swelling of pride and adoration
biting into the shield he'd taken years to forge. He imagined
how she'd spent the last nine years, where she'd lived, the
occasions when she was cold or hungry or lonely for aught
but the company of a reserved old man. She asked for
naught, would give away her very soul if you needed it. And
Ran wanted to return what she'd lost, shower her with the
luxuries she'd missed yet cared little about. He wanted to
give Aurora happy dreams and chase away her nightmares.

"He is near, Ransom," she whispered. The white wolf of
her seer box, he recalled, and looked down at her. "You see
why I must leave?"

'Twas impossible to get her to land. Not the land she
wanted. "What is his name? Mayhaps I can help?"

"MacLaren, Angus MacLaren."

He was confused and looked it. "But . . . ?"

"Lassiter is me mother's mother's name. I dinna use Mac-
Laren for I fear . . . he'll run from me if he kens who I am."

At least she realized her father might not want to be
found, he thought, then asked, "Would you recognize
him?"

"Me memory is that of a babe, and as I've changed, so
must have he. But his hair is red," she said tugging on the
crimson strands at her temple. Ran pressed a kiss there, and
she turned into him instantly, cupping his jaw and taking his
mouth, sinking her tongue deeply atween his lips and drawing him down to the bed. She kissed him with desperation,
with need and hunger, whimpering against his mouth; and

he let her have command, let her extinguish her fears and grief, for he felt shattered and floating, not recognizing himself, yet solid and grounded, too. The crust of bitterness and anger ripped away, shredded and dried to the winds, for his broken past, *any* pain he suffered was suddenly inconsequential, pathetic and spiteful compared to the harsh life she'd lived in the name of a lost father. And when she softened, spent, her lips moving slower as she shuddered with the residue of her tears, he wisely slid from the bunk, snuggling her into its coverings.

Ran settled on the floor close beside her, brushing red strands from her temple with a gentle touch. Blindly, she reached out and clasped his hand, her eyes opening briefly.

"Do you think he will like me?"

It scared him; the eyes devoid of life, her voice painfully hopeful.

"Aye, little pest. He will love you."

An hour later he called for Shokai to sit with her, explaining what he knew and how he'd found her. Shokai didn't seem to be surprised by her turmoil, and his lack of sympathy for Aurora's plight infuriated Ran. It made him wonder exactly how convenient it was that Shokai happened to be so close when Aurora was attacked by thieves.

. . . .

Chapter Twenty-Three

The ship was silent but for the hush of water along her hull, a lonely whistle command, or the hiss of midnight wind through a damaged sail as the *Red Lion* chased her freedom.

Below decks, bare chested and barefoot, Ran stared at the jagged line of light radiating from a crack in the cabin door. She was awake and his hand shifted at his side, marking his indecision to rap. He hadn't spoken to her since she'd cried in his arms, catching only brief glimpses of her otherwise, and he found himself searching areas of the massive ship he rarely ventured, making silent excuses for being in the galley or outside her cabin, worrying that her nightmares tormented her. Her humming came to him, soothing and soft, and he exhaled deeply, leaning back against the wall.

It had taken him half the night to garner the will to venture this close, and still he hesitated. God's blood, he was a mess, he thought, raking his fingers through his hair. Turned wrong side out by a slip of a lass, and his tangled emotions destroying the visage he needed to maintain discipline and order with his crew. Doubling his effort to conceal them made him feel like a fraud. Yet, as he missed her teasing humor and bold talk or the scent of warm ginger always lingering about her, he knew 'twas unwise to fool with his good fortune.

He had, after all, confessed to murder.

And she'd begged off; out of budding fear or relenting to his repeated insistence that they had no future, he couldn't be uncertain, and though Ran watched her occasionally move from spot to spot on his ship, he realized she skirted *only him.* The privacy of his cabin did not bring him peace either, for she haunted him there as well. 'Twere small things, almost inconsequential and unnoticeable at first; warmed water in his pitchers when he went to shave; meals of poached fish instead of salted pork or beef; a bath prepared when he came off his watch, the steaming water lightly scented with sandalwood. Or the piping hot cup of tea laced with citrus and mint on his desk, as if she'd just left it.

He seemed to be a step or two ahead or behind her. But never in synch.

And he knew she meant it to be thus.

And he decided tonight, he did not like it.

Raising his fist to knock, Ran stilled at a soft shuffling sound, turning.

"Sahib?" Dahrein yawned, sleepy-eyed and looking every speck the motherless boy. "May I be of assistan—" He focused on his captain, the door, then the man again. He frowned, more like a protective brother than an untried lad, and Ran lowered his arm, feeling the silent rebuke as if he'd been caught with his breeches about his ankles. "You should not disturb mem sahib," the young Indian had the rocks to tell him. *"You* upset her karma."

Ran's biting look warned him off, and Dahrein's color heightened afore he pecked a bow and backed away, muttering something about adults and their childish ways.

Ran tilted his head back, staring at the knotted ceiling. Grievin' mothers. What was he doing here? He was mangled inside, not comprehending a pittance of what he was feeling. All he could pluck clear was that without her nearness he felt empty and cheated and alone, and it stood like a fortess of hope against the lessons of his past and years of emotional decay. All that seemed petty and meaningless after the harsh life she'd suffered, what he'd put her though in the name of his oaths; and his only concern for the past days now was Aurora—what she was thinking, feeling? Was she comfortable, unhappy? Did she fear him now, or had she, as he'd claimed he wanted, dismissed him from her mind and heart?

A sharp pain lanced through his chest at his last thought and he straightened, gazing once more at the fracture of light.

"Bloody damn," he muttered, afore heading back toward his cabin.

Aurora listened to the footsteps recede, restless and anxious to call him back. Restraint was not one of her finer qualities, her past encounters with danger proving she often rushed headlong into trouble without thinking clearly. And avoiding Ransom was like avoiding nourishment, for she grew weaker by the day. Och, 'twas odd this, missing him when they were ofttimes not but feet away. But 'twas as he wished. Closing her eyes, she waited for the fierce urge to pass, and without pause, her last image of him filled her mind; standing topside, the breeze fingering the length of dark chestnut hair grazing his shoulders, his booted foot braced on a crate as he surveyed the sea as if 'twould give him the answers he sought. He was power; contained strength screaming from every pore of his tall muscled form. He needn't wear the array of knives and flintlocks consistently jammed in his wide belt, for without, Ransom was threatening. It showed in the manner he carried himself, aloof, unapproachable, in command.

But Aurora was not fooled. Beneath the leather jerkin laced snugly across his chest lay the bruised soul of a man crying out to be loved, unconditionally.

And she did love him.

The true depth of her feelings hit her the moment he insisted she be put ashore.

And the realization of his came when he'd called her back.

Though he insisted he could not have her in his life, his private struggle was no longer submerged. It marked his features each time he looked at her, the weakness she represented, his jaded trust; and in those amber eyes she caught a brief glimpse of the young prince of English society, gambling, carousing with his peers, boasting of his prowess with the ladies, then cast aside because of his *father's* sins. And her heart broke for him, for the part of Ransom that died that day. How crushed he must have been, humiliated and angry. And who had been there for him? Who had listened to his pain, held him when he wanted to destroy his surroundings?

Who had loved him when he realized he'd killed an innocent man?

Obviously neither mother nor father were there for him, or mayhaps he would not be harnessing so much bitterness. 'Twas an accident of circumstance, beyond his control, Aurora decided, yet the scar was deep and still festered.

And he didn't want to heal. Not yet.

When he did, when he trusted her not to abandon him, he would know he could come to her. Wherever she was then, she thought, then forced her attention to the indigo fabric spread across her lap. The bolt of rich Egyptian cotton was on the bunk when she woke this morn, and with Dahrein's help, she'd cut and fit the fabric for a simple dress. She cared naught for fancy clothes, for she'd never had more than a dress or two in her possession, but Ransom had given her this fabric and the gift of it was more precious than if he'd whispered the emotions locked in his heart.

She had to believe 'twas so.

Or this heartache was for naught.

Ran leaned against the door frame of his cabin, arms folded across his chest as Aurora negotiated the corridor. His position was relaxed and negligent, yet his blood rushed at forty knots, his senses singing with her vibrance.

"Are you afraid of me now, lass?" He hoped there was the right amount of dare in his tone.

She stopped, bracing one hand on her hip, a cloth-covered tray on the other as she turned. Aurora felt trapped, the corridor shrinking around her, her heart pounding wildly, for she recognized the smoldering heat in his eyes.

'Twas a danger just looking at him; he robbed her of all thought save one—how madly she loved him. 'Twas *her* weakness, she thought, sketching the noble features she saw in her dreams, aching to feel the warmth of his work-roughened hands caressing her body. But he simply stared, unmoving.

It made her restless.

"You would never harm me, Ransom," she said with a tilt of her head, realizing he'd sought her out.

"Yet for days you've avoided so much as looking my way." Always occupied in the company of Shokai or Dahrein or grouped with attentive crewmen, he gnashed, but never alone.

" 'Tis a bit ashamed I am, that you found me," she glanced at the deck, "wailing like a babe."

"Your tears were deserved," he said sympathetically and her gaze flew to his.

"Dinna hand me pity, Ransom," she said briskly. "For I dinna want it."

"Nor I yours," he countered, always surprised by her flashes of temper.

"Good. Pity is for those who canna help themselves."

His brows rose, her challenge lying atween them and ten years of suppression rushed to a dangerous boil. He could feel it driving up his spine, and this wild Highland sprite could draw it to a reckless spill in one finely worded sentence, or with one long thorough look. The ones he craved, the bold sultry stares that bespoke her pleasure and want and the patience she exerted to have it.

She may have avoided him, but her eyes gave her away. Aurora Lassiter could not lie. The capability was not within her. Nor did she play games, and each time she met his gaze Ransom saw a spark of a faint dream he once harbored and wished he had the strength to pursue—or walk away.

It was a choice he couldn't make.

Slowly, he pushed off from the doorway, advancing til she had to crane her neck to look up at him. Unwaveringly she stared back. He didn't touch her, his eyes churning with a dark golden fire, and Aurora wanted to leap on him, wrap her every limb around his big body and hold him until the tender ache crowding her chest was soothed. *When will you let me love you?* her heart cried. Excitement tugged at her nerves, patience pulled it snugly back. And still he stared, his breath quickening. Her tongue darted out to moisten her lips and his eyes flared. It was a predatory look, a hunter on the prowl. Thirsting, ravenous.

"Aye?" she said expectantly.

How could she be so composed when he felt like torn sails twisting above decks! "Who do you cater to?" he asked, nodding to the tray, though he cared not.

"The bosun, Connor Lockewood. He is below."

"Lockewood is always below decks." By God, he wanted to kiss that cool look off her face. "Unless in the company of Lougière. Most times the pair are inseparable."

" 'Tis good to have a friend like that," she managed when he was staring at her with such unbridled heat and hunger she could hardly push the words out her mouth. "Though I've never met the bosun."

"He's a quiet old chap," Ran said.

" 'Tis best I go," she muttered, yet didn't move.

"Aye." And neither did he.

"Ransom?"

A sable brow arched and the damp air crackled atween them.

"Dinna be lookin' at me like that."

"And what way is that?" His expression didn't alter a fraction, his gaze holding her prisoner.

"That if I'd no meal in me hands you'd toss up me skirts and have at me like a rutting buck."

He grinned, a flash of white teeth, the image she presented making him hard. "Is that so?" came out strained.

"And dinna think I'd mind, either," she said unblinkingly, and he groaned, bending closer. She watched his mouth draw near, unconsciously wetting her lips. "But we want different futures." Closer. "You've made it clear I dinna fit into yours, and I am not a stupid lass." Her voice lowered, a lover's brazen plea. "A wise woman doesna stay," closer, "and taunt a wild creature," her fingers capped his lips, "but she flees." Her brow arched. "Neh?"

"Have you not heard," he said against her fingers, "of soothing the savage—"

Someone cleared his throat, and Ran drew back, cursing the interruption. Aurora held his gaze for a fraction, then immediately twisted away, moving quickly to where Lougière filled the companionway, Lockewood behind him. She slowed her step, gathering her composure and staring beyond the quartermaster, her brows scrunching tight. Without realizing it, she offered Lockewood the tray. He took it, met her gaze briefly, then turned back down the corridor.

"Don't mind Connor, lass," Lougière said, limping toward her. "I think staying in the for'c'sle with naught but his own company makes him skittish."

Aurora nodded, rubbing the chill from her arms, never feeling this way afore. She couldn't pinpoint the sensation . . . cold, dark with rage? Or remorse? Or was it hatred? How many men on this ship carry secrets, she wondered, looking at Lougière. Both men were older than Ransom, gray haired, though Lougière's locks were liberally laced with the honey blond of his youth. He was congenial, quick witted and an incorrigible flirt. But she strongly sensed 'twas a mask, and natural curiosity made her accept his offer to escort her into the sunshine, but when they turned toward Ransom, Aurora did not mistake the jealousy in his eyes, the muscle flexing in his jaw. It pierced her like a blade, for she wanted naught but to stroll on his arm, lie within the strong circle and love him the way he deserved.

Yet Ransom Montegomery could not be coaxed or cajoled from the cloak of his past, and certainly not into falling in love.

Nay, certainly not.

Chapter Twenty-Four

The shout from the crow's nest sent men scurrying, yet their captain remained impassive, standing on the poop deck, the spyglass to his eye.

Land.

They'd made excellent time considering the destruction the *Lion* had suffered, yet Ran was not anticipating this moment. Even less so when Aurora burst onto the deck, shielding her eyes to gaze out onto the sea. Her blue gown puffed in the breeze, looking nearly black in the waning light, her unbound hair whipping about her skirts; and a tightness pulled in Ran's chest. He hadn't been this close to her since the moment in the companionway two days ago.

And she would dice him to ribbons over this.

She rose up on her bare toes at the rail, and Ran knew she could see naught in the coming twilight and moved to stand beside her. It was a moment afore she looked up at him. The impact of her stare drove through him like a sword to paper, severing and smooth.

" 'Tis true, then? Land?" Disappointed, then hopeful.

"Aye."

"But where?" She scanned the horizon in all directions, and he almost smiled. Almost. He held out the spyglass, gesturing for her to give it a go, and she accepted, focusing.

"Och, 'tis but a speck." And the sight of it tripped a wrenching in her chest. Land meant their parting was near.

"And will remain so til morn."

She lowered the glass, squinting in the distance as she handed it back.

"So we will sail past?" she assumed in a low voice, toying with her amulet.

"Nay, lass, we are heading to it," he said, and saw her stiffen.

Cheese and crust! She hadn't expected them to limp into port so soon! Not with the British chewing up the sea to find them. But she trusted Ran's instincts and knew there was reason behind going ashore now. Ashore. Blast. How she'd hoped that with time—

"Does this land have a name?"

"Sanctuary." A pause and then, " 'Tis my home, Aurora."

Her head snapped to the side, blue eyes wide with surprise. "Home?" She glanced around, the brief sweep of her gaze telling him she'd thought the *Lion* his only residence. "You have a *real* home?"

Real. Ran wouldn't know. 'Twas a house with occupants, naught else. But 'twas the way she said the single word, with awe and envy, harboring a wealth of longing, that made his heart cave in. Would she like it? he suddenly wondered. Would she find it austere and bleak?

"Aye," he finally answered, gazing into her liquid blue eyes and feeling them swallow him whole. " 'Tis protected by a reef and has but one path inland to the coves. We'll not make shore afore dark and must anchor and wait til sunrise."

One night, she thought, nearly choking on the knot swelling in her throat. One night and she would be parted from him. 'Twas as he wished. "I see." She lowered her eyes to the open vee of his shirt, then turned away.

Ran frowned, catching her arm. "Aurora? What ails you?"

"Naught, naught." She kept her head bowed, having little left but her dignity and determined not to make herself a fool when he'd not asked her to come with him. His home. He was going home, to friends, a haven of rest; and she would continue with her search. Och, dinna be feelin' sorry fer yerself now, lassie, she scolded silently. Yet it clawed at her heart to know there was no room in his life for her. 'Twas a foe she could not fight.

"Look at me, pest."

She wouldn't, the private name jerking the ties to her composure. " 'Tis pleased, I am, for I can search again for me father," she said, pulling free and running to the hatch. Ran started after her, then halted, his shoulders drooping.

"Why did you not tell her?" Domingo said from his side, and when Ran looked up he realized more than one crewman had overheard the conversation, Shokai included, the old man scowling at him like black thunder.

"And speak what, Dom?" came in a low hiss. "That after nine years of searching I have taken her to a place where she will never find her father? Marooning her on an island with no chance of freedom for weeks?" He shook his head, mashing a hand over his face, then plowing his fingers through his hair. The unhappiness she tried to hide dropped his heart to his knees. After all the occasions when he'd pushed her off, spouting his inability to commit to her or to alter his obligations for her, now he was doing just that. They would be miserable. She would be furious and hurt that he'd kept his plans from her, plans that would stagnate her life again because of his mistakes, his oaths. His need to protect her.

Yet she had to remain with him, for Ran suspected that to set her on *any* shore would find her dead within days.

Though she would not believe it if he insisted upon the matter, he was certain someone played a deft hand in her misfortunes. And the culprit lingered close enough to Ran or one of his crew to put her in his path in the past months. Aye, Foti could have betrayed them to the British, and even Aurora to the slavers after that fiasco in the dingy inn, but that did not explain how anyone had known her exact whereabouts after returning from Rahman's camp, or why she was separated from the other women aboard the *Black Star*. None of it detracted from the fact that they—whoever they be—had killed Castille and nearly slain Lougière to have her.

Who harbored enough vengeance to want her out of the

Maghreb that badly? And why? For the woman would never knowingly harm another living creature. Ran considered that Shokai might have been the intended target. Or mayhaps her attacker assumed she'd no one who cared if she disappeared from the face of the earth? The thought made his knees weak. What could she possibly know or have done that would warrant such foul retribution?

"I think you have underestimated the lady, Ran," Domingo said, breaking into his thoughts. "After a fortnight at sea with you, she might welcome the rest."

Ran did not see the humor in the jest and his glacial look bespoke his lack. "Perhaps she'll vanish into the jungle as you wish," Domingo needled, popping nuts into his mouth in regular tempo. "It is a large island."

"Get you to hell, Dom," Ran rasped, staring at the uncharted isle. Sanctuary. At least three hundred souls called it home, and that did not include the natives or the wild creatures noising up the nights. But Ran had never considered it a home in the way Aurora referred to it, for he found little peace even here. Which was why he spent a goodly part of his life at sea. The stone and wood structure represented a permanence he could not attain, not if he pursued his way of life. He would like, he realized, for it to be different.

Yet he'd sooner perish than put her back in harm's way for the sake of his oaths. For the utter disappointment he saw in her eyes then was too agonizing to witness again.

"Send two longboats ashore to prepare for our arrival."

Domingo nodded, then said, "Shall I inform Sayidda you'll be having a guest?"

"Tell her what you will, Avilar," he growled. "I care not."

Ran left the deck, descending into the passageway to his cabin, the slam of its door ringing throughout the ship.

Night fell quickly, the crew's relief after the dangerous voyage and their impatience to be home coming out in incessant chatter and music, the jaunty notes of flutes and mouth harps filling the warm evening. The *Lion* rocked in calm waters like a child's cradle, a gentle breeze kicking at the sheer netting surrounding the great canopy bed where

Ran lay atop a coverlet, hands clasped beneath his head. Sleep escaped him. His mind would not be still, darting from what Aurora must be feeling to the tasks he'd left undone, to how Mistress Ortiz had fared. And what Sayidda would have to say when she saw Aurora.

Every moment spent with her scattered like cracked chips of ice, clear, sharp, then melting into another: finding her trapped and chained, her fearless walk to save Shokai, their soul-wrenching kiss in the blackened alley, the disappointment in her eyes when she thought him a slaver, and her quick acceptance when he asked her to trust him.

His lips quirked as he recalled her blatant and frequent acknowledgment of his arousal and her part in it, then thinned, her fury over Shokai's sickly condition overshadowing the image. She never ceased to surprise him, he thought, though finding her naked in his cabin gave new meaning to granting secret wishes.

Pictures darted through his mind, smiles and sultry looks. Aurora, unfettered and brazen, massaging his temples and scrubbing his back. Aurora, sharing his apple and kissing him into madness, shoeless and full-breasted and luxuriously erotic. Aurora, speaking spells over flowers and herbs and a dying young man who'd wanted naught but her death and then begged for her help. And she gave it. Like her compassion and her forgiveness and her desire, she offered all that she was without hesitation. She hadn't asked for his help, his company, nor to be kept aboard, never demanded so much as a meal or clothing or special considerations from him. Naught but his heart, he thought dismally. Naught but to give her all he kept locked away.

Give.

'Twas like cutting away his skin.

Ahhh, but I ache for her, he admitted silently, craving her tender loving, now, afore the realities of his world came crashing in. God above, he was tired, of clinging to his past, of denying his feelings for her. And he wanted to experience her; the vibrance of her personality, her nurturing spirit, the incredibly sensual grace of her body. Her presence coveted his every move, his thoughts and he remembered the guilt and hopelessness swamping him when she'd disappeared from the inn, the ripping agony that stayed locked in his gut, eating away, unrelieved til she gazed up at him from the belly of the slaver.

She cried for a murdered mother, hoped she'd please a wayward father, and . . . desired a bastard pirate with naught to offer but a bitter soul and a few tattered pledges.

And he'd pushed her away when he wanted to claim her for his own.

His own.

A faint, tinny sound shattered his thoughts and he listened harder and the flex of a sad melody leadened the air in his lungs.

Sweet Jesus.

The pipes.

He lurched from the bed, tearing the netting in his haste to get to the door. Yanking it open, he grabbed hold of a passing sailor.

"Tell the bastard to cease the bloody piping! Now!" he snarled, then thrust the terrified man aside and headed toward Domingo's cabin. Rapid footsteps thumped the coarse deck and he saw her an instant afore she slammed into him.

"Oh, Ransom," came in a tiny wretched croak. "Hold me." Whispered and frightened.

" 'Tis all right, pest." He swept her up his arms. "I am here."

She hugged his neck, burying her face in his throat and using her arms to shield her ears as he stepped into his cabin and closed the door. He held her snugly, warmly, pressing his lips to her forehead, and he felt as if his entire world lay trembling in his arms.

"Ah, pest," he soothed against her hair. Her breathing was unnaturally rapid, brisking with every note til the piping was abruptly cut short. " 'Tis but old dreams haunting you."

She nodded, gasped for air, clinging to him, and he felt a brittleness in her, an urgency he couldn't touch. He released her legs and she tilted her head back.

Tears, filling her wide eyes, spilling down her smooth cheeks. And her silence twisted like broken glass in his chest. He wanted to hide her away where naught could hurt her. He looked down at her and knew she would not leave his arms tonight, knew his resistance was spent. She was the only one who mattered. He swallowed repeatedly, stricken.

He'd not keep his vow this night.

'Twill make you stronger.

The realization staggered his breathing. His composure chipped away, crashing into nothingness.

"Aurora." Hushed, yielding.

"I need you, Ransom. I do," she choked on a whisper, her hands at his neck driving up into the fullness of his hair, rough and impatient, desperation riding for she'd have but this one night to love him. And she would steal it like a banished thief, seeking the crack, the tiny spot that might give her back the man she loved more than life. She urged him closer.

"Come to me this one night. Don't push me away," she tumbled against his lips and he claimed the words, darkly, fiercely, his thick arms enveloping her, his knee insinuating atween her thighs. Aurora bore down, whimpering softly as she licked the sharp line of his lips, tugging erotically afore pushing her tongue inside. He tasted like Cognac and winter, and his arms tightened, hands driving beneath the borrowed shirt and dragging her up the hard length of his muscled thigh. She rocked against him, warm and anxious to have him there, and Ran trembled, answered the motion, his groin thick and pulsing, a groan of fiery pleasure and acquiescence rumbling in his chest as he advanced toward the bed.

Ran knew he'd regret this, knew 'twould bring them pain, but aught else had the strength to keep him from her. 'Twas Aurora he'd break his vow for. Aurora he ached to pleasure and give to and adore. A sequestered part of him erupted like a creature long buried beneath the earth, sensation rushing through his veins, pure, unharnessed, without bitterness, without regret.

He couldn't wait to set it free.

A thin shirt separated her plush skin from him, the buttons haphazardly done, and the force of his kiss drove her back over his arm as he tore at the closures. She moaned delightedly as he swept the fabric from her body, and she threw her head back, naked and lusciously female as he smoothed a hand down her chest, across her breast, cupping the plump flesh as he lowered his head. His lips closed over her rosy nipple, drawing it into the wet suck of his mouth and she gasped, heat gathering, blistering through her with every liquid sweep of his sandy-rough tongue, and she clawed at his shoulders, aroused and hungry and moist for him as he bent a knee to his bed.

Ran held her there, suspended, straddling his thigh, savoring the luxury of her skin beneath his lips, the scent of her excitement as her fingers liquidly circled his nipples, splayed and molded, one hand riding down his stomach, sliding atween his thighs.

He flinched, meeting her gaze. Somewhere, a hatch slammed.

His arm tightened about her hips.

Breaths mingled, carnal and damp.

She shaped his erection, slowly, firmly, womanly pleased and earthy.

"Give me this power," she panted against his lips, thumbing open the buttons of his breeches. Ran swallowed, his breathing rapid. The taut tips of her breasts rubbed his chest as she spread the fabric, freeing him. There was no hesitation in her, no fear, only desire, only her crystal blue gaze holding his as she wrapped her fingers around his erection. His heavy groan vibrated through the cabin, his mouth crushing hers savagely, his tongue plunging, and her hair spilled across the sheets like blackberry wine as he eased her to the bed. He held himself above her, his great body shaking with the rushing power of his desire, but she groped at his rib cage, pulling.

"Nay," he breathed against her lips. "I will crush you."

"Then crush me, m'lord," she panted, peeling his breeches down. "For I need to feel your weight upon me."

mall hands slid around to mold his buttocks, hastening
im atween the spread of her thighs.

"Ransom." An anxious breath. She could feel the luring
eat of his sex, rampant against her thigh, and she pulsed.

"Nay, lass, slower." He kicked free of his breeches, his
air brushing her cheek.

"I canna." She squirmed, reaching atween them, her
and wrapping around his arousal. Ran bucked, sucked air
ito his lungs, stone hard and stretching in her palm. He was
olid and smooth and vulnerable, and she molded him,
avishly, intimately, guiding him atween her thighs. "Come
ito me, Ransom," she breathed against his lips. "Fill me
ith your magick."

"Oh, grievin' mothers, Aurora!" He wasn't going to
nake it. Too long he'd waited, been tempted. The tip of him
ntered her wet center. His eyes flared hotly. His every
nuscle was tense and flexing wildly. He swallowed, amber
ools smoldering over the woman stripped bare and open
eneath him.

Raw. Brazen. Incredibly loving.

He pushed. Her breath shuddered. Eyes locked. He shiv-
red violently, the unbelievable tightness of her daring his
omposure. A breeze stirred the netting. She arched, press-
ng him deeper, bending her knee.

"Cease. Oh, God, cease!" he gasped for air, catching her
troking hands, threading his fingers with hers and slowly
lrawing her arms above her head, spread wide. He locked
is arms. "Look at me, love," he whispered and her gaze
lew to his, her heart in her eyes. By God, she was exquisite.
\nd Ran struggled for control, wanting so badly to be all
he desired, yet needing to love her like this, for if she
ouched him, he'd be destroyed. It had been too long, he
hought, his need driving him to near violence. He sank a
raction further, retreated, smoothly, loving her with his
eart, his body, over and over, deeper, her body stretching,
vet and burning, gripping his thickness. More, she wanted.
More she took, her legs wrapping his hips, the sharp tug
orcing him fully inside her.

"Aurora," he moaned, squeezing his eyes shut, missing

the pain streaking across her features. He withdrew, plung
ing again. And again.

Bronze marble against creamy alabaster.

Slick, supple, buffeting joy and promise.

And Ran watched, drowning in her, in the musky scent
and luxurious feel of her holding and releasing him, the way
her hips rose to meet him, the darkening of her eyes, and the
seriousness of her look as years of celibacy crashed over him
in torturous waves. He shoved and her legs clutched him
demanding he hold naught from her. He stroked her flesh
and she whispered encouragement, how she'd longed for
this moment, how glorious he felt moving inside her, hard
and heavy and gentle.

And she stretched beneath him, bone-gripping heat
sweeping roughly through her like warm red wine. Her
blood sang with the intense power of him, the tenderness of
this mighty giant as her body drew tighter and tighter, the
sweet threat of ecstasy clenching her muscles.

Her fingers tightened, her feminine muscles flexed, and he
slammed into her, regretting his harshness yet unable to
contain his passion. It climbed through him like a raging
animal, pounding the blood in his ears, and he pushed and
pushed and she accepted and Ran threw his head back, his
sable mane fanning his shoulders as he growled low, a dark
roar of primal release, his huge body quaking with liquid-
hot tremors, the savage burn of his climax grinding through
his body, erupting and flowing into hers.

And he watched her follow him, biting her lip as he
withdrew, the slick glove of her calling him back, and he
plunged, her pleasure spreading across her features, sharpening, then softening her beauty. Her lips parted, a ragged
burst spilling, and he captured the womanly sound, sliding
his tongue atween her soft lips and drinking in the rich
magic of Aurora.

Chapter Twenty-Five

Harsh breaths filled the cabin. The ship lolled on the crest of a wave, then settled as Ransom sank his weight onto her, slowly, quaking still, his kiss gentling as he released her hands. His arms slid weakly around her, and he buried his face in the river of hair. And Aurora smiled against the dampness of his shoulder, the warmth and tremors of fulfillment still ripening through her body. She blinked back sudden tears. Ahh, *Lord* and *Lady,* such a gift you've given me. She pressed her lips to the curve of his throat as her calf slid luxuriously over the slope of his buttocks.

He made a pleased sound, dark and lusty, breathing hard.

"You sound a wee bit winded for a man your age, Ransom."

His shoulders shook and he turned his head, giving her a one-eyed stare. "Give me time, love." He rose to his elbows, toying with streamers of black hair, looking shy and boyish for such a seasoned man. "I've not done such in ten years."

Her eyes widened, her fingers plowing his sable hair back as she searched his features. 'Twas a vow he'd broken, sworn in defiance of his father's roguish ways, she realized, and the impact of his restraint and sacrifice drenched her lonely soul.

She smiled beautifully, saucily, curling her finger around his ear, tugging at the gold loop piercing his lobe. "Och, a virgin, are you now, Ransom?"

"Hardly." His brow arched cynically, yet he rubbed his cheek against her palm, her feathery touch banishing the flare of bitterness. 'Twas her own magic, he thought, and something akin to fear flickered in her eyes, a spark quickly smothered afore he shifted to his side, taking her with, still rock hard and snug inside her and damned unwilling to relinquish the pleasure. Yet her sudden fascination with shaping the carved bulge of his chest made Ran frown and he ducked his head, seeking her soft mouth and nudging her with insistent kisses to look him in the eye.

" 'Tis a wee bit of time you've waited for me, then?" The conviction in her voice left his pride in shambles, her teasing fingers stirring the embers of desire.

"Aye, little pest," he murmured in a tight voice, willing to do aught to keep the loving look in her eyes. "A wee bit." He draped her leg across his hip, his hand fanning up the lush flare, gliding to her breast. His thumb brushed her nipple and she covered his hand.

"Well, it appears, my giant," she drew her hips back, his arousal firming with amazing speed, " 'twill take more than once to appease the beast denied. And, och," she breathed, pushing against him. "you'd best be about it."

"Sweet mercy, Aurora!" Strained, half laughing, half pained.

"Fatigued, m'lord?" she challenged tartly with another push.

Suddenly he rolled to his back, taking her with him. "Aye, spent like an old cannon." A smile ghosted across his lips as he shifted back against the carved headboard.

He made no move to touch her, and a tiny frown knitted her brows. "You've that look about you," she said with a wary glance, pushing herself off his chest, straddling his hips. Her eyes widened, a gasp sucked into her lungs. "God of Thunder!"

He chuckled, gave a nudge; and she slapped her arms around his neck, capturing his lips in a soul-stripping kiss, her tongue lazily outlining his lips, scoring his teeth afore sinking inside.

"Aurora," he murmured into her mouth, gripping her hips and giving them motion.

"Aye, aye, give me the beast."

And the hunger came, intense and molten, the craving for more than the hot gush of excitement, but the feeling that she was loved by him, in this life, on this earth and not in her dreams. One night. One night to covet over and over, and she felt wicked and beautiful, staring into his dark eyes as she rode the staff of his flesh, hard and unyielding. Here he was free. Here in her arms he lost the darkness, the heaviness of his past.

"Bring us there again, my heart." And his soul broke open, filling with her essence as he filled her body. My heart. My heart. Oh God. If she could only love him after . . .

His broad hands charged insistently over her body, kneading her buttocks and thighs and breasts as she rocked, swift and wet and untamed; and Ran loved her, loved her eagerness and lack of inhibition, her fingers combing through his hair, her shapely body draped over him like hot satin, luxurious and wanton.

He held her hips, his thumbs meeting over the center of her sex. He rubbed and she slammed wildly against him, clinging, coaxing, her damp body jerking and flinching with the sharpness of her passion. Her legs clamped, her womanhood clutched him, and he shuddered in her arms, his climax flexing through him with stinging spasms. He thrust upward and she cried out, a ragged moan, leaning back, grinding hip to hip, hair sweeping his thighs, and Ran caught fistfuls, driving his hands up her back to hold her head and devouring the untamed gush of her desire with the ferocity of a starving man.

They remained locked, limbs intimately entwined, breathing hushed and quick, and when dawn dared break over Sanctuary, Ransom was still loving Aurora.

Ran opened his eyes to find her propped on her side, her head in her palm, staring at him.

"You look the babe when you sleep," she said softly.

His gaze caressed the length of her nakedness. "You, madame, do not." Pleased and rough with sleep. Dawn was just coloring the sky a deep magenta.

" 'Tis well since you had your way with me so shamelessly." Saucy, grinning, her gaze parading down his bronze body. " 'Tis a fine appetite the beast has."

He rolled toward her, wrapping his arm around her and dragging her against him. Her breasts were cool pressed to his dark skin.

He kissed her leisurely and she wiggled closer, smelling of ginger and mint, and he adored the rosiness of his loving blushing her skin. And then he saw the stain upon his sheets.

His gaze flicked atween the blood and her eyes. "Aurora." Accusing, humbled. "What have you done, lass?" He was shamed by all the unkind things he'd assumed about her.

"Dinna be angry, Ransom," she said as if he'd no reason to be upset she was pure afore this night. "I'd naught else in this life but to give you the only prize I could."

Angry? He swallowed thickly, his voice a crowded whisper. "But 'tis a husband's gift." And he was bloody unworthy of it.

She shook her head, slowly. " 'Twas mine," she whispered, her fingers fanning his lips, holding back his words. "I gave to the man who crossed a desert to rescue me from the Bedouin. The one who searched for me lavender and shared his apple and his books and swam atween a war to take me back." Her smile slowly returned, mischievous and kittenish, wiping away his brooding scowl. "And a fine job you did at the wrappin', m'lord."

Abruptly he pressed her to her back, his big body sinking her into the feather mattress. "Sweet saints, Aurora," he said with wonder. "You are the most brazen virgin I've ever known."

She punched his ribs. "Like you've had many, you big ox."

He nudged her legs apart. "Ox, am I?"

"Aye, and— Ochaii!" She laughed as he thrust into her dewy softness, strong and solid. "The beast is restless, I feel."

"Aye, hungry." He left her fully and plunged again.

"Roarin', thinks I," she gasped, and his pace quickened

inside her. "Oh, Ransom, my heart, aye, aye. Love me awake."

Ran fastened his breeches. "Come from the bed, love, and be dressed." He dropped the freshly pressed gown across a chair, effectively keeping his distance from the temptation of her.

"Nay, thinks I." She stretched languidly, a willowy twist of slender limbs.

"Aye, says me," he countered, smiling.

"Uh-ah." She tossed the sheet aside, revealing her supple splendor.

"Aurora." Tight and dry, his amber gaze moving thirstily over bare skin.

"I dinna wish it." Pouty, sensual, her fingertips skimming atween the fullness of her breasts, the indentation of her waist, the soft plain of her belly.

He went rock-still. "By God, woman, I am not a saint!"

She crawled across the bed, catlike, slow, unruffled. "I know." She sat back on her calves, her legs tightly closed, yards of sleep-mussed hair clouding her body.

Ransom grew harder by the second.

And she knew it.

"You are taunting me a'purpose." He advanced slowly toward the bed, a look of sensual retribution in his eyes.

"Aye."

"Have you no shame a'tall?" he asked, gazing down at her from the bedside.

She looked confused for an instant. "Shame comes when you regret behavior." Her voice lowered to a throaty purr, driving him mad with desire. " 'Tis a magick we make, Ransom, and I dinna regret the spell."

He reached out and with a squeal of laughter she streaked across the bed, but he was quick for all his bulk and caught her about the waist, slamming the breath from her and kissing her savagely.

"Once more," she breathed into his mouth, freeing his

arousal from its confines, and he growled lustily, pushing
her onto the bed and burying himself deeply within her.

Their loving was raw and primal, bordering on violent,
each clinging desperately to the fracture of happiness they'd
found within the Lion's den.

Aurora stepped on deck, unnoticed for a moment. 'Twas
long enough to gather her composure. She'd delayed this,
bathing, tidying the cabin, luring Ransom into her arms.
'Twas where she wanted to live, but they were approaching
land. Their parting was inevitable. And she needed to find
her father, for 'twould be her only consolation to living
without her lusty pirate.

A lump swelled in her throat and she swallowed, plaster-
ing a smile on her face when her presence created attention.
She felt like a fraud.

Her stomach churned, more from the potion she'd ingested to prevent conception, understanding 'twas the sole
reason he'd kept his celibate vow.

He wanted no bastards with his name.

Repeating his father's mistakes would destroy Ransom,
and she would never hurt him like that. No matter the cost
to her heart.

But then she saw him.

He took her breath away, the midnight hours of their
loving spreading over her like the warm sensual cloud of
memory as he advanced, booted feet thumping. His massive
torso was tightly wrapped in the long leather vest he fre-
quently wore, the wide lion-crested belt circling his waist,
and to look upon him made her heart leap a few beats. She
watched his approach with feminine appreciation, a lover's
eyes taking in the rolling gate of his hips, the indecent length
of his corded legs. The wind spiked his hair as he stopped
afore her, gazing down. There was something different
about him; the secretive way he looked at her, the relaxed
set of his shoulders. He was always reserved, especially
beneath watchful eyes, yet now he seemed genuinely unguarded, almost tranquil.

A spark of hope burst in her chest. Had loving his body truly unfurled his tightly wrapped heart?

"Good morn, Aurora." A low growl, saturated with intimacy.

"Ransom," she acknowledged, breathless, tugging a strand the wind sent across her view. He looked past her to the land and his posture stiffened. "Do you not need to guide her in?"

His gaze dropped back to her, a wolfish grin on his lips. "We will take the tide a moment longer, then aye, I must man the wheel." His hands itched to touch her. "You may sit here." He gestured to a crate lashed to the rail. " 'Tis a magnificent sight."

She shook her head, leaning closer, her eyes taking on a softer sheen. " 'Tis not so pleasant to be seated this morn."

Tender humor and sympathy spread across his features. And the impact of what she'd given him in his bed last night melted through him like warm wax. He had the ridiculous urge to flex his muscles and roar.

"I would bid you kiss me, but I ken you willna afore your crew." She wanted one more, always one more, and refused to spoil the moment with thoughts of life without him.

Suddenly he slid his arm about her waist, her breath catching on surprise, her hands gripping his thick biceps. With two fingers, he tilted her head back, gazing into her eyes afore he captured her mouth in a slow smoldering kiss.

Crewmen cheered. Domingo chuckled. Aurora moaned. And Shokai noisily cleared his throat.

Slowly Ran drew back, adoring her dazed look.

"Were we alone," he murmured. "I would do more than kiss your saucy mouth."

Her smile dared him to make good the promise, and he was about to speak again when the coxswain called for his captain. Ran released her, judged the distance to the island, then spun away, taking several steps afore he halted and glanced back at her. His gaze swept her from head to toe, possessively, lovingly, afore he headed to the damaged quarterdeck.

Shocked at his uncharacteristic behavior, Aurora's gaze

followed him til he manned the wheel; then she faced the
rail. Her small hands gripped the polished wood as they
sailed closer, skirting the submerged reef, seeming to pass a
slate gray cliff sparsely dotted with bursts of green and the
hook-shaped tip of rocky land jutting out into the sea. Then
the *Lion* came sharply about, listing around a break in the
reef line, then heading inland. She caught her breath, her
gaze darting disbelievingly to the dangerously jagged reef
she could see beneath the clear water, to the craggy curving
land, then to the cliff.

Great Goddess. He would sail atween! 'Tis not wide
enough, she thought, fearful, then forced herself to relax.
'Twas Ransom's home, and he knew best what his ship
could do.

The *Red Lion* slipped atween the flat-faced mountain
rising out of the sea on the left and the curving boulder-
cuffed shore like a fat thread through the eye of a needle.
'Twas a narrow passage for a great ship, and she could
almost touch the wet side of the two-hundred-foot cliff as
the *Lion* negotiated the channel, slipping effortlessly into
the basin. The surrounding water was midnight black with
depth, remaining so well into the cove, and she realized why
Ransom chose this approach, this place to build his home.
'Twas nearly invisible from the sea, blocked by the overlap
of the jetty and the cliff.

Then she saw the pirate lair called Sanctuary.

Vibrant green vegetation blanketed the land, lush cloud-
capped mountains spiking the blue sky. Water spewed and
foamed as it hit the jetty, then rippled into the cove like
fluttering white silk across a glass floor. The sand was pink,
she swore, rising from the sea to give birth to a profusion of
plants and vivid flowers. But 'twas the house that caught her
attention. Perched in the center of the mountainside, high
above a village that skirted it like a raveled hem, the two-
story house was grand and pristine white, appearing carved
from the earth, with wood brown archways shaping the
doors and windows, railed porches and balconies stilted on
posts to accommodate the uneven terrain beneath. A
boarded walk led from the sandy shore to a wide path cut

atween the jungle and disappearing beneath the greenery to
emerge again afore the steps fountaining from the home's
porch. The heavy fragrance of wild flowers scented the
warm damp air and Aurora felt engulfed in the activity and
excitement radiating from the tiny city.

And the homes. Hundreds, with gardens and gates and
horses tethered, like the offspring of the white palace, small,
well kept, protected. Even a barracks. And the people,
thrice as many called and waved scraps of material, while
children, och, lovely sun-brown children ran the length of
the shore and back, hopping and dancing and shouting
"Papa." The noise from the ship was no less deafening in its
exuberance, and she glanced back over her shoulder to see
grown men, waving madly, swinging from the rigging, one
or two weeping with joy. A pang trapped in her chest, and
she gathered the love she felt from these people as if gathering fresh pungent blooms.

She returned her gaze to Sanctuary as small boats left the
shore, the dropping anchor rumbling the deck of the *Lion,*
the splash bubbling like a sigh of relief.

She felt Ran standing beside her, hovering and protective,
as men scrambled to let down rope ladders and boats and
greet their families. Nearly twenty ships of various sizes and
shapes littered the lagoon's dark waters.

" 'Tis yours?" Her wide eyes absorbed the happy chaos.
She never imagined Ransom could live in such a lovely
place.

"Only the house, pest." Look at me, he silently begged,
and he thrilled at the pleasure lighting her face.

"Och, Ransom." She elbowed him. "You dinna tell me
you were the pirate *king.*" His sarcastic expression told her
what he thought of her royal ideas.

"I'd heard rumors of this world." The elegant sweep of
her hand indicated the small village. *"Ahmar Asad,"* she
introduced him on a teasing laugh. "Red Lion and his kingdom."

"I command ships, not private lives."

She cast him a side-glance. "Oftimes, one canna escape

the cloak others bestow, Ransom. You are authority and protection to these people, whether you like it or nay."

He didn't comment, but stared at her for a moment longer, recognizing her curiosity. Leaning his forearms on the rail, he watched as men greeted their wives and children, and thought of the families who would have no one returning for the loss of the *Morgan*.

"Society does not want these people, has already turned their backs on them, and they have turned to me and my ways for the chance of a good life once taken by the strong hand of slavers."

" 'Tis all you've set free?" She waved toward the villagers.

He shook his head. "Most are returned to their homes. Those who do not wish it, can remain. We share this land with each other and the natives." There was caution in his tone as he turned and braced his hip against the rail, facing her. "They live in the hills and do not care to be but a small part of Sanctuary, yet do not begrudge us a place to live and work."

"You have gained the wrath of kings and sultans for your thievery of their 'cargo.' " The last came tinted with her disgust.

"Aye," was all Ran said, sinking to her gaze.

" 'Tis a quality in you I admire, Ransom. Your strength of conviction."

"Even when it has caused you pain?"

" 'Tis done." She shrugged minutely. "To dwell there is to live in mistakes. I canna abide such nonsense." 'Twas a warning, subtle and certain, and guilt pressed down on Ransom.

"Sanctuary is an island," he blurted.

"An isl—" She looked at the land, searching for the lie. She'd felt foolish for she'd thought it the Guinea coast, yet she'd never regret giving herself to him, never, yet now she found herself marooned, hundreds of miles from Rabat and her father!

"Why did you not tell me?"

He shrugged, almost boyishly. "I could not speak the words," he rushed to say, "for I've kept you from your search, taking you aboard and now, because of my problems," he inclined his head to the damaged ship, " 'twill be weeks afore I can allow a ship to leave."

With the heel of her hand she thumped his forehead. " 'Tis been over nine years in delay, a few weeks wouldna be so long a wait." He blinked, a flush creeping up his neck. "For a learned man you act the nitwit far too often," she said quietly, and his shoulders sagged. How much more would she forgive?

"Mem sahib. Mem sahib!" Aurora twisted around, and Ran watched her face brighten as Dahrein skidded to a halt afore her.

"A wee excited, are you now?" She grabbed his shoulders when he continued to hop from foot to foot.

"Oh, mem sahib, wait til you sample Léonie's cooking. I am most sick of tasteless food." Aurora exchanged a grin with Ran. How like a youth to think with his stomach. "You will love our island. It is most clean and cool and . . . and, I will show you everything," he said with feeling.

Aurora did not gainsay him. "Then we best be off afore you pop out of your skin," she said on a laugh, grabbing up her sack and accepting his escort to the rail.

Ran folded his arms over his chest, observing with pride how she calmed the lad, then made him feel the man, allowing his solicitation when every soul aboard knew she could scale the hull like a cat. She descended, her gaze briefly catching his afore she vanished from sight.

He frowned, peering over the rail, his heart suddenly pounding harder in his chest. He didn't mistake the sadness in her expression, and he felt as if she'd severed herself from him in the single glance. It made him uneasy.

Shokai moved silently to the rail, hands planted on narrow hips as he glared at the long drop with his usual distaste; then he lowered his ancient body over the ledge muttering, "Steal money you're a thief. Steal a country, you're a king."

Ran's lips twitched and after he'd posted a watch in the crow and made schedules to remove the stores, he too, joined the flotilla of longboats rowing atween shore and ship.

Aurora was already disembarking, Shokai behind her.

"Ran?" Domingo gestured with a frown, and his captain twisted to look at the shoreline, his oars skimming the water.

The shore was populated with crewmen and their families, but 'twas Aurora he focused upon. And she was having an argument with Dahrein, the lad tugging at her hand, urging her toward the horses tethered for their use, yet she refused, finally pulling free and starting down the beach, Shokai a few feet beyond.

Dahrein turned his gaze to Ran, and he realized the boy was fighting tears. Ransom dug the paddles into the water, the strength of his strokes yanking the boat across the surface. The crowd quieted, the crewmen who knew her as more than a face, strode closer.

As the hull scraped the shore, Ran leapt from the craft and strode after her. Her dismissal of his protection, again, felt like a dismissal of all they'd shared. Was he wrong in thinking she might return his feelings?

"Aurora!" She continued walking. Ran's stride ate up the beach and he caught her arm, spinning her about, his first instinct to unleash his anger on her, but he was numbed by the devastated look in her eyes.

"Where do you go, love?"

"With Shokai," she said as if he ought to know. "Send a messenger when the path is safe to leave."

She wanted to leave him. He couldn't believe it. "Do you not come up to the house?" he asked softly.

Her gaze flitted to the white structure, majestic and beckoning. Och, to know the comfort of a home with Ransom, she agonized. But for how long? Til 'twas safe enough to sail? Nay, her heart would not survive the cut, and he truly did not want her there.

"I canna."

"Damn your independence, Aurora!" he gritted, feeling a hundred pairs of eyes on them and a quick glance confirmed it. "Sanctuary is not the *Lion,* I cannot control it!"

"Then you mustna feel obligated to me," she said simply, and the look on her face said she'd find a way to vanish.

"How can you speak so?" he growled, spiriting her out of earshot, the rushing heartache that she'd leave him so easily sanding his bones. "Sweet saints," he hissed. "I took your virtue."

"You dinna take a thing from me *I* dinna wish to give, Ransom Montegomery," she said, losing his grip. "You willna gain your father's reputation from me, for 'twill be no child of our loving. I have seen to it." His scowl darkened, an unfamiliar pain burning in his chest. " 'Tis as you wished, so you needn't feel—"

"Do not tell me what I *feel,* Aurora," he cut in, grasping her arms and wanting to shake her. She offered freedom, no ties, and he didn't want it. He wanted her. And she was slipping away; he could feel it. "My God, pest, how can you turn away from me," he asked, searching deep into her eyes, "after the incredible way we loved last night?"

The mention was like a lead dart to her breast, and her composure disintergrated.

" 'Twas unfair, Ransom," she accused in a small voice. "And I dinna ken you." She gazed up at him, confused and trembling and crumbling inside. "What do you wish from me that I have not given?"

He paled.

"You swore there was no room in your life and I accepted thus. I think you have naught to make you happy, and I find this." The flick of her hand encompassed the island, the people, his home. "I am pleased for you, but dinna ask me to come with you," her voice broke, "for you truly do not wish it."

A stone of regret sanded in his throat.

"Ah, pest, think you I am so heartless," he whispered. He'd carved nay so often atween them she did not assume a place in his life, imagined he hadn't wanted her near simply for his lack of asking, even on the island with nowhere else to go. Even after she'd loved him from his angry vows.

God, he felt damned unworthy of this woman.

These feelings were new to him and he wasn't certain about any of it, except that he wanted her to come with him, freely, wanted to see whatever she saw that made her want so much from him. He knew it was unfair, for returning to Sanctuary reminded him he was an outlaw, that he could die without ever experiencing again the magic they shared. And after tasting its sweetness, he wanted a bigger slice.

"Aurora, look at me." Her lashes swept up. "Ah, do not weep, love," he moaned helplessly, unmaned by the sight. "I've not the elegant words to soothe the wounds I've caused, but know that you have freed a part of me I did not know existed." He drew a breath, smoothing the hair from her cheek, his fingers sinking into the inky cloud and clutching fistfuls. "I adore you, pest. Nay, do not bludgeon me with those sharp eyes, for I know I've spoken otherwise, but I ask that you do not dismiss what has begun atween us. I know 'tis selfish of me but," he swallowed, "but I find I am losing my soul."

Aurora rapidly searched his features, this moment unmatched, for he'd never admitted such afore and she knew, oh, Goddess, she knew the courage it took. How could she abandon him when she'd sworn to be there when he asked?

Ran stood on needles, waiting for her to speak. Ebbing waves sloshed at their feet.

"Have I truly a piece of your heart, Ransom?" Her voice broke. "For if 'tis so, I willna give even that back."

He smiled at the tartness in her tone, the threat that she'd beat him if he'd lied.

"I see I must work at convincing you." He gathered her in his arms and kissed her trembling mouth, slowly, a wet roll of lips and tongue, unceasing til he felt her legs crumble and her body press sweetly against his. The crowd of onlookers rumbled, pleased.

Someone called out, a figure pushing through the crowd, and Aurora stepped out of his suddenly tight hold, catching his annoyed look afore she saw a woman robed in a white *abayeh*, veiled and coming toward them.

"Have you no sense?" the woman asked, moving across the sand like a Spanish galleon in full sail. "Get this poor child out of the sun afore she turns pink!" She came to a halt between Aurora and Ransom, sweeping the veil from her face and head and draping it over Aurora's bare shoulders. She smiled sweetly at Aurora, then turned a disappointed stare on Ransom.

"Your manners appall me, Kassir," she scolded softly, almost hesitantly, and Aurora lifted her impatient gaze to the pirate, folding her arms belligerently and fidgeting with her warming toadstone ring.

Ran expelled a breath in a harsh burst, briefly tilting his face to the sky afore meeting her gaze.

"Aurora Lassiter, may I introduce Sayidda Ashran." His lips thinned, his next words a caustic rasp. "My mother."

Chapter Twenty-six

Aurora's jaw dropped, her gaze shooting atween mother and son.

Kassir. The resemblance was nearly nonexistent but for the golden skin and the sculpted look of his features.

Sayidda Ashran. That meant Ran was half Moroccan or Tangierian or—She snapped her mouth shut and smiled wanly at Sayidda.

"Good morn, m'lady." Aurora curtsied.

"Please, not so formal, child," the woman's voice was low and sultry.

Aurora's gaze slipped over Sayidda's face, smoothly youthful and flawless, only the silver streaking her black hair giving way to age. A beauty, she thought, looking to Ransom.

Her heart sank. Any trace of the man who begged her forgiveness had vanished, leaving behind the pirate who'd stormed the Sultan's palace, wielding fist and sword for her freedom. Chilling, arrogant.

"Go back to the house," Ran snarled at his mother, Aurora gasped at the rude command, her gaze flashing with censure, though Sayidda seemed unaffected, a blank look on her solemn face.

Ran reached for Aurora, but she jerked her arm back, the motion sending her right into another body.

"May I be of assistance?" The hint of a Spanish accent colored the words, and Aurora turned. A small and slender woman stood with hands clasped in the folds of her skirts.

She was lovely, yet 'twas hidden in the drab gown and scraped-back black hair. They made her look severe and unapproachable, Aurora thought, flicking her gaze to Ransom.

Ran hooked his thumbs in the back of his belt and briefly glanced away. "This is my half sister, Rachel," he muttered, feeling the words had to be ripped from his throat. God, he'd hoped to prepare her for this and could see Aurora was not a'tall pleased with him. Damn and blast.

"Sister? What a pleasure," Aurora said, beaming at the young woman, then giving her a light hug. She felt Rachel's instant retreat and sensed a remoteness in her.

" 'Tis fortunate you are, Ransom, to have so much family and so near."

Inwardly Ran cringed at her acid tone, and though her expression was smooth and serene, he felt as if a keg of powder was about to go off. On him.

"Enough, it is far too hot," Sayidda declared. "Discuss whatever you wish later. Come to the house, little one, come." Sayidda slipped her arm around Aurora's shoulders, ushering her up the sandy slope, and for once, Ran was thankful for his mother's insistence, for he doubted Aurora would have complied so easily.

"You be a blackheart of the first water, Ransom Montgomery," Aurora threw over her shoulder.

Sayidda's round eyes darted to Ran, expecting a caustic retort, but he said naught, a pleased look about him she hadn't seen afore. Sayidda turned her gaze to the woman beside her, listening to her happy chatter, recognizing the friendship she'd formed with Domingo and Dahrein. Looking once more to her only son, and though he completely ignored her as always, Sayidda was delighted to see a flicker of longing in his eyes. Allah be praised, she thought, turning her attention to Aurora. People crowded, one woman even catching Aurora by the arm to stare intently at her face afore turning away. Sayidda shrugged at Aurora's silent inquiry, and they continued on to the house.

Ran folded his arms over his chest, his expression struggling atween a grin and a scowl.

"In a quarrel, both sides should be punished," Shokai said from his side.

" 'Twas a misjudgement, Shokai. Mine."

Shokai snorted as they headed up the hill after the group. "Ahhh, you dig the well when you are thirsty!"

Ran arched a brow, looking down at the old man. 'Twas an accomplishment to understand his cryptic remarks, Ran thought, waving off the stable boy's offer of a horse and following leisurely behind the villagers. Aye, the damage was done in a poor apology, and Ran disliked his inability to eloquently express himself to her.

"Victims of the same disease have much to talk about," Shokai muttered and Ran found himself struggling to keep up with the old man's short rapid steps.

Did Shokai feel Aurora cared for him as much as he her? The thought made Ran extraordinarily pleased, for though Aurora may be free in his bed and willing to speak the same, he was never certain as to how she'd react to most anything, one moment calm and wise, the next prepared to use him for shark bait.

Along the path to the house, Shokai found a crooked length of wood, tapped the base on the ground, inspected it critically, then grunted approval and used it to tick off his steps.

"Have you given any more thought to who might want to harm her?" Ran asked as they strode beneath the cool shade of vines and palm trees.

"No one can keep one eye in the back of his head."

"Damn you, man!" Ran hissed, brushing aside a lush drape of flowers and ducking beneath. "Have you no caution, no concern for her safety?"

Shokai stopped abruptly, Ran's bent body giving Shokai the opportunity to stare at him directly.

"Often when the nail raises its head, my lord, we can hammer it down." Shokai shuffled past, slipping around the side of the house and disappearing into the jungle.

Ran sighed. He was correct, of course. One could do naught unless the culprit showed his hand, and Ran was certain none would dare on his island.

* * *

Ransom's home was surrounded by several smaller struc-
tures that rambled down the mountain on either side; a
small stable, a smokehouse, a huge cistern to catch fresh
rainwater, a dry storage shed, and a cookhouse. And as
Aurora stepped beneath the arched doorway, nearly stumbling as she took in her surroundings, she knew she'd never
seen anything so magnificent. Vaulted ceilings rose above
her; windows lined the walls facing the ocean, spilling light
into the wide spacious rooms. The fragrance of flowers and
the tang of the sea hummed on the air, mixing with the
delicious scent of roasting lamb.

"Och, 'tis like Bealltainn!" she whispered, turning and
staring.

"Your pardon?" Sayidda asked, frowning.

"Springtime," Aurora explained as Sayidda ushered her
past a parlor elegantly furnished in warm shades of beige,
coral, and soft brown, beyond a closed door and into the
center of the house. To her left was a massive dining room.
In it a polished table surrounded by over twenty chairs, airy
drapes sweeping the floor with the breeze. 'Twas lavish,
finer than anything she'd ever seen; sideboards, wheeled
carts, a silver tea service, and from somewhere beyond the
wide service door, she could hear voices laughing, dishes
clattering, children squealing. Her smile widened.

Directly ahead and beyond the first-floor landing, a corridor stretched the length of the house, and she noticed
through the arched doorway, the hall was lined with more
doors.

"Your home is lovely, Sayidda," she said, gazing up the
staircase winding to the second floor with something akin to
awe.

"Kassir's home," Sayidda corrected, then looked away.
Aurora's brows knitted but she didn't have time to comment before a round red-cheeked woman burst through the
service door from the noisy kitchen.

"Ooooh, Domingo said you were a beauty!" the woman
exclaimed, introducing herself as Léonie, the cook and

housekeeper. And, from her size, Aurora inagined she ex-
celled at her job. "Come, come," the cook said, waving
toward the stairs and mounting them with a groan. "I have
a bath prepared in the blue room," she said to Sayidda, half
in question.

Sayidda nodded, smiling, lifting her skirts and passing the
two women.

"I will bring up a meal and then you may rest," Léonie
said, bustling down the hall.

"Rest? 'Tis the middle of the day?"

Léonie glanced up as she opened the door. "You are not
fatigued?" she asked, and Aurora caught a trace of a French
accent.

"Nay, and you needn't cater to me." She glanced atween
both women, then moved into the room. "I'll be doin' me
share."

"But you are a guest!" They said in unison, following her
inside.

Aurora scoffed, tossing her bag aside. "Shokai would tell
you even fish and guests stink after three days."

Léonie grinned and Sayidda laughed as Aurora gaped at
the bedchamber. As on the lower floor, naught was spared;
a canopy-draped bed, lush deep blue curtains, puffed and
elegantly tied, a sitting area, vanity, commode, chest, and
armoire in pale birch and Aurora felt she'd stepped into a
dream. Sighing pleasantly, she faced Sayidda as the woman
crossed the room, sweeping the *abayeh* from her body and
tossing it on the bed.

How many Moslem and continental ways blended in her,
Aurora wondered, admiring her stunningly simple gray
gown. It fit her slightly plump figure splendidly, the shade
accenting her golden skin and dark hair, and Aurora
couldn't help but stare as the older woman scented the
water, tisking over Aurora's lack of footwear.

Ransom's mother.

Ransom's home. Did he ken how lucky he was, she wondered as Léonie cajoled her behind the dressing screen, out
of her gown, and into the warm tub.

"I would bid you stay a wee bit," Aurora urged Sayidda, gesturing to the delicate chair when she made to leave.

Sayidda nodded, once and slight, and Aurora recognized the gesture matched Ransom's.

"My thanks for your kindness, m'lady," Aurora said, scrubbing her arm as Sayidda sank into the chair.

"You, little one, are most welcome. Now," she folded her hands on her lap and leaned forward a touch, "tell me, Aurora Lassiter, how did you meet my overbearing son."

Aurora glanced up and grinned. 'Twas clear Sayidda had a captive audience and wanted answers. Well, Aurora thought, settling back into the bubbles, so did she.

Ran listened outside the door to Aurora chat happily with his mother, sending a rapid fire of questions about the island, the people, the children. And Ran considered how often her search denied her feminine company, for 'twas over three months since he'd found her in the Sultan's palace. When had she last been in a private home? The thought of her being denied such simple pleasures humbled him even as he was outraged that her father had not come for her, at least to end her tormenting search. Aurora would never find peace until she knew one way or the other.

Rachel approached cautiously, carrying a tray, and her timidness annoyed Ransom.

"Would you like me to tell her—?"

"Nay," he cut in, glancing over her features pinched back by her tightly scraped bun. "You've fared well?" he felt compelled to ask.

"*Si,* it has been a delight to live here, brother."

Ran stiffened.

"I thank you." Hastily she swept into the bedroom, her presence drawing Aurora's attention.

" 'Tis sweet of you, Rachel, but you needn't have—" Her gaze darted beyond. "Spyin' isna polite, Ransom," she warned briskly, feeling his eyes penetrate the thin robe. He looked different, his hair brushed back and damp from his bath, his cream shirt and buff-colored breeches claiming wealth and elegance. Only the gold earring revealed the pirate lurking beneath.

"But the subject was too lovely to pass by."

"Och, dinna be wieldin' that glib tongue near me, you big ox." She shooed him. " 'Tis a wee bit peeved I am."

"I know, love," he said somberly, his eyes only for Aurora.

" 'Tis well deserved, Ransom."

"Aye."

She tilted her head. "Come beggin' me forgiveness, have you now?"

"Will I get it?"

She stared at him for a moment. "Aye." He smiled confidently and she rose from the vanity bench, crossing the room to him. "Och, dinna be lookin' so pleased with yerself. Forgivin'," she said for his ears alone, "and lettin' you into me bed are'na the same." She gave him a shove, his expression drooping as she closed the door in his face.

Sayidda gaped in shock. Rachel blinked, the teacup clicking in her trembling hand.

"I do not believe you did that?" Rachel gasped.

Aurora shrugged. "His breeches are a wee too tight, thinks I," she said philosophically. "They be squeezing all that bloody arrogance to the surface."

"Aurora!" Sayidda scolded. "You dare toy with Kassir."

Aurora's brows rose as she glanced atween the two women, recognizing fear and caution in each. "Ransom would never harm me, Sayidda. Never," she said, returning to the bench. "Nor you," she said to their images in the looking glass.

Rachel immediately lowered her eyes, and Sayidda resumed her brushing, masking her doubt. The easy interplay atween the couple surprised Sayidda, and that Kassir had sought out Aurora, especially while in her presence. Yet 'twas his manner that spoke volumes, the negligent way he leaned against the door frame, the warm look in his eyes as he focused on Aurora. For years she'd hoped to draw anything but contempt and coldness from him, and had selfishly prayed that if he could find love in his heart, he might find some for her.

"Sayidda, are you ill?" Aurora asked, noticing her tears.

"No, I am fine." the older woman waved, sniffled; and Rachel frowned, rising from the bed and shaking out the altered dress.

"I wish I could wear this shade," she said wistfully, handing over the claret-hued garment.

"And why not? We are the same coloring." Aurora offered the dress.

"No, thank you," Rachel murmured, curtsied, and swept from the room.

"Such a shy flower," Aurora whispered.

Sayidda made a sound, of agreement or disapproval Aurora couldn't be certain, but when she raised a questioning brow, Sayidda remained stoically silent.

How many people has Ransom alienated with his cool demeanor, Aurora wondered, wishing they could know the man she loved.

Ran found Aurora's borrowed shoes tucked behind the open door, yet could not locate the woman. A day apart felt like a week, and though he'd thought it wise to give her time after she'd shut the door in his face, he needed to talk with her. He'd searched both floors afore the sweet smells of baking drew him toward the kitchen. Pushing open the door, he found the white-walled room swelling with people. Domingo was perched on a tall stool, eating Léonie's latest confection with relishing moans and cheek bulging approval, as two maids moved from table to counter to the wide hearth, fetching, mixing, and pouring.

Dahrein sat at the high cook table, his chin scarcely cresting the edge, his fork poised to devour an indecently large slice of cake, white cream already smeared across his lips. Five loaves of freshly baked bread lined the edge of the table, followed by heaping platters of fruit, aged cheese, lacy tea cakes and berry tarts.

Ran plucked a tart from the closest pile, sinking his teeth

into it with a groan, drawing the occupants' attention. He smiled sheepishly, licking thick berry filling from his fingers. Léonie paused, glancing from him to the tart, and he nodded, his mouth crammed too full to speak. She grinned, setting two more on a plate afore him.

Ran swallowed. "Have you seen Aurora?" He held up the delicate beaded slippers.

"Lost her already, have you?" Domingo teased, and Léonie turned away, hiding her smile.

"Lougière," Dahrein said around a chunk of cake, then poked the air, indicating outside.

Ran's gaze narrowed on the windows and the scenery beyond.

"That look gets you into trouble with her, Ran," Domingo warned. "And you've been locked in that study since we arrived yesterday." He shrugged. "Perhaps she was bored?"

Nay, she's likely furious, Ran decided. After all, she'd spent last evening befriending his mother. He grabbed a second tart and, with the slippers tucked beneath his arm, headed out the door.

"*La petite* is angry with him?" Léonie offered Domingo a sample of roasted lamb.

"I honestly believe there isn't an angry bone in her body, Léonie," he said, gazing out the window where Ran questioned anyone he passed. "Just a few annoyed ones." Domingo bit into the meat, murmuring approval and giving Léonie a well-deserved kiss.

"Look at this, Mr. Lougière, have you ever seen such a flower." Her fingertips fluttered over the sharply formed petals shaping a star.

"Not as lovely as you, lass."

She cast him a side-glance, stunned and blushing. "You're flirting with me."

He smiled, his pale eyes sparkling as he moved closer, plucking the bloom and slipping the stem behind her ear. "Lovely," he murmured, arranging a strand of hair. Sud-

denly his expression fell and he abruptly stepped back, his
attention focused on the jungle beyond the path, and Aurora didn't mistake the guilt shaping his handsome features.
Did he seek to woo her, then remember his captain? Confused, Aurora realized his attention made her uncomfortable, for he looked at her as if he sought another face in
hers.

"Ho, Mistress Lassiter!" Her gaze shifted past the quartermaster to see Mister Buckland striding up the worn path,
wheezing horribly.

"I thought," he gasped, "mayhaps . . . you could show me
how to make use of the herbs and plants."

"I dinna know if we'll find many here," she glanced
around. "But aye."

Buckland smiled, walking beside her, carrying her basket,
Lougière limping behind, a disgruntled look on his angular
face. Aurora wasn't conscious of her moves, her grace, her
animation when she found a plant that was familiar. Despite her lavish gown she gathered her skirts and stepped off
the path. Lougière and Buckland exchanged a smile over
her lack of footwear as she pulled her dirk from her skirt
pocket, then squatted.

"I give thanks for this flower, its leaves and roots and the
aid 'twill bring."

Buckland and Lougière frowned at her as she dug in the
earth, raising the roots with the blade. She instructed the
doctor on exactly how and why she was being so careful.

"You must harvest them yourself, physician."

"What difference does it make who plucks them from the
ground?" Lougière asked, hovering as she gently brushed
the dirt free.

" 'Tis but a certain part of the herb that makes a tea, or
mayhaps a stem that holds the potency for healing." She
offered him a sniff of lemon balm and he smiled, pleased.
"Each must be carefully selected and, if necessary, dried in
a manner so that they will not lose their strength. Fresh is
best, of course, for pulverized as with purchased herbs," she
warned with a glance at Buckland, "you dinna ken what's
what." She let the physician examine the plant. " 'Tis the

root you must crush and boil. Strain the leaves as you would a tea. 'Twill ease a stomach upset and calm the nerves.''

"And the stem?" Buckland questioned.

"Discard. 'Tis useless and, if used, will make symptoms worse."

Buckland nodded, sketching in a diary, making notations. "Will you aid me further?" he asked, still writing, then looked up, almost embarrassed. "I wish the knowledge you possess, mistress."

Aurora smiled, nodded, placing the root in the basket and her hand on his arm.

"Mister Lougière?" She inclined her head and Markus quickened his stilted pace. They spent the next hour collecting and categorizing herbs, plants, and flowers, and Aurora was surprised at how many they found. The trio ended in Buckland's home, preparing several concoctions for storage. Aurora wiped her hands on her apron, peering into the simmering pot.

"We will allow this to cool, strain it, then jar the tincture for later." Buckland nodded, Lougière stirred, and Aurora was taken aback by their interest.

"Camomile is a sedative, often effective for easing the pains of childbirth," she said to Buckland, and his look of relief made her laugh. "Too much and 'twill cease all together. Administer in increments and wait to judge the effect afore increasing."

Buckland scribbled, pausing only to dip his quill in the well, then gesture with the feathered tip to another plant.

" 'Tis used to prevent conception, but is unreliable. Sheep intestines are better," she said without flinching. Lougière looked at his feet, but Buckland was curious. "Colonel Cundum's sheaths," she explained. Both men reddened, and she laughed. "Och, a prissy lot you are. And you, m'lord surgeon? How many women have birthed too many children and died from it?"

"I'd not want to count," he said gravely.

"And help is as simple as a tincture rinse or a length of knotted lamb intestine slipped over . . ." Her words faded as their eyes widened. She chuckled to herself. "Prudes," she muttered, turning to pour the mixture through a sieve and finding Ransom filling the doorway, suppressed anger etched on his dark features.

She smiled. "Good day, Ransom."

"Might I speak with you, Aurora?" Politely spoken yet edged with temper, she thought, easing Buckland's concern with a gentle pat afore she swept round the table edge and went to Ransom. Lougière's pale eyes shifted atween his captain and the lady, then met Buckland's as Ran ushered her from earshot.

"Good God, Aurora, I cannot believe what I heard?" He dropped her slippers on the ground afore her.

"Then dinna eavesdrop."

"How can you speak to them of such private . . . things?" he managed to get out.

"For 'tis a part of life, Ransom. Be it loving for a cost or nay, 'tis the right of man and woman not to become diseased nor live a lifetime with the consequences when 'tis only a wee bit of pleasure they seek."

How simple her thinking, Ran thought, wishing he could see the world through her eyes.

"You, of all men, must see that?" she needled. "And 'tis the woman who often pays."

He looked to the sea, his body rigid. He knew where this was leading, and he didn't care for the path of her thoughts.

"Have you been here all day?"

"After foraging a wee bit, aye." She stepped into the slippers, making a face at the confinement.

He met her gaze. " 'Tis improper for you to be in the company of unmarried men."

She laughed, light and short. "Och, Ransom, 'twas improper for me to be in the company of two hundred and forty men, yet I was."

But that was afore we loved, he wanted to say, yet couldn't. "Come to the house with me."

"Nay, I canna."

He scowled.

"To leave the mixture as it is will be a waste."

"Then waste it."

"Nay," she hissed, though her expression was without anger. "I willna take from the earth and discard the rewards simply because you are'na pleased and dinna ask Sayidda where I was."

Ran grit his teeth, without a handy retort.

"If you'd care to wait?"

"I do not have the time," he said, impatient.

"Well, then," Aurora sighed, dispirited. "Mayhaps you should return to your duties and I to mine?"

He stared down at her, wanting to smother her with kisses, take her to his bed, and love her until she truly forgave him. It seemed to be the only place he could master her.

"How long do you seek to make me pay for my misdeeds?" came softly, tinted faintly with hurt and confusion.

"Och, Ransom, I dinna wish to punish you," she said as if he'd asked the impossible, stepping closer, her hand smoothing up his chest, resting warmly in the center. Yet he remained like a statue, staring down at her, his hands on his hips. "Only to love you."

He exhaled sharply, his shoulders sagging. Slowly his arms wound around her and she came to him, tilting her head back. His lips met hers, softly at first, desire and longing burning bright atween them like fire to paper, swiftly burned to white ash. It felt like years since they'd touched. She moved restlessly against him.

"Aurora," he moaned against her lips. "I need you, love." He kissed her hotly, slick tongues and wet lips and loving. "If I come to your chamber, tonight . . ." He hesitated, breathing deeply. "Will you bid me enter?"

"Oh, aye, Ransom," she whispered, her hand sliding down his hip, skimming close to his manhood, and he groaned. "For I canna resist the beast in you."

Chapter Twenty-Seven

Smiles were secret and ripe with promise, and Aurora anticipated the coming night, her body lively with want and excitement. She would lie in Ransom's arms this eve, wrapped in his strength, but for now she focused on her dinner. 'Twas hard, for he relaxed in the chair, his intentions undisguised in the smoldering way he studied her. She felt her skin pinken, heard his low pleased chuckle, and sent him a scolding look as she forked a morsel of meat.

The dining table was bursting with guests, the linen-covered surface overflowing with food; pigeon pie with currants, couscous topped with braised lamb, vegetables and fruit, saffron-spiced chicken stuffed with almonds, dates and lemons, steamed grains seasoned with cumin and cinnamon, and blended onion, carrots, and broad beans. Aurora's favorite was Moroccan *Bisteeya*, a blend of egg and chicken wrapped in a thin flour pastry. Conversation along the grand length of polished wood was animated, dishes and goblets clinking, diners singing praise to Léonie's talents. Léonie beamed, offering a platter overflowing with sliced lamb to the ever silent Lockewood. He stabbed a chunk and politely handed the platter to Lougière, who then passed it on to the far end where Ran sat at the head.

From across the elaborately set table, Aurora watched Dahrein shovel food into his mouth without ceasing for air and worried he'd choke. Puir lad, 'twas as if he hadn't eaten in weeks, and while Ran merely smiled at the lad's exuberance, Aurora was educated enough to see his table manners were appalling. She did not want to embarrass the boy and lightly tapped him under the table with her foot.

Dahrein looked up, his cheeks bulging, his jaw working slowly. Aurora's gaze shifted from his plate to hers afore she carefully cut a cube of meat, bringing it to her mouth and chewing, daintily, patiently. Dahrein watched her for a moment, his features pulling tight with realization, and after chewing and swallowing, he mimicked her moves.

Before his blunder was recognized by anyone else, Aurora turned her attention to Sayidda seated to her right. "Do you sew?"

"Very little and with less efficiency than Rachel."

"Truly, Rachel?" Ran's sister nodded, and Aurora realized she'd found a route to draw the shy woman closer into the household. "Wonderful. Think you could find some fabric for—"

"If you've a need, love, you only must ask," Ran interrupted, and Aurora turned to the head of the table. " 'Tis not for me, but Dahrein." The boy's head popped up, and Aurora smiled proudly at his efforts to contain his zeal with his dinner. " 'Tis time, do you not think, that he had a man's clothes? Dahrein, how goes that with you?"

"Truly, mem sahib? Like sahib?" he said in awe, glancing over Ran's garments with envy.

"Aye, my laddie. Whatever you wish." Under the table she nudged Ran, and he agreed.

Aurora turned toward Rachel. "I will offer my help, but admit I am poor at stitchin'." Aught but flesh, she thought, then felt the intense chill of someone's stare, as if touched by it. She glanced covertly across the table. Lockewood. And his penetrating glare confused her, for she'd not so much as chatted with the man.

"*Si,*" Rachel said, then looked shyly at her lap.

"I've some fine strips of leather I can weave for a belt, Dahrein, but it needs a clasp," Sayidda said, then hesitantly looked at her son. "Perhaps Kassir could aid me?" she added, hoping he'd offer. But Ran settled his attention on Aurora, rudely ignoring the request.

"I shall provide whatever you desire, lass."

"I do not need it, Ransom," she gestured to her right, "your mother does."

Ran glanced benignly at his parent. "She gains naught from me."

Sayidda paled and rose abruptly. "Allah bids me," she murmured, and Ran made a disgusted sound as she left the table without a backward glance. Aurora stared after Sayidda, then turned her blistering gaze on Ransom.

His expression remained bland and remote.

"Mem sahib?"

Aurora focused on Dahrein.

"It is not necessary."

Och, the burdens of a child to salvage the hurts of adults, she thought, smiling disarmingly at the youth. "Aye, Dahrein, 'tis so. Rachel and I will fashion the like of Ransom's if 'tis your wish." She leaned over the table. "Save a wee spot for Léonie's cake, and we'll have it on the porch," she whispered conspiratorially.

He nodded vigorously.

She sat back, glancing to the others, meeting smile for smile. Domingo nodded ever so slightly. Lougière was busy studying Rachel, who was consumed with playing with her wine goblet. While Lockewood and Buckland devoured their meals with nearly barbaric relish. She looked to Ransom, but he didn't appear the least regretful that he'd offended his mother.

Slowly Aurora rose, excusing herself to the dinner guests.

"Aurora?" Ran caught her hand.

"I find the need for prayer, too," she murmured to Ransom, deftly loosing his grip. "For me thoughts are a *wee bit* unkind."

She left the dining room, Ran's gaze following her til she disappeared from his sight. Slumping back in his chair, he threw his napkin across his plate, feeling the accusing stares numbering round his table. The worst he felt from Dahrein, who'd resumed eating, glaring atween forkfuls.

God's blood! he thought, pushing away from the table and coming to his feet. She was interfering in a matter that was not her concern, but he didn't want to face off with her, for he'd just begun to rebuild what his deception had lost. He'd no notion of what would happen now, for he'd never seen quite so much venom in her afore.

Aurora paced Ran's study and considered briefly going to Sayidda, but the woman had suffered enough humiliation this day and did not need her apology on Ran's behalf to magnify it. Yet the memory of Sayidda's face when she'd looked hopefully at her son cut Aurora so deeply she swore rage bled through her veins. She paced, fists clenched, bare feet marking a soundless rut in the fine carpet. Knickknacks clinked.

Cheese and crust! She could feel it building in her.

The latch rattled and she marched to the door, flinging it open. Ran stared down at her, his brow rising at the rosy flush of her skin, her lips pulled tight.

Her blue eyes were unusually bright.

"I dinna wish to have me words heard, Ransom," she said briskly, flicking a hand for him to get inside. He did and she shut the door, facing him. "I dinna care for the man I see afore me." Her foot tapped with impatience.

Ran crossed the room, slipping behind his desk. Sunlight silhouetted his tall form against the mullioned window. "I am the same as I was this morn, lass, and last eve when we shared my bed."

"Oh-ho nay, Ransom." Her unbound hair shimmered black against her maroon skirts. "That man wouldna be so cruel as to humiliate his own mother afore a dozen guests!" she ended on a snap and a ledger flipped open, the pages fanning in a nonexistent breeze. Ran briefly frowned at the broad book, then twisted slightly away, grabbing the neck of a crystal decanter from the low sideboard, then snatching up a glass.

"What is atween Sayidda and myself, is not your concern," he said, a well-tooled edge to his words. He yanked the stopper.

"I am your *mother's* friend, Ransom, a sight more than you can claim." Aurora tilted her head back, struggling with her temper, and when she looked at him as he splashed brandy into the glass, the gleam in her eyes startled him and he missed the lip, spilling drops on the polished wood.

"How can you treat me so dearly and the woman who gave you life so poorly?"

"Because you didn't give that life away." Monotone, emotionless. Ransom.

"If she is such a source of pain, then why do you have her here?"

"She is not the source," he growled into the glass. "She is a reminder of it." He gulped the brandy.

Aurora gasped. "Why?"

"Every time I look upon her I see the hand she played in my life." Ran sent her a cool, measured glance. "She was weak and allowed herself to be sold to the highest bidder. A friggin' concubine," he hissed, pouring more liquor.

" 'Twas not her choice. 'Twas that or death, and you are a man who has seen that a slave will do aught for the chance they might find freedom." Her voice held a challenging bite.

"By God, she," he jabbed a finger toward the door, "gave away her own flesh and blood to save herself!"

"Nay! To see that you lived!" she cried, and a racked book slapped on its side. "She was not the Pasha's favored, but a slave. In the ways of Islam, the Qur'an, men control, even the children are theirs. You ken it well, Ransom. Like the child I tended in the Sultan's palace, a tiny babe is a threat as large as war," she rushed to say, "and your life was at stake for Ali insisted 'twas his son Sayidda bore. Ah, I see you dinna ken this," she said at his sudden skeptical look. "But 'tis true. She told me herself. She was only to dance and serve for Granville, but they loved, Ransom, for that one night your mother and father loved."

Her words kicked him in the gut. "One night makes her more of the whore she is!"

"Does one night with you make me the same?" A drape whispered without a breeze.

"Nay! 'Tis different atween us." He dropped into his chair.

"We had no more than your parents," she said, shaking her head. "So you canna sit so high and regal and be the judge of her past, pirate." Her hands on her hips, she stared at him from across the wide carved desk and tried for calm. "Can you not imagine how she felt to birth her son, then be forced to hand him over the wall to a man she knew only once? Knowing well you would vanish from her arms forever! 'Tis a choice no mother must make." Tears blurred her vision and she clutched at the polished ledge. "She could have passed her child as the Pasha's, giving herself a better life, but found the courage to give you to your father, to give you more than she could!"

He tossed back the brandy in one swallow. "She gave me naught but a tortured childhood," he swiped his lips with the back of his wrist, "and a faithless wastrel for a father."

"Ochaii, you are a cold stubborn man!" Papers swooshed off the desk as if swiped by an angry hand. " 'Tis a prison you've locked her in! A prison she's willingly accepted." She paced wildly, and out of the corner of his eye Ran saw a vase totter, the ink well rattle in its holder. Slowly he set the snifter aside. "She came with you, knowing you blamed her for what happened in England, yet wanted naught but to be near her son."

"And if she had not been weak I would not have grown up believing that cold *bitch* was my mother!" He rose slowly. "If she had kept me with her, I would have never accused David of lying, never demanded satisfaction on the green, never put a bullet in his heart!"

Aurora whirled about. "But she dinna pull the trigger, Ransom." She pointed at him. "You did!" And with the words came with a sudden crack, the bell-shaped snifter splitting in half, rocking on its curved sides. Ran gaped at the snifter, then her, but she ignored the occurrence, caught in her anger. "You seek to live a life on *what if 'twere different*. But 'twill never be." The vase hovered off the shelf. "By the Gods, do you not see that with every vessel you attack, every man and woman and child you set free, you are avenging her? Championing Sayidda so no other will suffer as you have!"

"Nay, Aurora, nay," he said with unbelievable calm. "For I care not that she suffers." He leaned over the desk.

fists braced, his body tense as a bow. "And now that you have spoken your piece, I will tell you only once, Aurora Lassiter McLaren," he threatened in a deadly voice, "stay out of it!"

"God of thunder!" she hissed. "You are not a bastard by birth, Ransom Montegomery," her voice rose, "but a bastard of your own makin'!"

A pane of glass shattered, sending glistening fragments spewing like a rain of fairy tears over his head. Aurora staggered, the color draining from her face. Ran looked from the jagged pane to her and back, then shook his head, a mist of glass dusting the air. They stared. Ran reached for her, but she curved her body away from his touch, glancing from broken glass to strewn papers to severed snifter. Ran blinked as the vase settled back on the shelf, precariously close to the edge, and when he looked back to Aurora, she was gone, the door banging against the wall, her maroon skirts disappearing around the jam. A moment passed afore he shifted round the desk, following, colliding with Dahrein on the front steps.

Ran gripped the boy's shoulders to keep him from falling as he scanned the area beyond. He caught a glimpse of her afore she veered off the path.

Dahrein glared up at Ran, muscling out of his grasp and heading into the house. Léonie stood on the section of porch outside the dinning room, disappointment marking her round face as she stepped back inside.

Domingo sighed, shaking his head. "She only wants to see you happy, Ran."

Ran did not have to ask if they'd heard. The maiming glances from the departing Buckland and Lougière and even Lockewood were like gun blasts delivered with lethal accuracy.

Ran shoved his fingers through his hair, then leaned back against a support post, expelling a harsh breath.

Suddenly, he felt completely alone.

A moment later, Shokai shuffled by, stopped, and looked Ran dead in the eye. He made a disgusted sound, then said,

"Small mind, big mouth, often found together," afore continuing on his way.

Poor in pockets and rich in friends, Ran thought, when he came upon her. She sat on the ground, uncaring of her fine skirts, a newborn lamb cuddled on her lap. The animal baaed sweetly as she stroked its downy coat, smiling as another lamb tottered toward her, a small gray kitten darting atween its hooves. Suddenly a bird with a long, draping red tail swooped down, settling regally on a low branch, tilting its head curiously at the intruder to his domain. Yellow light dappled through the canopy of trees, bathing her secret place with an ethereal glow, and Ran remained out of her sight, watching.

Another bird, no bigger than his thumb perched itself on Aurora's shoulder, peeping happily. The kitten batted at her hair, tangled itself; and she leaned over, ribbons of silky black hair spilling off her shoulders as she freed the bundle of fur, then let him do it again.

She's a creature of living things, he thought, half expecting elves and fairies to be flitting about her. Or kelpies, whatever the deuce they were.

"Where is your mama, little one?" she asked the kitten, teasing its whiskers with a blade of grass. "Is she nearby or aboard the *Lion* gathering mice for your supper?" Her voice broke and Ran realized she wasn't as composed as she appeared. "Ah, Goddess, what I wouldna forfeit to have me mother near, to tell her how much I have missed her, to crawl upon her lap like a little girl and feel the gentleness of her arms." She tilted her head back. " 'Tis a gift he has in his hands," she whispered, and a knot worked in his throat as Ran listened, envisioning her world, empty and narrow, and how valiantly she shielded him from it.

"Och, to have precious time and be wastin' it to old anger," she mused aloud, and Ran left her alone, feeling every inch the bastard he was for treating her so wretchedly. 'Twas no wonder she talked to her Goddess, for he'd no defense to her accusations.

Her words rang in his head over and over. Your life was at stake . . . A threat . . . Could have passed you off as the Pasha's son . . . They loved . . . 'Tis a prison you've locked her in . . . and still she stays.

Ran had often wondered why Sayidda came with him that night in Crete. His father had led him there. Granville had always known where Sayidda was, had taken her away from the Pasha and given her a new life. Without her son. Had she begged his father to bring him back? Had she asked of his health, his friends? Did she know Anna was spiteful and distant to her son? Grievin' mother, he thought, I've learned it from a master.

He kicked at the dirt, sending a pebbly spray over the path and frowning when he heard voices. Looking up, he saw two figures in the distance, near the side of the cookhouse. Maintaining his slow pace, he squinted against the sun to recognize the pair. Two women, he decided, realizing one was his half sister. Rachel had not so much as set foot outside, he'd been told, and was so reserved she spent considerable time in her room or with the friar, praying.

The smaller woman, slender and pale skinned, left, her shawl-covered head bowed, her quick steps kicking out her striped skirts. Rachel entered the cookhouse. And halfheartedly he wished he could muster feelings for the timid woman, then decided he'd much rather a man come along and take her from his care. Four women in his house was enough, especially when one was Aurora.

Ran strolled without direction, without purpose, and came upon Shokai, setting up house in a cave. The old man paused at the vine-draped entrance, glancing benignly at Ran, then shrugged and ducked inside. Ran interpreted that as an invitation. The cool damp cut in the mountain was already filled with old pots and crates, neatly arranged discards. Candle stubs lit ever fissure and crack, and as Ran ducked inside, a strange sensation made him roll his shoulders. His height wouldn't allow him to straighten completely. He cleared his throat, but Shokai didn't look up from where he knelt on the floor aside a smokeless fire, a cracked pot simmering atop a grate.

"There is room in the house, Shokai, why do you live here?" Ran recognized the quilt making a pallet in the corner. 'Twas Sayidda's.

Shokai prepared two cups of tea. "Heaven can not use two suns, nor a house two masters." He poured, then gestured to the woven mat opposite him.

"Aurora will not be pleased." Ran settled to the ground.

"Women and small men are hard to handle, my lord."

Ran snorted, accepting the cup, giving the green contents a suspicious look afore tasting. It was slightly bitter but sweet, too. "She's ah," briefly he looked away, "bloody furious," he confessed, his shoulders shifting.

Shokai chuckled knowingly. "Ahhh, when the dragon fights the tiger, both get hurt."

"You've spoken with her?"

Shokai shook his head. "Old pigeons know not the dreams of swans."

"Do you ever *not* speak in riddles?" Ran asked, irritated.

"Ancient words are the wisdom for the ignorant, my lord."

Ran glanced up, his amber eyes narrowing til he detected the curve of Shokai's thin lips. "Good God." Ran smiled. "You are as blunt as your mistress!"

"Better the arrow in your breast than in your back, neh?" the old man said with the lift of a hairless brow.

"Grievin' mothers, aye," Ran said with feeling. "I believe I've been pierced by a few this day."

"Spare me your sparrow's tears, my lord," the old man waved him off unsympathetically, "for even with devils, we prefer the ones we are used to."

Damn and blast, who hadn't heard of their fight? "Think you I *enjoy* feeling this way?"

"*Hai,* for you can stand the severest pain ten years, when someone else is suffering."

"I did not intend to hurt Aurora, old man."

"Aiee, you are a blind man peeping through a fence!"

Ran's gaze sharpened. "Sayidda has influenced you, too, I see."

Shokai exhaled an impatient breath. "Often we can see seven faults in another and not one of our own ten."

"I know I am not innocent, but you cannot ask me to forget everything."

"To know a parent's love and depth of forgiveness, you must have a child."

"Bloody unlikely," Ran muttered into the cup, drank, half anticipating Shokai's unsolicited advice.

"Ahhh, but you have already witnessed this, thief of slaves, outlaw, pirate, ravisher." He folded his arms, waiting til the words sank home and Ran realized not only Aurora but his mother consistently forgave misdeeds and harsh words. "See," Shokai nodded, aware of his enlightenment, "to teach is to learn, neh? My Empress does not judge only by what she hears or sees, but by what she feels here." He thumped his thin chest. "This I've always admired," Shokai said with complete candidness, then shrugged thin shoulders. "There is no weakness in admitting the boasts of the heart, my lord, yet find courage in the words once uttered. Often it is the language that wins the lady. Mother and lover."

Ran stared intently at the fire.

"Sooner or later you act out what you truly think and feel," Shokai added.

They drank in silence, Shokai gazing at the English captain, Ran staring at the liquid dance of red flames.

"My lord?"

Only Ran's gaze shifted.

"You will know the heart of another only when you see inside your own."

Ran expelled a tight breath, then slowly climbed to his feet. "My thanks, Shokai." Shokai acknowledged the remark with a slight bow, his spine incredibly rigid. "Should you need aught," Ran said, glancing at the meager furnishings, "come to me."

"Every extra thing I own is extra trouble."

Ran nodded, turned away, yet paused at the entrance to look back. Shokai freed the forked silver comb securing his topknot and stared at the razor-sharp prongs. And Ran knew his presence was recognized.

"To give ground, my lord, is sometimes the greatest victory."

Alone, Shokai released a long breath, then moved to the pallet, aged bones cracking and popping as he sank down to rest.

"Ahh, even the tallest trees," he muttered on a soft chuckle, "are leveled by a small storm."

Chapter Twenty-Eight

Sayidda Ashran was a strong woman. But 'twas a forced strength, born out of love for her only son. She'd endured much since that night in Gran's arms; birthing her son with the aid of a sympathetic eunuch, waiting days for word to reach Kassir's father, then the wrenching moment she'd handed her newborn child over to him, that the baby boy might survive the first year of his precious life. The painful beatings she'd received for her treachery against Ali could never compare to the acid remarks from Kassir and the dismissal of his affection. And though Gran had rescued her from death, often she considered that Allah had intended her to perish that night, and her punishment for twisting her fate was to experience never-ending sorrow.

"Here, my child," Sayidda answered the insistent call, pausing at the top of the staircase, grasping the bannister. The stairs looked unusually steep today, she thought as Aurora mounted the steps, smiling. Always smiling. "You do not wear the gowns?"

"'Twere a wee too delicate for diggin' in the dirt, m'lady." She shrugged, glancing down at the white dress Ransom had given her aboard the *Lion*. "I dinna wish to ruin them. And I apologize for soiling the other."

Sayidda waved negatingly, her lips curving. "We will find you something suitable for play in the mud, then." She met Aurora on the staircase. "Threadbare and too large," she tisked, plucking at the skirt. Dizziness suddenly swept her and she gripped the bannister.

"Sayidda? You are unwell?"

"It is nothing." She shook her head to clear the haze.

"Come belowstairs and sit," Aurora coaxed.

"I am fine," Sayidda replied, taking a deep breath. "But you? You've argued with my son?" Sayidda suspected 'twas over her. "It could not have been pleasant."

Aurora's expression slowly shattered. "I trod where I shouldna, Sayidda. And left marks on his back, thinks I."

"Do you love my son, Aurora?" came bluntly.

Aurora's gaze flew to Sayidda's. "Aye," she said with feeling. "Aye. But a man canna love back with half his heart."

"It may be all he has," Sayidda whispered, blaming herself.

"Nay," Aurora answered firmly, turning to ascend the stairs just as Ransom entered the house. "I dinna believe that." Her foot shifted on the step, throwing her off balance, and she reached for the bannister.

"Kassir!" Sayidda screamed, lunging as Aurora's hand swiped at air.

Aurora tensed, anticipating the impact to wood, yet hit solidly against Ran's chest, his strength keeping her from suffering no more than lost breath and a quick shot of terror.

His arm circled her waist and he buried his face in the curve of her neck, breathing heavily. Seeing her tumble backwards off the step had sent his heart into his throat, and it took him a moment to regain his bearings.

"Aurora," he gasped, his gaze lifting briefly to his mother.

Her skin blanched of color, her hand over her heart, Sayidda whispered, "Allah be praised."

Ran swept Aurora up in his arms, turning and carrying her down the remaining flight and into his study. Gently, as if holding a sliver of crystal, he laid her on the settee, then knelt aside her.

Immediately she popped up, elbows bracing her torso. "My thanks, Ransom, but I'm unharmed." He flipped back her skirts and examined her ankle, running his thumbs over the instep and arch. She giggled, squirming. "See there now," she said, tossing the muddy hem down. The gown slid off her shoulder and she shrugged it back up. "You're making a muck of naught, Ransom. I slipped, 'tis all." He stared at her with an intensity that scared her and slowly she swung her legs over the side of the settee. "Why do you look at me like that?"

The pounding in his chest had returned to normal, yet in his mind, her backwards tumble replayed again and again. How easily she could have died, he realized, and when she tried to stand, he pointed a finger in her face. "Nay! Stay put!" he ordered, and afore she could retort he quit the room, bellowing for the maid.

Ran knelt on the staircase, smoothing his hand over each step, searching. The wood gleamed, the scent of beeswax still heavy in the air. Aurora was not a graceless woman; Ran straightened, using the toe of his boot to prod each step where she'd stood. He tapped, and Sayidda, still on the steps above, watched as he sent more force into the kick and wood separated, the tread tottering a fraction.

Sayidda gasped, and his gaze flew to hers. "Who would do such a thing?" she whispered.

He didn't know. But even Sayidda recognized the deliberate tampering, the cut hidden beneath the carpet runner. "Keep this atween us," he murmured lowly afore their privacy was interrupted.

"M'lord?" A speck of a lass, blond and petite, bobbed a curtsy.

"When did you polish this last?" He flicked a hand toward the accursed stair.

"Two days ago, m'lord," came a timid reply.

"See you this?" He nudged the wobbling piece.

"Aye, m'lord, but wuddn't like that then, I swear, I swear."

" 'Tis fine, Meggie," he said calmly, though she didn't relax. "You're certain?"

"Aye, oh, aye. Would 'ave tol' someone, m'lord. 'Tis dangerous, that."

He'd no reason to doubt the maid, for she traveled the

same path daily, he reasoned, dismissing the servant. He
headed back down the stairs, then paused, turning toward
his mother. They stared for a moment afore Ran offered his
hand. Sayidda blinked, staring at his open palm, his face,
then back again. Carefully, almost afraid he'd snatch it
back, she placed her trembling fingers in the warm center.
His fingers wrapped gently and without meeting her gaze, he
aided her over the break in the step, releasing his hold the
instant she met the landing and advancing toward the study.

He froze.

Aurora stood in the doorway, hands on her hips, a
strange look on her face. He walked til he was a few feet
afore her, his heart leaping in his chest. God, he thought,
what had he done now? She seemed prepared to cry. He
hoped not. He always felt utterly useless when she did.

"What, love?"

She smiled, wide and bright, and he couldn't help but grin
back, though he found naught amusing about her mishap.

She looked around him to Sayidda. "Excuse us," she
said, then grabbed his hand, yanking him into the study and
shutting the door.

Immediately she wrapped her arms around his neck, his
hands gripping her waist as she pulled him down to meet her
mouth. She kissed him hungrily, happily, with such exuberance Ran felt his knees soften. His hands rode heavily up
and down her back, pressing her closer. She was so angry
with him afore and now . . . He didn't waste a moment and
swept her up in his arms, never breaking the kiss as he
carried her to the settee, dropping to the cushions with a
jolt.

She drew back, gazing adoringly into his amber-rich eyes.

"Aurora!" he demanded, impatient and confused.

" 'Tis a grand thing you've done, my heart. Grand." Her
fingers drove into his hair, holding him prisoner for another
wrenchingly heady kiss, the small concession a victory over
his past. "I'm proud of you," she hummed against his warm
mouth, wiggling round to straddle his hips.

Sayidda, Ran realized suddenly, stunned as she pecked
kisses over his forehead and cheeks. "Helping her down the

stairs has made you *this happy?*" He pushed her back to see her face.

"Oh, aye, aye," she said, then attacked his jaw, the warm column of his throat. "I dinna 'spect you to do it so soon." She looked at him. "But I kenned you would."

Would her faith in him always be unyielding? he wondered, sinking into the cushions, silently thanking Shokai for his wisdom.

"What are you 'tempting here, lass?" He stroked her back, then her shoulders, brushing the gown lower, aware of her position and the delicious advantage it offered.

"You," she panted, stripping open his shirt and molding the sculpted hardness of his chest.

"In here?" His skin jumped to her touch.

"I canna very well take you to my room." Her voice lowered. " 'Twould cause a stir, hearin' all that pantin' and the 'oh Ransom, aye, touch me again's and especially the wonderful roaring you do when you— Och, I've made you blush!"

He was, didn't know why, but he was! God knew he wanted her, but his household lacked certain manners, servants having no compunction about walking into an unlocked room. He glanced at the door. "Perhaps we should wait."

She made a sour face, sliding her hand down to his waistband and his stomach flexed beneath her fingertips. "I want you, my heart," she whispered, the sweet words moving against his lips and he groaned darkly, the lush push of her breast weakening him.

"Ahh, you deal me into madness, Aurora. You know that." His breathing quickened, his hands running up and down her arms.

"Then come with me, Ransom, to a spot created for us."

A sable brow rose in question.

" 'Tis deep in the jungle."

Afore he could protest again, she wriggled off his lap, uncaring of the bulge she'd created in his breeches as she grasped his hand, pulling him along. She threw open the door and, like a loving puppy, he followed.

* * *

Markus Lougière flattened himself against the wall, briefly closing his eyes, then backing away from the open window. He left the porch, slipping alongside the house, then into the jungle. Several yards away, Shokai stepped onto the path, silent and unnoticed, even by the breeze.

They climbed higher onto the mountainside.

"I found it when I was gatherin' herbs." She brushed aside a low branch, ducking beneath. " 'Tis magical, Ransom." She released the limb, smacking him in the chest.

Ran stopped briefly, shaking his head and whacking the branch aside. "Then, of course," he said dryly, grinning, "we must go there."

Her excitement was catching, the anticipation of loving her driving through his bloodstream and straight to his groin. Even her sultry walk and swishing hair invited his fantasies to run wild. He wanted her now, here. In the forest where she belongs, he thought, his vibrant creature of life. Yet as she slowed her step on the narrowing path, veering off to the right, Ran frowned, glancing back to memorize their trek. He hadn't ventured in this direction afore. 'Twas an area mostly inhabited by the natives.

When he returned his gaze to Aurora she was too far ahead for his comfort and he hastened his pace. "Slow down," he called, then sharper, "Aurora!"

She looked back over her shoulder, the command holding enough caution to make her stop. She waited, leaning against a tree, his tall form partially hidden by the thick vegetation.

High above birds squawked.

The damp breeze waved palm fronds, separating them in a sheer curtain of green.

"You heard something?"

He shrugged, glancing left and right. His gaze halted on something in the distance, and she squinted into the brush to see.

Suddenly he lunged forward, breaking through the jungle, knocking her to the ground, shielding her with his body just as a soft hollow thump passed overhead. The leaves rustled briefly, then ceased. He didn't move, his gaze snapping in all directions, then halting suddenly. His sharpened features pulled taut, terror and rage bursting through him. Naught but four feet above them, a small thin dart protruded from the trunk of a tree.

Mother of God!

Abruptly Ran sat up, taking her with him, his hands running over her face and throat and arms, eyes searching for a prick on her skin.

"What is it? Why did you do that?"

He ignored her question, twisting her to see her back. "How do you feel? Were you struck?"

"Nay, I am fit."

"Do you feel dizzy? Is your throat dry?"

"Ransom!" She gripped his arms, giving them a telling squeeze. He was terrified, and it left her stunned.

He searched her upturned features for the length of a heartbeat, then nodded to the tree only a foot away.

She inhaled sharply, reaching for the dart.

"Nay!" He caught her wrist.

She looked at him, startled. " 'Tis poisonous?"

"Deadly." He cradled her hand against his chest, and she felt the panicked beat of his heart.

"Why would anyone do that to us?"

"I would not venture a guess," he said, keeping his suspicions to himself as he stood, then helped her to her feet. 'Twould be unjust to accuse without proof, he thought, hurrying her onto the path.

"But you said the natives dinna bother your people." She spoke over her shoulder, walking ahead. "And 'tis clear 'twas not the weapon of a pirate."

"None have dared travel so deep into their area afore, lass," he said, trying to keep the edge from his voice.

"I have." He latched onto her arm, spinning her about, his eyes harsh with demand. "With Mister Lougière," she explained. "Only this morn."

"Here?" He gestured. *"Exactly* here?"

"Not quite." Aurora pointed off to the right, moving around him. " 'Tis this way." Afore he could stop her she left the trail, ducking and picking her way through the jungle. Ran followed closely, frowning as the vegetation thinned enough to recognize a footbridge strung across a narrow ravine. A small waterfall fountained from the hill, misting the air. She stepped onto the swaying bridge, then turned and held her hand out to him. Water rushed along the dark cavernous floor, soothing frayed nerves. 'Twas beautiful, Ran admitted.

"Och, we are almost there, my heart." A jolt spirited through him every time she called him that, and although he had his doubts on whether the ropes would support their combined weight, he would not risk her life by dallying in the forest.

"Someone shot that dart, love," he said measuredly. "Come back with me." He waggled his fingers, beckoning, and she sighed grumpily, taking a step.

"Later mayhaps?" A teasing smile on her lips, she reached out, her fingertips grazing his as the bridge ropes snapped.

One by one, from the other side.

For a heartbeat she looked startled, suspended.

Ran dove for her hand as she lurched wildly for purchase. He clamped her wrist, yanking, but the loss of support beneath her slammed him to the ground. He grappled to keep from going over the edge, his free hand snagging in the vegetation for anchor, but mist-dampened skin and the spongy ground beneath him, taunted him to the mushy rim.

"Aurora!" Dirt and stones sprayed the top of her head, and he thought she was unconscious. "Aurora!"

She tilted her head back, swallowing afore she spoke. "I am fine, Ransom," she gasped, and he realized her free hand gripped a cracked slat. "But I've naught below my feet to aid me," she said, apologetic and frightened.

"Do not move. Let me," he warned, inching back, aware that if he struggled, he'd lose her on the unstable ground. He pulled, cautiously, his soft voice reassuring her that he'd never let go.

Please God. I beg you. I cannot lose her.

Her head crested the edge of the ravine, her hand clawing the earth. He clamped both hands on her arm, working hand over hand and as soon as he could reach near her waist, he grabbed a fistful of her gown, dragging her away from the edge and into his embrace.

She clung to him, trembling, and Ran tightened his arms about her, his breath rushing against the top of her head.

"Aurora, oh, thank God." He pressed his lips to her temple, her forehead, and she tipped her head back, gazing into his amber eyes and working her hand atween their bodies to touch him. She rubbed a finger over his cheek, across his brow, brushing his lips. Great Goddess, how she loved this face and wanted to erase the fear lingering there.

"Fionn's fairies, Ransom, 'tis thankful I am, yer such a braw lad."

He smiled tenderly. "More that you are a speck, love."

She glanced at the twisting rope, all that remained of the bridge, then lifted her gaze to Ransom.

"I'm feelin' the need for one of your kisses, Ransom," came almost shyly.

And he gave her what she desired, his mouth and tongue and body speaking all he could not in the hot fiery release. He kissed her and kissed her, hard and driving, the horror over seeing her fall melting into the shame that he hadn't told her he loved her.

"Aurora, Aurora, my love," he murmured huskily onto her mouth, and she drew back, gasping for air, her hands running over his chest, his shoulders, then cupping his face.

"Take me home, Ransom. This place," she glanced beyond the ravine, "has lost its magick."

Chapter Twenty-Nine

Ran couldn't believe she was taking this so lightly.

"Anyone could have been in our place then, Ransom," she said in a reasonable tone, walking ahead. "You're peeved because you dinna have your pleasure with me, 'tis all."

"Don't be absurd." He stopped her on the trail, gazing down at her dirt-smudged face. "I have learned restraint over the years, love." He plucked a pebble from her hair, tossing it aside. "Much as I'd like to dally in the woods with you," he murmured, his gaze taking in her lush shape in one hot sweep, " 'tis dangerous. And know 'tis truth when I say that," he nodded toward the forest, "was deliberate. As was the crack on the stairs."

"You dinna look surprised at your findings." She tisked over the tears in his shirt sleeve.

"I'm not." He ushered her down the hillside. " 'Tis one reason I brought you here, to keep you safe."

She frowned, mulling over his words, then snapped a look at him. "You never intended to take me back," she realized, and he heard the storm gathering in her tone. "You spouted about your bloody obligations, but you'd nary the intention of returning me to Morocco!"

"Aye." Without a shred of guilt.

"You'll be tellin' me why, Ransom Montegomery." She blocked his path, her hands on her hips, dirt clods sagging her dress.

Now was not the time to laugh, he warned himself. "We . . . I am wanted."

Her brows rose sharply, her features pulling taut. "Think you I'd betray you to the authorities?"

"Nay!" Quick, sure. "But I am not the only one involved." He lashed his arm toward the village. "And to put you ashore would see you dead."

She scoffed at that, but his narrowing gaze warned her to listen.

"You did not cross my path so often without aid, Aurora. Rahman and Achmed may be a separate matter, but Foti and whoever killed Castille know you have been in my company, my confidence."

"You mean in the Red Lion's company . . . the peacock pirate's," she clarified.

"Aye, aye. I do not know if these incidents are directed at me and you are simply a vulnerable target, a weak spot by which to gain access. But I could not risk harm befalling you," his voice lowered, "because of me and mine."

"I ken," she sighed, conceding the point. "But if 'tis true, then is a vengeance mislaid. I've done naught to warrant threats." A pause and then softly, firmly, "I willna believe Rahman had aught to do with your troubles."

"Mayhaps." His hand at the small of her back, he urged her to continue their return home, keeping her close. "But do you understand I've made many enemies? I am a criminal in England and can never go back." His words were precise, laying the impact of his deeds against the lack of a future, any future, at her feet for her to see.

"You are an outlaw here, too." She shrugged. "And I dinna see the matter."

"The day will come when I must pay, pest." By hanging.

"Yet you escaped Newgate or the hangman . . ." When his expression remained impassive, her words dropped off, her brows knitting tightly. "Were you tried, Ransom?" she asked cautiously, and he nodded.

She stopped walking. He didn't.

"Then how be you here if you've been convicted?"

"I have been exiled."

She stared at his back for a heartbeat, her eyes growing wide. "You are titled!" she gasped.

"Stupid of them, wasn't it?"

"So, you truly are the pirate's lord."

His gaze flew to hers, the laughter in her voice startling him, and for a few steps he walked backward, grinning as she lifted her skirts and hurried to catch up. How often, he wondered, did he expect one response from her and receive completely the opposite.

"Dinna fuss over naught, Ransom. I canna return to me Highlands either." She wouldn't look at him. " 'Tis against the law to practice witchcraft."

A moment stretched, his narrowing gaze scrutinizing her profile afore he asked softly, "You weren't attacked by thieves when you left Scotland, were you, pest?"

"I was banished," she said, then glanced at him through a curtain of hair. "Och, dinna be looking at me as if I'd roasted children, I simply scared a few of the more timid souls, 'twas all."

"Is that so?"

Aurora reddened, yanking her dress back up on her shoulder, flipping her hair off, which only served to loosen the gown again. "I apologize for breaking your pane," she muttered, looking anywhere but at him. She rubbed beneath her nose, leaving a mud mustache behind.

He grinned hugely.

"Cheese and crust!" she hissed, quickening her pace.

"Aurora, the house is that way." She stopped and turned. He pointed to the left and she huffed, veering off the street, heading to the village and up the incline. Ran caught up with her, lightly catching her arm.

"Do not speak of the dart, nor the bridge, love."

Her look questioned his reasons.

"We have been betrayed, somehow," frustration and anger bit into his tone, "and I must find the bastard afore he strikes again." He paused on the hillside, gazing out over the cove at the ships rocking in the calm water. Who has done this? he wondered. What ship had they come on? Were they stowaways or had he truly disloyal men in his forces?

Didn't the bastard realize they would all die because of it? He looked down at Aurora, pulling her into his arms and crushing her mouth beneath his. The kiss was hard and wild, a wet slid of lips and tongue, steaming with passion riding on fear and delayed by treachery.

"Aurora, Aurora," he murmured, raining kisses over her face and throat. He wanted her badly, needed to assure himself she was still here. "I *am* peeved."

"Yer showin' that boldness again, too." She slid her hand where only the trees could see, shaping over his manhood. His eyes flared, the tempo of his breathing rushed. And as he bent to steal another kiss, he heard the call, his gaze shifting beyond her to the house. His mother, half sister, and Dahrein strode toward them.

"Sweet saints!" He looked down at her. "You create a brick in my breeches and seek to embarrass me afore my family."

Family. 'Twas the first time she'd heard him say it. Did he believe it or was that simply said for her benefit? When he muttered something about reputation and honor, she turned in his arms, pressing her back to him, then glancing up. "Your reputation is shielded, your *lordship*." She laughed, his narrow look bespeaking his concern for *her* reputation, what there was of it.

"Don't call me *that*," he hissed in her ear, resting his hands on her shoulders with a gentle weight.

"As you wish, my heart." He kissed the top of her head afore company arrived, Domingo striding lazily up behind his half sister, a knowing look on his face.

" 'Twas an accident. A fall down the mountain, 'twas all," Ran said when they questioned their appearance, and Aurora was grateful his tone brooked no argument. Sayidda met her son's gaze, a silent warning in her dark eyes, afore she solicitously urged Aurora toward the house.

As the group departed, Domingo stepped in front of Ran. " 'Twas either the wildest loving a man could hope for," he said, looking over Ran's torn and soiled garments, "or you've lied for the sake of your mother."

Why, Ran wondered, didn't he include his half sister in that statement?

Sayidda flinched when she noticed Kassir standing in the doorway, though he wasn't looking at her. Quietly gathering up the soiled gown, she crossed the room to her son. "Behave. She is tired," she whispered as she passed him, and he followed her retreat, then looked back at Aurora.

He leaned against the door frame, ridiculously pleased to simply watch her brush her hair. By God, she was beautiful. The robe clung to her curves, and he knew as her arms rose to wind the mass of hair into a rope, she was bare beneath. The knowledge drove pure lust through his blood.

"Will you lolly there all day, Ransom?" she said, her eyes on the ribbon she threaded in her braid.

Ran pushed away from the frame and stepped inside. "Did you not tell me you saw a twisting rope in your seer box?"

Aurora glanced up briefly. "Aye, but what I see there isna always meant for me. Most often the visions concern people I do not know a'tall."

Ran closed the door, the click of the key in the lock sending a tingling up her spine. She looked at him.

"Och, yer soilin' yer reputation, m'lord."

"I want to soil yours," he growled, crossing to the vanity, and anticipation spirited through her. She would let him. She would give him aught he wanted, she loved him so much. When she'd dangled over the ravine she could think of naught but Ransom, how much he'd changed, gentled, and that she could not pass to another world without loving him like he needed. And as he bent, slipping his arm round her waist and placing a soft kiss to her throat, she felt loved and adored and snuggled back into his embrace.

Even if he never spoke the words, even if he could not relinquish his outlaw life, he belonged with her, in her heart, in her bed. His lips against her throat were moist and heady, his breathing quick with readiness, and she tilted her head and reached up to sift her fingers through his hair. The silken sleeve slipped back and he caught sight of it in the looking glass. Instantly Ran sank to one knee aside her, shifting her on the bench and gently cradling her wrist. He examined the purple bruise, his face marked with guilt.

"I willna hear of you apologizin', Ransom."

He nodded, smoothing his fingertip over the marks. "Did my mother see these?"

"Aye." His gaze flew to hers. "She can be trusted, Ransom. Nay, I dinna tell her all 'cept that you caught me when I went to fall." She looked down at her arm, drawing it from his grasp. "I dinna like fibbin' to her. She has been awfully kind to me."

"We cannot trust another, pest."

"But you've told Domingo," she sniped, and he looked bewildered. She smiled. "I dinna ken til just then."

"Crafty wench." He shifted her on the bench, curling his fingers beneath her knees and spreading her legs. "Domingo holds the same opinion as I."

"Does he now?"

"He agrees I should keep close watch on you."

Ran pulled at the sash, letting the silken fabric slide through his fingers, and then opened the robe. His gaze caressed her nakedness, his breath sucking in atween clenched teeth.

"You do that unwrappin' so well, Ransom," she commended, leaning forward, the heat of her freshly bathed body drawing him closer as she kissed him, her tongue outlining his lips, then pushing atween.

He went still, his shuddering breath tumbling into her mouth.

"Dinna be stoppin' now," she begged, and his hands slid up her thighs, thumbs diving to the sensitive inside, then up to enfold her breasts.

She sank into the warm pressure, loving him with her mouth as his thumbs circled the delicate blushing peaks, slowly, so slowly, and Aurora felt she'd burst apart with the pleasure of his touch. He made her feel sensual and adored, her body moving of its own accord, answering push for caress, tuning to his needs, and she never felt so desirable.

"Aurora," he said against her mouth, and she moved restlessly on the bench, urging him closer, heat to heat, and he lowered his head, lifting her full breast and taking the tingling peak into his mouth. She gasped, a feminine inhale of satisfaction, as he drew her nipple deeply into the tender suck of his mouth.

She threw her head back as he laved and kissed, his hand gliding down to her hips and around to tuck beneath her buttocks, lifting, his fingertips seeking the warm feminine flesh. And he found her, wet and wanting, and it drove every thought from his mind but satisfying her.

She pressed against his invading touch, clawing him closer, closer, and Ran whispered, "Wrap your arms around my neck," and she complied as he stood, her legs following around his waist. He carried her to the bed, laying her on her back, stripping the robe from her body and his garments from his own, never taking his eyes from her as she twisted and squirmed, begging him to come to her, to hurry.

She rolled onto her stomach, reaching to draw back the coverlet, but he stopped her, leaning his weight onto her, nudging her thighs apart.

"Ransom, Ransom," she cried softly, pushing back against his invading hardness. He whispered in her ear what he would do to her, that he intended to love her body until she could not stand it, and he grasped the pillows and stuffed them beneath her hips, her feline smile daring him to try. The position felt wicked and carnal, magnifying the passion racing through her blood and she wanted him to fill her, now, but he didn't. He lay half on her, gently, his hand slipping 'atween her and the pillows and finding her dewy softness. Lightly he stroked her, manipulating slickened skin, rocking passion-hard flesh to soft, whispering praise for the extravagant curves of her body, praise for her tiny gasps, of how sweetly she rode his mouth the first time he held her naked against him, and Ran felt her climax against his hand, an opulent pulse of pleasure and heat. She shuddered liquidly, and when she regained her breath, he began loving her in truth.

He licked and caressed the set of her shoulders, the curve of her spine, spreading grinding kisses over every inch of skin exposed to his gaze til her body was again strung taut with ripening hunger and begging for release. But he wouldn't give in, toying with her, dragging her senses to a lush peak, then letting her hover, throb, her skin aching for him.

"Ransom!" she whimpered, biting the pillow. And he positioned himself behind her, sliding his arm beneath her hips and slowly entering her, inch by inch. Aurora could not be still. The pressure was luxurious, sharpening her nerves, clamping on every cell, and as he withdrew and pushed again, she rose up, grasping the headboard and looking back at him. He met her gaze and wound his arms tightly around her, tucking his knees 'atween hers, smoothly rising with her with every thrust and memorizing her body with his hands.

Her hands clenched the wood, and his gaze fell on her bruised arm. He could have lost her today, and the pain of it scored his heart like the claw of a beast. *He* clung to her, *he* needed to feel her skin molded to his, *he* ached to preserve this moment when bodies clashed and hearts were rent open, flooding, giving, loving. She rested her head back on his shoulder, her breathing rasping, and hungrily he took her mouth, sinking his tongue deeply, his fingers slicking over the tender core of her, and she bucked and pushed and ground against him, and he shoved, burying himself deeply, spilling his seed, a secret lonely part of him praying he gave her his child.

And knowing she prevented it . . .

Chapter Thirty

Too bloody damn many people in this house, Ran thought, for it felt like a week since he'd been alone with Aurora. 'Twas not for lack of trying, he mused grumpily, although she gave him her complete attention when they were together. But she was in demand, with Buckland and his patients, his mother, and Dahrein and as Ran strode down the staircase, he considered this a conspiracy to keep them apart. He paused to be certain the carpenter had repaired the break in the step.

"I think Aurora loves him," he heard Léonie say, and smiled to himself.

"There is no question that he adores her." Sayidda's voice. "Or he would never have let her cut his hair."

Ran frowned at that, continuing down the stairs.

"Look at them." Léonie gestured to the window, laughing, and Ran moved silently behind them, tension drawing his shoulders. Lougière stood on the lawn, partially hidden by palm fronds. His appearance was unchanged, and he was talking to someone obviously smaller than he.

Ran's entire body clenched. He bypassed Sayidda and Léonie to the open doors and then froze in his tracks, a grin splitting his face. Aurora and Dahrein lay on their backs on the lawn, arms out, eyes closed. Dahrein was without his turban, and Ran could see his black hair was sheared.

"Can you feel it?" Ran heard Aurora ask.

"Yes, yes," Dahrein said, awed.

" 'Tis the energy of the earth," she whispered as if 'twere some great secret.

Ran shoved his fingers into his hair, his shoulders jerking with a silent chuckle as he turned back into the house. He came face to face with his mother.

"May I speak with you?" She gestured sharply to his study and Ran nodded, frowning at her terse manner for she'd never so much as gainsaid him in the last years, though he'd given her cause.

She preceded him into the room, pausing to allow him to pass, then shut the door.

They stared.

She was exceedingly pale, Ran thought, and much thinner.

"You have something to say?" he prodded, settling his rear against the desk.

"I saw you leaving her chamber the other night."

Ran stiffened.

"I do not wish to know what transpired, only that you do not shame her. Aurora is a fine woman, Kassir, and she deserves to be treated well."

"And I suppose you shall tell me I have not done so?"

Sayidda glanced to the side, marshaling her courage. They'd come so far in the past days, actually having civil conversations on his part, and she didn't want to ruin it. But Sayidda adored the Scotswoman, and he had to see what his less than honorable behavior was doing.

"Aurora is being spoken about."

Ran straightened. Whatever was being said, 'twas clear by the look on Sayidda's face he would not like it.

"Some have said you've brought your personal whore with you."

"Bloody friggin' hell."

"Kassir!"

" 'Tis not true!"

"Of course it is, for that is how you have treated her."

" 'Tis a damned lie!" His fists clenched.

"Have you not openly shared her bed in this house, without vows?"

His skin colored slightly. "Aurora knows I respect her."

Sayidda harrumphed, folding her arms. "Kassir," she said, with a calming breath, "I am most aware of what this can do to a woman's life, whether she cares or not."

"Did you care?" he asked suddenly, softly, his voice catching. "Did you *ever* care what happened to *me?*"

Sayidda's eyes bloomed with tears. "You have waited long to ask, my son."

"Did you know how cruel she was to me? How she despised me, because I was not her son?"

Sayidda shook her head.

"I never understood why a mother would be so heartless," his voice hardened, his next words bitterly tight, "til the morn I shot David Chalmers in the heart."

"I did not choose to keep your heritage from you, Kassir. Your father thought it best, assured me in letters you were well cared for."

Letters, Ran thought, a strange release flooding through his chest. She *had* kept in contact.

"I spent my life in hiding, from Ali, and could not subject you to that risk. No, no, listen," she commanded vehemently when he started to interrupt. "When I gave you to Granville, I gave away my heart. You were all I had!" She swiped at her tears. "Do you not think I hated that *she* watched you grow," came angrily, "that *she* held you in her arms when you were hurt or frightened."

"She didn't," he growled. "The servants did."

Her expression crumbled into absolute despair. "I never knew," she whispered, and Ran felt the jab of his bitterness, knowing he'd taunted and ridiculed his mother as Anna Montegomery had done to him.

"Was not your father—?"

"Off wenching." The words scraped past his throat. "And God knows he still is."

"Stupid infidel, he promised!" she muttered at the floor, then looked at Ran. She took a step closer. "You are *my* son," she said righteously, as if no one else could lay claim. "And I love you, Kassir." He looked startled. "I would not withstand your deplorable behavior toward me, *and* Aurora, if I did not."

Ran held her gaze for a moment longer, then sighed, tiredly pushing his fingers through his hair. "I cannot wed her."

"Why?"

"Because I am wanted in a fistful of countries!"

"The pirate *Red Lion* is wanted," she said pointedly.

"I could hang, *will* hang!" He backslapped the air. "What future is that to offer her?"

"We could die tomorrow. Any one of us. Have you not learned anything in the past years? Can you not see the riches Allah has given you?" She waved toward the windows, Aurora and Dahrein's laughter filtering in from outside. "Is yours the example you wish Dahrein to follow into manhood?"

Ran twisted around to gaze out the blurry glass. Aurora hugged the lad, and Dahrein blushed, but Ran could see the happiness in his eyes. She mothered him, lavishing the youth with the gentle nurturing he'd been denied since birth, yet treated him with respect for the man he would someday become. And he'd already shown the makings of a fine one, voicing his concern the day after their mishap with the bridge. Ran never lied to Dahrein and had confided the truth swearing him to secrecy, and Dahrein seemed to grow two inches after they'd clasped hands, sealing their bond and appointing himself Aurora's personal guardian. Though Ran held her promise not to venture away from the house without escort, he silently commended Dahrein's persistence, his pride in the lad fierce and unyielding, like that in a son. Aye, Ran thought, wanting better for Dahrein.

"Would you allow your own son to be called bastard?"

Ran snapped a hard look at her. "Aurora's skills have prevented . . . that."

Disbelief shaped her features. "But you are your father's son, Kassir."

Potent, she was implying; and he was trusting their loving to potions and herbs.

"And if Allah wishes it, it will be done."

Ran remembered three nights ago and how selfishly he'd wanted a child with Aurora. *To bind her to me,* he realized, yet he did not consider how she truly felt. "Grievin' mothers," he hissed, pounding his fist against his thigh, "what do I know of being a husband, regardless?"

"There is no secret. And from all I've witnessed, you understand rather clearly the duties required." The sarcastic rebuke nailed him. 'Twas the first time he'd been dressed down by his mother, and he could tell she was harnessing her temper. "I needn't tell you that Aurora is a very special woman, and had she not entered our lives, we would not be speaking now." There was a pause, mother and son gazing at each other from across the room. "You are a fine man, Kassir." Something shifted inside him then. "And I will not tell you how to live your life, only that you must consider the effect of your actions on the innocent." Abruptly she turned away, her skirts rustling softly as she moved to the door.

"Kassir?"

He glanced up. "Aye." Her back was to him, her fingers shaping on the latch. A moment passed unchanged and then, "If you choose to abandon Aurora, do it quickly."

Sayidda left the room, and Ran's shoulders drooped at the soft click of the sealed door.

Abandon her? God Almighty. He couldn't. But after struggling not to, Ran realized he was repeating his father's mistakes. He might not have fathered bastards across the countryside, yet his sins were no less severe.

And what, a voice asked, will you do to atone?

'Twas bleedin' long enough, Aurora thought, walking down the upstairs hall. Even Dahrein had noticed Ransom's brooding silence since yesterday, and Aurora considered that by spending most of the afternoon afore and evening with the lad, Ransom might be upset with her, mayhaps even a bit jealous. Or was he still concerned over their mishaps with the dart and the bridge? Her protective spell was sufficient precaution, but he wasn't convinced.

'Twas time to ask him, she decided, negotiating the bend in the hall. A gurgling noise caught her attention and she halted, listening, her brows knitting when she realized it came from Sayidda's chamber. Rapping softly on the door gained her naught but louder retching, and concerned, Aurora let herself in. Immediately she rushed to Sayidda, supporting the older woman as she hung over a chamber pot, emptying the contents of her stomach.

Aurora soaked a cloth, blotting her brow as the bout gradually subsided, and Sayidda slumped into a chair, her skin so pale 'twas nearly yellow. Aurora made no comment as she poured her some water to rinse her mouth, then covered the pot and set it aside.

Sayidda swiped her face with the damp cloth, breathing heavily.

"How long has this been happening?" Aurora asked.

Sayidda shoulders moved sluggishly. "Perhaps a week, maybe more. It always comes in the morning, after I've dressed and bathed and breakfasted."

Aurora glanced at the tray; the half-eaten rolls, crock of jam, and a pot of tea, untouched. She lifted the pot lid, bending to sniff. Naught unusual, she thought, yet her toadstone ring was warming.

"Could you, mayhaps, be with child?" she asked, replacing the china top.

Sayidda laughed shortly. "Aurora!"

" 'Tis possible."

"Nay, child," Sayidda said, straightening in the chair, "For I have not known the pleasure of a man since afore Kassir was born."

Aurora blinked. Ransom's celibate vow held naught to Sayidda's thirty-three years of abstinence.

Ran thought the same thing as he flattened against the wall outside the door. He closed his eyes, utterly ashamed of himself. How miserable he'd made her life, he thought, then straightened when he heard footsteps. Pushing away from the wall he headed toward the stairs, bidding Rachel good morn as she passed. He glanced back as she slipped into

Sayidda's chamber. He'd made progress with everyone but her, he thought, ascending the steps.

"Is there something amiss?" Rachel asked, not venturing farther than the doorway. She clasped her hands in the folds of her dark skirts, waiting.

"Come, sit with Sayidda," Aurora gestured, then looked at Ran's mother. "I will get you something to ease the upset?"

Sayidda nodded and Aurora left, returning to find the women unmoved. Setting her bag on the vanity bench, Aurora rummaged, removing bottles and pouches.

"Your medicines," Rachel said, almost excited. " 'Tis why I've sought you. There is a girl. She has fallen under a man's spell." The other women looked up questioningly, and Rachel wrung her hands nervously, glancing briefly to the floor. "She is with child and unwed. He will not claim her, and she is terrified. I feel she will harm herself."

Aurora set a bottle down slowly, frowning. "What do you wish of me?"

"Mister Buckland said you have tinctures?"

"Aye, but they dinna work that well and are dangerous, Rachel."

"Show me the dosage and I will see it done."

Aurora shook her head. "Nay, tell her to come to me. 'Tis too difficult to judge without—"

"Nay!" then softer, "Nay, please," Rachel begged. "I have sworn not to reveal her identity."

"You would encourage her to rid herself of the child?" Aurora was confused. "But your teachings, the convent?"

Aurora and Sayidda exchanged a frown, and Rachel drew herself up regally.

"This girl is stricken and I fear for her life. I can help. You can," she clarified. "And I know," she swallowed, "my God is directing me to help the unfortunate." Her voice took on a defiant edge. "I will do whatever I must."

"You are certain she is with child?"

Rachel nodded, and Aurora looked indecisively at the small bottle, reluctant to help without seeing the girl yet firm in her belief that 'twas unnecessary for a woman to suffer a

lifetime for the pleasure of a man. Without a word, she
meted the proper dose into another bottle, giving instructions that it was to be taken at intervals and to come to her
immediately with any problems. Rachel gratefully accepted
the tincture, thanking her in her quiet dignified manner, and
Sayidda and Aurora stared after her as she left the room.

Sayidda lifted her gaze to Aurora. "She is lying," she said
briskly.

Aurora raised a brow, silently admitting Rachel was a
distant woman and difficult to sense, yet . . . "I gained no
such feeling."

"I did," Sayidda replied firmly, afore her expression suddenly twisted with pain. She clutched her stomach, every
speck of color draining from her face. "Aurora," she
moaned. "Help me. 'Tis worse than—" Sayidda covered her
mouth and Aurora shoved the basin beneath her.

A half-hour later Sayidda lay comfortably on the bed,
drifting into a painless sleep as Aurora examined the remains of her breakfast tray, then inspected the bottles littering her vanity, sniffing powder, creams, perfumes, and even
the scented soap. Naught was amiss. Tucking the coverlet
around Sayidda, Aurora touched the back of her hand to
her forehead and cheek, watching her breathing and mentally listing symptoms and searching for the cause.

"Aurora, what goes here?"

Aurora met Ran's gaze, then looked once more to
Sayidda afore she came to him, pushing him out of the room
and closing the door.

"Your mother isna well," she whispered. "Let her rest."

"What is wrong?" he asked, his low tone betraying his
panic.

She placed her hand on his arm. "I am not certain, but I
believe she's ingested a poison."

"What?" he blasted and she clamped her hand over his
mouth, nodding down the hall. "Are you certain?" he asked
when they were clear of being overheard.

"Nay. But 'tis unintentional," she assured. " 'Tis likely
naught but eating a bit of spoiled meat, or a reaction to a
new food—"

He grasped her arms. "Can you help her?" The plea in his eyes betrayed aught he'd said in the past to Sayidda.

"I will try, Ransom. This I swear." She laid her hand on his chest. "But with the cure, she may become worse afore she is better."

Ran swallowed, looking beyond her to the closed door hiding his mother. Not now, God, he pleaded, *I've* punished her enough.

"I can help," she assured, sensing his fear.

His gaze lowered to Aurora and after pressing his lips to her forehead, he abruptly turned away.

Rachel briskly walked the path from the village, her gaze darting from bush to cluster of flowers, to every tree, her head snapping at the slightest sound. Lowering her gaze when anyone dared meet hers, she clutched the empty bottle in her fist and quickened her pace.

Chapter Thirty-One

Ran threw open the door to his study and was assaulted with a barrage of questions from his captains, the appointed heads of the village.

"Gentlemen!" he said sharply. "I cannot very well answer at once, can I?" He stepped back, allowing the seasoned pirates to file past as Aurora crossed the hall from the dinning room, bearing a cloth-covered tray on her hip, and munching on a crust of bread. Aurora stopped, chewed, swallowed, watching as Ran nodded to each man entering his study. His gaze darted up, then returned sharply to meet hers over the shorter men's heads. His expression immediately softened, and she took at step closer.

"Captain," someone called from his office, "this proposal of yours, what—?"

"In a moment, Mister Hawthorne." His eyes remained fixed on Aurora.

"Good day, Ransom," she said, breathless. She hadn't been this close to him in days and she missed him. Yet she realized only this morn that he was purposely avoiding her. It stung and confused her. "I've a need to speak with you." She felt as if she were requesting an audience. "Later mayhaps, when you can spare moment." There was no bite in her tone, only hope.

"Aurora, I don't . . . ah," Ran stammered, glanced to the side, then met her gaze; and she frowned at his apprehension, the sadness, and stepped closer, but insistent voices beckoned him inside.

A maid called from the top of the stairs, motioning excitedly, and Aurora turned quickly away as Ran slipped into the room. With a sigh, he closed the door and faced the men gathered at his request. God, this had to work.

Aurora stood over Sayidda, watching as she slept, the woman's brows knitting and smoothing as she wrestled with pain. Her illness had escalated and Aurora felt helpless to ease her discomfort. Inspecting her food and drink, even going so far as to prepare it herself to be certain 'twas untainted, had not relieved the pain, nor revealed the source. Yet 'twas poison. Aurora was certain, for her toadstone ring warmed to the point of burning her finger, forcing her to take it off. Sighing dispiritedly, she gathered the tray, touched the back of her hand to Sayidda's face, then left the room. In the morning she would again inspect aught she came in contact with, and confer with Mister Buckland. This, Aurora decided, was not in her realm of knowledge.

She padded quietly down the corridor, ascending the stair with dangerous haste and heading straight to Ransom's study. She stopped. The door was ajar, and after peering inside she could see the room was empty.

"Aurora?" She turned to find Léonie standing quietly by. "The tray . . ." She gestured and Aurora handed it over with thanks. "He is gone to the mountain," Léonie said as if reading her thoughts.

Aurora's shoulders stiffened, her eyes narrowing on the view out the open doors. "If you should see his *lordship,*" she said crisply, "tell him I'll be requestin' another audience. If he can spare a moment for the wee folk."

Léonie's brows lifted at her acid tone, and she watched as Aurora left the house, calling for Dahrein, and the pair headed toward the sea.

Facing west, the lookout had a perfect three-quarter view of the island, the east side populated with natives and the trek to the west arduous and unhealthy for the unseasoned.

The natives, Ran knew, had often proven themselves worthy of keeping invaders from reaching the shores in their domain. They trusted Ran to do the same in his.

Three sailors stood by, stiff shouldered and silent, as Ransom stooped to check the cannon, staring down the empty barrel with one eye closed, deciding 'twas well tended, then straightened and strode amongst the kegs of powder, glass and grapeshot readied for attack. Stones crunched beneath his boots. 'Twas his usual tour, weekly, and the few men without families enjoyed the relaxing shade and having naught to do but take the watch for oncoming vessels.

'Twas a dull time free from the rigors of shipboard life.

But as on his vessels, Ran would not tolerate laziness or disrespect for his orders, and when he bent and snatched a dark slipper from behind a barrel, the sailor flinched. Ran let the telltale footwear dangle from his fingertip, his gaze darting to the two who'd drawn the watch this week.

" 'Tis . . . ah . . . mine, well, not mine," the sailor rushed to say, red faced. "But . . . ahh damn me sir," he yanked his cap from his head, "two days up here is enough, and when she brought me dinner, well, I coaxed her to stay and well . . . ." The sailor cleared his throat uncomfortably, and Ran realized he was terrified, trembling. By God, did everyone fear him?

"See that it does not happen again, Mister Pellum," Ran said, tossing the slipper at the sailor afore turning away. The stunned man gawked at his captain's back, then his comrade, his eyes finally shifting to the first mate lounging against the stone wall. Pellum let out a long relieved breath.

"Change the watch to one day on, one off," Ran said to Domingo, then glanced back at the three gunners. "Your replacement is coming up the hillside. Mister Avilar and I will see to the post til they reach us. Dismissed."

The sailors nodded and grinned, handed their captain the spyglass, then took their leave without hesitation.

Domingo chuckled softly as the men raced out of the wide granite mouth of the cave, scrambling over boulders and skidding down the hillside as Ran moved atween the two end cannons. He recalibrated their range, then with the spyglass in his hand, stepped from beneath the cool shade into the sun. Picking a mango from the watch stores, Domingo watched Ran survey his island. Even though the captain insisted otherwise, he was lord and master here.

Ransom scanned the sea, empty and endless and glaring white, then turned the glass to the cliff, the shore. Ships rocked like tired guards, quiet and lonely in the cove, but the village was alive with activity, children running, dogs and goats annoying the folk hard at work; and through the glass he noticed Shokai emerging from his mouse hole, heading toward the village.

Ran shifted left, to the mountainside where workers cleared the land for planting. Sugar cane, he'd decided with the agreement of the other captains. Aurora was right, he supposed. He seemed to be the authority they often sought, yet 'twas their accord he sought this past week. Sugar was a small start, he knew, and wondered what she'd think of the enterprise. God, he always wondered what she was thinking.

"She is over there," Domingo said, and Ran glanced at the Spaniard, spyglass still poised. Domingo gestured with his chin to the sea as he pared off a slice of a mango. "In the tidal basin," he pointed with the knife, "as she has every morning since you did I-don't-know-what and won't talk to her."

"Have you an opinion to express, Mister Avilar?" Ran asked, putting the glass to his eye and focusing on the cove and the sandy break making a pool in the lagoon. His heartbeat jumped at the sight of her. She looked as a mermaid might, willowy streamers of black hair floating on the surface, marking her swim, draping her as she stood.

"Damn her!" he hissed, his fingers clenching on the spyglass. She wore naught but a chemise, the wet fabric clinging and molding. She might as well be bloody damn naked! By God, did the woman not realize the risks of her reckless parading? He breathed a little easier when he saw Dahrein sitting on a huge boulder, his back to Aurora as he surveyed the area, protecting her as she dove beneath the surface.

Ran realized he could see her from his position on the mountain, yet no one else could gain an unrestricted view, for the boulders shielded her.

He relaxed a little more.

"I've never known a woman with more love to offer and such an unlikely candidate to receive it."

Ran watched her swim into dark waters, dive, and come up a moment later with a fat shiny shell. "Are you saying I am unworthy of Aurora's love, Mister Avilar."

If it would go to fists, Dom thought, he would have his say and be done. "I'm saying you're unwilling. And breaking that celibate's vow, which I've consistently thought was preposterous—"

"So you have told me—"

"—was only the start."

"Of what, Domingo?"

"Shaking you free of this unreasonable link you have with your father's sins."

Ran lowered the glass and stared at the Spaniard.

"Three people love you unconditionally, yet you barely spare a moment or a civil word, to the point that they avoid you," he lashed an arm toward the lagoon and Aurora, "instead of suffering your black moods."

"Would you care to heap another helping of my disgusting behavior for your inspection?"

"Have you a big enough spoon?"

"Dom." Tired, pleading.

"Marry her, Ran, have fat babies, forget about the slave ships. You've done your part."

Sailors climbed into the granite cave, effectively severing conversation. Two men in threadbare breeches, boots, and naught else stood afore their captain.

"Mister Cross says he'll have the land cleared for plantin' by week next, sir," a sandy-haired man said to Ran, huffing for air atween each word. "And the carpenter says the *Lion* figurehead can be changed to whatever you need cause it's big 'nough." He turned away, then stopped. "Oh, and the schoolmaster asks that you be speakin' with the lad, for the last time 'e was in class, the young whip cut out afore they opened their primers." This amused the sailor.

"My thanks, Ducks." Ran patted him on the shoulder, giving it a rough shake. "Well done." Ducks smiled, showing two missing teeth, his spine straightening as captain and first mate turned out of the cove and forged down the mountain.

Frowning with confusion, Domingo's gaze shot to the area cleared, to Aurora, the house, the ships. Suddenly he grabbed Ran's arm, stopping his descent. Ran twisted to look at him.

"You're . . . retiring?"

Ran scoffed. "Don't be ridiculous," he said, then continued down the trail.

"I swear on my mother's grave I will not reveal a word," Domingo prodded, following like a child eager for a treat.

"Your mother isn't dead, you lying Spanish wastrel." Ran grabbed a branch to steady himself. "And Aurora will hear of it first."

Domingo snorted. *"If* she'll speak to you."

Ran glanced back, frowning. "And why would she not?"

Domingo moved alongside Ran as the path widened. "Ahh, my friend," Dom chuckled, shaking his head and dropping his hand to Ran's shoulder. "You've been without the sweet gentle creatures too long, and I believe 'tis time to discuss how poorly you handle your women."

Shokai plucked sticks of broken furniture from the pile, stacking them neatly on the wide strip of leather, then tying off the bundle. He nodded to Leelan Baynes as the young man strode quickly down the street, pausing to raise his arm and prove it well healed. Ahhh, Empress, you have succeeded once again, he thought, offering a bow and a facsimile of a smile, then slinging the faggots of wood onto his back, positioning the binding strap across his forehead. The villagers gawked, but he paid them no mind, walking slowly, his hands free to tick off his steps with his staff.

The streets were few in number but clean and hard

packed, scampering children kicking up dust and sand.
Homes and shops lined the avenue to the broad stone well,
women of varied shape and size and heritage gathering to
fill jars and kettles and to gossip.

Clacking hens, Shokai thought, with a brief glance, then
focused on the path afore him. He was tired today, sleep
coming less easily for his aching bones, and he stopped to
adjust the strap more comfortably. His gaze fell on a man
leaning against the stone well, drawing water for an old
woman. Shokai's weathered face wrinkled in a frown, a
familiarity hidden in the man's bearded face.

"Boy," Shokai called, gesturing, and a child of six or
seven edged up to him, glancing back at his friends, who
remained a protective distance away. The boy clenched his
fists at his sides and bravely lifted his chin. "At the well, the
man?" was all Shokai said, and only the child's gaze shifted.

"Be the *Lion*'s bosun, sir, Connor Lockewood. He don't
talk much."

Shokai nodded as if he understood the significance of
that, then foraged in his loosely wrapped coat. With a speed
that startled the child, he pressed a coin in the boy's trembling hand, then continued on his way, his lips curving when
he heard the boy's swear laced with awe and the happy
shout to his comrades over such easily captured booty.

Thin almond-shaped eyes darted to his surroundings,
marking the lane ahead, Shokai's refined senses taking in
the bosun's appearance, stripping away the bulk and leg of
mutton–sized arms, switching the dark hair for a brighter
shade.

"You can change your clothes and face, old friend," he
whispered to himself, "but not your character."

Shokai followed at a distance as the man called Lockewood left the well, tipping his cap to the ladies on his stroll
toward the mountainside. That Shokai had not seen him
afore now was no surprise, for the pirate lord's ship was
large, housing well over two hundred forty men, and the
bosun kept to himself as did Shokai. But his empress . . . she
should have sensed the man's presence. Or had she and not
mentioned it to him? The consequences of this angered him.

The Spaniard appeared around the edge of a building, his stride relaxed as he visited from lady to lady; chatting, snatching a piece of fish off the fire, and getting his hand slapped. He kissed a maiden, boldly cupping her buttocks, and received a smile and a soft caress across his cheek. Shokai shook his head. The man's only talent is eating and pillowing, he thought; then frowned, for although the Spaniard spoke to the women brazenly tempting them with his affections, Avilar's gaze shifted from nook to doorway to the hillside. Suddenly he bid the ladies good day and hastened off.

Shokai, still walking, glanced indecisively atween Lockewood and Avilar.

Lockewood could not leave the island without notice, so he decided to make Avilar aware of his findings. Shokai approached Avilar, yet halfway to the heavy jungle skirting the house grounds, the Spaniard turned off the trail. Shokai followed, his step unheard behind Domingo as the Spaniard brushed down a cluster of ferns and froze.

Shokai's eyes narrowed to mere slits. His fist tightened on his wood staff.

In the seclusion of the viney jungle, a man and a woman lay in naked splendor upon the green carpet, her slender limbs wrapped about his hips, sweat-slicked bodies undulating in the throes of fierce bone-pounding sex.

Domingo sighed, shook his head, and released the branches, turning back. His body clenched when he saw the little man a few feet away.

Shokai's thin gaze shifted past Domingo, the guttural sounds of coupling muffled, but distinguishable. "Even the clearest mirror cannot see the back, neh?"

Domingo spared a brief glance over his shoulder, his expression marked with suspicion. "I ask that you hold your tongue on this, Shokai. For now."

Shokai nodded mutely, shuffling back toward the trail, and with a disappointed sigh, Domingo followed, leaving the *Red Lion*'s quartermaster alone with Ransom's sister.

Chapter Thirty-Two

Ran poked his head into the kitchen, glancing around. The servants ceased their work to look at him, yet only Léonie moved closer.

"Have you seen Aurora?"

Léonie smiled knowingly. He's misplaced her again, the poor dear. "She was in the garden when I came from the cookhouse."

Ran entered the kitchen, snatching a lemon tart from a heaping platter as he passed to the door. He paused on the threshold.

"Alone?" he asked, taking a bite, and Léonie nodded.

Blast! She'd promised not to move beyond the house without escort!

As Ran stepped into the garden, his expression darkened. Naught but herbs and vegetables neatly rowed within the stone confines greeted him, and as his gaze shifted to the gate, he glimpsed a thin shadow moving across the ground. Aurora, he thought, finishing off the tart as he slipped out the iron gate. Beyond the walled garden, he stopped abruptly, his gaze searching. Damn me, he thought, where was she now? Farther down the sloping ground was the smokehouse, then the summer kitchen used mostly for roasting and baking; and after checking the former, he stepped inside the summer kitchen, unnoticed by the young girls basting a lamb.

Ran cleared his throat, startling the matched pair, his gentle inquiries answered with blank stares and directions to the root cellar. The terrified looks his servants consistently gave him were starting to annoy Ransom. He'd wanted to shake the pair, then nearly laughed aloud at the thought, for 'twas likely what they expected of him.

"Good day, ladies," he said, smiling what he hoped was his best smile and giving them a jaunty salute. He walked away, enjoying their surprised gasps and giggles.

Rounding the corner of the garden wall, Ran found the root cellar, full of jars and bottles, dried fruit, barrels of beans, apricots, rice, couscous, salt, kegs of wine, ale, and various assorted spices and sundries . . . but no Aurora. Grabbing an apricot from the barrel he sank his teeth into the soft fruit and climbed the steep steps, banging his head on the door frame.

Rubbing his abused skull, he glanced left and right. He was getting nervous. How was he to keep her safe if he couldn't find her?

Though his stride was long and relaxed as he moved down the incline, Ran was anxious and, he admitted, even a little scared. With his inability to get the woman alone, he felt as if his future was unraveling and he couldn't stop it. He wasn't convinced Domingo's advice of pretty words and gifts would work on Aurora. Ran knew her better. She would see through the flimsy gestures and demand words, confessions, his heart. God above, she has it, he thought, but Ran needed more.

He wanted permanence, for the first time in his life he wanted to remain here, with her, with his family. Family.

God almighty, he never thought he'd have one, even want one, but since Aurora tumbled into his life, what he assumed about himself and others, insisted he wanted and needed to survive, was never what his heart spoke.

Shokai was right. Sooner or later we act out what we truly feel.

And Ran had to get to her afore she discovered what he'd done.

* * *

From the pebbly road, Aurora stared at the ship being readied for sail, her heart beating furiously. Cheese and crust! The *Lion* lay dormant in the water like a fat princess, the repairs slow, but this other vessel, och, sailors crawled over her like hungry ants, testing line and winch, sail and tackle, able hands hoisting kegs and barrels over the side to replenish her stores. Was it truly safe to sail? Ransom would pack her off on that vessel, she realized. He'd tried to rid her from his life afore, even when they both knew he did not want it. Kelpie's mischief, had she been wrong? Sudden anger drew her shoulders back and she spun about, smacking her nose into a broad hard chest. Warm hands steadied her.

"You have been quite the elusive woman this week, Aurora."

She lifted her gaze, meeting dark amber eyes. "No more than you, m'lord." She rubbed her nose.

"You promised not to visit unescorted."

She twisted out of his grasp. "Dinna be speakin' to me of protection and guards and such rot when I witness that!" She lashed a hand toward the ship.

Ran's gaze darted over her head to the *Ruben*. "She sails for the Maghreb."

"And when were you to tell me of this?" Aurora asked crisply.

"I'm telling you now."

Hurt burst across her features. "So this is why you have been struttin' round as if the axe were about to fall on your neck?" He hadn't the nerve to confess his plans.

His lips pressed tight and he glanced away, not wanting to have this discussion in public, and she took his silence for confirmation.

"Ochaii!" She threw her hands up. " 'Tis the last occasion you'll be treatin' me in this manner, Ransom Montegomery." She turned toward the lane leading up to the house, her pace brisk. "If 'tis gone you want me, then I'll be packin'!"

Ran blinked, stunned, his gaze bouncing from Aurora to

the ship and back. Packing? "Aurora," he said calmingly, striding up behind her. "You can not leave."

She scoffed. "And why not?"

Tell her. Ran swallowed, his tongue feeling suddenly dry and thick in his throat. *Tell her.* He couldn't. "Sayidda needs you, and what of Dahrein? The lad has come to look upon you as the mother he never knew," he rushed to say, and her steps slowed. "And you cannot ask Shokai to travel in the heat and the desert, not after the beating he suffered. He's an old man, love."

She sent him a hot look that said she'd go it alone, if need be.

"Damn your stubbornness!" he blasted.

"Dinna curse at me, pirate, you give me no choice!"

He ignored the stares from the villagers, hearing only the pain beneath her anger. Sweet saint! Would he never learn? "Aurora?"

"What of you, Ransom? Am I such a hindrance to your missions, you'd send me off without askin' after my wishes?"

His will crumbled at the catch in her voice. "The ship is sailing to search for your father."

She stopped, and Ran had taken a few steps past her afore he realized it.

She gazed up at him with wide eyes. "My father?" came soft and bewildered.

"Aye." He inspected the toes of his boots, his long hair falling to shield his features. "The *Ruben* will not return unless she carries information or the man himself."

Aurora's expression softened, her heart swelling with joy. He appeared the reluctant champion, unsure of her reaction. She peered closer. "Why do you this for me?"

His head jerked up, his gaze clashing with hers. "Selfishness," he said, straightening, and her brows furrowed. "Because I want you to stay," he hesitated, shoving his hair back and inhaling a deep breath, "with me." Her features pulled taut and he grasped her arms, drawing her near, his gaze anxiously searching her upturned face. "Will you?"

Fear. She never thought to witness it in him, but 'twas

there, stripped and barren for her to see. *Stay with me*. The
words held a wealth of emotion, speaking the volumes he
could not. For Ransom had a hard time of it, the shield
atween himself and his heart in place too long. Yet the
darkness in him was dimming. He was seeing with new eyes,
a new heart; and her happiness for him swept her into tears.

"Aurora!" Anguished, impatient, his fingers flexing on
her arms.

She laid her hands to his chest, palms splayed wide over
sculptured muscle. "Aye, aye," she whispered, feeling the
thundering beat of his heart. He'd commissioned an entire
ship simply to gather information for her, and he'd done it
aforehand in the hopes she'd have no reason to argue the
matter. The gesture made her love him more. "I dinna wish
to leave, anyway."

"Is that so?" His voice lowered to a husky growl, his head
tilting, nearing. God, this close to her, he didn't even know
what he was saying.

"And 'tis well you've all that muscle," her hands slid
down his chest to grip his waist, "for to shove me on that
ship would take a wee bit of doin'."

"A wee bit." Her every breath pushed her bosom lightly
against his chest.

" 'Tis a home I've come to love, your Sanctuary." She
moistened her lips, anticipation skimming through her.
" 'Tis magical."

"Magical," he repeated, feeling the faint heat of her
mouth brush his.

"Capt'n Montegomery!"

Ran groaned in disappointment, briefly pressing his forehead to hers, afore releasing her. He glared at the sailor.

"Mister Hawkins asks that you come aboard the *Ruben*,
sir." Ducks doffed his cap, aware he'd interrupted an intimate moment, but smiled cheekily just the same. "Somethin' 'bout the route yer wantin'."

Ran sighed. He had to attend to this matter. "Aye, aye,"
he said, agitated, turning to Aurora as Dahrein raced down
the lane.

"Mem sahib?" Dahrein called, skidding to a stop aside

her. "It is almost three," he reminded her excitedly. "We will be late." He shifted from foot to foot.

"Canna have that, can we now?" she said, lightly patting his cheek, then looked to Ransom. Eyes met and locked.

"Coming, Capt'n?"

"Mem sahib?" Dahrein grasped her hand, tugging.

She shrugged helplessly, sidestepping away.

"This is not finished," he told her, watching her leave afore turning toward the shore.

He'd taken only a few steps when he heard, "Ransom?" He stopped and faced her. She back-stepped up the hill, swinging her braid like a reticule. "If you wanted me to stay, all you had to do was ask."

Ran made a sound, half chuckle, half groan as he shook his head. Ask. Bloody damn novel approach, that.

Ran strode up the lane, looking left and right.

Damn and blast. He'd dispatched his affairs with Hawkins in rude haste in the hope of catching her afore another soul obstructed his path or insisted they needed Aurora's attention.

Well, damn them all, he needed her. It wasn't as if he wanted to ravish the woman— Well, he did, but a consenting ravish, he thought, a smile lighting his darkened features when he heard her laughter. Shokai's cave, Ran realized and hastened off to the left. Peering into the murky cavern, he found it empty, his brows drawing down. Blast.

He spun about when he heard a grunt, followed immediately by the definite impact of something hitting the ground. Poking through the trees, he stilled when he saw Aurora, climbing to her feet and dusting off her hands.

What was she up to now? And, good God, where did she find breeches?

Pushing atween the fronds and ferns, Ran stepped into the clearing. Shokai was face to face with Dahrein, instructing him on the precise movements of his feet.

Suddenly Aurora rushed forward as if to attack the old man, and Ran swallowed his tongue as Shokai shifted slightly, his light slap to her shoulder sending Aurora flying past, headfirst across the ground. Ran raced to her, but she was already sitting back on her calves, brushing herself off.

"Good day, Ransom," she said brightly, and he offered his hand, his gaze skimming over her body as he pulled her to her feet.

"Do it again," Dahrein begged, his eyes wide with amazement.

"Nay!"

"Certainly."

Ran and Aurora spoke in unison.

Shokai chuckled, calling the boy to come try as Aurora lifted her gaze to Ransom's.

"Dinna be lookin' to scold me this time," she said tiredly. "Dahrein kens more of this than me. See," she added proudly as Dahrein aptly defended himself with fists and his agility. "Shokai's father learned from a priest from China."

Ran didn't spare teacher or student a glance. "I do not care how or where he learned what, Aurora, I do not want to see you dueling fisticuffs with a boy!"

"You'd rather it be you," she challenged tartly, stepping closer, and when he folded his arms, his expression smug, Aurora gazed up at him adoringly, then hooked her foot behind his knee and jerked hard, toppling him to the ground. Ran blinked, catching his breath, and in a heartbeat Aurora dropped aside him, her forearm braced across his throat.

" 'Tis twice I've landed you on your back, pirate." She arched a brow, her turn to be smug.

"I would rather push you onto yours," he growled softly, his free hand cupping the back of her head and pulling her closer for a kiss, his mouth rolling over hers in a shameless slide of tongue and lips, swift with banked hunger. God, he'd missed her, he thought, drawing back. He chuckled at her dreamy look.

Her eyes flashed open. "Arrogant beastie," she muttered.

"Aye, and the beast is hungry." He lifted his head to kiss her again.

Shokai made a noise in his throat, loudly, and Aurora's

gaze shifted atween her scowling *sempai* and a grinning Dahrein.

"Cheese and crust." She scrambled off Ransom, waiting til he stood.

"Nay," he said in all seriousness. "I prefer softer delicacies to that." He reached for her and she batted his hand away, enjoying his teasing, yet urging him to watch the lesson. Aurora observed, Shokai instructed, Dahrein listened, and Ran focused on her breeches.

"Those," he pointed to the pants cinched with a bit of rope, "are highly, *highly* improper."

"I ken why you English dinna wear a kilt," she said, ignoring his chastising. " 'Tis convenient this." She plucked at the baggy breeches. "And comfortable."

"That is not what I meant," he hissed, and she knew it, the imp.

She tossed her braid off her shoulder, sparing him a mild glance. "You dinna like them for you canna toss them up, 'tis all."

Ran choked. "By God, you are a lippy woman!"

"That I am."

Dahrein paused to stare at the feuding couple until Shokai dropped him to the ground with a single jab to his chest, then wagged a warning finger in his face.

A pistol shot rent the air, then another, and Ran was thrashing through the jungle afore the third successive blast. He came upon Domingo shoving his flintlock into his waistband as he stood over a body, one of the natives on the opposite side.

Domingo looked up as Ran approached.

"Who is it?"

"Hard to tell. A woman."

Ran bent, his expression souring. "God almighty!" The body was mangled, skin torn from throat and arms in strips, a chunk of flesh gouged out of its side, exposing rib bones and spilling organs. Claws, Ran realized.

His gaze snapped to Domingo. "A lion?"

"Po-tahd thinks so." Domingo inclined his head to the native standing motionless, a spear clutched in his fist. The native revered the animals as Gods, actually bringing infant cubs in canoes from the outlying islands.

Aurora came up behind Ransom, sucking air into her lungs. He immediately stood, pulling her away from the gruesome sight.

She wriggled free. "I am fine," she said determinedly, stepping closer, frowning.

Dahrein entered the clearing, Shokai at his side, and at the brush of leaves, Aurora twisted. "Nay, go back to your lessons," she ordered, and when Dahrein looked to defy her, she added more firmly, "Do not gainsay me, Dahrein, please." The boy stole a quick glance, then left with Shokai.

"He has seen worse, Aurora."

She met his gaze. "He's a child, Ransom, and I would keep his memories happy and pleasing afore he grows to a man."

"Remind me to tell you of his past," Ran said sadly.

"I care not, only that he be spared this," she looked at the body, "nightmare."

Ran let the matter fade, focusing on the victim, but he had to clench his fists to keep from pulling her back when she knelt and sanded a torn piece of skirt atween her fingertips. Aurora lifted her gaze to Ransom afore returning it to the body.

Something was odd, and she sensed it, he knew.

"She looks familiar."

"Aye," Ran agreed, now that she'd mentioned it. His gaze drifted over the striped skirt, but he couldn't place it. "Good God, Rachel?"

"Nay, nay," Aurora assured. "This woman is shorter."

"She is Helena," came in a low whisper.

Aurora jerked to her feet.

Connor Lockewood stood a few feet away, his gaze on the dead woman. He strode closer, regret in his eyes.

"If you know her, man, speak up," Ran insisted, watching his face.

"I did not. But Markus did," he said, the words weighing heavy on his tongue. He lifted his gaze, looking first at Aurora, then to Ransom. "They were lovers."

Domingo nudged his captain, inclining his head for Ran to follow. Ran eyed Lockewood for a moment, then strode over to his first mate. They stood with heads bowed.

"What!" Aurora heard, and she glanced at Ransom. Ran cursed, looked to the sky, then at the body. Domingo nodded and disappeared into the woods.

The warning shot brought Mister Buckland, huffing and clutching his bag as he picked his way atween the clusters of rocks and trees.

"My word!" he gasped, stopping beside Aurora.

Without looking from the body, she said, "Tell me what you see, physician."

Together they stared down at the blood-soaked remains. "She hasn't been dead long. Died here from the look of it," he said, then lifted astonished eyes to hers.

"Dinna speak it aloud," she whispered, slyly meeting Ran's gaze, then shifting her eyes to Lockewood.

He hadn't moved, his stare fixed on the victim, and Aurora felt the strength of his sorrow. He looked at her then, and she caught her breath, so intense was his gaze. Did he care deeply for the girl, for 'twas a love lost she sensed in the quiet man? She hadn't time to wonder further, for the area quickly filled with spectators. Ran banished them to the village, and Lockewood made to join them. Ran stopped him.

"We must bury her. Domingo will return with a horse in a moment." Lockewood nodded solemnly, turning away to wait in private as Ran halted beside Aurora. Her attention was on the body.

"You are a strange woman, love, to stare at that," he said with disgust.

She ignored his distaste, lifting her gaze to his.

"I thought lions would not attack unless starved or provoked?"

"Aye," Ran said, recognizing the line of her thoughts. "The pride has lived peacefully with us and the natives for years."

"They've never attacked afore?"

"A lamb once, I think, but naught else that I recall."

"She did not anger this beast, Ransom." Final, certain.

"What say you, lass?" He scowled, confused.

"Look at her legs." She pointed. "Not a scratch. Would not the lion attack there first, or her back, to bring her to the ground? And the wounds on her arms and throat," she indicated with a wave and he frowned, unable to see what she wanted, "there is little blood flowing from them and even less on the ground around her."

His features pulled taut. "She was dead afore the lion touched her," he concluded.

"Aye," Aurora agreed quietly. "Freshly dead, for the lion would touch naught but a recent kill."

"Sweet mother of God." Ran shoved his fingers through his hair, meeting her gaze. Murder.

Chapter Thirty-Three

In the waning hours of daylight, Ran and Domingo questioned bloody near every soul inhabiting the island save the babes, yet turned up little, for Helena had kept to herself. Except on occasion, Ran was beginning to learn. Seated behind his desk, he toyed with a small blade, and Aurora, sitting across the room on the settee, was entranced as he rolled the knife over his knuckles and around his fingers as if 'twere a living thing. Lamplight winked off the silver, keeping her spellbound.

"By Jesus! Why do you question me like this? Have I once in two years given you cause to distrust me?" Lougière bellowed, thrusting to his feet. It startled Aurora and she looked up. "I tell you I am not the only man on this island who has lain with Helena."

"Yet rumor has it she fancied herself in love with you." Lougière's expression fell into shock, but he quickly recovered.

"She was attacked by a wild animal for God's sake!"

"I do not seek to blame, Markus, only to find answers as to why she was even in the jungle." Ran's tone was calm, remote. "You were her last acquaintance."

"Happenstance," Markus said, his fists clenched at his side.

"Did you notice aught different in her mood, her manner?"

Markus frowned, struggling to remember. "She was always a bendable lass, simple, patient," he said with some

fondness. "Her English wasn't clear enough for much conversation." A lusty smile pulled at his lips til he recalled her
fate.

"From where did she hail?" Dom asked, his gaze ripping
over Lougière.

Markus felt it and his expression went suddenly blank.
"She never told me." He shrugged. "A land north of the
Caspian Sea," he said vaguely, not meeting Ran's gaze.
"Mayhaps Russia, for her accent was Slavic." He shrugged
again, and Domingo's eyes narrowed, pinning him.

"Dismissed, Mister Lougière," Ran said, and Markus
spun on his heels, quitting the room.

"I wonder if his tryst with Rachel was intentional, the
discovery, I mean."

Aurora shot out of her seat. "Rachel?" Her gaze bounced
atween the door and Domingo, and he explained what he'd
seen, leaving out that Shokai had also witnessed the affair.

"I cannot believe 'tis so," Aurora said, "being a novitiate
of a convent."

Ran made a nasty sound, a foul sneer, and it made Aurora realize she hadn't been near Rachel enough to sense
her. The woman was always so timid, keeping to herself, not
spending more than a moment in Aurora's presence other
than at meals.

"You willna speak of this with her, Ransom."

"Nay," he agreed with a tired sigh, straightening in his
seat. "Not and be a hypocrite." He met her gaze from across
the desk, longing coloring the look.

"There is little else we can do this night, Ran." Domingo
didn't believe either heard him, and he smiled for the first
time that evening, leaving them alone.

Aurora moved around the desk as Ran stood. A knock
rattled the door, and Ransom moaned almost childishly at
the interruption, then snapped a terse command. Aurora's
hand covered his, her expression scolding as Léonie peered
around the door.

"Thought you might want to know Mister Buckland is up
with Sayidda, miss, and Dahrein has eaten and is in bed."

"Rachel?"

"She has taken a tray to her room."

Aurora moved to the door, glancing back briefly. "Speak with Dahrein, Ransom; ease his curiosity." Ran's smile was tender, and he moved to catch her hand afore she slipped from the room. He brought it to his lips, kissing the back, then the warm center, closing his eyes.

"When will you think of us, Aurora?" he whispered, tugging her closer, his mouth a fraction from hers.

She gazed into liquid-gold eyes, her body blossoming with vivid desire. She longed for his touch, for the feel of his strength wrapped around her.

A maid called her, urgently, and she smiled, disappointed and apologetic, then swept around the half open door, leaving Ransom alone, again.

Doctor Buckland covered Sayidda and stepped back from the bed. He took her pulse, watched her shallow breathing, then tucked her arm beneath the coverlet. Lifting his gaze to Aurora, he shook his head.

"I cannot understand it. She's worse in the morning."

"Aye, by noon she is at least sitting up and taking tea, but by nightfall she is like this." Aurora nodded to the woman lying so still in the bed, her skin bearing a yellow cast. "I can ease the upset and the pain."

Buckland's brow wrinkled. "What makes you think 'tis poison?"

Aurora glanced to the side, biting her lip. She took his hand, bringing forth a single digit and touching it to the smooth stone topping her ring.

His eyes widened. " 'Tis not simply warm from your wear, but hot."

" 'Tis tellin' me beware of the taint," she said. "Now, go home, Doctor," She ushered him toward the door afore he could ask any questions. "I will stay with her." Aurora yawned hugely, her eyes tearing.

Buckland's lips curved in a tender smile. "You look prepared to sleep standing, miss." He patted her hand. "Send for me if there is any change."

* * *

Plans were falling apart, years of waiting, of covert messages and faceless couriers bleeding the Emperor's funds. And the blame would lie afore one pair of loyal feet. The royal bloodline must be extinguished, leaving no claim to the throne, no threat to the reigning Emperor and his bride.

Belowstairs in a room off to the back of the house, Ran sat at the foot of Dahrein's bed. The lad didn't seem uncomfortable with the late visit, nor with Ran's position, though both knew he'd spent little time in the lad's room. It bespoke the quarters of a child of one and ten: a small chest of secret treasures, shells, and odd little pieces of sea-smooth glass lining the sill, a discarded map nailed on the wall, an adventurous path marked across in dark graphite. Ran smiled, for he'd done the same at Dahrein's age.

But the curtains and coverlet were recent acquisitions, Ran realized, along with a wardrobe and rug. It shamed him that he'd been so thoughtless to the boy's comforts, and he knew, without doubt, Aurora had seen to the furnishings.

"Sahib?" Dahrein peeked beneath Ran's bowed head and Ran smiled, shifting his knee onto the bed, bracing his back against the footboard.

"I bid you call me Ransom." He tested the mattress with a couple of shoves.

Dahrein's eyes widened. "But not even the bosun calls you that!"

"But you are not the bosun. Mister Lockewood and I are not friends."

Dahrein beamed, sinking down into the covers. A soft knock and Aurora opened the door, slipping inside, a tray in her hand, a glass of goat's milk and a moderate slice of Léonie's cinnamon cake resting in the center.

"Hungry, Dahrein?" she said in mischievous whisper, coming around to the opposite side of the bed and setting the tray on the commode.

"Aurora," Ran admonished, " 'tis too late to be eating that."

"A sweet snack offers sweet dreams, Ransom, and *you* are not a growing boy."

Dahrein's gaze shifted atween the two as Ransom frowned and Aurora offered the treat. Delighted, he accepted the milk, draining half afore he put it aside to indulge in his midnight feast.

"Have you any questions, Dahrein? About what happened?"

He stilled, the fork halfway to his open mouth as he considered her request. "Helena was nice to me." Slyly he met Ran's gaze. "To everyone."

Ran pursed his lips, his eyes warning, and Aurora huffed, her hands on her hips. Ran dared a look at her, then shrugged sheepishly.

"But I do not think she liked Miss Rachel."

"Why do you say that?" Ran asked.

Dahrein politely finished chewing. "Helena argued with her outside the cookhouse, the day you . . ."

"Go on, lad," Aurora urged, glancing briefly at Ran.

His pale gaze shifted rapidly atween the adults. "The day you argued over Sayidda."

Ran's features stretched tight, recognizing time and place and why he'd thought her familiar. He'd seen the pair that afternoon.

Aurora waited without comment until Dahrein finished his treat, then tucked him snugly into bed.

"I think the *Lion*'s new figurehead should be a great spreading hawk," Dahrein said, yawning.

Ran motioned discreetly for him to be silent, but he failed to make his point when Aurora twisted to look at him.

"New figurehead?" A brow swept up, her gaze shifting atween both males.

"The *Red Lion* was sunk this last voyage, mem sahib," Dahrein said, highly amused at the tall tale as he snuggled beneath the sheets.

"Dahrein!" Ran groaned.

"You did not tell her?" he peeped, then realized his blunder.

"Remind me never to share a secret with you," Ran chuckled, leaning forward to ruffle the lad's hair. Dahrein sighed, certain he was forgiven.

His stomach full and his body exhausted from his lessons, Dahrein was nearly asleep when Aurora dropped a kiss to the top of his head. Ran stood by the door, watching as she lightly brushed hair from his brow, her expression so adoring a spark in his chest caught and ignited. To have had that love when he was child, Ran thought as she took up the tray, bracing it on her hip and preceding him out.

Ran closed the door, expecting her to be near, yet finding her moving down the hall and into the dining room.

"You're angry, again." Her hips swayed enticingly, capturing his attention.

"Nay, peeved," she said, and he caught her elbow, taking the tray. "Ransom, I've work to tend." She reached for the tray.

"I want to play," he countered huskily, setting it on the long table.

Before she could utter a protest he pulled her into his arms, his mouth crushing hers, his arms swallowing her in his strong embrace. His lips were warm and smooth, and he tasted of lemons and brandy, his tongue pushing atween her lips and sweeping deeply inside.

She opened wide for him, clutching his shoulders, moving restlessly against the long sinewy length of his tall body. She ached, her urgent whimper speaking for her as his hand slid up her back, driving into her hair. His kiss grew wilder, hungrier, low moans and a ticking clock the only sound in the sleep-quiet house. Fabric rustled. Soft sighs pleaded.

Yellow candlelight threw the figures in shadows.

Aurora drew back a fraction, breathing heavily. "You think to sweeten me with kisses?"

"And more," he said dipping his head, his mouth skimming the flesh of her throat, then lower.

Desire spread hotly through her, distracting her. "Nay, nay, nay," she pushed out of his arms.

"Aurora," came in a frustrated growl as she avoided his reach and picked up the tray, heading to the kitchen.

Ran followed, the rattle of dishes giving way his affect on her.

"The *Red Lion* died this past voyage," he pleaded his case as she carefully settled the soiled dishes in the wash tub. "The ship will sail into British waters with a new figurehead, her new crew spreading the word that the pirate, Red Lion, perished, going down with his damaged ship." She looked at him with beautifully wide eyes, wiping her hands on a cloth. "The unexpected victory will please them, thinks you?" He smiled.

She didn't. "You will sail with her?" Breathless, afraid.

"Nay, love. And the *Ruben* will bring the rumor of my 'death' afore the *Lion* sails."

"Ransom," she warned as she left the kitchen. "I dinna ask you to change, only to bend a wee bit."

He followed.

"So dinna be givin' up your cause for me."

He loved it when she was full of spice and indignation. "I'm merely rerouting my priorities." He shrugged negligently. "And handing the task to Domingo."

She paused at the foot of the stairs. "You canna tell me sitting idle on this island will satisfy you." She waved to the lush greenery beyond the walls, and the corners of his mouth quirked rakishly.

"I find I am more than content to be the planter." He propped an elbow on the bannister, his chin in his palm. He grinned.

The land freshly cleared, she realized, searching his features for confirmation, the shifting breeze flicking candlelight across his square jaw. "Ransom. Dinna be teasin'."

He straightened, his expression gone serious. "I sailed for the wrong reasons, love, and when I asked you to stay here," his voice lowered, "I did not mean alone."

" 'Tis a house bursting with people, Ransom." She patted his cheek, thrilled with his admittance. "Neither of us would ever be lonely, thinks I." She spun away, rapidly mounting the stairs.

"I know, says me," he muttered, ascending after her. "By God," he hissed softly, "will you cease for one moment and talk with me!"

She paused on the top landing, looking back. "I've a bit of work still," she reminded.

"This house is silent for the evening, love, and you need to be sleeping." He paused at her eye level. "With me."

Her brow arched sharply. "An invitation, is it now?"

Ran slipped closer, his broad hand on her waist. "Will you accept?"

She glanced to the side. "I have tried to preserve your wishes, for I ken you dinna want a babe with me, but I canna be responsible should—"

"Are you increasing?" he asked indelicately, his fingers tightening.

"Nay."

His brow furrowed. "You speak with certainty."

"I am." She turned out of his touch and negotiated the lantern-lit hall. "And if you'd spoken to me but once these past days, I would have told you thus."

Damn. Her monthly, he thought, marching up the remaining steps.

His head down, hands braced behind his back, Ran was momentarily lost in thought as he walked the corridor til he heard Aurora moving around in Sayidda's room. She was plying a cloth to his mother's forehead, her own sharply marked with concern.

"Aurora."

"Hold this, Ransom. I need to freshen the water." She picked up the basin and with a Betty lamp in the other hand, slipped behind the dressing screen. Setting the light on the commode, Aurora poured the lukewarm water into the tub, then reached for the pitcher shelved beyond the tub. Her foot kicked something and she frowned, grasping the pitcher and bending to see. "Cheese and crust," she muttered. 'Twas too dark, and she set the crockery aside and, with the lamp in hand, squatted. She held it out, her gaze scanning the darkness. The light caught on a flash, and a fractured memory tripped to the surface as she knelt and stretched to reach the sparkling glow. A pear-shaped bottle lay on its side atween the commode and the copper tub, close to the draped curtains framing the private bathing area. The fabric shifted with the strong night breeze and as she stood, Aurora considered the bottle was meant to be hidden behind the drape, for she'd never seen it afore.

She turned the fat vial over in her hand, holding it to the lamp. 'Twas beautiful, carved crystal with a glass stopper shaped like a bird, and she made to set it on the richly polished commode when a stinging raced through her body, piercing her from the inside out. She closed her eyes, breathing deeply, clutching the vial.

The vision came quickly like the flash of summer lightning, without sound, without warning, gone in an instant. The urn in the *keek stane.*

Opening her eyes she hastily set the Betty lamp on the commode and uncorked the stopper. She dipped her finger inside. 'Twas empty but for a drop lining the bottom and she stretched her finger, feeling the liquid coat the tip. It numbed, and she frowned, bringing it to her nose. She sniffed, then immediately wiped it clean, yet the sensation lingered. Dizziness swept her in a hot rush, and when Ran called to her, it seemed from a great distance.

She moved sluggishly around the screen, the bottle clutched tightly. Sayidda was awake, smiling weakly at her son, and Aurora imagined the pleasure she must have felt to find him at her bedside.

"You do not look well," he said, rushing forward and helping Aurora into a chair.

He poured her some water, kneeling by her side, his face a mask of sudden fear. Aurora drank deeply, then handed back the glass. She held out the vial, blinking to focus as she explained where she'd found it.

"Rachel gave that to me," Sayidda whispered hoarsely, and both looked at her.

"When?"

Sayidda struggled to remember. "The day you arrived. She used it to scent my bath water."

Ran's eyes snapped to Aurora. "Dinna think such thoughts, Ransom, for she may have been gifted with it."

"I will find out!"

He made to take the vial, and she held it out of his reach. "Nay, *I* will."

Ran held her gaze, battling with his need to see this matter solved and Aurora sheltered from harm. Realizing she would gain more from Rachel than he, he nodded.

Aurora stood, using Ran's shoulder for support, then walked to Rachel's chamber, pausing afore the threshold to gain her bearings. She heard crying from within, muffled heart-wrenching sobs, and when she pushed open the door, she found the slim woman on her knees aside the bed, her folded hands on the coverlet.

"Rachel? Are you ill?"

"I will be fine." She sniffled, rising off the floor to plop dejectedly on the bed, and Aurora, too upset to wait for her to gather her tattered composure, thrust the bottle in her line of vision.

"Where did you get this?"

Rachel blinked, then lifted her gaze. "It was a gift."

"From Markus?"

Rachel looked at her as if she'd been slapped.

"Aye, I ken you've been with Lougière."

"Does Ransom?" Rachel asked timidly.

"Aye."

She crumbled a bit more. "He is upset?"

"Disappointed mayhaps, but your brother hasna led the pristine life to become your judge, and neither have I." A pause and then, "Was Helena the lass who asked for the medicines?"

Rachel glanced to the side, her disheveled hair shielding her face. She didn't answer.

"Why do you hide the name if the lass is dead?" Aurora persisted, and Rachel broke her silence, bursting into fresh tears.

"I told her the dose, but she grabbed the bottle from me afore I could take it back. She drank it all!" Rachel wailed.

"I see," Aurora said unsympathetically. "And you helpe(
Sayidda with her bath daily, usin' this?"

"Si," she muttered, frowning at the quick change of sub
ject. "I did not care for the scent."

Aurora's spine stiffened as she stared down at the pitifu
creature. Rachel was hiding something, and though her own
emotions were pulling her in two directions, Aurora wa:
certain of it.

But this woman was Ransom's sister. She'd given n(
cause for doubt, and Aurora realized she scarcely knew her

Rachel hesitantly tilted her head back, ashamed, dispir
ited; and Aurora said naught. As she left the room, Rache
flopped onto the bed, sobbing hysterically.

Ransom stood when Aurora entered the chamber, imme
diately noticing the stiff, tight set of her shoulders.

"She is in pain," he said, concerned for his mother.

Aurora's shoulders drooped. Though Sayidda was sleep
ing, she'd curled up like a child, attempting to ease th(
agony.

Aurora thrust the bottle at Ransom. "Markus gave it t(
Rachel. A gift she says."

Only his gaze shifted. "You doubt her?"

" 'Twas filled with the sap of a milk plant, thinks I
though well refined and scented with lavender."

"Dear God!" Ransom seemed to wither, dropping into a
chair, his head bowed. 'Twas deadly and, he realized, from
Africa.

"If Rachel and Markus are lovers, why would he be givin
her something so deadly?" Aurora shook her head, answer
ing her own question. "Nay, Helena gave it to her, thinks
I."

His head jerked up. "To poison Rachel? Why? Jealousy?'

Aurora told him of the abortive Rachel had given Helena
that even after the warnings, Helena had taken too much a
once. It likely killed her.

"Mayhaps Helena committed suicide," Ran suggested
"Love unrequited?"

" 'Tis possible. One canna assume the depth of another':
pain, and being with child, realizing she'd lost Markus'

heart to Rachel, and that she'd failed with that," she gestured to the vial in his hand, "she may have welcomed her death."

Aurora would never understand that train of thought, but considered the possibility.

"But Helena was dead afore the lion caught her, lass, and something or someone provoked it to attack."

"To mark her death a murder?"

"Mayhaps to blame another."

"Rachel or Markus?"

Ran shrugged, too tired to think on it. "They were the bane of her misfortune." He turned the bottle over in his hand. "You saw this in your seer box." 'Twas a statement, lacking doubt.

" 'Twas absorbed through her skin, mayhaps every morn in her bath water, then again at evetide to cool her when the fever rose." It angered Aurora that she hadn't sensed the poison until it entered Sayidda's body. "Now that none will pass to her again, mayhaps we can sweat it out and with a blood purifier . . ." Her words trailed off, and he looked up, hope shadowing his handsome face. Aurora knew what was necessary and, suddenly, so did he.

Ran stood, gripping the bottle so tightly the stopper cracked. "I will ready a bath for you, love." He stared deep into her eyes. "Prepare your altar."

Ransom did not lay witness to the ritual, remaining outside the room, but he heard the now familiar Pict chant of incantation, ancient words calling on the powers of the earth and spirit. And in that moment, however brief, Ransom Montegomery believed in what could not be explained.

Chapter Thirty-Four

Aurora slipped into the chamber. "Ransom?" she whispered, believing him asleep. With no response, she searched the darkness and found him standing on the balcony, his back braced on the open door frame, his big body thrown into shadows. The blue-gray light of midnight splashed down over the carved muscles of his chest, his folded arms, the sinewy length of his thighs. Her body jumped to life, a primal heat singing through her bloodstream.

He was naked but for a bath cloth drawn around his hips.

She studied his face, half-shadowed, his gaze lingering on the view to the sea, and she sensed a yearning in him and—A painful scraping drove through her, catching in her chest, clawing up to her throat.

He must have heard her gasp, for he jerked a look at her. She stood in the center of the chamber, her unbound hair a vivid contrast against the flowing white nightrail, her fingers crunching the voluminous folds.

"Come here, love," Ran said, holding out his arm, and she flew to him, clinging, her body pressed tightly to his, and Ran kissed the top of her head, enfolding her in his embrace.

She trembled and he tucked his fingers beneath her chin, forcing her to look at him.

His gaze searched hers. "What is it? Sayidda?"

"Nay, she sleeps, but . . ." Her stare faltered.

"You're frightened," he marveled. "What has done this?"

She met his gaze. "You."

His brows rose a fraction.

"One moment you beg me to stay with you and then I see you longing to be gone."

"Ah, love," he brushed the backs of his knuckles across her cheek. "I look at the life I led for my own selfishness."

" 'Tis a valiant cause, Ransom, and I dinna wish to see it perish."

He smiled crookedly. "But I am no longer satisfied to be the champion. And I gladly bid it good voyage."

She searched his face for the truth and smiled. "I willna be left behind if you've the need to sail and conquer something."

He grinned, slow and rascally. "I would not dream of conquering aught without you." She smiled sleepily, and he bent closer. "I have missed you this week," he murmured, brushing his lips back and forth over hers.

"I ken I've not been near, but Dahrein, he—"

"I know, pest." He deepened the kiss, briefly, smoothing his hands over the curve of her spine, and she moaned, resting her head on his chest. He could spend his life just like this.

Ran wanted to wake on quiet nights with his mind hopping from subject to subject and be able to talk with her, listen to her profound reasoning. He wanted her near because his house was alive with her in it, because he was alive only with her. He wanted her plump with his child and warm in his bed. He needed her serenity, her zest for life, to keep him from slipping into the darkness of his past. He needed to know that if he were to set sail again, she would join him or await. 'Twould make him cautious, he knew, and anxious to return, but he cared only that Aurora loved him, that she would not leave him, would forever cradle his heart.

He wanted a future. He wanted her for his wife.

And when he'd realized his desire to have it all was greater than his need to return to his missions, Ran's singlemindedness had nearly pushed them apart. 'Twill take years to learn the workings of her mind, he thought.

She sagged against him and he tilted her face up, smiling

with tender humor. She was asleep. Gently he lifted her i
his arms and padded softly to his bed, laying her in th
downy center. She snuggled into the coverlet and he inche
it beneath her, then shielded her from the breeze. Ranson
stepped back and settled into a chair. Long into the night h
sat there, watching her sleep, so in love with her, and won
dering when he would have the courage to tell her hov
much.

A slim prince perched atop his sandy kingdom, Dahrein
sat on the boulder, cross-legged, his back to Aurora as sh
swam in the basin.

"Mem sahib?" he called over his shoulder when he didn
hear her splashing.

"Dahrein," she warned kindly, flicking water at his back

He hunched at the cold wet contact. "It is difficult to cal
you that . . . Aurora. It is most familiar."

"Friends are familiars, neh?"

He grinned, incredibly pleased. "Many thanks for th
fighting lessons."

" 'Tis not fighting, Dahrein." Aurora hovered in the blue
green water. " 'Tis to defend oneself."

He nodded sagely, the strong breeze ruffling his newly
cropped hair.

"Of the thirty-two ways to defend," she said, "the best i
to flee."

His chuckle was low and decidedly masculine for hi
young age. "You sound like Shokai."

Aurora smiled, her arms fanning the water as she swam
out. "He is a wise and gentle man, Dahrein, and 'twould do
you well to listen to his ways. 'Tis solution, and warning, in
his funny little phrases."

"He is very proud of you, Aurora." The name moved
easier on his tongue.

"As I am of his new student."

The corners of his mouth bowed in a bashful smile, and
without thought he twisted to look at her, his eyes bursting
wide as saucers. "Aurora!" he screamed his throat raw.

* * *

Leaning out to gain leverage, Ran snapped the reins and urged the plow horse along the rut in the field. His arms strained to keep the hulking jumble of leather and metal straight, his muscles flexing. Bloody backbreaking work, he thought, but after two days, he found himself more pleased with the accomplishment than if he'd salvaged a thousand slaves and sunk ten enemy ships. He felt exhilarated. The sugar plants, gifts off the Sultan's barge, sat like miniature guards to the sloping land, awaiting their chance to root in dark moist soil.

Suddenly he yanked back on the reins, rolling his shoulders, not from the work but for a tingling racing over his spine like slap. Lockewood strode by, nodded, and kept going; and Ran scarcely acknowledged him as he snapped the reins over the handles, searching the area and working his fingers from the gloves. He turned, facing sea and shoreline, squinting into the distance and wondering why he felt so strange. Immediately he reached behind his back for his knife, withdrawing the long curved blade. He worked the bone grip in his fist, amber eyes searching. 'Twas fear he felt, untold terror, yet not his own. Then he heard Dahrein shout and took off running toward the shore, ignoring the men calling to him. Ransom forced his legs to move swiftly, his chest heaving frantically. The villagers stared as he raced by and scrambled around the boulder to where he knew Aurora was swimming.

His heart slammed against the wall of his chest.

Aurora stood hip-deep in the water, Dahrein on the shore.

A shark circled her legs, slowly, the dorsal fin blading through the water.

"Nay, Dahrein! Stay back!"

"But he will attack!"

"Nay! I am protected, he will not!"

Aurora watched the dark fin slip closer and closer, and she chanted, prayed to the Goddess to protect her.

"Oh, Rom," Dahrein swore. The shark bumped her leg

and Aurora flailed wildly for balance and Dahrein splashed into the water to catch her. The shark sang through the sea with amazing swiftness toward the disturbance.

"Run! Dahrein!" Aurora shouted, helpless. Dahrein tried to turn back, but the depth hindered, and the shark clamped its jaws on the boy's calf. He screamed, his head thrown back for an instant afore he was dragged into the water. And Aurora searched the sandy bottom for a rock, a shell, anything to help as the big fish shook him violently, wanting only a piece while she was forced to listen to him beg for help.

Ransom help me, Ransom, she silently called, trying to narrow her thoughts to free the jagged teeth from Dahrein. Panic refused to yield to her powers. Blood colored the water. Dark blue running red as Ransom skidded to a halt on the sand. In the space of a heartbeat he took in the horror and met her gaze.

"Help him!"

Ran held the knife by the blade point, his gaze shooting atween Aurora and Dahrein and the second fin cutting the surface. He drew his arm back and threw, the blade whisking downward into the water, striking with such force the shark bowed in the water, releasing Dahrein afore it flopped wildly.

"Hurry!" she cried, backing up cautiously. Ran scooped the nearly unconscious boy from the water, bringing him to shore. He clamped his hands on the mangled flesh and muscle. Blood fountained atween his fingers and he pressed tighter, feeling bone. Aurora backed out of the surf, then ran to Dahrein, dropping to her knees. She checked his eyes, then his leg, showing him no emotion over the wound. Immediately she stripped off her chemise and wrapped it around his calf, pulling tighter and tighter, then knotting it off.

"Aurora," Dahrein gasped. "You're safe?"

"Aye, lovey, please do not talk." She met Ran's gaze. "To the house, quickly."

Ran stood, his face creased with worry; then he looked at her, it just dawning that she was naked.

"Aurora, you cannot—"

Her gaze cut to his, razor sharp. "I dinna give a rat's arse, Ransom," she said acidly. "Take my boy to the house!" Ran cradled Dahrein in his arms and Aurora walked alongside, her gaze narrowing on the hands wrapped over the wound. She would use aught in her power to save Dahrein, and focused her thoughts, channeling them to ease his pain, to stop the bleeding.

A crowd had gathered, and Domingo shouldered his way atween, barking orders and stripping off his shirt. He draped it around Aurora's shoulders.

Ran glanced solemnly at Dom, then spoke to the boy, calling his name as Aurora, barelegged, moved alongside. Lockewood appeared, pulling a horse forward, and with Dahrein in his arms, Ran swung up onto its bare back, wheeling about and racing up the hill to his home. Aurora ran behind, buttoning the shirt and begging for someone to send for Buckland. She was breathless and sobbing when she entered the house. Dahrein lay on the dining table, motionless, and Ransom looked at her, helpless, his stomach and breeches covered in Dahrein's blood.

"Boil water! Bring me cloths, needles, thread, blankets, and my sack," she gasped atween breaths, swiping at her tears. As Léonie and Domingo sped off to do as she bid, Aurora crossed to Dahrein. She gazed down at the terrified youth and gently brushed wet hair from his forehead. He was shaking.

"Och, me brave young lad," she whispered sadly, her tears on the edge. "Nay, dinna speak. I ken it hurts." His lips pressed to a bloodless white, his pale blue eyes begging for relief. "I promise I will make it stop."

She lifted her gaze to Ransom and swallowed. "Hold tight to the wound and do not let go." Her voice cracked and she struggled for evenness. "I'm needin' strips of cloth and a piece of wood. Now."

Léonie tore her apron, then reached to the mantel, snapping off the candle from a wooden stick and handing it to her. Aurora made a tourniquet, slowing the flow of blood to the wound as Buckland entered the house, pausing to take in the scene, the surgeon becoming the consummate professional in the breath of a glance.

Aurora was relieved.

She worked quickly, preparing a sedative and cradling Dahrein's head as she forced him to drink it. He slipped into a painless world as Aurora met Buckland's gaze across the table.

"Nay!" she hissed angrily, softly, easily reading his doubt. "Dinna be even thinkin' it! We can do this! The limb stays."

He gathered strength from her determination, and together they set about to fight for Dahrein's young life.

Ransom watched for a moment, admiring Aurora's ability to maintain calm as she plucked broken shark's teeth from the gaping wound, her chanting words mouthed silently as Buckland plied his instruments to the torn flesh.

Ran quit the room, stopping on the porch and sinking to the step. He held his head in his hands, Dahrein's suffering striking him with the force of a cutlass. Over and over in his mind the horrible moment replayed, the split instant of indecision when two lives so precious to him were in danger. His stomach rolled loosely, the scent of blood filling his nostrils. God keep the boy safe, he prayed.

Ran stood abruptly, leaving the porch and striding to the horse left grazing. Snatching up the reins, he mounted.

"Ran?"

Ran jerked a look at Domingo, the horse sidestepping afore it heeled to its master. "In all the years we've lived here, Dom, have you once seen a shark venture into the basin?" Ran reined around and the beast lurched taking him swiftly to the basin.

On the rocky shore Ran searched the tranquil area, unsure of what he'd find beyond a bloody trail, the dead shark floating, half devoured by its mate and sloshing against the smooth boulder where Dahrein had kept his vigil. The stone formation marked part of one side of the pool; toward the shore was the shallow break scarcely hidden beneath the surface, and toward the sea lay the dip in the jetty where water channeled in at high tide. The only other open area of the basin flowed into the cove along the edge of the jetty. Not about to wade into the water, Ran climbed over Dahrein's perch, leaping the break and picking his way farther down, onto the curving finger of land separating the cove from the sea. His face deeply creased, Ran stood atop the rocks, searching beyond the jetty's tip. Salt water surged violently. Naught different, he thought, though he'd no cause to come out here afore now.

Discouraged he sat down on a pile of rocks, his gaze sliding over shore and ships and the cliffs rising to his left. The cove was filled with ships, the dark blue water hiding hull and anchor. Sharks had never been sighted, yet it did not abolish their existence in the warm water. If the shark had entered the channel atween the cliffs and jetty, then . . . He left his seat, striding quickly to the crusty break aside the tidal pool. Climbing onto the rocks, Ran maneuvered over the top, step by step coming closer to the churning surface. His gaze skimmed the water. His feet braced wide apart, he waited for the surge to roll back out to sea. His arm shot out, his curse vicious as he pulled the remains of a lamb from the water.

A rope dangled from the carcass, its end anchored securely to a rock with a seaman's knot.

His gaze narrowed, shifting to the path leading to this point as Domingo maneuvered toward him.

"I found footprints," he said, jerking a thumb behind him. "They stop just afore the basin." Domingo gazed out at the sea; his voice clipped with anger. "They are distinct, Ran."

"Your opinion, Mister Avilar?" The words snapped with the crack of a whip.

Domingo's gaze collided with Ran's. "The bastard's gait is uneven. He drags his right leg a bit."

Ran's eyes took on a savage gleam, primitive, predatory, scraping over the terrain of Sanctuary. Lougière. "Yet I saw Lockewood leaving from just that spot," he rasped, nodding to the path Domingo had followed.

"You think they've designed this together?"

Ran tossed the carcass on the sand. "I do not know,

Dom, yet 'tis nay doubt 'twas Aurora who was meant to die, and Dahrein," his voice faltered, and he swallowed, "was caught in the trap."

"What could she have done to warrant this?" Dom asked, both men climbing down to inspect the tracks behind Dahrein's perch. Ran's gaze traveled from the soft sand to where they ended at the boulder. The tide hadn't a chance to wash them away yet, but as Ran stood motionless, the sea spilled atween the boulders, bleaching them into the sand.

Rage scored through Ran's bloodstream, pounding in his temples, tightening his breathing. Betrayed. His family was threatened, hurt, lying bleeding and fighting for survival.

Lockewood and Lougière.

Ran would kill them.

And like it.

Chapter Thirty-Five

Ransom hadn't calmed down by the time he reached the crest of the hill, and the horse sensed his agitation, rearing back at the poor treatment. Ran immediately loosened his hold on the reins, settling the beast. He couldn't look toward the house. He wanted to keep his anger fresh and biting. He wanted to exact blood for blood, yet could do naught but recall Dahrein's face, his odd blue eyes silently begging for help, begging not to let him die. Ran swallowed repeatedly, his Adam's apple bobbing like a cork. The lad cried out. Ran looked away, grinding his teeth.

Dahrein did not deserve this. No one did, least of all this gentle-hearted boy. Fate was the thief of his childhood from the day the half-English, half-Indian babe had been abandoned, orphanages shuffling him from one cruel hand to another until he was old enough to hold a pick and be sent to the diamond mines, into darkness. Into a forgotten corner of hell.

Ran remembered the filthy child caught lifting his purse in Bombay, pale blue eyes staring bravely back in the face of his outrage. He claimed himself Dahrein, no surname, only that, and insisted 'twas enough for he was too small and insignificant to have more. Dahrein had been in Ran's care since.

And now he would die. Without knowing how strong he could become, without seeing the world beyond the Mahgreb, without experiencing the glories of loving a woman like Aurora.

Damn and blast.

Ran shouldered the blame, for if he'd seen the incidents over the past months as a whole, he might have realized treachery existed at his back and Aurora was the target.

Slowly he tipped his head back, his amber gaze narrowed and sharp with venom. And he knew now where to find the answers.

Sitting back on his calves, Shokai adjusted the roasting pigeon over the low fire, fat droplets spattering the flames. The hiss broke the silence, white smoke spindling up to the craggy ceiling.

"My lord," Shokai said, not looking up as he turned the bird on the spit.

"Have you eyes on the top of your head, old man?" Ran ducked into the cave, instantly feeling the cooler temperature.

"Fools and father's do not hear the steps of a comely man."

Ran's lip quirked, his foul mood lightening a bit. Shokai could be counted on to make one think just a little harder.

"Sit, my lord." He gestured to the spot adjacent to him, and Ran recognized the elegant brocade wrapping his body. Who had fashioned the garments traditional to his country? 'Twas not Aurora, for she'd included Rachel in the stitching of Dahrein's new clothes to bring the woman closer into the household.

"The boy?"

Ran's gaze shifted. "Aurora labors over him."

Shokai waved off his concern. "Then do not brood like a lonely stallion. The defeated often become the rebels."

Ran smiled weakly. Aye, Dahrein had the inner strength, if he survived.

"I know you do not come for my tea, my lord." Shokai poured from his cracked kettle, offering the cup to Ran.

Ran rolled the cup in his palms, sipped, then expelled a long sigh. "Do you recall the night in the hostelry?" he began, clearly and concisely relaying his findings and theories to the old man, including last night's discovery of the vial and the suspects. Shokai listened, nodded, grunting occasionally, but did not interrupt.

When Ran finished Shokai appeared entranced with the flames licking at the pigeon's skin. When he spoke, the sound of his voice startled Ran.

"Ask yourself why the woman would help her lover's mistress?"

Ran scowled, family pride rearing to defend Rachel, but Shokai put up a long gnarled finger, halting comment.

"Why would she admit her deed if the girl was dead?"

Ran shrugged. "Guilt that she may have had a part in it?"

"If he gifted the vial to one woman, then it fell to another, he would not be suspect, neh?"

Lougière gave it to Helena, yet perhaps she truly was aware of the contents and gave it to Rachel? God, his head ached to think on the conspiracy.

"Finding the quartermaster and the woman pillowing was intentional."

"Why?"

"Were they not together when the girl perished?"

"An alibi," Ran muttered. " 'Tis weak, Shokai, even you can see that."

"Hai, but my Empress's first fault is trusting goodness in everyone when three faces seek to blind."

"Three?"

"Listen carefully my lord, for I am old and to repeat exhausts my brain." Shokai grasped the stick spitting the pigeon and set the bird on a plate of leaves, unmindful of the heat as he shoved it off the stick.

"I'm listening." 'Twas the first time Shokai did not speak in riddles.

Shokai shot him an annoyed glance. "A young handsome man-witch was shipwrecked on the shores of Scizore, discovered by Cassiandra, the daughter of the Emperor." Ran's features tightened. "While she nursed him, the couple fell in love, but he was a barbarian, a commoner with only a handful of gems and magic spells to offer. And to mate with the Empress was forbidden, for such a bond would taint the pure bloodlines."

Ran made a disgusted sound, and Shokai's lips quirked. "A crime of death, *hai,* but they risked it. Their love was discovered, the barbarian sentenced to death." He shrugged as if 'twere destined. "Cassiandra could not bear it, and she begged an emissary to the Emperor's court to aid their escape. Secretly in love with the beauty, the emissary willingly did as she bade, taking them to the home of the barbarian."

Shokai poked at the flames with a stick, pensive, then offered Ransom a portion of his dinner. Ran accepted the bite, waving off the rest.

"The couple lived in secret, protected by ancient magic, hiding in fear they'd be discovered and killed for the crime of loving. Cassiandra gave her husband a child, and though the babe was raised by the ways of his family, both knew the infant must also be kept secluded, ignorant of her identity."

Aurora, Ran thought, stunned. Shokai sighed, taking a bite of meat, swallowing afore he continued.

"Cassiandra's father was murdered in his sleep, and all believed the daughter would be left to the life she chose. But the emissary discovered the self-appointed king's plans to assassinate the couple, wiping away the final claim to the throne. The emissary traveled to warn them, yet encountered the cloaked assassin, wounding him afore he escaped." His voice weakened, so low and filled with regret Ran had to strain to hear. "He turned his concern to the Empress, but was too late. With her last breath in this world, she begged him to protect her daughter, who was hidden in the base of a tree." Shokai sighed, his voice coming stronger. "Without question he took the child to safety. The barbarian returned from a hunt, finding his love massacred, his child stolen, and, in his grief, fled into the hills."

Ran compared the story to what Aurora told him, and wondered if Shokai had confessed his part in her legacy.

"The girl child was left to the care of an elder, in the hopes that such rearing would erase any notion of her true and rightful past. The emissary kept the Empress' wishes, remaining near, watching her child grow into a woman, forced to make himself known when she began her dangerous journey."

"You were the emissary."

"Ahhh, his mind is not so small," Shokai said, without looking up.

From the entrance, Aurora sighed, and Ran glanced up, then leapt to his feet, his gaze shifting past her. "Where is Domingo?"

"I am here, Ran," came from outside, and Ran relaxed. Aurora shot him a sour look, still not believing 'twas she that was in danger.

Ran cradled his anger to himself. He'd yet to tell her of the carcass.

"Dahrein?" he asked, a hopeful demand.

"He will live, Ransom, and keep his leg." The air went out of Ran then. "But I fear he will limp a wee bit."

Ran swallowed, looking away, overcome. "Knowing Dahrein, he will struggle to best the wound."

"Aye, he will sleep for several days, I pray, for naught will ease the pain he'll suffer when he wakes."

"You overhear so much corn will grow in your ears, child," Shokai berated Aurora and her gaze fell on him, a message of years passing 'atween them. Ran suddenly felt like an outsider.

"You loved my mother?" she asked.

He shrugged thin shoulders.

"All these years and you dinna tell me?"

"You seek a father, not a dreamer."

Ran could tell Shokai was uncomfortable with the questions. "Yet you've royal blood in your veins," he said to Aurora with a lift of his brow.

She snorted indelicately. "I wish naught from a country that would kill their Empress."

She was still looking at Shokai, seeing him differently and loving him even more as she moved close to bend and drop a kiss to the top of his head. He scoffed and fussed, brushing aside her hand, yet met her gaze like a loving parent. Her lips pressed tight, Aurora abruptly turned out of the cave, Domingo hurrying her back toward the house.

Connor Lockewood stepped out of the thicket, eyed the retreating pair, then the glow radiating from the cave afore he backed into the brush, his gaze fixed on Aurora's back.

At the yawning entrance, Ran paused. "What will you not speak afore her?" he asked softly, feeling in his bones that Shokai was hiding yet another precious bit of information.

Shokai pulled the forked comb from his hair, the topknot unwinding slowly. "A *sai,*" he indicated, shaking his head, the cascade of long iron gray hair giving him a powerful appearance, sinister and cunning. "Observe." Shokai held up the pronged comb, flicked his wrist; and Ran's eyes widened as it shot across the cave, the triple points embedding deeply in a wood crate.

Shokai fixed narrowed eyes on Ransom. "The nail has raised its head, my lord. And it bears an old wound, here." He clapped a hand over the back of his thigh, yet nodded to the *sai.*

Cassiandra's assassin, Ran thought. "Do you expect me to ask every soul on this island to drop his breeches?" Ran wanted to shake him, and Shokai sensed it.

"The face was cloaked. To accuse wrongfully allows a killer to be free!" Shokai snapped, then calmed. He was silent for a moment and Ransom almost departed, but the old man looked up, remorse creasing his features. When he spoke, his voice was tired and worn. "For two decades I have asked myself, why did the barbarian leave them unguarded when he knew the risk?" His tone hardened, razor sharp with accusation. "And why did he not return to find his only child?"

Ran understood the burden Shokai carried, accompanying Aurora on a search for the man who might have murdered her mother. It was as Ran suspected when she first told him the tale. He closed his eyes briefly, praying 'twas untrue and her father was not near.

It would destroy her to know he was and had not made his presence known.

Aurora sat beside Dahrein, taking the last stitch in a poppet filled with powerful herbs, then tucked it under his pillow. She hummed softly, a babe's lullaby, and he stirred on the bedcovers. Pouring a dark mixture into a cup and adding water, Aurora cradled his head and forced him to sip, sending him gently back into the painless void. Constantly she checked his wound, reapplying the poultice, and praying she'd found all the broken shark's teeth.

She sensed a presence and looked up. Connor Lockewood was peering inside, his forearms braced on the sill.

"Good day to you, Mister Lockewood," Aurora said and he nodded, his gaze lowering briefly to her amulet. It seemed to warm against her skin.

"You've a fine hand with healing," he complimented, his eyes on the boy.

"He's strong." She soaked a cloth, laying it across Dahrein's brow. "But he dinna deserve such agony," she added, her face mapped with sorrow.

"You know the captain suspects me of a part in this?"

"Aye." She resoaked the cloth, his presence giving her the oddest sensation . . . as if he didn't want to be so near her. "Why were you near the basin, Mister Lockewood?"

He shrugged. "A feeling for trouble, I suppose."

Her gaze snapped up. "Causin' or delayin'?"

The door opened sharply afore he could answer. Aurora turned and Connor looked up as Ransom stepped inside.

Ran's gaze darted atween the two, stopping on Aurora. "You look tired, love."

Lockewood's green eyes narrowed, shifting 'atween the pair.

"A wee bit." She rose and came to him. "I need to see to your mother."

He stopped her from moving around him. Out of the

corner of his eyes he noticed Lockewood leave, saw that Aurora sensed his departure. "She sleeps without pain, love. I have spoken to her," he assured and she sagged a little.

"Rachel?"

"She hasn't left her room since last eve."

Aurora nodded. "I need to speak with Shokai. Nay, dinna deny me this, Ransom. Come with me if you must, but I will see him."

Ran pulled her into his arms, hugging her snugly, pressing his lips to the top of her head. She had questions that only Shokai could answer, of the mother she never truly knew, and he couldn't deny her.

"Let me find someone to sit with Dahrein, and I will join you."

"Quickly," she said, meeting his gaze. "I dinna ken why, but all is not at peace here." She looked to the empty window, her delicate forehead wrinkling softly.

Lockewood was disguising something vital, but Aurora couldn't name it. 'Twas a block atween her and his feelings, strong and powerful with heart-rending pain. And he was still on her mind when she left the house, Ransom a few feet behind her, speaking quietly with Domingo. She felt his eyes on her and smiled, casting a glance over her shoulder. He winked, and despite the troubles they shared and the harm to the ones they loved, Aurora's heart felt suddenly light.

Her step was jaunty as she found the path toward the cave, calling for Shokai. He appeared at the entrance. His gaze held hers, slipping beyond to Ransom, then to their surroundings.

He stepped out and she quickened her pace.

A whispery sound made her freeze.

Abruptly Shokai flinched, briefly, like a marionette yanked on his strings, afore he crumpled to the ground.

"Shokai!" Aurora screamed, running, batting aside branches and vines, Ran directly behind her as she slid to the ground.

"Sempai?" she crooned frantically, turning him over. "Oh, nay! God of Thunder, nay!" A dart protruded from the side of his neck, moving with the pulse of his heart. She

plucked it free, cradling his head in her lap as Ran knelt beside her.

"My bag quickly! Please." Ran didn't move. "Ransom!"

Ran carefully picked up the dart, sniffed the tip, then met her gaze. The hope he saw there cut him in two.

" 'Tis Giant Milkweed, love." Fatal. Twenty times stronger than what Sayidda suffered. "And 'tis taken into his blood."

"Naayy!" she cried, tears falling. "Nay! Oh, Shokai, look at me, please!"

Thin almond-shaped eyes opened.

"See, Ransom, see. Get my sack!"

"Love—"

"Shhhh," Shokai said sluggishly, his breathing rapid.

"Dinna leave me, Shokai," she sobbed, shaking him.

Weakly, he covered her hand, clutching it tightly. His blurry gaze shifted briefly to Ransom, then back to Aurora.

"He is wise who knows what is enough, my child."

He slumped in her arms, his fingers unfurling as his last breath rattled atween still lips.

"Shokai!" Aurora screamed, a low tortured howl of a wounded animal as she clutched him to her breast, rocking him in her arms. And Ransom felt utterly helpless as she sobbed how much she loved her *sempai*, how she'd never have survived the years without him. She remained on the ground, hugging her dead protector, rocking him into the afterlife; and her every sob, every spasm of her shoulders, or flex of her fingers ripped at Ransom's soul, making him a part of her agony. His eyes burned, his throat tight and hot, and he could not find the will to pry her from the body.

He stood a few feet behind her, Domingo at his side as Aurora mourned her guardian, the man who'd loved her mother so deeply he'd offered his life to be near her child.

When the sun began its descent, Aurora was silent and still, holding Shokai in her arms, her cheek pressed to the top of his head. Ran separated her from the old man, and she fell loosely into his arms as he lifted her from the ground. She didn't open her eyes, and he decided she'd worn herself into a much-needed sleep. He took her home, removed her clothing, and tucked her in his bed.

She did not stir.

The moon rose and vanished, and Buckland was summoned. He could find naught wrong and begged Ransom to have patience. Ran was fast running out of his share, for no amount of shaking would rouse her and when the silver moon began its climb into the night sky, Ran knew Aurora's spirit was no longer in the room.

Chapter Thirty-Six

He was losing her, to a world he would never understand. Aurora was not inside the body lying in his bed, but in a mystical place only she could touch.

Ran wanted her back.

He wanted to curse her for leaving him.

And he was helpless to bring her home.

Sitting on the edge of the bed, he gazed down at her still face. Her breathing was almost nonexistent, her skin translucent, pale. He tried to recall all she'd said about her world of magic and healing, searching for a clue to help her home, his mind continuously slipping back over the days and nights they'd shared—to the moment he'd first found her imprisoned in the Sultan's dungeon.

For saving a life.

Aurora was a champion of wounded hearts and tired souls.

And how could he champion her, he thought, if he could not find where she'd traveled?

God almighty, pest. Come home, he agonized. His heart felt torn in half. And he resisted the temptation to hold her in his arms, the memory of her bonelessly falling into his embrace still tormenting his burgeoning fear. He searched her calm features for a flicker, a blinking lash, the spark she always showed him, uninhibited, bright.

The flame brightens afore it fails.

Sweet Jesus, I sound like Shokai, he thought, regret swamping him. He'd buried the ancient man on the moun-

tain top yesterday, deeply saddened by the loss. His familiarity with the man was new, yet Ransom recognized the
wisdom in Shokai, unmatched by anyone he'd met, save
Aurora. Shokai hadn't coddled Aurora, for he'd known he
would not always be around. Ran felt immeasurably proud
that Shokai had thought him worthy of her.

What information was so vital it had cost Shokai his life?

And why was Lockewood always near when something
happened? Was it he who'd planted the carcass? Had he
masked his deeds by falsifying footprints?

And Lougière? How did he fit into the puzzle? He did not
appear to be a man who'd consciously give a deadly poison
to a woman, especially one he'd spoke so fondly of. And
why would Rachel help Helena rid herself of a child, a child
that would bind the woman to Lougière? 'Twas doubtful
Lougière was the father, for Helena had bedded several
men, but Rachel may have felt 'twas so, and Ran had no
evidence to gainsay the claim.

And what if any of them were lying?

If Lougière gave the poison to Helena, and she, realizing
what it was, gave it to Rachel, hoping to kill her, then why
ask Rachel for Aurora's potions? Why not turn her venom
on the man who sought her death?

God, he thought, propping his elbows on his knees and
cradling his head in his hands. His brain ached, and atween
seeing that Dahrein remained in the painless void she'd
prescribed, and being at her side, Ransom was drained.

He needed Aurora, her help, her insight, her uncanny
power to see beyond the facade into the lies.

He needed her to keep on living.

He needed to love her.

He mashed his hands over his face, releasing a long
breath afore he thrust off the bed.

Ran paced, anxiety building with every long stride. His
gaze flicked to her with every turn of his heel, his shoulders
hunching tightly. He felt caged and angry and restless. He
wanted to scream. The room grew darker, yet Ran hadn't
realized it until a soft knock rattled the door. He flinched,

stopping briefly then striding to the door. He yanked it open.

"Why are you not abed?" Ran barked, and Sayidda blinked up at him.

"Because I am much better, Kassir," she said softly. "Will you eat?" She offered a cloth-covered tray. He took it from her, ushering her inside and closing the door. Setting the tray aside, he practically pushed her into the chair positioned aside the bed.

"I am your mother, Kassir, not a babe," she scolded, loving his attention just the same. "And I have seen to Dahrein," she assured him when he made to leave and his shoulders sagged with relief.

He stared down at her. The misery he'd caused this woman, he thought, plowing his fingers through his hair.

"Kassir?" she panicked, glancing at the still form lying in the grand bed. "Has Aurora—?"

"Nay, 'tis no change." Worried, weary. Dejectedly he sank to the floor, bracing his back against the side of the bed, knees bent, elbows propped there. He stared at nothing, his fists clenching and unclenching.

"Oh, Kassir." His mother had never seen him look so haggard. He appeared to have slept in his clothes, his hair tangled and wild, his eyes bleary. She grasped his hand and he gripped back, gazing at the slim fingers wrapped around his for a moment afore lifting his gaze to hers.

"Can you forgive me?" When she blinked, obviously stunned, he plunged ahead. "I have been an utter fool," he hissed vehemently. "A blackguard of the first water by far, but I swear, I did not realize what I was— Nay," he shook his head sadly, "I *did* realize. I wanted to hurt you. I wanted you to feel the pain I suffered, for I blamed your giving me to my father for every moment of it."

"I know, Kassir," she said sympathetically, and he looked surprised.

"Then why did you not tell me your reasons?"

"Would you have believed me, if I had?"

"Nay," he said without doubt. "Not then." Not afore

he'd learned to love Aurora, he knew. "Why did you come with me that night in Crete?"

She leaned back into the cushions, drawing her hair to the side. "Whatever you suffered I blamed on myself, Kassir. I did not know Anna was cruel, and I'd hoped your jackal of a father would keep you from such ridicule." She shrugged. "I simply wanted to be near my child, whatever the price."

"Even my rage?"

"When you have a son of your own you will understand how much you can endure for him."

To know the love of a parent, you must have a child. Shokai had said and Ran's voice was soft, hesitant. "I know I do not deserve to ask." He held her gaze, swallowing deeply afore taking a breath. "Will you—can you—find it in your heart to forgive me . . . mother."

Her tears were swift and burning, and she reached out, feathering his hair from his brow. She gazed into his eyes, golden eyes so much like her grandfather's, and loved the man he'd become, always knew he could be.

"Of course, my son," caught on a sob and he closed his eyes, grasping her fingers and placing a kiss to the back, whispering his thanks. He stared at the ceiling, his head braced on the bed. He found a soothing comfort in her presence.

"She will come back to you, Kassir." The statement broke the long silence.

"God, I miss her," Ran rasped at the ceiling.

"Then tell her."

His head jerked upright. "She cannot hear me." he doubted.

Sayidda briefly looked past him to the bed. "Aurora sees and hears more than any of us, I've found."

His lips quirked. "Aye. When I first met her I believed she could read my mind, for ofttimes she spoke my feelings when I tried to hide them." His expression fell into absolute hopelessness. "I have begged her to come back, but still she . . . sleeps," he said, rubbing his hand over his face, frustrated.

Sayidda leaned forward, gripping his hand and forcing

him to look at her. "Then you must beg again, Kassir. Beg til you've nothing left to offer. Til your throat is raw and your strength depleted." She squeezed, her words strong with conviction. "We get so few chances to love, do not allow this one to go without doing battle."

She kissed his cheek, then released his hands as she stood, glancing once at her son afore leaving the room.

Her journey was long and slow to the place of gathering. For a time Aurora did not feel the earth beneath her feet, nor did she care.

The ground cushioned her steps as she stopped, knowing she'd reached her destiny. Tranquillity settled into her being, cradling her without pain. A tawny deer loped through the forest beyond. Winged creatures, as translucent as rain, danced upon the earth, spirited through trees and nipped at flower petals. The squawk of birds noised the breeze.

'Twas cool and moist, the mist of a waterfall dampening her skin, and she tilted her face toward the rushing clear liquid, smiling softly. It pampered her, the spray sheening over her body, clinging sweetly to her skin, her robe. The sunlight dipped and beamed through the high trees, playing off the crystal water in a bright dusting of color. The mist churned like fine white smoke and a figure appeared in the wet air, cloaked in gold and silver and blue. Immediately she recognized Shokai.

I am home, Empress. Let no one avenge me whispered through her mind though his lips did not move. She nodded to his request, and he said naught else but waved her back toward the way she'd come, smiling a smile she'd never seen afore. She bid him good-bye, her heart gladdened for his peace as he melted into the mist, the colors of his robes becoming a part of the fall of water, flowing into the brook.

She did not go back. 'Twas not time yet, she recognized, so she walked, sensing a presence behind her, making her aware of the keenness of her powers. She could feel the heartbeat, the steps pressing into the soft earth, the breath of the beast that followed, not stalking, but patient for her to turn and look. She didn't; not a refusal of the force bending her world but a decision to understand why.

" *'Tis time to go back,*" the beast said, yet Aurora did not turn. *"You have mourned enough."*

Still she did not turn. The white wolf.

The need to look passed, and with it, her nine-year quest. She no longer experienced the drive to search for him, not here, not anywhere, for she knew 'twas not the lost father she'd always sought, but a place of belonging and a love that could find her, even here.

Beyond the magick.

She turned. The white wolf sat patiently.

And she recognized the beast with in the strange colored eyes.

"Why did you not show yourself to me?

"Those who took your mother seek you, through me."

"Why did you not come back for me?" she asked, and the beast bowed his head sadly.

"Shame kept me, child. I was unworthy to claim myself your father, a coward, for failing you and Cassiandra."

"But I was alone!"

The wolf tilted its head to look at her. *"Nay, girl, never alone."* And Aurora touched her amulet.

Suddenly a lion appeared, edging around a tree, over a low boulder, a regal prance as it ceased afore Aurora's feet. It crouched low, as if readying to attack, and when Aurora laid her hand atop the bushy red mane, the cat-beast settled, wary, protective, scorning the wolf.

"Return to those who love you."

Aurora reached out.

Like falling dust, the wolf vanished.

Aurora lowered her arm slowly. The lion was gone.

"Come to me, my love."

Ransom. His voice was strained and pleading, and she smiled, running.

"Part of me wishes I could join you, pest, for surely 'tis better than this misery I feel now," he murmured; then he sighed, long and heavy, the burdens of his deeds haunting.

"I am a selfish man." Tightly he closed his eyes, his voice soft, angry at himself. "I have lived a life of believing in naught but what I chose to see, chose to call witness to, and 'twas hard, God, bloody hard, to face what I've done to those around me." His shoulders moved restlessly. "I imagined myself, arrogantly so, as I'm sure you'll tell me, a man with his life patterned. But you proved otherwise, didn't you?" A hint of a smile curved his lips, and he braced his fists on either side of her, his gaze lovingly skimming her face. "A gentle bashing, you've done me, love, to make me see beyond images and falsehoods I hid behind. And to learn this from a woman who has known little love in return is damned humbling." Naught changed, and despair raked him. He couldn't lose her. "Oh, God, pest, I need you," he rasped, his shoulders slumped, his head bowed low. "I cannot go back. I *cannot.*" His voice cracked and he swallowed dryly. "But I need you to go on."

Aurora opened her eyes, blinking, aware of her surroundings and that Ransom hovered close. His dark silhouette was outlined by the magenta twilight of dawn.

"But I am here, my heart."

His head jerked up, his gaze colliding with hers.

"Aurora." Ecstatic, disbelieving. He trembled, almost afraid to touch her.

"Oh, Ransom," she whispered, seeing tortured pain in his eyes. "I heard you." She slid her fingers over his face, his lips, and he reveled in her touch, nudging into it.

"You terrified me, woman," he said roughly, chastising.

"I will never leave you, Ransom."

"Swear to me." He bore down and she heard the tenuous hold on his emotions.

"Ransom?"

"I love you, pest."

Aurora blinked, not sure she heard correctly.

"I love you," he repeated, the words bursting softly from his lips in a wind's caress. "Madly." He enfolded her in his arms. "Wildly." He drew her upright. "Desperately," he ended on a groan, pulling her across his lap. She fell against him, a cushiony press of woman curves, and his hands smoothed up her sides, beneath her arms, lifting them around his neck afore traveling slowly back to her narrow waist.

He searched her features, memorizing every hollow and crease, adoring her from her sleep-mussed hair to the glassy sheen in her eyes, to the streams of flame fountaining from her hairline and marking her fiery temper.

To simply look upon her gave him a strange mix of peace and possessiveness and fear.

"I am in love with you, Aurora Lassiter MacLaren."

" 'Tis a recent discovery, this?" came in breathless joy.

"Aye," he growled. " 'Tis a powerful feeling in me."

"Och, trustin' those feelin's, are you now?" She tisked, toying with his gold earring. " 'Tis a dangerous thing, Ransom Montegomery. 'Twill gain you naught but me love."

The air locked in his lungs. "Oh God, Aurora—"

"You canna be thinkin' I've stayed for aught less than your heart?"

He looked sheepish.

"You big ox." She yanked on the earring. "Be screamin' it to the world afore you believe, thinks I."

He clutched her closer. "Whisper it, says me." He trembled against her, the eagerness in his eyes bringing tears to her own.

"I love you, Ransom Montegomery," the air left him in a rush of breath against her lips, "in this world and the next."

"I prefer this," he growled, then kissed her, crushing her to him, and she yielded, soft and plush and banishing the misery of the past nights. His mouth rolled over hers, and she opened for him, hungrily answering his desire, as his hand swept the length of her, hot and claiming.

"I love you," he panted over and over, showering her face and throat with kisses, wanting to strip off her gown and feel her skin against his. "Are you ill? Do you hurt? Are you hungry?"

She smiled, cupping his jaw and pressing her forehead to his. "Nay, nay, and a wee bit."

He frowned, trying to recall his questions. "Food," he

said like a revelation, then kissed her, deeply, erotically, afore hesitatingly releasing her. Aurora sighed, deliriously happy, allowing him to plump pillows in a mound behind her.

"You were," he caught her gaze, "healing yourself, weren't you?"

"Och, you be thinkin' like a *Wiccan,* neh?"

"Or I would have gone mad," he admitted, plumping another pillow afore he left the bed to light the bedside lamp. Aurora's smile fell suddenly, her gaze shifting around the room as Ransom stuck flint to a wick. Briefly he met her gaze, a frown wrinkling his brow, his senses keenly aware. Then he twisted away, lunging for the shadowy figure near the balcony.

"Ransom!" Aurora cried as he slammed the intruder against the doors. Glass shattered, moonlight bending off a blade of silver, and Ran caught the assassin's wrist, smacking his fist against the wall. Instantly the weapon clattered to the floor. Angrily Ran jerked the man onto the balcony, into the moonlight and stared into the face of Connor Lockewood.

Chapter Thirty-Seven

"You bastard!"

"I do not come to harm her, Captain," he said calmly and Ran realized Connor did not fight him, had not from the first, and his gaze darted to the blade. His heart rammed against the wall of his chest, his skin prickling over his spine. On the carpet lay a blade identical to Aurora's ceremonial dirk.

Ran looked at her.

"Let him go, Ransom." Calm and without question.

Ran thrust Connor away and stepped back, scooping up the knife. His gaze skimmed over the silver, darting to Connor, then back. Dread filled him.

"I ken how well you handle a blade, Captain. I willna attack."

Ran's gaze flew to his, then narrowed. "You never had an accent afore."

Connor folded his mammoth arms. "I dinna say much a'tall, did I now?"

"You're MacLaren!" Ran snarled, outrage bursting through him. "Do you know what you have done to her? She gave up her life to find you!"

"She should have forgotten me," Connor said without preamble, glancing at his daughter.

"You righteous son of a—" Ran lurched and Lockewood waved his hand. Ransom step blunted, as if something struck him in the chest, knocking the breath from his lungs and holding him there. His eyes widened. He couldn't move.

"Release him!" Aurora demanded hotly, scrambling from the bed, and Lockewood lowered his arm. Instantly the pressure eased and Ran rubbed the spot. Sweet saints! He never imagined her father would be . . . a witch! 'Twas then he noticed the difference in Connor's appearance. The beard was gone, his usually quequed hair lacking the dull matty brown—of henna, Ran realized—the strands now a dark vivid red, long and shaggy.

"Ransom," she said, stepping closer, her gaze clinging to Lockewood.

In three strides, Ran was beside her, pulling her into his arms. She clung to him, shaking.

"You knew, didn't you?" he said, searching her face.

"After a fashion, aye." She shrugged, her gaze shifting beyond to Connor.

Slowly she pushed out of Ran's arms and moved to her father.

"You should have stayed in the Highlands, daughter," he said, not unkindly.

Aurora swallowed tightly. "You are my only family," came in a fractured whisper, and Ran's heart shattered for her.

"Dinna let blood be a bond. It killed your mother." Connor gazed into eyes so like Cassiandra's, aching to ease the torment lingering there. "Your birth was a secret, lass, for your mother and I knew you'd be killed for the blood in your veins. Your search brought my name afore the new emperor and he sent off his spies. I dinna care for meself, but you—" His words broke off and he shrugged. "If you could not find me, then they could not know of your existence. But you came upon the *Red Lion.*" He looked at Ransom, his expression filled with worry. "Your path was mine. And know that naught will stop King Stephan. He holds the throne by fear, not decree."

"Tell me all you know, Lockewood," Ran demanded.

Connor sighed heavily. "Helena was from Scizore." He looked at Aurora. "She must have recognized you for the likeness to your mother," he said with a half smile, and Aurora touched her face.

Ran was oblivious to the exchange, his mind sifting and straining details. "Mayhap Helena discovered 'twas Lougière who has come to kill Aurora—"

"Nay! Markus would never harm her!"

Ran's eyes narrowed, predatory. "Does he know she is your daughter? Cassiandra's heir?"

"Nay, 'twas too much of a risk to tell anyone."

"Does he ken you were Cassiandra's *husband?*" Aurora asked, and Connor met her gaze, his features softening.

"Aye. But not her heritage."

"Lougière was in the room when Shokai and Aurora were taken to the slaver," Ran said, thinking aloud. "Castille died that night."

"He disappeared," Connor clarified.

"Nay, Father, he is dead," Aurora said and Connor realized she had the sight of his ancestors.

"But Markus was injured, too," Lockewood defended.

"Minor." Ran waved off, his mind churning facts. "When Shokai came upon Cassiandra's assassins, he wounded one in the leg. Lougière limps."

"I saw that cut inflicted in Bombay! 'Twas when we first met!"

"Mayhaps," Ran contemplated, "he received a second atop Shokai's? To cover the first, for he knew you were Cassiandra's husband?"

Connor's expression didn't change.

Ran scowled, dropping into a chair, and Aurora went to him, settling on the arm. No one spoke. "They have tried to kill Aurora and have failed," Ran said to the toes of his boot, then lifted his gaze to Aurora's father. "The bastards have left a great deal to chance, Connor. Could it be that an old friendship hinders a killer's heart?"

Connor clenched his fists, refusing to give up his friend to his captain.

A bell clanged. Five quick successions. A ship approached. And Ran lurched out of the chair, glass crunching beneath his soles as he strode to the balcony. The sun struggled on the horizon, battling gray clouds for supremacy in the morning sky. A ship sailed toward the island.

A hinge-rattling knock pounded the door afore it burst open. Domingo strode inside.

"She's British— Aurora!" he said, startled. "You're awake!" He gave her a hug, pecking a kiss to her cheek afore he went to Ransom, handing him a spyglass. Ran sighted, sensing Aurora moved up beside him.

"They are out of cannon range," he said, his brow knitting. All who knew the path into the cove were on the island. "Her gun ports are closed."

"They've let down a longboat." Domingo pointed.

"Cocky bastard." Ran clapped the spyglass down. "Two squads to the shore, and I want Markus Lougière in irons immediately and a guard posted at Rachel's door."

Domingo didn't question the order. "The village is secure, but what of here?" He gestured to the house.

"Send the panicked into the cellars, but they will not get this far," he said with all confidence, then looked to Connor.

Lockewood pushed away from the wall. "I will protect my daughter, Captain Montegomery."

"Daughter?" Domingo gawked as Ran nodded to Connor, handing back his silver dirk.

Ran kissed Aurora deeply, murmuring his love, then glancing over her head to Connor afore dragging Domingo from the room.

"Daughter?" Dom squeaked again as they closed the door.

Connor gazed down at Aurora, love hidden now freed.

"I have missed you, child."

Ran sawed back on the reins and slid from the horse's back, tossing the leads to Leelan Baynes, then striding down the beach. Behind him, the village was silent, its inhabitants sequestered in cellars or lining the barracks walls with freshly loaded weapons. Above, on the mountain top, cannons were regaged on the dormant British ship. Ransom stood afore his men, armed, blades thrust in the back of his waistband, flintlocks primed and loaded in the front. Better than twenty men were on the shore on bended knee, muskets aimed at tender chests. The visitors, Ran realized as he sighted through the scope, were unarmed, six oarsmen, one astern, and two aft.

None wore uniforms of the Navy or they would have been blown from the water afore they rounded the jetty.

Oars slapped the water, the surf scarcely causing a ripple. Ran's shoulders hunched as the longboat approached, recognition dawning.

"Lower arms," he growled and stepped away from his men, angrily clapping the spyglass closed. The boat scraped the shore and men leapt to drag it safely in. A figure aft of the craft, stepped out, splashing through the surf.

Ran would have recognized that arrogant lazy stride anywhere.

"Father," Ran said, utter contempt in the single word.

Granville Montegomery halted afore his eldest son, pride in the powerful young man making him smile. "You look fit, Ransom."

"What do you want, Father?" Ran folded his arms over his chest.

Granville arched a brow at the acid tone, matching his son's stance. "Only to see my son."

Ran snorted a laugh. "Haven't you enough bastards to call upon?"

Granville released a breath, his broad shoulders sagging. "I had hoped we could amend matters and return to the relationship we had afore Anna told you the truth."

"Surely you think me a fool?"

"Anna is dead."

"Pardon my leave if I do not mourn her."

Granville scowled. "What is the meaning of your animosity, Ransom? For surely 'tis not due to my unexpected arrival."

Ran thought he had put aside all his anger, but it seemed one aspect remained. His father was a wastrel, charming and roguish but a hedonistic rakehell who believed only money made life simpler. Aurora had proven to Ran that money meant naught when waged against happiness.

"How many of your bastards will come to *me,* pleading for funds and lodging in *your* name?"

Granville drew himself up, eye to eye with his son. "Do not think you are old enough to question me, for I have provided well for each of my children."

Ran shifted his weight to one foot. "What of Rosa's child?"

Sadness briefly cloaked Granville's features; then he frowned quizzically. "How do you know of Rosa?"

"Your daughter sought me."

" 'Tis impossible," Granville said slowly, warily. "The child died, Ransom. I have only sons."

Ran's features yanked tight, his eyes searching his father's for the lie. Immediately he spun away, his heart thundering wildly as he headed up the beach. God, what an idiot he was! The letters were forgeries, and Ran blamed himself for not examining them more closely. And Rachel! Sweet Jesus, her deception was flawless . . . He feared what evil truly lay beneath the demure shell.

Domingo's horse skidded to a halt, hooves clattering. "Lougière has disappeared."

Ran grabbed the reins and mounted his horse. "Keep her safe, Connor. Please," he whispered to himself, digging in his heels.

Connor frowned at his daughter's sudden lack of attention, his gaze following her as she rose from her spot on the bed and went to the balcony.

"Careful of the glass, poppet," he said, and she sidestepped the mess, rubbing her arms.

" 'Tis been an evil unearthed, Father." She watched as men filed out of the longboat, dragging it ashore.

"In those men?" he asked, coming to her side.

"Nay, 'twas here, all along, dormant—"

A knock rattled the door, then it opened without invitation. Rachel smiled demurely, and Aurora felt icy cold spiral up her arms. She opened her mouth to speak. Rachel leveled a pistol and fired.

Connor stepped in front of his daughter, the bullet impacting with his yielding flesh. He felt it rip through muscle and sinew afore exiting his shoulder, and he called on his powers to keep it from striking her. He wasn't quick enough and heard her cry of pain afore he lost consciousness and sank to the floor.

Aurora crumbled behind him, catching his weight against her. His warm blood fountained over her chest, sliding down her belly and atween her legs to pool beneath her. She groped for the wound, trying to seal off the flow, but she couldn't keep her eyes or thoughts focused beyond the pain in her head. A wetness trickled into her ear. *Ransom,* she called, sinking deeper into the dark painless hole.

"Damn," Rachel muttered, striding into the room.

"Connor!" came from behind and Rachel turned, a second pistol aimed.

"Get in here and help me," she snapped at Markus, waving the pistol. "The shot will alert everyone."

Markus strode inside, kneeling by Connor. "God's eyes Donette, you didn't need to do this!"

"I am weary of doing your work, Markus," Rachel said with amazing calm, primly brushing her hair from her face. "We'll have to do it afore we leave for the ship."

"You fired a gun. You can't think to get away now Ransom—"

"Pick her up," she warned softly, pressing the barrel against Connor's forehead. "Now."

Markus rolled Connor off his daughter and lifted Aurora from the floor. Her head hung limply over his arm, her nightgown red with Connor's blood. It dripped from her fingertips as he took her from the room.

Her gown lifted high, Sayidda stopped abruptly, gaping from Rachel to Lougière, her gasp of shock alerting them

"Allah be merciful!" Sayidda's gaze shifted from Aurora to the gun. "What have you done?"

"Not enough," Rachel said dismissingly, and as Sayidda lurched for the pistol, she caught her in the cheek with the stock, sending her reeling back to smack against the wall.

"The horses are out back," she said afore Sayidda hit the

floor, already descending the stairs, arrogantly ignoring the servants fleeing the house like frightened children. She couldn't wait to leave this horrible little island, and if Sayidda hadn't suspected she was not who she claimed, this would have gone much smoother. The poison would have killed her afore Aurora discovered the source. Damn the chit for looking so much like her mother. Helena had immediately recognized the girl as the rightful heir and had threatened Rachel with revealing her position in Stephan's court. Poor girl underestimated Rachel's devotion to her King. "Lord, how I've hated this postulating act for these fools!" she said to no one, then paused when Markus wasn't aside her. "Hurry up."

Markus moved ahead.

Sayidda rushed down the stairs, dizziness sending her into the wall. She stalled, gripping the banister as Connor stumbled at the landing, catching the rail. Softly he called her name and her eyes widened at the crimson stain running all the way to his knees. She flattened against the wall as he raised his arm, squinting, narrowing his thoughts for true aim.

"Goddess forgive me," he gasped and threw the blade. The dirk whispered through the air, sinking into Rachel's side.

She screamed, lurched forward but did not fall, stumbling out the back of the house. She caught the horse's bridle, then twisted to look, pain jumping up to her chest.

"Nay, nay, get on the horse!" she snapped when Markus made to free the knife. He turned away, draping Aurora over the mount's withers as Rachel wrapped her fingers around the blade and yanked, air hissing through her teeth. She closed her eyes briefly, gripping the knife afore sliding the dirk into the waistband of her skirts.

Markus mounted his horse and froze. The guard lay on the ground, his throat cut from ear to ear. 'Twas his quartermaster's mate.

"Damn you to hell, woman! Why don't you simply be done with it now?"

Rachel mounted shakily, blood darkening a path down her skirts.

"I want her head." Markus' eyes widened. "Oh, do not look so squeamish. You took her mother's finger, her ear. I want Stephan to know I've succeeded where you failed. Consistently." Rachel cruelly jammed her sharp heels into the steed's side, and the beast lurched away from the house, up the path to the far side of the island. Markus followed.

Her head. Donnette Rostoff, the consort to the King, would do it, her loyalty to Stephan proven in the severed head of the last Empress of Scizore. The thought made her positively giddy.

Chapter Thirty-Eight

No daughters.

Ran spat a curse, riding the horse onto the porch, the clatter of hooves rattling the walls as he slid from the saddle. Shouldering the door open, he froze.

His mother sat on the landing her back against the wall, her cheek swollen, her lips bloody.

"Oh, sweet saints!" he moaned, sliding to his knees beside her.

"Help Lockewood," she sobbed, blood spilling from cracked lips. Several feet up the staircase, Connor lay sprawled as if he'd fallen, trying to rally himself and come to Sayidda. Ran went to him, helping him down to a seat at the bottom step.

"Rachel killed the guard at her door," Connor said dismally, his palm covering his wound as he slumped against the bannister post. "She has Aurora." Blood seeped atween his fingers. "She tried to shoot her." Ran's gaze shifted to the bullet hole and knew Connor had taken the shot meant for his daughter.

"*Madre de Dios,*" Domingo whispered as he came to Sayidda, lifting her gently, wincing when she collapsed against him.

"Baynes, Pellum, Ducks!" Ran bellowed as he straightened and the men scrambled into the foyer. "Gather the *Lion* crew to search," he said to Pellum. "They have nowhere to run but over the mountains." Pellum did as ordered.

"What is going on here?" Granville said as he strode inside. "Who has done this? Why?"

"Be quiet, Father," Ran snarled, then turned to Baynes. "Send twenty men to the shore. Let no ship sail. And fetch Chief Po-tahd. Tell him what has happened, to alert his people. They are headed into his lands." Baynes nodded, racing off as Ran turned into his study. He threw open a cabinet, arming himself with a machete and pistols while his father stood by, wrapped in awe over the ruthlessness he witnessed.

Ran quit the study and strode into the parlor, where Léonie tended Sayidda. "Kassir, Kassir," his mother cried, reaching out, and he went down on one knee, grasping her hands.

"I will find her, Mother."

"Allah keep you," she whispered, kissing his cheek. Ran's gaze moved to Lockewood, and the stillness in the man amazed Ran, for Buckland poked and probed his wound with less than gentle fingers.

"She's hurt, here," Connor said pointing to a spot above her ear. Ran's features sharpened, horror and fear and rage burning through his veins when Connor spoke again. "I heard them. Rachel wants a prize, proof for her king." Connor swallowed. "Her head."

Amber eyes cooled with a predatory gleam, Ran's lungs expanding to bring sudden calm. He would rip them limb from limb.

"Lougière?"

"With her." The defeated sound of his voice knifed Ran. How could this man not know such evil lurked in Lougière? Ran stood, touching his mother's shoulder afore he headed out the back of the house.

"Sahib?" Ran halted, gazing into the darkened hall as Dahrein limped into the light.

"Grievin' mothers, lad, you should be abed!"

Braced by the wall, Dahrein lifted his chin, his pale eyes bright with tears. "I will join you," he said, and Ran's heart swelled with pride and love for the boy as he knelt, gently lifting him in his arms and calling for Léonie as he took him back to him room.

"Do you not trust me to find her?" He laid him on the bed as Léonie rushed inside.

"Most definitely, but—"

Léonie quickly poured Dahrein's medication into a cup and pressed it into his hand. "I will tell her how bravely you offered your help," Ran promised, turning away, and when Dahrein protested again, Léonie touched the bottom of the cup, tipping it to his lips.

"Do you want to hear the scolding we will both receive if you become ill?" Ran asked, half out the door.

Dahrein shook his head, gulping the drink. "I do not want to live without her, sahib," Dahrein whispered, and the fear in the boy's eyes mirrored his own.

"We will not have to, lad." Ran left, striding out of the house to search for tracks.

He found the stable hand, staring up at him with sightless eyes, and Ran sank to his knees beside the youth. Mother of God, he's just a year or two older than Dahrein, he thought, mashing his hand over his face. He stood, stripping off his shirt and covering the lad's face afore he checked the count of horses.

A keel of rope clenched in his fist, he left the stable.

His father met his stride.

"Should you not be seeing to my mother?" Ran said caustically. Overhead the sky dulled with clouds.

"Sayidda is fine. I found their trail. They headed up that way," Granville said, pointing to the slope behind the house, and Ran looked at him with a jaundiced eye afore confirming the path.

"What did Rachel think to do?" he muttered to himself. "Traverse the mountain, then go over the side of the bloody cliff?" Then he snapped, "Nay!" when he saw Granville holding the reins of a horse. "Your reputation of bastards brought Rachel here!"

"You would deny my help for the sake of your damned pride?"

Would you risk a limb for the sake of a physician's pride?

Aurora's words haunted him. Ran shook his head, almost smiling.

"Take five men, up this way," he nodded north, to the visible trail Rachel had left.

"You do not follow?"

"This is my home, Father, and there is more than one way to the top." Ran arched a brow, a sinister smile toying at his lips as he reined around and headed west.

Word traveled like a brush fire, islander and pirate fanning out to search. Pale clouds brewed darker, tinting the land like twilight. Torches ignited and prayers whispered, as the aged and the young combed their island. The heart of the Lion was in danger.

Muscled flexed and jumped with power as Ran hacked through the jungle, the machete slicing liquid-filled vines and brush. The rope slung over his head and beneath his arm, he groped for vegetation and twisted tree limbs to draw himself up the west face. Sweat beaded on his forehead, trickled steadily down his back. He ignored it.

Rachel and Markus were headed for the peak, then the gulley, a deep valley gouged on the north side of the island, which led to the sea. 'Twas their only escape, yet to reach the peak on horseback they had to ride the winding trail up the mountainside.

Ransom was climbing the cliff. Straight up, it felt like, in the hopes of reaching the summit first. From his position Rachel, Markus, and Aurora were somewhere to his far right on the trail, above him was the summit and beyond that, over the top, the valley and the sea. Ran jammed his boot into the earth and pulled himself higher.

On the other side, the natives had cut a narrow trail into the escarpment, from the pinnacle above the valley straight down to the sea. 'Twas dangerous, steep, no more than a lip hugging the cliff; an endless drop to the left and the ivy-cloaked rock face on the right. It could only be taken by foot.

Ran had only seen it once. Its beginning marked atween pirate and islander.

Ran had chosen to live on the south side of the island for its defenses, the treacherous path into the cove. The natives preferred the north west, for its access to the sea and escape. They'd been overrun too often by British, Portuguese, and Spanish, and believed 'twas safer and quicker to flee by canoe to the outer islands, waiting til their conquerors perished from fever or poisonous snakes or lions. The lion pride was sacred to the natives, and they considered it a sign that Ran's vessel was named *Red Lion*. Unwilling to seek trouble where peace could be forged, Ran had accepted the native's belief that he was some manifestation of their red lion and left it at that. The beast was merely a legend. And it had kept peace on Sanctuary.

Connor Lockewood lay on his back on the bed, his wounds stitched and dressed. He knew he hadn't the strength to go after Markus, but he could find them. And help. Closing his eyes and laying his arms at his side, Lockewood cleared his mind and left his earthly body.

The heat was oppressive, settling thick and wet with the threat of rain. Clouds rolled overhead, darkening the jungle. Lightning ripped the sky without a sound as Ran climbed, his face chiseled with determination.

Ransom.

His features sharpened.

Aurora? He dashed back the terror licking at his spine, muscles tensing as he groped for hand holds. He struggled to position his booted feet and slipped. Dried branches snapped, stones scraping his chest and arms as he fell. He grappled for purchase and latched onto a vine, the sharp stop tearing through his shoulder. He fitted his feet into the soft ground, holding tight and catching his breath.

Ransom, Aurora's voice whispered through his brain, and he shook his head as if to clear it.

They've bound me.

For an instant he thought he was going mad and experienced the briefest smack of fear, yet the odd connection intensified.

Open to me. Help me.

Where are you? his mind asked.

Nearly at the top.

The summit, he thought, resuming his climbing. A primal instinct drove him, strength and power coming with the hint of her voice in his brain. He prayed it meant she was alive, and kept the need to exact blood for blood submerged, afraid that to question the thoughts filtering through his mind would destroy his link to her.

His heart pumped steadily, his fingers clawing in the earth. The air moved in and out of his lungs, stirring, unearthing a primitive rush of energy. His thickly muscled limbs felt suddenly sleeker, elongated, his feet landing agilely where he needed, his balance uncanny. He moved faster, swifter, and out of the corner of his eye he saw the lion, rippling power and golden red. It didn't startle him, as if he'd sensed he was never alone. It moved with him, seeming to direct his path, and Ran accepted, climbed, scaling the steep mountain. Blood pounded, his breath calmed. He felt the savageness in him, the taste of the hunt. Anticipation. His back curved, muscles bunching and flexing. His hands fit into fissures and cracks, his booted toes finding sure shelves.

He moved in synch with the beast, cresting the summit, crawling across the ground, low, patient.

Stalking.

The rain came, a mist at first. His shot and powder would be damp now, he thought, and discarded his last pistol, one already lost in the climb.

He paused to catch his breath, bracing his hand on a tree. Water sheened over him, sounding like scattering pebbles in the dense jungle. The lion awaited in the thicket several yards away. It stared at Ran, amber eyes meeting amber afore the beast dipped its regal head, then disappeared into the jungle.

Ran's skin prickled. And though the lion was gone, he was not alone.

The withers cut into her stomach, the jolting gait of the horse bruising her with each step. Aurora concentrated, narrowing her thoughts, and tried to loosen her bonds, but her head pounded unmercifully, the side of her skull above her ear stinging. She struggled to keep conscious, the heat stifling her already tight breathing. The horses charged up the slick incline, lathered and winded, and she knew the exhausted beasts would not last long at this pace.

The mist grew heavier, soaking her gown, the scent of her father's blood metallic in her nostrils. She feared he was dead. And his killer rode her mount with a regal air, unaffected by the rain and humidity, her smile serene and artificial as the gray daylight. *But she bleeds.*

Rachel lacked hatred and anger, only impatience and determination filling her now, and why Aurora had not sensed this in the woman, she didn't know. But she was certain 'twere too many faces lurking in Rachel to count one afore another. She'd used those carefully carved facades to hurt Aurora's only family, and Aurora knew she had to stop them afore they descended into the valley. Or Ransom would not be able to reach her in time. Aurora had no intention of losing her head to some self-appointed king.

Drawing on her remaining energy, she shifted with each lift of the animal's hooves, then abruptly thrust back, falling to the ground in a heap.

Her cheek and shoulder impacted with the wet muddy ground, scratching a burn across her skin. The wound above her ear throbbed incessantly, and she rolled to her side and tried to stand.

The horses stopped. Rachel cursed.

"Bloody hell, I think she is unconscious," Markus said.

"Do not think, Markus. It is what fouled this plan." His features stretched tight, and he eyed her with malevolence as he dismounted. *"You* were supposed to remain near Lockewood til she came for him," she said, delivering a slap to the horses' rumps. The lathered pair lurched, heading the way they'd come. "If you had reported to our King often enough to suit, I wouldn't be in this wretched pest hole."

Rachel faced Markus, her eyes glossy. "God, I loathe the heat," she said as the Empress struggled to her feet.

Markus steadied Aurora, gripping her arms from behind.

"Let her be," Rachel snapped, holding her wounded side. "A head is easier to cart than her. Do it." She held out a knife, gesturing with the hilt. "I want to watch." She stepped back to view, staggering slightly. "My King will ask every detail."

"Mayhaps you should, then," Markus goaded. "Stephan will be pleased when you tell him you did it yourself."

She waved him off as if he'd offered her a second cup of tea. "Helena and that horrible little man was enough this trip."

Aurora lifted her head, staring at Rachel with such rage the woman recoiled.

"My, my, the flower blooms," Rachel muttered. "Aye. Blow guns are very effective at a distance. Most times," she said as if missing Aurora and Ransom were an embarrassment. "Helena's mother was the last Empress' handmaid and she recognized your likeness to Cassiandra from a portrait her mother revered." Rachel sauntered over to Aurora, gripping her jaw and squeezing. "I admit the resemblance is uncanny," she marveled, critically examining Aurora's features. "She heard the rumors that Cassiandra gave birth and the child lived. And I'm not unknown to Stephan's subjects." Rachel shrugged, sliding her hand down to dig into the jugular veins of Aurora's throat. "Stephan is a most determined man." She squeezed and Aurora's vision blurred. "Once your existence was discovered, he vowed to wait years to see you wiped from this earth."

Aurora clenched her eyes shut, pain screaming in her head as she resisted the urge to send a kick to Rachel's gullet. She could not fight them both, dizzy as she was. And she wanted to live. "You're a fool to believe King Stephan will want a woman with so much blood on her hands," Aurora said softly.

Rachel's eyes flared and she slapped her. "Shut up." Her body shook with rage. "What do you know of Stephan? You—peasant!"

Ran approached slowly, brushing aside branch and bough, the heavy rain muffling his approach. Then he saw her, his heart dropping to his knees. Grievin' mothers. She was covered in blood, the rain pelting the fabric to her body, draining the red to pink. Blood trickled into her ear, down the side of her throat. She was grazed by Connor's bullet, he realized, rage swamping him. Her legs wobbled and he wanted to cut off the hands that touched her, held her prisoner. The three stood near the ravine, their backs to the divide atween it and the narrow lip of the trail curving downward to the sea.

The drop-off was too close to charge, Ran thought, searching for a way to draw them from the dangerous edge.

The ocean crashed against the shore beyond and below, the earth vibrating.

Rain came harder, flooding Aurora's feet.

Concentrate.

In his mind Ran chanted her name and suddenly she looked up. The gesture did not go unnoticed by her captors, and Markus pulled her against his chest, the knife at her throat. Damn.

Ran bent, slipping a blade from his boot, catching the tip lightly atween two fingers. He hesitated. The three still hovered too close. He couldn't risk sudden movement and hit Aurora.

"Do it now," Rachel commanded over the storm, her gaze snapping to the surroundings. "Or I kill you!"

Markus clutched the dagger beneath Aurora's slender throat, tilting her vulnerable neck to the blackened sky. Rain saturated them.

Ran balanced the blade tip atween two fingers and drew back his arm.

*   *   *

Lockewood stepped from the forest.

"Dinna be hurtin' her, Markus."

Lougière whirled, Aurora pinned against his chest.

Rachel frowned, recognizing Markus' panic. "What is it? Did you hear something?" Her gaze scanned the terrain, but could find nothing.

"Come to see the Empress perish, Connor?" Markus said to the air. "Just like your wife, you can not do a thing to save her."

Lockewood edged close. " 'Tis me daughter, mon. You canna hurt me flesh and blood."

"What do you care? You didn't want her to know."

"Who in hell are you talking to?" Rachel snapped, but Markus ignored her.

"Her crimes are'na mine, Markus. I'm beggin' you, mon."

The sounds of thrashing, the voices of men came from the path they'd taken, and Rachel moved past Markus and onto the trail.

"Do not think this will delay us, you spineless fool. Markus!" Rachel shouted, yanking on his shirt.

Bend low, pest, Ran warned her. *I need your help. I cannot do this alone.*

Aurora hunched, but Markus fisted her hair, pulling her back against him. Her gaze skimmed the jungle, searching for Ransom or the image of her father.

Markus briefly closed his eyes, feeling twisted inside. He had a duty to fulfill. He had to!

"We are friends, Markus. We drank and ate together, we found women together. Please dinna hurt me precious girl." Connor advanced.

Lougière retreated. "Stay back or I'll cut her now!"

"Now, now!" Rachel screamed, not caring what demons took Markus as long as he did her bidding.

"I've naught else left," Connor pleaded.

Markus' stern expression faltered. "I didn't want to do it, Connor."

A step forward. "What, my friend. What?"

"Cassiandra, I . . . I . . ."

"Oh nay, Markus, tell me nay, you dinna." Cassiandra.

Connor's legs weakened at the thought of her. "Markus, nay!"

"Aye." Lougière stepped onto the ledge, inching backward with every word. "I was ordered to take her life, and yours too, but I couldn't find you," he admitted, as if it mattered.

"Tell your ghost you wore her finger about your neck as a prize!" Rachel laughed, fueling his torment. "That Shokai wounded you!" She swiped wet hair from her face, her voice in Markus' ear. "Do it now, Markus. Redeem yourself now!"

Markus looked from Connor to Rachel, the feral gleam in her eyes striking him hard. "Nay!" Markus shouted in her face. "Enough!"

And Rachel's face went molten with rage as she threw herself at Markus, slamming him against the jagged stone wall, sandwiching Aurora atween as she grabbed his fist, pressing the knife up against Aurora's throat. Blood colored the blade. Aurora couldn't move.

A streak of silver whistled through the pounding rain and Rachel twisted to the sound. The hollow bone-handled blade sank smoothly into her throat. She gasped, startled, disbelieving as Ransom emerged from the forest.

Rachel flailed wildly, for the blade, for purchase, the wet ground giving way beneath her feet. She fell backward, groping the air, but grasped Aurora's nightgown. A strange smile curved her blood-foamed lips.

Ransom dove, sliding in the mud as the force of Rachel's fall took all three over the edge of the ridge.

"Aurora!!" Her fingertips skimmed his touch, and he gaped in horror at his empty hand. "Aurora!" he screamed, raw. "Oh, God, nay!" He pounded the mud with his fist, agony ripping him apart. "Aurora!" echoed into the valley.

Ransom!

Ran blinked, swallowed, shoved dripping wet hair from his face and looked over the edge.

Below you. Hurry. I'm slipping.

Ransom scrambled out as far as he could.

Men burst from the jungle canopy, his father at the lead,

and Ran glanced back long enough to throw him an end of
the rope he wore wound round his chest.

"Hold on." Ran slipped down over the edge, head first.
Vines and thick brambles tore at his skin. Then he saw her,
clutching an exposed root, dangling out like a thread on a
branch. Rain battered her face as she stared up at him.

His heart in his throat, Ran forced his gaze away from the
terror in her eyes and inched himself down. The rope went
taut and he stretched, reaching. His wet fingers closed tight
over her still-bruised wrist.

The root snapped, her body jerking against his grip.

"I'm slippin'!" she cried, clinging to his arm.

"I have you."

"Ransom!"

"Aurora!" he commanded harshly. "I will not fail you.
Hold on, love, hold tight." Ran tried to draw her up. "She's
caught," Ran shouted. "Something's keeping her back!"

Domingo skidded down the thin lip to see. *"Dios,* Markus has her by the ankle!"

The rain-weakened ground shifted, spraying pebbles and
mud over Aurora's face. Her wrist shifted in his grasp.
"Ransom!"

Connor was near, unable to touch or be seen by anyone
other than Markus.

He concentrated, forcing a gnarled limb within Markus's
reach. "Grab it, Markus," Connor begged. "Quickly, afore
you both die!"

Lougière tilted his head back and met his gaze.

"Nay!" Connor panicked, recognizing the resolution in
his eyes. "Nay dinna—!"

"Good life, my comrade."

Connor stared numbly as Markus Lougière released his
daughter, smiling as he sailed the wind to his death.

Ran dragged Aurora up enough to grab a fistful of her
gown, twisting it for leverage and she used his body like a
ladder, climbing to safety. Aurora fell back against the
green-covered rock face, her breathing rapid and short as he
inched himself onto the ledge.

Ran lay face-down in the mud, his back rising with each

gasping breath, and she touched his wet hair. He lifted his head, staring into her eyes, and her lip quivered as he drew himself up to his knees. Her hand trembled atween them, rain rinsing mud from her fingers as she touched his face, his lips. She choked down a sob. And Ran pulled her into his arms, his hands scrubbing wildly over her body for injuries, sweeping up to her shoulders, her throat. He cradled her face in his broad palms, shaking, his gaze raking her upturned features. Water splashed her pale skin.

"I love you," Ran rasped, his voice fracturing. *"I love you."*

"I know," she said, swiping her fingers across his cheek, wet with warm tears.

"God almighty, pest, I thought I'd lost you! Again." Agony still taunted him.

" 'Tis not possible, my lion heart," she said, soft and confident. " 'Tis power we share. Not even death could part us."

"Good God," he choked, his eyes burning hot. "Does that mean you'll torment me even after I'm gone?"

"If you be needin' it, aye. But," she swallowed, her body quaking, "I'm needin' one of your kisses, Ransom."

His mouth touched hers, timid, quivering, afore he deepened the kiss, his strong arms swallowing her, and Aurora sobbed against his mouth, clinging fiercely.

Beyond them Connor smiled, then melted into the mountainside.

The jungle rumbled with slapping brush and thrashing people, pirates and half-naked natives bursting from all directions, torch and lantern lighting storm dark land.

"Mother of mercy!" someone said as the cat emerged from the thicket, muscular and graceful, with a coat of deep red. It moved slowly, circling in front of Ran and Aurora, then settling afore the pair. Natives fell to their knees, postulating, and even seasoned pirates backed up a few feet.

"So now you show?" Aurora scolded. The lion tilted his head back and roared, scattering the islanders. "Hush now." Aurora reached out, sliding her hand smoothly over his wet fur. "Aye, you're forgiven," she said, then looked at

Ransom. "Are you believin' in the power of magick now?" she asked, gazing at his muddy face.

Ran smiled, the corners of his eyes crinkling. "I believe in you, love, and 'tis enough magic for me."

Epilogue

Several months later

Ran stood on the long dock extending off the end of the jetty, awaiting the final moorings to be anchored. The ship was large and sleek and black from sail tip to her sculptured bow. She'd arrived with her gun ports closed, flying white from her topmast. He'd no reason not to allow her a berth, but the twenty cannons ashore reassured him of his decision.

He grinned when he heard his name called and turned. His smile withered.

"By God, woman, do not run!"

"I am not running," she said, huffing for breath. " 'Tis but a brisk walk."

Sayidda, Granville, and Connor were not far behind, each looking horrified and worried over her behavior.

"Can you not control yer wife, mon," Connor complained. "Gives me a bleeding start every time she takes to bustlin' off like that."

"She's your daughter," Ran countered, sweeping his arm around Aurora's distended waist and snuggling her to his side. She moved restlessly, and afore all he bent, kissing her leisurely. "And controlling my wife is simply not possible." He kissed her again, his forehead knitting slightly. "Dahrein?"

"He climbs the mountain," Aurora said, and Ran's gaze shifted beyond to the summit, his smile laced with pride.

"Kassir?"

"Ransom," Granville corrected.

Sayidda's nose tipped the air. "Kassir, who is our guest?

Shielding his eyes, Ran turned to see a figure climb to the ship's rail and, without lowering the gangplank, drop to the dock with a shuddering thump. A strange prickling rose up his spine, fanning out to his arms and legs.

The man straightened before Ran, and they stared at each other, examining face and form and eyes with intense scrutiny.

"Goddess of Light," Aurora whispered. " 'Tis like a bleedin' mirror."

Ran gazed into the face so like his own, the prickling intensifying.

"I am called Royce Tremayne." Wind whipped coppery brown hair.

"Ransom Montegomery." Ran bowed slightly. "My wife, Aurora," he introduced with a nod, still staring. He is younger, Ran realized.

The tall stranger grasped her hand, bringing it to his lips. "A pleasure, madame, to find you here. Evan Pierce sends his regards and his thanks for saving life and limb."

"You're an American!" Aurora said, and he flashed her an easy grin.

He turned his gaze to Ransom. "Evan insisted I'd find my past in the face of a pirate king."

"It appears," Ran muttered dryly, then glanced back at Granville. "I believe 'tis time for a full and accurate accounting of your affairs, Father."

Granville arched a single brow, offering no comment, and Aurora decided 'twas an affectation of the Montegomery men, for she'd seen the like in Dahrein.

"Father?" Royce asked, his gaze skimming the man with undisguised curiosity.

Granville stepped forward. "You are Angela's son." A pause, then, "and mine." Royce's face split into a heartstopping smile, free and generous, sire and heir staring briefly afore Granville enveloped Royce in a backslapping hug.

"Och, my heart," Aurora whispered to Ran, leaning her head against his broad chest. "For a man who wanted naught of family, look how full your table is now."

Ran smiled down at her, then kissed the top of her head. Royce stepped back, facing Ransom, and both men flicked hair off their brows with the same arrogant toss. Aurora laughed, soft and knowing, studying Royce with a critical eye.

"Aurora!" Ran gave her a quelling look, full of jealousy and love.

She elbowed him. "The lion's heart is enough, thinks I."

Ran chuckled and slung his arm around Royce's broad shoulders, urging him toward the house.

"So. Tell me, little brother, have you met Rahman?"

About the Author

Amy J. Fetzer lives with her family in San Clemente, California. She is the author of two previous Zebra historical romances: *MY TIMESWEPT HEART,* a 1992 Golden Heart Finalist, and *THUNDER IN THE HEART.* Amy has also contributed to two Zebra anthologies: *MY SPELL-BOUND HEART,* currently available in bookstores, and *TIMELESS SUMMER,* a time-travel collection which will be published in August 1995. Amy is currently writing the sequel to her first book, Ramsey O'Keefe's story, and loves to hear from her readers. You may write to her at PO Box 274, San Clemente, CA 92674. Please include a self-addressed stamped envelope if you wish a response.